Vi

for

Victory

Rosemary J. Kind

Best wishes

Rosemary Kindy

Printed in the United Kingdom

First Printing, 2021 Alfie Dog Limited

The author can be found at: ros@rjkind.com

Cover design: Katie Stewart, Magic Owl Designs
http://www.magicowldesign.com/

ISBN 978-1-909894-47-1

Published by
Alfie Dog Limited
Rose Bank, Snitterfield Lane,
Norton Lindsey, Warwickshire, CV35 8JQ
Tel: 07712 647754

DEDICATION

To women footballers everywhere.

AUTHOR'S NOTE

This book, and the one which precedes, would not exist without the story of the Dick, Kerr Ladies Football Team. However, the novels are not about that team, but are an entirely fictional story set against the backdrop of events in the period 1915 - 1921. I have deliberately begun the story ahead of the Dick, Kerr team taking to the field; they were not the first team during WW1 but were undoubtedly the most famous and most successful. Libra Lines was a well-known Coventry player as early as 1912 and continued to play throughout the war.

To put the numbers of supporters in context, on Boxing Day 1920, 53,000 spectators attended the Dick, Kerr Ladies Team match at Goodison Park whilst there were thousands more outside the stadium unable to get in.

The teams playing in this story are all fictional, although I make passing references to the Dick, Kerr team but in fictionalised circumstances.

When I first came across the story of the real Dick, Kerr Ladies Team I felt compelled to look into it in some detail. As a child, I loved playing football. I was a 'tom boy'; I spent all my time on the field with the boys playing football. When I was about 10 years old, on behalf of a number of the girls at school I approached our teachers to ask if we girls could play football instead of netball and have an official girls' football team. This was about 1975 and the answer was a plain and simple 'no'. Girls were only allowed to play netball. It was a sad indictment of the times. I wish I'd known about the Dick, Kerr Ladies Team back then. Maybe I wouldn't have given up.

For information: - the news headlines used are to give a

flavour of what was being reported around the time of each chapter. They do not always correlate to the specific day the chapter begins. I have taken them primarily from *The Daily Mirror* and *The Sunday Pictorial* because those were the newspapers Billy and his father read. The songs used are music hall and other popular songs from the time.

NOTE:
The characters are all fictitious and any resemblance they may have to persons alive or dead is entirely coincidental. This book is not intended to suggest that the events portrayed happened in reality. It is purely a work of fiction, rooted in elements of real history.

CHAPTER 1

Silent night, holy night!
All is calm, all is bright.
Round yon Virgin, Mother and Child.
Holy infant so tender and mild,
Sleep in heavenly peace,
Sleep in heavenly peace
Stille Nacht Heilige Nacht - Joseph Mohr 1816

Saturday 23rd December 1916 - The King on our War Aims - 'Vindication of Rights' - The Daily Mirror

Billingbrook, Lancashire
Violet Dobson took her young son's hand as they walked down the steps from Billingbrook Hall Hospital. She needed the comfort of holding on to him as much as he needed her. Neither one of them wanted to leave Billy behind. She turned in case Billy was looking out of the window, but all she could see was the nurse's back as she wheeled him away.

"Will Daddy come home soon?" Tommy asked as they walked.

Of all the questions she was expecting, how soon until Billy came home wasn't the first. She considered her words before answering. "Well, Daddy has to have an operation on his face first, to rebuild his nose."

"Can't he smell anything now?" Tommy looked at his

mam's face as he asked.

Vi smiled. It was as though Tommy hadn't seen the scarring and the disfiguration. All that mattered to their son was the inconvenience of his father's nose being flattened. She wished everyone could regard Billy's injuries in that way. "Yes, to help him smell. And they're going to give him a new leg so that he can walk."

It wasn't going to be easy when he came home, but they'd manage somehow. Would she have to give up her job at Caulder and Harrison to look after him? How would they manage for money if she did? She'd miss the factory. It wasn't that she enjoyed making munitions, not like when she'd worked making hats. What she'd miss was the camaraderie with the girls and, of course, being in the company football team; that was something she wouldn't give up easily. It had taken long enough to gain acceptance of her playing from Billy's mam; now she had, Vi wanted to make the most of it.

Tommy was quiet for a while and Vi appreciated the time to think. Eventually he asked, "Can we see Daddy tomorrow?"

"No, my love, but we'll see him the next day, Christmas Day. Tomorrow we're having Christmas with Nanna and Granddad."

It had been hard fitting everything in, even before she knew Billy was alive and in the local military hospital, and not dead in battle, as the telegram had said.

"Did Jesus have two birthdays?"

"Pardon?" Vi didn't immediately realise what Tommy was thinking.

"Can I have two birthdays?"

She laughed. "No, silly. He only has one birthday, but because we're seeing Daddy on Christmas Day, we'll have to see Nanna and Granddad tomorrow and pretend it's Christmas."

It was a shame her parents couldn't go with them to the hospital, but with Billy's parents as well, there'd be too many of them. Besides, if Matron found a way for Billy to attend the football match on Boxing Day, her parents would see him then. Fundraising through the football matches seemed more important now she knew Billy was amongst those who would benefit. She felt a jolt of excitement at the thought he'd finally be there to see her play.

It was late afternoon when they arrived home at Ivy Terrace and Vi was ready for a cup of tea and a sit down. They walked down the passageway to the back gate.

"I'm hungry, Mam," Tommy said, tugging at her coat sleeve.

"It's been a long time since lunch. I'll make you some toast when we get in." Vi suspected with the afternoon's excitement that Tommy would be asleep soon after eating. She'd talk to Billy's Mam and Dad about the visit once he was in bed.

"Is that you, Vi?" Billy's mam called from the back room as Vi went along the hall.

Vi poked her head around the door. "Yes, it's me. I'll see to Tommy and then come down."

She didn't feel much like the inquisition that was likely to take place, but until Billy's mam could straighten things out in her own mind, she wouldn't be able to move forward. Six months of Billy letting them believe he was dead was difficult for all of them to comprehend. Vi was hurt too. How could Billy not have trusted her love for him? How could he even think she'd be better off without him? The war might have broken his body, but it hadn't broken her love. She still wanted him for the man he was. When she thought about things properly, she realised none of them could judge his reaction when they'd no idea what he'd been through at the Somme. She suspected it was easier for Billy's dad to understand, having fought in the Boer War but he'd never talked about his experience, and she doubted he'd start now.

By the time Vi went back downstairs, Elsie was nowhere to be found. Alf was sitting in the dimly lit room, smoking his pipe.

"Where's Mam?" Vi asked as she sat down.

Alf shook his head. "Bed, I shouldn't wonder. How is he?"

"No different from when you saw him last week. Tommy climbed onto his knee and carried on as though he'd last seen him yesterday, rather than it being nearly two years." Vi smiled at the recollection.

Alf drew a deep breath through his pipe and blew the smoke out slowly. "I suspect that's what he needs us all to be doing. He hardly wants people pointing out his injuries. It's not as though he doesn't realise. I shouldn't think he wants questions either. Mam can't stop herself. The football will be a good thing. Just doing something together and not having to talk."

"I can see that," Vi said. With Billy still in hospital for a few months, there weren't going to be many opportunities for everyday activities.

Alf took a deep draw on his pipe. "Mam's not coping well with what's happened. It's not easy for her." He looked straight at his daughter-in-law. "She's had a lot to deal with over the years."

He looked back down at his newspaper and Vi saw the sadness in his eyes.

From the time Tommy woke the following morning, Vi would have thought it was Christmas Day itself rather than Christmas Eve. He knew Father Christmas wouldn't be visiting until the following morning, but that didn't stop his excitement at this being an extra celebration.

"Don't you go waking Grandma and Grandpa." Vi couldn't face Elsie being annoyed this early in the day.

She took the flannel and made it damp with water from the jug, then gently scrubbed Tommy's face and neck. He was unlikely to stay clean for long once he was playing with Bobby, her youngest brother, but he'd do for now.

Vi was washing their breakfast pots when the gate latch clacked. She opened the back door as their neighbour Tessie was about to knock.

"Am I early?" Tessie asked as Vi stood back for her to enter.

"It's easier getting myself ready for work than preparing Tommy to go somewhere. I don't think he's stopped talking since we got back from the hospital yesterday. I'll tell you about it on the way." Vi picked up her hat and a pile of presents that were standing on the kitchen table. "Tommy, are you there, love?"

Tommy came running along the hall and bowled straight into Tessie.

"Careful." Vi shook her head. "Sorry," she mouthed to Tessie, who had clearly made a great deal of effort with her clothes that morning. Tessie was wearing her Sunday best and, with makeup on, appeared much older than her nearly sixteen years. At work in her overalls she looked completely different and, but for the yellow at the front of her hair caused by the chemicals at the munitions factory, you could easily think this was a different person.

They were all easy to spot by their canary-coloured

hair. Vi was used to it now and made no attempt to cover it. It was almost a badge of honour, displaying their part in the war effort.

Tommy looked up earnestly at Tessie. "Are we really having two Christmases? Will I get presents on both of them?"

Vi pulled a face of despair in Tessie's direction and the girl laughed.

Taking hold of Tommy's hand, Tessie led him out toward the street. "Why don't you tell me all about seeing your dad yesterday?"

All talk of presents disappeared, and Tommy launched into a long explanation of what the hospital had been like and seeing Billy. Vi walked alongside, listening carefully. At no point did Tommy talk about Billy's injuries. He had his father back, and nothing, not even two days of presents, could make him happier. Once Tommy finished chattering he ran on ahead, which gave Vi a chance to talk to Tessie without him overhearing.

"Here, let me take some of those." Now Tessie's hand was free from holding onto Tommy, she took one of the bags that Vi was carrying. Tessie looked hard at Vi. "And how is Mr Dobson, really?"

Hearing Tessie call Billy 'Mr Dobson' was funny. Vi forgot how young Tessie was and how little she knew Billy. "Honestly? I don't know which is worse, how he's going to cope without an arm and a leg, or him thinking he'll just be a burden to us. I suppose the hospital will help him with some of that. His mam's finding his injuries hard to accept, but if I have to nurse him for the rest of his life, I'll do it. He's still my Billy."

Tessie was quiet for a while. Then she said, "I could help you sometimes if you'd like."

Vi smiled. She was lucky to have such a good friend. "Thank you."

The conversation stopped when Tommy ran back to them, full of happy chatter about Christmas — the presents he might be given and what food there might be to eat. "Will there be a pudding?" His eyes were round in anticipation.

"You'll have to wait and see," Tessie said, her face alive with amusement at the boy's frustration with her answer.

As Tommy ran on ahead again, Vi picked up the conversation. "I don't want to eat too much pudding if I'm going to be in any state for the football match."

"Give over, you've got tomorrow to recover from that. Do you think the Manchester team will be any good? I don't want to lose with everyone coming to watch us."

By everyone, Vi knew that what really mattered was how Tessie looked in front of Vi's brother John, who she was walking out with. "They're a big team with a lot of support, but so are we. We can beat anyone when we play well." She went quiet for a while. "The football's the one thing I wouldn't want to give up if I have to nurse Billy. I do love playing."

When they arrived at the tiny back-to-back house that was home to her family, Vi turned to take the bag from Tessie and realised how shy the girl had suddenly become.

"I've not met your eldest sister yet," Tessie said.

Vi nodded. "You'll be fine. She'll love you."

Vi wasn't surprised John hadn't introduced Tessie to Ena and Percy; her sister's husband could be mean-spirited at the best of times. Vi would do what she could to protect her friend.

John came out to meet them, looking as awkward as Tessie. Vi left them to have a few minutes to themselves.

Inside the house, Mam was busy at the stove in the corner of the room, while Dad was on his knees by the table.

"Hello, love," Dad said, getting up and waving a wad of paper in the air. "I was trying to get this one to stop wobbling." He indicated the small table carefully positioned at the end of the dining table. Even in the middle of the room and fully extended, the table would struggle to seat them all. "I borrowed it from our neighbour, but it's got a bit of a wobble. She did warn me." Having kissed his daughter's cheek, Frank Tunnicliffe returned to his task of levelling the table.

Vi put the food bag down. "I'll take these presents upstairs out of the way and then come down to help. Where are the others?"

Queenie Tunnicliffe blew a strand of hair out of her eyes and pointed the wooden spoon toward the ceiling. Vi understood that the younger children must be in their bedroom at the top of the house. Kate was nine now and perfectly capable of keeping an eye on the others.

When Vi returned to the kitchen, Mam said, "We'll put the children on the end table. Now, before your sister gets here, why don't you tell me how Billy's doing?"

Vi had barely finished tying her apron when Ena and Percy came through the door. She went over to greet her sister. Ena was pale and her eyes darted around the room. Vi knew better than to ask if everything was all right, but simply gave her a peck on the cheek and went back to help Mam.

"And who have we here?" Percy wandered over to where John was sitting with Tessie.

Vi was about to answer, but Tessie, her normal confidence reasserting itself, beat her to it.

"Hello, Mr Mayberry." She turned to Ena. "Mrs Mayberry, I'm Tessie Brown." She stuck her hand out to shake first Percy's and then Ena's hands. "I've heard ever so much about you both from John."

Vi was glad that Tessie hadn't referred to any of the things she'd told her about Percy.

Percy perched on the arm of the chair where Tessie was sitting and Vi groaned. At least Tessie was forewarned and wouldn't fall for any of his charms.

In Vi's eyes, Percy was a no-good scoundrel. He'd avoided his army call-up by being signed off as unfit, though none of them believed the doctor's report for a minute. What really hurt Vi was Percy pointing out that if Billy hadn't fought then no harm would have come to him.

"Billy joining us for dinner?" he asked, turning his head to Vi. "I'm sure one of us could feed him."

Vi bit her lip and counted to ten before replying. "That's very kind of you, Percy, but he's not ready for that yet." She turned back to her mother before the threatening tears began to fall. She couldn't let Percy get to her; he wasn't worth it. Besides, if she responded with what she really thought then it would be Ena who was likely to suffer for it, and she didn't want that.

As she turned, she heard John squaring up to Percy. "Leave it out."

She'd never heard her brother stand up to an adult before. She wondered if it was having Tessie there, or simply the fact he idolised Billy.

"I was only saying." Percy got off the arm of Tessie's chair and moved to the fireplace.

Vi felt some of the tension drop away from her shoulders and tried to be more cheerful. That was made easier by the sounds of clattering, as the children ran down the stairs and into the room, all talking at once. Vi began to smile with real pleasure.

"By the sound of that lot, it's a good job I've cooked plenty of potatoes." Queenie Tunnicliffe laughed heartily.

Vi loved the warmth and good nature her mam exuded, and it wasn't long before Percy's comment had been washed away on a tide of family jollity.

Frank Tunnicliffe took out his accordion and began to play carols. "Righto, let's do everyone's favourites in turn. You start, Vi love, what's it to be?"

"Dad, that's a lovely thought. I'd like *Silent Night*, please." Vi sang along quietly as she and Mam continued to prepare the dinner. Ena's voice could be heard above the others; it was such a beautiful sound, and Vi could have listened to Ena and their dad for hours.

CHAPTER 2

Sunday 24th December 1916 - How the Fighting Men Came Home for Christmas Yesterday - Sunday Pictorial

Despite his tiredness from the previous day, Tommy was awake bright and early on Christmas morning.

"He's been. Did you see him, Mam?" He lifted the stocking onto the bed and began to take out the small gifts.

"It must have been after I'd come to bed." Vi chose her words so she didn't exactly lie to her son.

She didn't mind being woken early today; there was a lot to do in the Dobson house before they went to the hospital later. She would have loved to have Christmas dinner with Billy, but the nurses had a big enough job on their hands without feeding relatives as well.

Vi went downstairs to light the fires and put the kettle on to boil. Tommy followed her down, clutching his orange in his hands. Vi supposed he was going to want to eat it now and wouldn't want to wait. She reached a plate down out of the cupboard and then turned to take the orange from him.

Tommy pulled away. "Can I save it and give it to Daddy for Christmas?"

Vi smiled and nodded, but struggled to get any words out. She put the plate away and took down a bowl to give Tommy cereal instead.

"Happy Christmas, love." Billy's dad came into the

kitchen to fetch tea to take back upstairs to Elsie. His face looked strained.

"Are you all right, Dad?"

He gave a weak smile. "I'm fine, love. Mam's not quite herself. I think she's worrying about going to the hospital." He sighed heavily and went toward the hall, carrying a tray on which Vi had put their tea and some toast.

At least Alf didn't say that Elsie wouldn't be going with them. That was Vi's first fear. Getting her there was half the battle.

Although Vi cooked a dinner with all the trimmings for Christmas, it was a very quiet affair. It was hard to know what to say to Elsie, and Alf said more through the looks and nods he gave Vi than through any words. She guessed he was being careful not to upset Elsie.

Tommy was so wrapped up in the excitement of going to see his dad that he barely seemed to notice the strained atmosphere, for which Vi was thankful.

Once she'd cleared away and fetched her coat and hat, the four of them set off toward the hospital. Tessie waved to them out of the window next door and mouthed the words 'Happy Christmas', which made Vi smile as she waved back.

She was grateful that the pavement was only wide enough for two to walk comfortably side-by-side; it meant she walked ahead with Tommy skipping beside her, and Billy's parents followed just behind.

The walk took around half an hour, but after their big lunch Vi was glad of the exercise.

On top of her excitement that Billy was coming to the following day's match, it would be the first time her own mam and younger sisters had watched Vi play, and Billy's mam come to that. She hoped her nervousness at them being there wouldn't affect her game, for the team's sake as much as her own.

There were lamps shining from almost every window as they approached Billingbrook Hall; even Elsie's mood seemed to lift. One of the soldiers was stationed at the front door to greet all the visitors, and for a moment Vi felt like an arriving dignitary rather than just Billy's wife. They heard the sound of a string quartet playing carols come drifting from the direction of the library, whilst the more mobile patients directed each arriving family to the location of their relatives.

The hospital was bright and there were paper decorations strung across the main dining room. "It gives the patients something to do," a nurse confided as she showed them through. Vi took hold of Tommy's hand, so he wouldn't go running on ahead, and followed the nurse. In some corners there were soldiers who sat alone. Vi wondered if they had families who didn't know they were here, or ones who couldn't face coming. She was becoming all too aware that this was the reality of war. It was no good saying you supported what your country was doing and then closing your mind to the effect it had.

They were taken through to a smaller, quieter room. There were three family groups already there and Billy, waiting alone in the far corner. Tommy tugged at Vi's hand, clearly desperate for her to let go, so he could run to his dad. She smiled and walked a little faster.

"Dad," Tommy called, and Billy looked up.

A sense of relief seemed to break out across his face, and Vi wondered if he'd been worried they wouldn't go. "Happy Christmas," she said, bending down to kiss him.

Billy reached out his left hand and Vi felt a thrill and warmth as her own hand met his.

Elsie and Alf were a few paces behind, but soon caught up.

"Happy Christmas, lad."

Billy took his hand back from Vi so he could shake his father's hand. Vi felt disappointed to lose that contact, so moved a chair around to Billy's left side and sat where she could put her hand into his when it was free again.

Alf moved aside to allow Elsie to come forward. Vi watched her mother-in-law intently as, with faltering steps, she approached her son. There was so little colour in Elsie's face that Vi wondered if she should put a chair behind the older lady, but she didn't want to move and disturb the moment. Elsie's hands were shaking as she reached out to her son, and Vi held her breath. Finally, Elsie moved a step closer and put her arms around Billy. There were no words, but she could see tears glistening on Elsie's cheeks.

Vi would have waited for as long as Elsie needed, but Tommy's impatience could only be contained for so long. "Dad, I've got a present for you." He put his hand out to Vi so she could give him the orange.

Vi moved slowly, allowing Elsie to pull back in her own time. Billy's mam said nothing, but sat next to Alf, who took hold of his wife's hand in an unusual show of affection.

Thankfully, Tommy's chatter filled the void. "Happy Christmas, Daddy. Father Christmas left this for me, but I want you to have it."

Billy broke into a broad smile. "Thank you. You know, that's reminded me of something. Can you put your hand into the pocket of my jacket on this side?" He indicated the right, where his missing arm prevented him from doing it for himself.

Tommy looked uncertain, but with some encouragement from Alf, who was sitting on that side, did as asked. The boy's face broke into the widest smile. "You've still got it." He drew out the small smooth pebble that he'd sent to his father the previous Christmas.

Billy nodded. "I don't know how I managed to keep it through everything that happened. I think it must be a magic pebble. Maybe that's how I still come to be alive."

He might be saying that to make Tommy happy, but from the way he spoke Vi wondered if Billy half-believed that himself. Tommy wrapped his arms around his father and held him tightly.

Elsie spoke for the first time since they'd arrived. "Well, I've never heard such…"

Alf put his hand on her arm to quieten her and she stopped. "… a lovely story," Alf added, finishing the sentence a little differently than Elsie might have intended to say.

The next hour passed happily, with Tommy being the main focus. Laughter and chatter from other parts of the room helped, and Elsie said very little.

Vi could see that Billy was beginning to tire, so she got up. "Perhaps we should go."

Billy exchanged a grateful smile with her and nodded.

"Will you be up to coming to the football tomorrow?" She bit her lip as she asked. She so wanted him to be there, but it was clear it would be quite an ordeal for him.

"I'll look after you, Daddy," Tommy said, hugging him again.

"I thought you were looking after me tomorrow," Elsie said, looking relieved to be getting up from the chair.

"I can do that too." Tommy frowned at his grandmother as though that was obvious, which made them all laugh.

It was a good point to leave, and Vi tried to keep the smile on her face as she said her goodbyes. There was nothing she wanted more than to take Billy home right now. She could care for him as well as any nurse, couldn't she?

Tommy was tired from the excitement and Vi was surprised and relieved when his grandpa Alf offered him a piggyback for the rest of the walk home. That left her falling into step with Elsie, and she hadn't the faintest idea what to say to her mother-in-law.

They walked in silence until Elsie said, "Will we have to turn the parlour into a bedroom?"

Vi felt herself relax. Elsie seemed to be coming around to the idea that sooner or later Billy would leave the hospital and be back with them. "I don't know. It's hard to think what he'll be capable of when he comes home."

Elsie nodded, and whilst she didn't say anything further Vi could see that she was mulling things over, and that at least was good.

Vi was awake even before Tommy the following morning. The idea of having her entire family watching her play football was both exciting and terrifying. She sat up in bed and took a few deep breaths. What did she need to do? Her kit was ready to go; she always repacked it once it was washed and ironed. She would go to the Billingbrook United ground with Tessie, and Billy's parents could bring Tommy in time for the match.

Leaving Tommy sleeping, Vi went downstairs. She was still lighting the stove in the kitchen when a tap at the window made her jump. She opened the back door to find Tessie standing there in her dressing gown. "What in heaven's name has happened? Is your mam all right?"

Tessie giggled. "Everything's fine, silly. I saw the light from my bedroom and thought I'd come round. I bet you're excited, aren't you?"

Tessie was becoming a regular visitor to the Dobson house, although usually she got dressed first. Whilst Vi continued to light the stove, Tessie filled the kettle ready to heat.

"How's Billy's mam?" Tessie was sitting at the kitchen table, watching Vi as she moved around the tiny room.

Vi turned and rocked her hand from side to side, but said nothing.

"I reckon," Tessie continued, "today could do her loads of good. You know, being out with Billy doing something normal."

Vi broke into a smile. "There's not much normal about Elsie Dobson coming to watch us play football. I never thought I'd see the day. It doesn't seem five minutes since I was worried she'd throw me out if she found out I was playing." She shook her head. "How times change."

The match was starting at two o'clock. Vi always liked to be there in plenty of time beforehand, so she made up sandwiches to take for lunch and wrapped them in paper. As she was finishing, Tommy came in.

"Hello, sleepyhead," Tessie said to him, and he climbed onto her knee and wrapped his arms around her neck.

Then he pulled his head away and looked from Tessie to his mother and back. "You will win today, won't you? I'm bringing Grandma and Daddy to watch, and I really want you to win."

Vi smiled as she prepared his breakfast.

"Well, we can try," Tessie said as he climbed down and onto his own chair.

When Vi arrived at the Whittingham Road ground she was more nervous than she'd been before any match. She could see an area which had been especially reserved for the soldiers who were coming from the hospital, and any family who came with them. If everyone came with as many family members as Billy, they'd need a larger area.

Major Tomlinson was arranging transport for the injured servicemen, and Vi expected they'd be there close to kick off.

As the girls warmed up, spectators were arriving, and Vi kept an eye out for hers and Billy's families. She would only be convinced they were all coming when she saw them.

"John's here," Tessie shouted, pointing to a group moving along the terrace.

Vi waved madly as she saw her mam and dad and the four children following where a steward was directing them. Then she saw Tommy, holding tight to his grandma Elsie's hand, and for the first time let herself believe they would all be there to watch. There was just Billy to come now. She tried to concentrate on what the team was doing, warming up and getting into the right state of mind to play, but all the time her thoughts kept going back to her family and looking across to the stand.

Suddenly the crowd started applauding, and a way opened up between those who were standing.

"Is that Mr Dobson?" Tessie asked, shielding her eyes from the low sun to see across to the stand.

Vi broke into a broad smile. "Yes, it's my Billy."

Patients in wheelchairs were being rolled into position by more able-bodied soldiers, each of whom was being given a seat behind his charge. Vi could see Elsie bustling through the crowd to see her son and hoped the rest of the family would be able to move nearer to him too. This was real. He was actually here.

Tessie went running over in their direction and, on shaky legs, Vi followed.

"Welcome home, Mr Dobson," Tessie shouted, waving madly from the edge of the pitch. "See you all later."

Vi gave a shy wave. She felt funny having him see her in her football kit, but she guessed he'd already seen photographs, so maybe it wasn't so strange.

Once the whistle blew Vi's nerves were forgotten and all that mattered was beating the team of Manchester girls. She threw herself into the game, looking for opportunities to pass the ball and finding space so her teammates could pass to her. She had one shot at goal in the first half, but the Manchester goalie was good and anticipated where she'd kick the ball. Vi would have to do better than that if she was going to score.

Early in the second half she had possession of the ball without the attention of an opponent. She surged forward. There were still thirty-five yards to go to the goal and Beattie was being closely marked. Vi had to go it alone. She didn't think she'd ever dribbled so fast as she moved the ball toward the goal. Once she was close enough, it was just her against the goalkeeper. She could see one of the opposition girls only paces away; there wasn't time to hesitate. She glanced toward the top left corner, in an attempt to mislead the goalkeeper, then flicked the ball toward the opposite corner of the net. When it crossed the line, Vi punched the air. She could hear the crowds cheering, but all she cared about was that she had shown Billy what she could do.

The remainder of the second half was less eventful and the game finished in a draw. As soon as it was over, Vi went to find her family.

"Great goal, love." Her dad was looking very cheerful.

"Well done," Billy said quietly.

Vi's heart jolted. He didn't look as happy as she'd hoped. She wanted him to be proud of her, but he seemed distant. Just as she was about to ask him if he was all right, Major Tomlinson came over and shook her by the hand.

"Fine performance from you gals. Good show. Must be getting back."

When Vi turned to speak with Billy, he was already being wheeled away. She hadn't even had the chance to say goodbye, and was about to run after them when Tommy put his arms around her legs.

"Will you take Tommy home?" she asked Billy's mam. "I want to go up to the hospital."

Almost before Elsie had the opportunity to reply, Vi disentangled herself from Tommy, gave him a quick kiss, and rushed away to the changing rooms. She'd have gone to the hospital as she was if it wasn't likely to be more trouble than it was worth.

"What's wrong?" Tessie called as Vi passed her.

"I'll tell you later," Vi replied. She didn't want to waste time explaining.

It was dark long before Vi reached the hospital.

"I think Private Dobson may be sleeping," the Voluntary Aid Detachment nurse said after opening the door to the Hall when Vi rang the bell. "He's had a tiring day."

"I know, but I have to see him, please?" Vi wouldn't settle until she'd been able to talk to him.

"Mrs Dobson." Matron was passing through the reception hall and spotted her. "I think it might be best to leave Private Dobson for today. He was rather upset when he came back."

Vi quite forgot herself. "But I didn't even have a chance to say goodbye to him. No wonder he was upset. He must think I don't care."

Matron gently took her arm and guided her to a quiet corner.

"Mrs Dobson, this isn't about you not saying goodbye. You must remember that everyday things can remind a man of what he's lost. When your husband came back, he was feeling pretty sorry for himself. It's not easy to come to terms with the things you're never going to be able to do again when you're still so young. You're going to need to give him time. In my experience, with your support, he'll come around."

Vi's shoulders slumped. "I just wanted him to be proud of me. I hadn't thought of it from his point of view. He must miss being able to walk, never mind run and play football. How stupid have I been?"

"Come and see him on Saturday. I'm sure by then he'll have had some time to think." Matron guided Vi back toward the door and out into the damp evening air. "It will get easier, Mrs Dobson, trust me."

Standing on the steps of Billingbrook Hall on a cold December afternoon, Vi found Matron's reassurance hard to believe.

CHAPTER 3

Wednesday 27th December 1916 - Empire War Conference — British Force Closing in on Kut - Daily Mirror

"Private Dobson."

Billy looked up from where he'd been dozing to see a nurse standing a little way away.

"You have a visitor."

Before Billy had time to say he really wasn't in the mood to see anyone, the nurse moved aside and his father stepped forward. He was holding his hat in his hands and turning it around over and over again.

"Dad." Billy felt a bolt of alarm. "Is anything wrong?"

As the nurse withdrew, Alf Dobson moved toward him and turned a chair so it was facing Billy before he sat down. "I could say the same to you, son."

They were both quiet for a moment. Billy presumed his dad wanted to say something, but wasn't sure where to start. He could feel himself tensing, waiting for a dressing down from a parent, but that had never really been his father's style.

After a while, Alf raised his head and looked his son in the eye. "When you left the match on Monday, I could see you'd found it hard. I've been thinking about it. You don't need to talk to me if you don't want to, but I can remember what it was like coming back from the Boer War. I'd seen things I couldn't unsee." Alf looked down at his hat as though he were seeing them again. Then, as if with difficulty, he focussed once more on Billy. "I'd done things I couldn't undo. I'm not proud of those things. I didn't do them because I wanted to. I did them because I had to." He paused as though gathering his thoughts. "I came home to Mam and you, and I didn't say a word about any of it. I locked it away. I didn't say much, to be honest. I was looking around me at a world that had been carrying on as if nothing had happened. Some days I just wanted to scream. Then your mam had another miscarriage, and the doctor told her she shouldn't be trying for any more children as it could be a danger to her as well as the baby. I felt like I'd woken up from a bad dream. I suddenly saw that Mam needed me — and more than that, you needed me. My son didn't deserve his father to be distant and absent most of the time. I won't say it was easy. I had to remind myself every day to be in the world I was part of. It did get easier though. Eventually it felt more normal, and I count myself one of the lucky ones."

Alf got up from his chair. "Anyway, son. I just thought the time had come to tell you." He nodded to Billy and turned to go.

"Dad, wait."

Alf turned back.

"How were Mam and Vi when they got home?"

Alf shook his head. "Don't judge them, son. They don't know what you've been through. Neither do I come to that, but I might have a small inkling. They were hurt. It meant a lot to Vi to have you there to see her play. She thought she must have done something wrong. And Mam? I've been married to her for over thirty years, and I haven't worked out how she thinks yet." He gave a shrug.

Billy nodded. He was about to reply, but the moment

was broken by one of the volunteers coming over with tea.

"I expect you'll be needing these," she said, winking at Billy and putting a small plate of Bourbon biscuits beside the cups. "Just don't be telling Matron that I'm spoiling you."

They went back to talking about more everyday matters and a little about the football itself.

"Vi's good, isn't she?" Billy said.

Alf nodded. "I don't think she really realises how good she is. She'd love to hear you tell her."

Billy felt a rush of love and guilt toward his wife. He could see why she was upset on Monday when he went. It was only later in the day that the nurse told him she'd tried to visit too. "Could you ask if she can come to see me on Saturday?" Billy couldn't meet his dad's eye. "Sooner if she's free." He looked up at Alf's gentle smile and thought how lucky he was to have this man as his father. Perhaps he could still be as good a father to Tommy as Alf had been to him.

Billy thought a lot about the things his father said, and the three day wait until Saturday seemed like an eternity. He asked the nurse to position his wheelchair in the window so he could see the drive; then he watched every coming and going from lunchtime onward, intent on seeing Vi approach so that he was ready to see her.

"Private Dobson, are you awake? You have a visitor."

He felt the nurse take the handles of his chair to turn him toward the room. He had no idea when he'd fallen asleep, but there she was in front of him. His own Violet. He blinked and suddenly felt shy. He'd practised in his head what he wanted to say. A full and unbridled apology for how he'd behaved, but when he came to it, he felt tongue-tied. "No Tommy?"

"I left him with Mam and Dad. He can play with Bobby this afternoon. I thought…"

He nodded. She was right, of course, but just then he'd have liked the distraction of Tommy being there. "I…" He stopped and looked at the love that shone from Vi's face, despite the hurt she was feeling. He reached out his hand. "I'm sorry. I…"

"Shh." Vi took his hand and the careworn look fell away, leaving only the love.

"You were really good, love. I'm not sure what I expected, but you're as good as any of the men in the Billingbrook United team."

Vi laughed. "Now I know you're having me on, but it's nice to hear you say it."

"I don't know how I'm going to get things straight, but I will try. I won't let you down, Vi."

He looked at the tears glistening in the corners of Vi's eyes. He hadn't meant to make her cry, but he did want to tell her he'd thought about things.

"Just be my Billy again. That's all I want." Vi moved her chair closer to his and leaned her head on his shoulder.

She was sitting on his left side, and he slipped his arm around her. For a moment, he felt almost normal.

Over the next few weeks, it seemed to Billy as though he and Vi were having to get to know each other all over again. Though he didn't talk about the war itself, they couldn't avoid talking about the fears and insecurities it had left him with.

"I still have dreadful nightmares. When I come home it might be better for me to sleep on my own somewhere," Billy said, in one of his more candid moments when

Tommy wasn't with them.

"In a house the size of Ivy Terrace? Don't talk daft. Besides, I want to be there for you, however hard it is."

They were fine words, but Billy wondered if Vi really knew what she was letting herself in for. Some nights were more night terrors than nightmares. On the hospital ward, a night didn't go by without one or other of the men screaming until they were all left wondering what fresh hell he was re-enacting.

Through the weeks Billy was in hospital, Tommy proved the most remarkable tonic; telling his father earnestly about everything that had been going on, and coming up with ways his father could take part just as he was, regardless of limitations.

"Why don't you have two pockets on this side, where your hand is?" Tommy said when Billy asked him to get something out of his other pocket.

"I don't know. Because the jacket came with one small one each side." Billy looked at Vi. "Could you change that?"

Vi reached across and lifted the material to see the back. "I could do that fairly easily, or make this one bigger."

"Two would be better, so I could find things without sorting through them." Billy shook his head. It just wouldn't have occurred to him. He realised how fixed some of his thinking was. It was far easier to approach a problem if you didn't start from the assumption that there was a right way it should be done.

Billy was happy to have some news of his own at Vi and Tommy's next visit. "The doctor says I'm ready for my operation," he told them one Saturday in February.

"What are they going to do to you, Daddy?" Tommy

asked.

"Well…" Billy paused and looked up at Vi.

He didn't know how much to say to his son. "They're going to make my nose work better." He thought that sounded less frightening than explaining they would reconstruct the bone.

"I like your nose," Tommy said simply.

"And I'm sure you'll still like it when it's been operated on." Vi smiled at him as Tommy continued to examine his face. She continued, "Daddy will be able to breathe more easily through his nose, and hopefully he'll be able to smell more too."

"It's not always nice when I smell things," Tommy said, before moving on to a different topic of conversation.

Billy was glad of the change of subject. He was worried about the operation, but he didn't want to share that with Vi. When he'd been close to the battlefield and his operations had been life-saving, there'd been little chance to think about the risks. Now he had all the time in the world to think and felt as though there was far more at stake. There were dark days, there probably always would be, but he no longer woke every day with the oppression of feeling he should be dead. Most of the time, he really believed he had something to live for.

Matron had said it would be time for him to go home once he recovered from his operation. Quite apart from dealing with his disabilities, eight months in hospitals, and fifteen months in the army before that, made the prospect of making decisions for himself a daunting one. He didn't know which he was dreading most, working out how to be a civvy or the risk his mother would treat him as a child. He'd talked to Vi about how he felt. They were trying to work things out together, although until they faced the everyday situations, neither of them really knew what would happen.

There were, however, some things he hadn't told her; things he wanted to keep as a surprise. He wasn't sure how his attitude had changed. It had happened slowly, rather than all at once. His dad's talk to him after Christmas was definitely the starting point, but he thought maybe it was Tommy's approach which had made a big difference. Tommy simply didn't see his disabilities as obstacles and expected him to find new ways to do things, rather than sitting about feeling sorry for himself. Before Christmas, his rehabilitation hadn't been going well. What was the point? He would never be able to do the same things he could do before. The change had been realising he didn't have to do everything the same way as in the past. If Vi could learn to play football and turn out to be so good at it, then he could learn to do new things too. She was his inspiration.

He thought of Davy, the lad he'd taken under his wing in the army. He and Davy could not have been more different; Billy the working class lad, and Davy having been to private schools. Davy might have seen Billy as a father figure, but while Billy was bunking off school with Stan, Davy had applied himself to his learning and could do almost anything if he set his mind to it.

After Christmas, when the nurse came to take him for his physiotherapy and training to walk with his prosthetic leg, instead of pleading tiredness Billy began to try.

It hadn't stopped him shouting when he'd fallen over, or giving up when he was in pain, but it had meant he went back to try again.

"That's right, Private Dobson, use the crutch to help.

We'll move to a stick when you're ready." The doctor was remarkably patient with the men. He'd clearly seen every injury in the book and firmly believed he could help. That encouraged Billy as well.

When Tommy visited, writing had started as a way to keep the boy quiet and occupied. Now Tommy and Billy sat side by side at a table, forming their letters. Tommy was already learning some of them at school, but his writing and Billy's, using his left hand, started out much the same. Billy was determined that he would develop a neat hand, however much work it took and, sitting next to Tommy, he couldn't throw a tantrum when it went wrong, as he didn't want to discourage the boy from learning. Instead, they pushed each other to improve.

"How are we going to get the wheelchair into the house?" Vi asked when she visited Billy shortly after the operation on his nose.

Billy was still bandaged and neither of them had seen whether the operation had improved the way he looked, but Vi was clearly ready to focus on the next stage. "Let's do one thing at a time, love." He was hoping if he kept working hard it wouldn't be an issue, but he wasn't ready to tell Vi that.

"Can you smell now, Daddy?" Tommy asked, looking at his dad's bandaged face.

"If I can, the only thing I can smell is bandage." Billy laughed and the others joined in.

It was March when the nurse removed the final bandage, and the doctor said his face was now healed. The nurse picked up a hand mirror to pass to Billy, so he could see the result. All the times they had changed the bandages he'd declined the opportunity to look, and today was no exception.

"No, I don't want to look yet. My wife's coming this afternoon. I want to see how she reacts. More importantly, I want to see what my son says. If he tells me my nose is good, then good it will be."

"Are you sure, Private Dobson? I thought you might want to see first."

"Thank you, nurse, but no, I don't. What's the point in me thinking I look all right if others around me don't? Or worse, if I spend the day sitting here convincing myself they won't want me again. I've been there, it didn't do me any good." Billy was quite set in his own mind that their verdict would be the only one that mattered. He did feel nervous about it, and self-doubt could be overwhelming, but deep down, if the last two months had taught him anything, it was that Vi and Tommy loved him for who he was, no matter what.

He hadn't been able to tell Vi that the bandages were being removed, as he hadn't known in advance. By the time he expected her to arrive, he was beginning to worry he was doing everything the wrong way.

He was sitting facing the door when they came in and he watched Vi scan the room, looking for him. She looked around twice and seemingly couldn't find him. Then she did a double take and covered her mouth with her hands as she gasped.

"Is it that bad, love?" He grinned at her.

Tears were rolling down her cheeks. "Oh, Billy, I never thought I'd see the day. You look like the Billy I knew before the war started."

Tommy came straight to the point. "Now can you smell?"

It was funny; until he asked, that hadn't been what Billy

had been thinking about. He leaned in toward his son and breathed in through his nose. He broke into a broad smile. "I can smell coal tar soap."

"Yuck." Tommy brushed his coat sleeve over his neck, and they all laughed.

Vi ran her hand gently down Billy's cheek. "What do you think?"

He shrugged. "I didn't want to look. Tell me honestly what it's like."

"Well," Vi said, studying him closely. "There is still scarring, but the doctors have done a wonderful job with your nose. Honestly, it does look the way it used to. Just like the Billy I fell in love with all those years ago. It's wonderful."

She stood back and looked at him again. "Something else is different."

He was still grinning but said nothing.

"Your wheelchair."

He nodded and waited for her to piece it together.

Vi's eyes were wide and her mouth fell open. "Your leg."

Billy thought his scars would burst open if he grinned any more broadly. He took a stick from where it was leaning against the table and, holding it carefully, levered himself to an upright position. "It would all have been much easier if I could have had two sticks, but..." He didn't finish the sentence, just nodded toward his missing arm. Then slowly, and with faltering steps, he moved forward. "Shall we go for a walk?"

"Really?" Vi looked hesitant, but Tommy was jumping up and down with excitement.

"Only to the other end of the library, but let me show you." Billy took a deep breath. He was still a little wobbly, but determined to show them the progress he'd made. He set off down the length of the library. When he got to the other end, he was very glad to drop into an empty chair.

"I had no idea." Vi was laughing and crying with happiness. "It's amazing. How long has it taken?"

"They tried to get me started soon after I came to the hospital, before you knew I was here. I didn't try very hard. I couldn't see what the point was for someone like me, already on the scrap heap. Then I saw you play football on Boxing Day, and I came back here and felt I was worth nothing to anyone. I didn't want to go to my next session of physio. I just wanted to give up. Then Dad came to talk to me."

"Alf?" Vi frowned in surprise.

Billy nodded. "For the first time he talked to me about his own experience, and it made sense. After that, Matron came and ordered me to attend physio and wouldn't take no for an answer. I think Dad might have spoken to her too. She said I might not be able to do the things I could do before, but there would be different things I could try. I was going to argue, but I thought about you learning to play football, and I remembered something Tommy had said about doing the things he could do and not worrying about the things he couldn't. I realised they were all right. I started to work hard and, well, here I am."

Vi sat in the chair next to his so she could hold his hand. Tommy was still in a frenzy of activity and couldn't sit still. Vi tried to stay the boy with her other hand. "And when you said you'd be coming home, you already knew all this."

Billy nodded. "Stairs aren't that easy, but I'm getting better. I am going to need help, what with the arm, but I'm not totally useless anymore."

Matron marched over to where they were sitting. Billy hadn't thought the woman was capable of smiling so broadly.

"I see our star patient has been showing off again." Matron drew up a chair to join them. "Now, Private Dobson will still need to come in once a week to begin with, for his physiotherapy session; that will be on a Tuesday at three o'clock. He's going to need help with washing and dressing, although he's finding ways to do more things one-handed."

Billy stared at Matron, but couldn't find a gap to ask a question without seeming rude.

"He does still need the chair for when he gets tired or longer walking, but that will get easier the more he practices. I have the paperwork all sorted, so I think that's about it." Matron put some papers on the table and made to stand up.

Billy could only splutter out, "Now? Today? But..."

"Yes, of course today." Matron was frowning. "Didn't the doctor tell you?"

"How am I going to get home?" Walking across the library had been hard enough. He couldn't walk all the way back to Ivy Terrace.

"In the chair, of course. It's in the hall ready for you," Matron spoke as though it were obvious. "One of the ambulances is driving you home today, but for your weekly appointments the number 15 bus stops right outside the hospital."

Billy looked at the anxiety written across Vi's face. "We'll manage, love." He was trying to sound braver than he was feeling.

Vi nodded, but her face looked grim. Gone was the smile of earlier.

Billy couldn't even begin to think what this was going to be like.

Matron stood up. "Good luck, Private Dobson. From what I've seen, you'll do very well. Nurse Parker will help you from here."

Of all of them, only Tommy looked excited about what was happening. This was it, Civvy Street awaited. The only thoughts in Billy's head, as he moved across to the wheelchair the nurse had brought over, were how his mam was going to react with no notice that he was coming home, and how was he going to get outside to the privy? He wondered if Vi was worrying about the same things.

CHAPTER 4

The nurse wheeled Billy's chair, with Vi and Tommy following behind. Once they reached the hall, Nurse Parker stopped and turned to Vi.

"Have you ever managed a wheelchair before?"

Vi shook her head and looked at Billy, who shrugged.

Nurse Parker continued, "Then before Mr Dobson goes home, it's a good opportunity for you to take over and I'll give you some tips." She stood back from the chair.

Vi looked from Billy to the nurse and back.

"I'll do it," Tommy shouted and went to take the handles of the wheelchair.

"I'm sure your daddy will be very pleased to have you help him, but you need to be bigger and stronger first. Let's help your mam, shall we?" Nurse Parker guided Tommy to the side.

Vi took a deep breath and moved into place. The first problem was what to do with her handbag and she looked around for somewhere to lodge it. Eventually she hung it over one of the handles of the chair.

The wheelchair was stiff and wouldn't move.

"I'm sorry, I should have said." Nurse Parker pointed to a lever. "When you stop, you must always apply the brake for the patient's safety. To start up, you need to release it."

The nurse showed Vi what to do and Vi had another go at moving the chair. Although still heavy, it moved rather more easily. She tried to steer in a straight line, but made very slow progress.

Nurse Parker turned to Tommy. "Young man, your first important job is to be ready to open doors so your mam can get the chair through." She indicated the front door and Tommy eagerly ran over to it.

The door was made of heavy oak and took all of Tommy's strength to open wide before Vi could wheel Billy out of the hospital. Ahead of the open doorway were the steps down to the path. Vi looked at them in horror.

"How do I get Billy safely down there?"

The nurse laughed. "Don't worry, Mrs Dobson, if you turn your husband around this way there's a ramp. You will need to learn how to do steps, but I'll explain that in a moment."

Vi hadn't noticed the ramp before and felt a rush of relief; that was until she reached the edge of the slope.

Nurse Parker said, "Before you start, you need to hold the weight of the chair as you go down, so your husband doesn't start running away from you."

"I don't think I'm going to be running anywhere just at the moment, but the chair might. What do you reckon, Tommy? It sounds fun, doesn't it?"

But Vi could hear the anxiety in his voice. "Don't you start giving him ideas, Billy Dobson. That's the sort of thing Stan…" Vi stopped. "I… I…"

"It's all right, love. We have to talk about him. He was my best friend, for God's sake. And you're right, he'd have found a way to have fun with the wheelchair. I just wish he was here to try." Billy reached his hand up for Vi to take.

"This bloody war." Vi felt suddenly lost and helpless.

Nurse Parker's voice was calm but firm. "When you're ready, Mrs Dobson, the ambulance is waiting for us."

Vi was grateful that she only had to take the wheelchair as far as the vehicle. From there, the volunteers who drove the ambulance took over.

"One moment," Nurse Parker called to them. "Can you just show Mrs Dobson how to manoeuvre the chair up and down a step before we go?"

Vi watched them, once again horror stricken. How would she ever do that safely and without tipping Billy out of the chair? She pulled herself together. When they were at home she'd take the chair out and practice with it empty, before having to try it with Billy's weight as well.

"Is there room for us to travel in the ambulance?" she asked, not wanting to make any assumptions. They could go back on the bus or walk, but if Billy arrived home ahead of them then she had no idea how his mam would cope.

Tommy, who had been asking how much longer it was all going to take, suddenly brightened up. "Am I going in the ambulance?"

The helper nodded to them, and they climbed in with Billy.

"You're going to have to sit still." Vi knew how much Tommy would want to touch things that he shouldn't, and hoped the journey wouldn't take long.

Once they arrived back at Ivy Terrace, Vi climbed out first. "I'm going to tell your mam and dad that you're here." She took Tommy with her. "You stay inside while they bring Daddy in."

She was barely through the back door before Tommy was shouting to his grandparents, "Daddy's home."

Vi let out a heavy sigh. That had not been how she was going to break the news to Elsie and Alf. Billy's parents came out into the hallway, but Vi didn't have time to say anything more as Billy had been brought to the back door. He was standing up from the chair, which would have been difficult to steer through the entrance.

"Hello, Mam," Billy said to Elsie, who was staring open-mouthed.

Elsie gripped the work surface. "Oh, my dear Lord."

Vi thought her mother-in-law looked as though she'd seen a ghost and it took a moment before she came to. Everything about Elsie changed and she moved into action. "Alf, get him a chair. Oh, Billy, lad, I never thought you'd come home. Come through. Alf. Alf."

Vi suddenly understood that Elsie hadn't wanted to visit Billy because she was still so scared of losing him. Now, she finally seemed to understand that wounded as he was, he was alive, and she still had her only child.

Tessie arrived as the ambulance was leaving and was behind the wheelchair, which was still in the doorway.

"Where shall I put this?" Tessie asked once Billy had gone through to sit down and Vi was putting the kettle on.

Vi looked at it. "I have no idea."

The girls laughed.

"It's not as though there's much spare space in here. I think we'll have to find something to cover it over and it can stand outside. I'll talk to Billy's dad."

Thoughts of the wheelchair were soon forgotten as Tommy came charging down the passage into the kitchen. "Daddy's home," he told Tessie, "and he says he's never going away again. Not ever."

Vi smiled, then looked at Tessie. "I'm guessing this will all be a bit of a shock to the system after the quiet of the hospital."

"Dad, Dad." Tommy headed back along the hall.

"See what I mean?" Vi shook her head.

Then Vi heard Elsie telling Tommy to slow down. "Leave your dad in peace, he'll need to rest."

"No, Mam," Vi heard Billy say. "All I've done is rest. I want to see Tommy."

"Well, that's as maybe, but mind he doesn't stay in here long."

Vi raised her eyebrows. "Well, maybe I was wrong."

For short distances around the house, Billy could manage. It took some help from Vi or Billy's mam to get him dressed and presentable in a morning and ready for bed at night, and Billy became frustrated easily. He could do some things for himself, but other things, like tying the lace of his shoe, weren't so easy one-handed.

"How are we going to get you to your appointment on Tuesday?" Vi asked. "I'll be at work."

"I'm sure I can manage," Billy's mam said.

Vi simply stared at her. This was the woman who did virtually none of the heavy lifting around the house, claiming her knees or some other part of her body simply wouldn't cope. How in heaven's name was she going to wheel Billy and get him on and off buses to travel to the hospital and back again?

Alf's work had an order on, which meant he couldn't help, and as Billy seemed to think the arrangement would work, Vi decided to keep her concerns to herself.

When she came in from work on Tuesday evening, she could hear the shouting before she even set foot in the house.

"It's no good you complaining every time someone

tries to help you, Billy Dobson."

"I wasn't complaining about them helping. I was complaining because you wouldn't let me do anything. I might be an invalid, but you don't have to treat me like I'm useless, and you don't have to speak on my behalf. I'm not a child, and I'm perfectly capable of explaining what I need for myself."

"Well, if you're going to be like that, you needn't think I shall offer to help in future…"

From the sound of it, his mam was going to drive him mad very quickly. Vi slipped quietly upstairs and found Tommy sitting up in bed, listening.

"Is Daddy all right?" the boy asked.

"He'll be fine, darling."

"Grandma wasn't being very nice to him."

"I think they're probably both tired. And so will you be if you don't get some sleep." She stroked Tommy's hair as, with the shouting having died down, his eyelids began to close.

"I could help Daddy," he murmured as he drifted off to sleep.

Vi smiled. If only things were that simple. She'd ask if she could work on Saturday instead of Tuesday the following week so she could take Billy.

Much as she would rather have asked the factory manager Mr Giffard than go to see Mrs Johnson, the overseer for her part of the factory, Vi would only pay for it in the long run if the dragon wasn't happy. Mrs Johnson had never appreciated the special treatment afforded to the girls who played football, and Vi as team captain was definitely not her favourite person.

"You know it'll be all right," Tessie said as they walked

to work on the Wednesday morning. "They want more people working Saturdays."

"As well as Tuesday, not instead of." Vi sighed. "The claxon hasn't sounded yet, I'll go before the shift starts." She changed into her overalls as quickly as she could and, as part of keeping the factory safe from the risk of explosion, left anything made of metal in her locker. Then she went up to her floor at a brisk walk, passing some of the other girls on the way. She called a greeting to them, but would explain at break why she couldn't slow down to walk with them.

Vi's heart was pounding as she knocked on the door to Mrs Johnson's office. The overseer looked up from her desk and nodded for Vi to enter.

"How is Mr Dobson?"

Vi was lost for words. Mrs Johnson never asked about any of the girls' home lives, unless as part of a caution on behaviour to the younger ones. "He's... he's doing very well, thank you." Her carefully prepared speech evaded Vi and she wasn't sure what to say next. Mrs Johnson was waiting for her to explain her presence. She took a deep breath. "Billy, that is Mr Dobson, needs to be taken to the Billingbrook Hall hospital on Tuesday. I was wondering if I could perhaps work on Saturday instead, so that I could take him?" Her hands trembled.

"Will this be every week?"

Vi almost said 'pardon?'. She'd expected an automatic refusal. "I don't know until I speak to them. I don't think so. Mr Dobson thinks it will be once a month now. He should be able to go on his own soon."

Mrs Johnson smiled. She actually smiled. Vi blinked at the sudden transformation.

"If you can let me know each week whether you will

need to switch shifts the following week, that should be adequate. Thank you, Mrs Dobson."

"Thank you." Vi backed out of the office, almost feeling she should be curtseying as she went.

"What's the matter with you?" Eva asked as she went back to her bench.

"Mrs Johnson — she was nice." Vi didn't know what to make of it.

Eva looked around her to make sure that Mrs Johnson wasn't watching her. "Haven't you heard? It's her son. He was missing in action early in the war. She never told a soul. Anyway, she's had a letter to say he's safe in a prisoner of war camp. After all this time."

Vi broke into a broad smile. "That's not so different from finding your husband's still alive when you thought he'd been dead nearly six months. No wonder she's happy." Vi went about her work, humming to herself. She hadn't felt this cheerful at work for a very long time. She didn't suppose for a minute that Mrs Johnson would be any less strict, but she was pleased for the woman all the same.

Although she tried to encourage Billy to leave the house, so far he had refused, except for his appointments.

"I want to be able to walk out of here under my own steam, not go in some chair," Billy said when Vi suggested they practice with the chair before Tuesday.

"And you're not going to be able to do that if you spend too much time sitting around in here." Vi walked out of the room and counted to ten. His spark seemed to have gone. Since he came home and reality hit, he seemed to have gone backward. She was hoping there would be an opportunity to bring that up at his next appointment.

They set off early for the hospital. Neither she nor Billy was clear how long it was going to take, and Elsie had found it so difficult the previous week that it gave no real measure. Vi knew what time the buses ran, but getting to the bus stop, changing buses in Billingbrook, and then going from the bus to the hospital at the other end could take minutes or hours.

They were both quiet as Vi tried manoeuvring the chair. If it hadn't been for her munitions factory work and football training, she'd never have managed the weight of it with Billy sitting there. The streets hadn't been built with wheelchairs in mind, and as soon as Vi arrived at the first kerb the problem became apparent. The bus stop was on the other side of the road.

"You need to do it back first," Billy said, obviously trying to be helpful.

"Oh, do I?" Vi said through gritted teeth as she tried to turn the chair around.

"Bloody hell, Vi." Billy gripped the arm of the chair as Vi tipped him back.

"We'll have none of that language," Vi reprimanded, although secretly muttering something similar under her own breath as she bore his weight.

Getting up the opposite kerb was going to be even more difficult.

"Billy, you're going to have to stand up to get on the bus, so perhaps it would be better to get out of the chair now so we can lift it up the kerb."

Billy began to stand up, but the chair moved. "For God's sake, put the brake on, Vi."

Vi silently counted to ten as she found the brake and applied it. They'd learn what the problems were and find ways through them together. At least she hoped they would. Otherwise, life was going to be impossible.

They boarded the bus with the help of the conductress, and the driver waited patiently for Billy to sit down before moving. Vi hoped the driver and conductor of their connecting bus would be as understanding. Then she thought about the last stretch of the journey. How was she going to push Billy up the drive to the hospital? Some of that was gravel. She sighed.

Despite her worries, the hospital was set up with wheelchairs in mind. There were boards laid across the gravel to the footpath which led from the gate. They'd made it.

Vi went around the chair to open the front door. As she passed his side, Billy caught her hand.

"I'm sorry, love."

She turned to face him. She could feel that her hair had tumbled down from the pins holding it and she felt damp with perspiration. As she looked at the sadness in Billy's eyes, all her frustration melted. How would she like it the other way around? She squeezed his hand. Then a thought occurred to her, and she smiled.

"When I started playing football with the girls, to begin with, we were all playing our own games. We didn't really know what we were doing, so all focussed on our own part. It was my dad who made us think about it differently. He was the one who taught us to think as a team. It wasn't always about what I could do, but what the team could do together. The girls started talking then, admitting the things we found hard or weren't good at. Once we did that, we became much better at working together." Vi stopped. She could see from the look on Billy's face that he'd understood what she was saying.

Billy looked rueful. "I think I'd better start. I haven't

wanted to go out because I'm scared. I'm scared of people feeling sorry for me, or of falling and not being able to get up. I'm scared of kids pointing at me. It's easier to stay at home."

Vi hadn't thought about any of those things. She was about to reply when one of the Voluntary Aid Detachment nurses opened the door and held it for them to go in.

"Later," Billy said to Vi as she went back around to the handles of the chair and took Billy into the hospital.

The appointment went well, although the doctor was concerned that Billy wasn't making more progress.

Billy nodded. "That's going to change, doctor. I just needed a bit of time to readjust." He smiled at Vi.

Vi thought about what he'd said. The reality was they both needed to do some readjusting, and the one thing they hadn't done was talk to each other about it.

As they came out of the front door of the Hall after Billy's appointment, he turned his head around to her and said, "Let's start again."

He didn't need to say anything more; Vi knew what he meant. She nodded. "If you look ahead at the hazards and tell me how you think they'd be best approached, maybe we can find a better way through. You know what it feels like in the chair, I don't."

"Right, down the ramp and off we go. I did think earlier that we might have been better on the road when we get near Ivy Terrace, rather than keep going up and down kerbs. I didn't think you'd appreciate me telling you."

"I probably wouldn't." It was funny admitting it, but Billy was right. Working as a team where she knew it was his job to tell her what lay ahead was one thing, but when she'd felt it was her responsibility she'd just felt he was correcting her and interfering. Teamwork would definitely be better.

When they alighted from the second bus Vi remembered to apply the brake to the wheelchair, so that Billy could sit down safely. "Road it is then," Vi said as she began to push the chair along the cobbles. "Are you sure about this? Kerbs are hard, but this can't be much fun either. It's certainly harder to push, and I can feel the bouncing of the chair through my arms."

"Hang on," Billy called to her. "I've got a better idea. Put the brake on and I'll walk this last bit."

As they came close to the house, Tessie ran out. "Here, let me help." She took over the chair from Vi so that Vi was free to help Billy.

"Thanks, Tessie," Vi said, giving up trying to pull the chair over the kerb to take it through the side passageway.

The pavement was uneven, and a couple of times Billy caught his foot. If Vi hadn't been there to support him, he could so easily have gone over.

"Looks like I'm going to need more practice. The doctor says it will get easier." He passed the stick to Vi and used the wall of the passageway for support instead. "I'm just going to have to work harder."

Vi sighed; it was easy to see why he'd felt like giving up. It was going to take a long time for him to build up the strength he needed.

CHAPTER 5

28th March 1917 - British Hospital Ship Torpedoed by U Boat -
The Daily Mirror

"I'm going to football practice this afternoon, but I won't be late home. I wish there was a way you could come with me." Vi kissed Billy before heading out to meet Tessie.

"I have to piss in a pot unless Mam helps me to the outhouse; how am I supposed to make it to the bloody recreation ground?" Billy sat on the edge of the bed and ran his hand through his hair.

Vi sat down next to him. "I'm sorry. I won't go."

Billy looked up at her, a serious look on his face. "You bloody well will go. I need you to inspire me, not wallow with me."

Vi nodded. She could see what he was saying, but it was hard to say the right thing when she was treading on eggshells the whole time.

"Go on, you get off. Tessie'll be waiting. I'll be all right."

Vi stood up, knowing that Billy probably wouldn't be all right, but there was precious little she could do about it. She wanted to help, but she just didn't know how. She could see from the stresses between Billy and his mam that taking over and doing things for him wasn't the answer. "See you later, love," she said and went out, feeling that somehow she was doing everything wrong.

"Where's your kit?" Tessie asked as soon as Vi came out into Victoria Street.

Vi grimaced and turned around to go back. She ran upstairs and into the bedroom, expecting to find Billy still sitting on the edge of the bed, but he'd moved across to the dressing table and was trying to find somewhere to put away his notes from the hospital.

"What are these?" he asked, holding up one of the sketches of hats that Vi kept at the bottom of the drawer.

Vi could feel herself blushing. "They aren't very good. They're just ideas of hats I'd make if I were a designer."

Billy frowned. "Unless I'm mistaken, they are good. I didn't even know you could draw. May I?" he asked, indicating the pile of drawings still lying in the drawer.

"I… oh, why not. I can't stop now, I only came back for my bag. We could look at them together later." She gave him a weak smile and ran back downstairs carrying her kit to catch up with Tessie.

The girls had a match coming up on Easter Monday. It was a return game against Calderley, a team who had beaten them by fouling when they met the previous year. The Billingbrook girls were determined to win and needed all the practice they could get. Wednesday afternoon training was easier for Vi to attend; she'd have been at work anyway. Saturday was harder, as it meant leaving Billy behind.

"We could do with you here," their coach Joe Wood said. "There must be some way you could bring Mr Dobson with you."

Vi sighed. "I just don't know how. I couldn't get the wheelchair over this ground and it's too far for him to walk at the moment, especially with the path being so uneven."

"I've got an idea," Maud said. "Dad's a greengrocer. He's just bought one of those motorised vehicles so he can deliver his fruit and veg more easily. He'll finish by lunchtime on Saturday. What if he drives Billy here and takes him back afterward?"

"D'you think he would?" Tessie asked. "Oh, Vi, what do you think? Would Billy come then?"

Vi decided to wait until Maud had an answer from her dad before suggesting it to Billy. The last thing she wanted to do was raise his hopes and then let him down. Besides, when she went home that night, she wanted to tell him about her hat designs and her dreams of making them; this time not in someone else's factory, but under her own name. It was a silly idea and would never happen, but she loved dreaming, and sharing it with Billy would be something special.

When Vi went down to the Caulder and Harrison yard at break the following day, Maud was already there and her broad grin said it all.

"He said yes. He won't be able to get the wheelchair in, though, so I don't know what Mr Dobson could sit on."

"There are some chairs in the social club at the recreation ground," Joe Wood said, looking as relieved as Vi was feeling. "Mr Giffard won't mind us bringing one of those out. Mr Dobson can always sit inside if it rains. That's the best place for Maud's dad to drive to anyway."

"I'll ask him tonight," Vi said, wondering how best to do it so that he would agree. Billy was very sensitive to offers of help and didn't always appreciate them.

Tommy was still not in bed when Vi arrived home that evening; he was with his dad and grandparents in the back room. They had already eaten, and Vi's meal was being kept warm. She decided to talk to Billy before eating, so went in to join them.

Tommy and Billy were sitting side by side at the table and it made Vi smile to see them looking in many ways so similar. Even the expression on their faces as she went in was much the same.

"Shouldn't you be in bed, young man? You're at school in the morning."

"I was helping Daddy with his writing." Tommy held up a piece of paper showing all his numbers up to twenty and the letters of the alphabet.

Vi grinned at Billy. "I'm sure Daddy is very grateful." Billy held up a page to show her, written with his left hand. He was making good progress and his letters already looked much neater than Tommy's. "I think I may have some more good news for Daddy." She turned to look at him face on and felt suddenly anxious. "You know you wanted to come to the football practice so that I didn't have to cancel going?" She paused, hoping he would acknowledge what she'd said, but he didn't react. "Well, how about if there was transport in a motor vehicle to take you there?" Vi's heart was racing. She had no idea which way this would go.

Before Billy had an opportunity to speak, Tommy shouted, "Can I go in the motor vehicle? Please let me?"

Vi shook her head. "No, love, you'd have to come with me. There's only one spare seat. Maud's dad has offered to collect Dad and bring him home afterward. What do you say, love?" Offered might be something of an exaggeration, but she thought Billy was more likely to accept on that basis. She could see by his frown that he was struggling with the idea.

It was Alf who filled the pause that opened up. "I've been thinking, with all this move to motor vehicles, being a cartwright isn't quite the job it used to be. I might like to take up driving, and I'm sure even at my age I could learn to be a mechanic. I could do with finding someone with a vehicle who might let me have a go. Do you think Maud's dad would be willing for me to try?"

Somehow Alf's words shifted the tone of the conversation. This was no longer about Billy being an invalid and needing help. This was about Maud's dad being the only person they knew with a motor vehicle, and something they all wanted to take advantage of.

Billy looked across at his dad and for a moment Vi worried he wouldn't give her an answer. "Perhaps I can talk to him about Dad when he gives me a lift."

Vi went over and hugged Billy. "It will be wonderful having you at the practice sessions. You can tell me how to improve."

Alf took a long draw on his pipe and Vi wondered if he'd meant what he'd said, or had just seen a way for Billy to give a reasonable reaction.

That Saturday Vi had to leave for practice with Tommy before Maud's dad would collect Billy. She wished she could be there, but it was perhaps best that she wouldn't be. He'd be happier if no one made a fuss; besides, she thought Alf was looking forward to going out and having a good look at the grocer's van.

There were no stands at the Caulder and Harrison recreation ground; spectators would normally gather around the field, but when Vi, Tessie and Tommy arrived, there was already a row of chairs neatly positioned along the edge of the pitch. What was more, they were all standing on wooden pallets so that they weren't on uneven ground, with planks as a walkway from the footpath to reach them. They looked for all the world as though they were always like that.

"Who? What?" Vi looked around at the grinning faces.

"It was Mr Wood's suggestion," Clara said.

"Mr Giffard thinks it's such a good idea that the Company will do it all properly in the next few weeks. He says he wants to make it possible for some of the patients at the hospital to come and watch if Major Tomlinson will agree," Joe Wood said as he positioned the final chair.

"It's perfect." Vi thought she was going to cry, but sniffed hard to stop herself. "I'd better change into my kit." She and Tessie headed to the changing room while Tommy went to sit on one of the chairs to wait for his dad to arrive.

Any anxiety Vi had was soon lost in hearing Billy shouting encouragement to her. With him giving her instructions on what to do when wheeling his chair, they were becoming good at communicating directions, and Vi could easily understand most of his ideas.

"You need to come more often," Joe Wood said to Billy as they all came off the pitch. "If that's how Vi plays when you're here, we need you as a permanent fixture." Joe hesitated. "I've not asked Vi if she'd mind this suggestion, but how would you feel about helping with some of the coaching?"

Vi bit her lip and looked eagerly at Billy. She'd love for him to help.

Billy was looking at Joe. "Can't you see that I'll never be able to run around the pitch?"

Joe burst out laughing. "I'm not stupid, mate. I wasn't asking you to run anywhere. If you can get the best out of Vi's play by shouting observations from the sidelines, why would you need to run? I reckon you could do just as well for some of the others. What do you say?"

"The only problem is getting to all the sessions." Billy's face had lit up at the prospect.

"That's sorted then." It was Maud's dad who spoke up. He'd stayed to watch the practice with Billy. "Our Maud loves playing and if you can help her to do even better, then it will be a privilege to be your taxi service."

By the time Vi arrived home that afternoon, Alf was outside admiring the Morris Oxford van belonging to Maud's dad, Burt. The bonnet was raised, and they were deep in conversation looking at the engine. Vi said hello and left them to it. She went inside to find Billy. She wanted to talk to him about the game, but when she found him, he was already fast asleep in a chair.

As Easter came around, Vi couldn't believe that it was two years since Billy signed up on his way back from watching Billingbrook United play. Now he was going to be on the sidelines at Whittingham Road and cheering for her and the rest of the team. At least at the football stadium they could wheel his chair up to the sideline, although that meant going on the bus, as it didn't fit easily into Burt's vehicle; at least not without completely unloading the van first. They became better at negotiating buses and roads as time went on, although, practising every day, Billy could walk further too.

Billy waved to Vi as she and the girls ran out onto the pitch. She waved back and felt a bubble of excitement. He'd already helped the girls to think about passing the ball ahead of a teammate so they could take it in their stride. He'd also encouraged them to mark opposition players more closely, giving them less time to think;

forcing their opponents to control the ball more accurately or risk losing it to one of the Billingbrook girls.

The referee was clearly aware of the history between the two sides and was stopping the game for any apparent foul. Within the first half, both teams were down to ten girls and Vi was starting to feel very frustrated. She wasn't happy that Annie had been sent off and would talk to her about that later. For now, she needed to focus on the game. Try as she might to find opportunities, they just didn't seem to come her way. She couldn't find space to pass to the other girls, nor could they pass the ball to her when they needed to. It was their first ever match to end with a no score draw.

"Don't worry, love," Billy said when she joined him afterwards. "Even Billingbrook United has games that go like that. You were really good, even though you didn't score."

Vi's spirits lifted. Billy's praise was worth more to her than all the goals she could have scored. She slipped her hand into his, while her dad and Billy's dad took turns to push the chair along the road. Tommy was helping push as much as he could, but would sometimes run around the group, clearly delighted to have his dad around.

Those first few weeks were difficult. Vi could see how frustrated Billy was with the things he couldn't do and by his mam's behaviour. His mam always had been one to interfere.

"You don't know what it's like, Vi."

Vi suspected she did, but bit her lip and listened.

"Every time I try to do something, she leaps in. When I go out for a walk, she tells me to stay indoors. I'm going mad. The doctor told me to walk every day to build up the strength in the leg and I'm doing well. It doesn't hurt so much and I can go further. I can even go out to the privy safely on my own, if she'll let me. I need to get out more, Vi. I want to go back to work." He ran his hand through his hair. "I want to provide for my family again. I feel... I feel... oh, I don't know how I feel. Less of a man." He thumped the table.

Vi chose her words carefully. He'd always been such an active man. "You might need to think about doing a desk job. How's the writing coming on?"

"Vi, I'm no good at schoolwork. Writing was never my thing. How am I supposed to learn now?"

He was right, she knew. He couldn't very well go back to the infant school with Tommy, or the secondary school come to that. "Maybe they'd have some ideas at the hospital." She also thought she'd ask around at work, but didn't want to mention that in case it came to nothing.

As the weeks passed, Billy's fitness improved until he could walk quite a good distance, as long as it was on even ground. His depression, however, increased, not helped by his mam treating him like a small and rather backward child.

"What kind of man am I?" he shouted at Vi when she came home from work one day in May. "I wish I'd died. I'm no use to you, I'm no use to Tommy. Stan was right not to come back. I should have carried on pretending I was him."

Vi had been patient up until now, but with working long hours and trying to help Billy, she was feeling strained and tired. "Tommy worships the ground you walk on. You've got a wife who loves you. Yes, your mam can make things hard, we both know that, but she loves you. Why not think about the things you can do and stop hankering after the things you can't? You are doing a great job coaching our football team. You'd rather moan than try to learn anything new. You might just find you like it. God spared you on the battlefield. You have your life ahead of you, Billy Dobson. Bloody do something with it."

She didn't stay to see how he'd respond. She picked up her coat and went out for a walk.

CHAPTER 6

Wednesday 9th May 1917 - British Withdraw from Fresnoy Village - The Daily Mirror

"Leave it out, Mam." Billy was fed up with his mother fussing. He was twenty-four, for goodness' sake, not eight. He did not need cushions plumped or his slippers bringing.

"You stay there, love." Mam carried on as though he hadn't spoken.

Billy was getting more and more frustrated. It was as though she wanted to keep him immobile. "Mam, I said leave it out. I might be disabled, but I'm not ill."

"Could have fooled me, shouting in your sleep, having nightmares all over the place."

Billy was quiet for a moment. The nightmares weren't as bad as they'd been at the start, but they still came; and when they did, everyone heard them.

"Who was Chip anyway?" Mam asked. "Shouting at him to get down, you were. Most insistent."

Billy laughed. A real belly laugh that he hadn't felt for some time. "What else did I say?"

"I don't know really, but you keep shouting for this Chip. Who was he?"

"Chip," Billy replied, grinning, "was a lovely little dog that Stan picked up. He was quite a character, I can tell you. We had some good times. I wonder what happened to him." Billy had an idea. "Is yesterday's paper still around?"

"It'll be in the kitchen. I'll get it for you. I was about to make it into firelighters."

"I'll get it. Please, let me." Whilst thinking of Chip had lowered his stress, he still didn't want his mam doing everything.

Mam looked disappointed, but Billy got to his feet and made his way to the kitchen. It was only an idea, and his mam would probably object, but he wasn't going to let that stop him. He lay the newspaper on the table and turned the pages. He couldn't find what he was looking for. "I'm off out," he called. Before his mam could find a reason to protest, Billy picked up his cap from the hall peg and set off into the street. Using his stick, he was getting about much better now, although uneven pavements proved a challenge.

Billy knew Vi was right. Life had to change, and much of that was about him changing how he viewed the world. He hated how things were. He'd been the breadwinner; that was how it was supposed to be. On his disability pension he could hardly put food on the table, never mind do anything more. He was scared to go back to studying. It hadn't really been his strength at school, and he was afraid he'd feel stupid; he hadn't even worked out how to sharpen a pencil one-handed. He'd coped better when he was doing his army training, so maybe it wouldn't be quite so bad. He was torn. He remembered the example that Davy had been and how he'd been willing to try anything. Perhaps he owed it to the lad to have a go; but failure was hard, and he didn't know how much he could take.

Before he turned his mind to what he could do about employment, Billy had another mission in mind. This one could be good for all of them. He knew he should talk to Vi first, but if he didn't act immediately the moment would pass. He'd talk to her as soon as he could.

As he walked, Billy remembered there were notice cards in the window of the greengrocer's shop. Although he'd had no reason to read them before, it might be a good starting point for what he had in mind.

It was Mam asking him about Chip that had done it. Billy didn't want to end his days sitting in a chair doing nothing. The stump of his leg was often sore if he walked too far, but over time he was building up greater distances. The hospital had told him that it would get easier as long as he kept practising. If he was going to walk further and more often, he wanted a companion to walk with.

He found the cards in the corner window of the greengrocer's shop. On one of them, in neat block handwriting, was exactly what he'd been looking for. 'Free to good home, 2 girls and 3 boys, mother terrier, father unknown.' The address was nearby, which was helpful. Billy headed in that direction before he could change his mind, hoping Vi would forgive him for not talking to her first.

"I've come about the puppies," he said when a woman answered his knock.

She stood in the open doorway and looked him up and down. "You'd best come in."

She led him straight through to the kitchen where a rather shabby terrier was nursing some young puppies.

"Boy or girl?"

"Pardon." Billy hadn't been listening. He stood looking at the little dogs and was certain this was the right thing to do.

"Boy or girl?"

"Boy," he replied automatically. He didn't know what looking after a girl would involve.

"Sit down," the woman instructed.

Billy perched on the stool indicated. Without ceremony, the woman put a small brown bundle in his lap. Billy dropped his stick as he had to make sure the little chap didn't wriggle and fall off. With his one hand, he lifted the pup up to his face and was promptly licked for his trouble.

A dog didn't care about the scarring or know he should have two good legs. A dog wouldn't stare at his missing arm or his wooden leg when he took it off at night.

"And they're free?" he asked quietly. He hadn't thought to see what money there was in the jar before he'd come out.

The woman stood with her legs wide, supporting her over-thick trunk of a body. "Well, he seems happy with the arrangement, so I suppose I am. He's a bit young to be leaving his mam, but if you don't mind waiting a week or so, he's all yours." For the first time since Billy's arrival, the woman smiled. She struggled down to lift his stick and hand it to him. "It's the least I can do in return for what you've been through." She looked at him more closely. "Are you Elsie's boy?"

He nodded and frowned.

"I knew you when you were a nipper." She shook her head as though remembering.

Billy smiled to himself. Without knowing it, she'd given the puppy his name: Nipper. At least waiting a week would give him the opportunity to talk to Vi before the little chap arrived. He couldn't wait to collect him. Nipper would be a wonderful surprise for Tommy, but he dreaded to think what his mam was going to say when she found out.

When Vi came home that night, Tommy was already asleep, but Billy still decided to talk to her downstairs in case the boy heard. He waited until Mam went through to the kitchen and his dad had gone for a pint.

"Vi, love, I was thinking, I need to get out walking more than I have been and it's not much fun on my own. How would you feel about us getting a dog?" Now Billy just hoped she didn't say no.

Vi's face lit up. "I'd say it's a lovely idea, but are you sure? They can be a lot of work and I can't see your mam being willing to do it. Are you...?" she trailed off.

"Am I up to it? Is that what you're going to ask?" Billy leaned back in the chair, deflated after the excitement of the day, and sighed. "I don't know, if I'm being honest. But I want to try, and I have the feeling that knowing the little chap needs me to do things for him might just be what I need."

"Chap?" Vi was grinning. "Does that mean it's going to be a boy?"

Billy felt sheepish and nodded. "I've already chosen him. I'm sorry."

Vi stood up suddenly and clapped her hands. "Is he here now?"

Billy felt a rush of love for her. She hadn't focussed at all on the fact he hadn't talked to her first. "Not yet. He's still too young, and if you'd said 'no' he could have gone to another home. We can collect him in a week. I want it to be a surprise for Tommy."

Vi nodded. "And Mam?"

Billy grimaced. "It's not so much that I want it to be a surprise for her and Dad, it's just I don't want to risk telling her and her say she doesn't want him here."

The week passed slowly as Billy waited to fetch Nipper. He decided to collect the puppy on his own. Vi would be at work and he wanted to surprise Tommy when he came home from school. As the little dog probably wouldn't be able to walk even as far as Billy could yet, he took a canvas bag that he carried on his shoulder, slung around his neck; that would still leave his hand free for his stick. After putting an old towel in the bottom of the bag so Nipper would be comfortable, Billy managed to leave the house without his mam realising. That at least avoided all the awkward questions he'd been expecting, for now anyway.

This time when he arrived at the house, the woman greeted him with a broad smile and showed him straight through to where the remaining puppies were playing while their mam looked on. He spotted Nipper immediately. It was the odd way his ear stuck up as though listening and attentive, even when he was doing something else. Billy wanted to get down to floor level to join the puppies, but if he did then there'd be little chance of getting up without help, so he took the seat offered and waited for Nipper to be passed to him.

The puppy had grown during the intervening week and was already getting more difficult to manage with one hand. Billy realised the stupidity of not talking to his parents about this. More than likely he was going to need some help, but it was too late now. He'd just have to use his charms and hope his mam came round. Nipper was licking his hand and Billy smiled.

The walk home with Nipper was harder than Billy had thought. He really needed a free hand to stop the bag from bouncing against his body, but he took the steps slowly and talked to Nipper as he went. Despite everything, the puppy seemed content in the bottom of the bag and slept as Billy walked. As they arrived back at Ivy Terrace, Billy took a deep breath. May as well get the introduction to his mother over with and find out just how bad it was going to be.

"What in God's name is that?" Elsie asked as he lifted Nipper so that his head was out of the bag. She peered more closely. "Well, you're not bringing him in here. He'll make an awful mess."

"Then I guess I'll just have to stay outside with him. I was rather hoping he would be living here now. Where he goes, I go. If he can't come in, then neither can I." Billy wasn't completely sure that he would be able to take Nipper everywhere he went and hadn't really thought about what would happen when he couldn't, but there'd be time to sort that out. His mother stood with her hands on her hips and her mouth open as Billy walked past, taking Nipper into the back room.

If he was being honest, Billy didn't know a great deal about looking after a dog, especially a small puppy. Stan's dog had fed itself on rats and as they were outside most of the time, there was little need to take it out for walks or the toilet. When Nipper woke up, the first thing he did was pee on the back room carpet. Billy sighed. Being on the wrong side of his mam wasn't going to make this easy. He picked up Nipper and took him through to the kitchen where his mam was doing some laundry.

"Is there a mop I can use? I'm really sorry, but Nipper's peed on the carpet." He put Nipper down on the floor by the back door and was about to take him outside when Nipper peed again. How could he go a second time when he'd only just gone? Billy looked up at his mam's face.

"Look, I'm sorry." He held up his good hand in a gesture of supplication. "I was wrong, and I should have talked to you first. I just thought having Nipper would help me to get stronger. I thought he'd just accept me as I am and that would help me come to terms with things. Perhaps I'd better take him back."

His mam looked first at Billy and then down at Nipper, who was sitting next to the puddle on the floor and looking back at her innocently.

"The back room carpet, you say?" Mam asked him.

Billy nodded.

"You take him outside before he causes anymore trouble and I'll sort it out." Mam moved the washing onto the side so that she could put the bucket in the sink and started to fill it with water.

Mam said no more about whether Nipper could stay, and Billy wasn't really sure what to do. He took Nipper outside into the back yard and let the little dog have a sniff around. He stayed outside for a while, but both he and Nipper were getting tired, so he headed back indoors. His mam was nowhere to be seen, but both puddles had been cleaned up and there was some newspaper down on top of the carpet. Billy grinned. That he took as a good sign.

When Billy heard Tommy run down the side passage coming home from school, Nipper was fast asleep on his lap.

As Tommy came in through the back door, he heard his mam say, "You mind you wipe your feet, I've just washed this floor." Billy half-smiled.

"Where's Dad?"

Billy could hear the sound of feet scuffing on the mat as the boy waited for a reply. Billy didn't want to call out and wake Nipper.

"He's in the back room, more's the pity."

His mam didn't elaborate, and Billy waited for Tommy to come charging in.

"Dad," Tommy shouted as he came through the door.

Billy put his finger to his lips and then stroked Nipper. The little dog lifted his head, yawned, and went straight back to sleep.

Tommy dropped to his knees in front of his dad. He looked at Nipper and then up at Billy, his mouth open.

Billy grinned back. "What do you think?"

"What's he called?" Tommy's eyes were wide.

"Nipper. I'm not sure he's got used to the name yet, but he will. Your Gran's not happy." Billy tried hard not to smile too broadly as he told Tommy what had happened. "I'm going to need your help with him, if that's all right with you?"

"Me? Really? Oh, Dad, yes, please let me look after him."

Billy nodded. "If we do all the work between us, then there'll be nothing for your mam to do, and nothing for your gran to complain about."

"She'll only find something else to complain about." Tommy groaned.

Billy knew he should reprimand his son for the remark, but he couldn't help smiling, knowing full well it was true.

Thankfully, when Alf Dobson came home, he took the arrival of Nipper with his usual equanimity. He seemed to rather like the little chap, but nodded at Elsie as she laid out her concerns.

At least Billy's mam seemed to have accepted that Nipper would be staying, which was enough for him to be going on with. There was just Vi left to meet the little chap and Billy was looking forward to that. He was glad Nipper wouldn't come as a surprise to her. His mam's reaction had been enough on that score.

Vi was tired when she came in from work; she always was. Her shifts were long and the work very physical. Normally she would say hello, then go upstairs to give Tommy a goodnight kiss before coming back downstairs to eat. Tonight was different. He heard both Vi and Tessie clattering in through the kitchen. Tessie was giggling and that made him smile. If she was bringing Tessie in now, it could only mean she wanted to meet Nipper, and if Vi had been talking about him, that showed just how excited she was. He'd made sure Nipper had already been outside to the toilet before Vi arrived. He didn't want a repeat of earlier, so he put the little dog on the floor to see what would happen.

When Vi came through the door, Nipper padded over to her immediately. Billy could see from the look on Vi's face that it was love at first sight, for both Vi and Nipper, and that made Billy happy too.

Over the next few weeks, Billy and Tommy taught Nipper all the basic commands he needed so as not to cause too much trouble around the house. When Tommy wasn't at school, the three of them would go out to play together or for a walk. Nipper's total acceptance of Billy gave him confidence not to hide away as much as he'd been wanting to before. Billy also thought that if Nipper could learn so many new things, then so could he.

He had one or two false starts where he set off in search of the adult school, but turned back and went home. He wanted to ask what help he could get with retraining, but he couldn't quite bring himself to go. The day of his third aborted attempt, he spent the rest of the day sitting at home reading the newspaper. Apart from catching up on what was going on in the war, there was nothing much that interested him except the sports pages. However, as he'd got nothing better to do, he read everything there was just to fill his time. That night, Vi was worn out when she came home and was almost falling asleep over her dinner. Billy looked at his wife and felt a sudden stab of guilt. While he'd been sitting doing nothing very much, she had been working hard to put food on the table for their family. That was his job. He had to stop making excuses to himself and get on with it.

The next morning when Vi left the house, Billy got himself ready and this time nothing was going to make him turn back before he reached the adult school. Someone there would be able to give him some guidance, he was sure they would.

By the end of the day he'd signed up to return to studying, and was determined to make it a success.

With Nipper around, Elsie was glad to have him out of the house for periods of the day, and he kept what he was doing quiet from Vi, for the time being. No one challenged him about taking the dog with him to his lessons and so, with Nipper by his side, Billy set about improving his writing ability with his left hand and learning the basics of mathematics, a subject he had frequently skipped at school. It was funny, it seemed a lot easier now. Part of that was having had to use numbers in working out his carpentry measurements before the war. They no longer held the same fear that he'd found when confronted with sums as a boy.

He had no idea whether he'd be able to find any work at the end of his studies, but if he didn't learn some new skills, then he certainly wouldn't.

Billy felt happier than he had done for a long time. He just wished Stan and Davy were there to share it all.

CHAPTER 7

Friday 3rd August 1917 - British Win Back Lost Advanced Positions - The Daily Mirror

"How's your Billy doing?" Eva asked as they were working.

It was unusual to be free to talk, but this was a rare day on which Mrs Johnson wasn't around, and they were making the most of the opportunity.

Vi smiled. "I can't believe how much difference Nipper has made to him. He's only had the little dog a few weeks and he's a different person. More the old Billy."

It was hot working in the factory at the best of times, but having to wear overalls all through August was stifling. Vi wiped her brow.

"It's good having him help Mr Wood with the football. I know he can't run about, but he's made a big difference with the things he's told us." Eva was packing the shell she was working on in between them talking.

Hearing each other over the factory noise was difficult.

"You should tell him. He'd like that." Vi was proud of Billy for his help with the football. However, she wondered where he was going during the daytimes now; he said he wanted to save that as a surprise, so she guessed it was something good. She didn't suppose he could get up to too much mischief. She hoped he might have found a way to go back to studying, but she knew how scared he was of failing. He hadn't said anything, but she'd noticed a big difference in his writing, and she hoped the two things were connected. She returned to the conversation with Eva. "I'm excited we're playing more football matches this year. I know we play to raise money, but I'd do it just for the love of the game."

"Mr Giffard says there'll be one a month through to next summer."

"Miss Podmore, please get on with your work and stop idling." Mrs Johnson had appeared back on their floor and the opportunity to talk was over.

When she turned to walk away, Vi wagged a finger at Eva and the pair of them had to hide their laughter.

The war might still be raging, and Vi's fringe was still the odd canary yellow from the chemicals they worked with, but she was happy. She and Billy took Nipper for walks together and Billy could walk much better now than when he'd come home from hospital. He still tired, but they could rest against a wall when he needed to. Despite all the good things she had, it was when she was on the football pitch that Vi really felt she came alive. At those times, she didn't worry about money, or providing Tommy with clothes; nor did she worry about the difficulty Billy was finding looking for work. It was just her, the girls, and a leather ball.

Vi was captain. The role stuck early in their playing, and everyone still seemed happy with the arrangement. She was the eldest in the team, so she presumed that was the reason, even though the others said she was best for the job. Some players came and went, but the core of the team stayed the same and they were all rather more expert than when they'd started. Not that you'd realise from any of the newspaper reports. Even after playing for a couple of years, the papers were still more concerned with what the girls were wearing and how they looked than they were with any tactics and skills. Vi hoped that if there was a women's cup or league, then reporting might eventually change, but so far there'd been no success on either score. She hadn't realised how difficult it would be to organise.

"You'll never guess what," Tessie said as they were walking back from work in early September. "Edith's been offered another job."

Vi gasped and turned to look at her. "Why? What's wrong with working at Caulder and Harrison? Will she be getting more money?"

Tessie shook her head. "She said she's fed up with her hair being yellow and not being able to talk when she works. I don't think that's really the reason. She's going to be a nurse. She'll get training and everything."

Vi nodded. She could see Edith taking care of people. She'd be good at it. "But what are we going to do for a goalkeeper? She's loads better than any of the others."

Tessie grinned. "Don't get your knickers in a twist. Mr Giffard's made arrangements so she can still play for us. He's even said they'll make up any wages she loses at her new place."

Vi let out the breath she'd been holding. Edith had really saved the day for them in a number of matches; it would be a nightmare for the team if she couldn't play. In training, it was always hard getting a penalty kick past her. She was the best.

"I don't really understand why the company pays us to practice. It's always seemed odd to me, but I'm not complaining," Tessie said.

Vi smiled. She'd wondered too, to begin with. "I was

talking to Billy and his dad about that. What they think is that the amount we raise in the Company's name makes them look good. We raise much more than the wages. They might even take our wages out of the ticket money before giving the rest to the hospital, as part of the costs of playing. That way, it doesn't actually cost them anything. Even if they did that, it would still be a good way to raise lots of money."

Because she'd become so much stronger over time, the work at the factory wasn't as physically difficult as Vi had found it at the start, but it still required concentration. From the point she clocked on in the morning until the claxon sounded for break, Vi generally kept her head down; well, except for the occasional exchange with Eva, but that didn't happen often.

One Tuesday they were working at opposite sides of their bench, as usual. Vi was just lifting a new shell case, ready to fill, when there was an ear-splitting sound like overhead thunder. The building shook so badly that dust and debris showered down from the ceiling.

Vi didn't hesitate. They'd been told what to do in an emergency. She left the shell case, jumped down from her stool and sat in a foetal position under the bench, covering her head.

"What the hell was that?" Eva shouted, still sitting on her stool.

Before she'd finished speaking, there was another thunder crack, with more dust showering down as the factory reverberated.

Vi wasn't the only one to get down. Other girls were under their benches and some of them were screaming.

"Get down here, Eva," Vi called. "Now."

Eva was looking a little dazed and shaken as she peered under the bench to Vi. Vi moved across and pulled her arm. "Get down here."

Vi's hands were trembling. She had no idea what to do. She waited to see if there was going to be another blast, but all seemed quiet. She was wondering if they should carry on working when one of the gate men came running onto their floor from the corridor and went straight to Mrs Johnson's office. If he wasn't paying attention to the 'no running' rule then something was seriously wrong.

After a few seconds, he ran back to the stairwell and out of sight.

Mrs Johnson was marching out of her office looking flustered; her skirts were bunched up from where she too had presumably been under a desk. Vi had never seen the woman look anything other than calm and neatly dressed.

In contrast to her appearance, Mrs Johnson's voice was commanding as she shouted to them. "Leave the building calmly but quickly, girls, and meet outside the front gate. Don't collect your things, just go straight out. All of you, move. Now. No running, but don't hang about. Come along there." She was walking the length of the benches, ushering all the girls away from their stations and from under the benches, out toward the exit. One or two of the girls seemed slower to react and a steely note crept into Mrs Johnson's voice. "Now, girls. Right away. Do not go back for anything."

Vi didn't need telling twice, and she and Eva moved quickly toward the corridor. They were about halfway to the exit when there was another almighty noise. This time, some of the windows shattered, and they were thrown to the floor. The screams of the other girls rang in her ears.

"Bloody hell, Vi, that's not thunder, is it?" Eva took Vi's

hand where she lay next to her in the mess.

"We've got to get out, Eva. We can't lie here." Vi tried to get to her feet but some of the glass had cut into her hand. She winced. That would have to wait until later. For now, she needed to get as far from the factory as she could.

"Eva," she shouted. The girl seemed stunned. "Eva." This time she looked around at Vi and nodded, clambering to her feet.

Vi half pulled Eva as she found a gap through the flow of people. They were used to moving nimbly around opponents on the field and they dodged the others in their rush to leave the building.

"Don't stand there," Vi said, when Eva stopped just outside the gate. "Let's get as far from this as we can."

They moved through the crowds of workers to the far side of the road, before stopping and looking back at the Caulder and Harrison buildings.

Vi gasped as she saw smoke coming up from where the roof of the end building should have been. "Tessie!" she shouted and made to head back in that direction to find her friend.

Eva grabbed her arm. "You can't go back."

There was another blast which confirmed what Eva was saying. Vi realised there must be a risk of the entire factory going up.

"But it's the wing that Tessie and Beattie work in. We need to see if they're all right." Vi was desperate to make sure they weren't inside.

"Are you stupid? You can't go back until everything's safe. You've just made me move away from the building, you can't go back there now. We'll have to wait to find out." Eva was shaking as she tried to hang on to Vi.

Vi slumped down onto the edge of the pavement. She

knew Eva was right. Please God, let the others all be safe. She chewed her lip and felt cold, even though it was a warm day. Eva dropped down next to her and they clung to each other.

"Did you really think it was only thunder?" Vi asked as she looked across at the still smoking building.

"I don't know. I just didn't think it could be anything else. I mean, I know we're working with explosives, but they're not meant to go off until they get to the battlefield. I've always thought they must be safe, really."

Eva's naivety made her seem much younger than twenty, and Vi wondered how many of the factory understood the significance of the work they were doing.

One of the gate men was going around with a clipboard, trying to mark off who had left the building. Vi scrambled up and went over to him.

"Tessie Brown. Do you know if Tessie Brown is out?"

He shook his head. "Sorry, love, I'm only doing our building. There are others covering the other buildings. You'll have to wait to find out."

Vi thanked him and slumped back down next to Eva.

From the crowds of people gathering who were not wearing factory overalls, word had obviously spread around town of what had happened. Although now that Vi thought about it, they would all have heard, and for that matter felt, the explosions. She didn't know Billy was there until there was barking and Nipper stuck his nose into her face. She lifted the little dog and stood up, searching the crowd for Billy.

He limped over to her. "Oh, thank God, Vi. I thought…"

As Vi wrapped her arms around him, she broke into sobs. "Oh, Billy, it was awful. The explosions were so loud.

We were terrified. I thought the first one was bad, but then when the second one happened…"

Billy pulled away. "Shut up, shut up, shut up."

"What? I could have died in there. I thought you'd at least care."

"Care? Of course I bloody care. Don't you think I know what it's like? We heard shells landing over and over through the days. Even now, when I go to sleep, I hear artillery guns firing through the night. I hear explosions as though shells are landing all around me. I see Stan and I can't save him. I can't do this, Vi." He turned around and limped away from her. Nipper ran after him.

"Eva, I'll be back," Vi shouted over her shoulder as she followed behind Billy.

Vi could move faster than Billy and caught up with him quickly.

"I'm sorry," she said. "I didn't think. Why don't you talk to me about it?"

They went to sit on a low wall, which was far enough away from the growing crowd of people.

"I can't talk about it. How can you understand when you weren't there? How can you have any idea what it feels like to see dead bodies when you close your eyes? Not even bodies, but parts of bodies, rotting flesh. I can still smell the stench of death. It's like it's stuck in my nose, and I'll never get it out."

He was crying now, and Vi simply held him. She kept her bleeding hand out of the way. There was still a shard of glass to get out and it was hurting, but what was that compared to what Billy had told her? She'd never really understood before. Of course, she realised that it must have been bad to lose part of his leg and his arm, but she'd never really thought about the reality of what had happened to cause it. It was unimaginable. Now that she thought about what Billy was saying, it was unbearable. While he'd been away, she'd only coped by not thinking. Since he'd been home, whilst she knew he had nightmares, she'd never let herself think about the things he might be reliving.

He looked up and she could see his green eyes glistening, looking far away.

"Then you come home and you're just scrap. No use to anyone, and you know you never will be. The men who died were the lucky ones. They aren't left to a living hell of constant battle. God, I miss Stan, and Davy come to that, but I wouldn't wish this on them."

Vi didn't know what to say. She was still desperately worried about Tessie and Beattie, but the things Billy had said put the events of the day into perspective. For the first time, Vi wasn't sure she felt so good about making shells. This war had gone on long enough. Too many men were losing their lives. Too many families were broken. She couldn't leave her job; they needed the money. Vi wondered what she was going to do. The only other things she knew were football and hat making, and no one was likely to pay her to play football.

CHAPTER 8

Wednesday 8th August 1917 - The Battle of Flanders - Tommy Gives Fritz a Light - The Daily Mirror

Vi's hand was stinging from the glass.

Billy was sitting slumped on the wall with his arm around her. "I'm sorry," he said, without looking up. "I shouldn't have shouted."

Vi stroked his hair. "No, it's me who should be sorry. I just didn't realise. I think I should look for another job."

Billy frowned. "But what about the football?"

Vi shrugged. "Maybe they'd still let me play. Edith's leaving the factory and they've agreed to pay her for practice on a Wednesday, and when she's playing for the company. Besides, some things are more important than football." A thought crossed Vi's mind and she looked inquisitively at Billy. "How come you got here so quickly? It would have taken you longer than that from home." She felt a small prickle of unease as to where he might be spending his time, but she was disarmed by the boyish shrug.

"I don't want to tell you yet, but I will soon. I want it to be a surprise." He looked down at Nipper and put his finger to his lips, as though telling the little dog not to let on. "It is a good thing. I promise." He got up from the wall and stretched his shoulders. "Did all the girls get out all right?"

"I don't know. I'd best go back to look for Tessie. We don't know about her or Beattie yet. The explosions seem to have stopped, anyway. Maybe it's safe. I need to find someone to look at this as well." She held out her injured hand.

"Ouch, let me see." Billy held the hand angled toward the sunshine and peered at it closely. "Should be able to get it out with some tweezers if you've got some."

"My bag's in the locker. I don't know if we can collect them yet. There's some at home if not. You go back, I need to see what's happening. I'm fine for now." She hopped down off the wall and looked at him with concern. "Will you be all right?"

"Old soldier like me? I have to be." Then he kissed her cheek and, with Nipper at his heel, started to limp away.

Vi watched him go and wondered if life would ever feel normal again. Once he was out of sight, she turned back toward the Caulder and Harrison factory. Whatever she decided to do about her employment would have to wait. For now, she needed to know her friends were safe, and that meant going back to the building.

She walked to where the others were still waiting for news. The overseers had brought some sort of order to their sections and were trying to keep their employees together.

"Any news?" Vi asked Eva, who was still sitting in the same place.

Eva shook her head. "Nothing."

"Right then, wish me luck," Vi muttered and took a deep breath. "I'm going to ask Mrs Johnson."

Eva raised an eyebrow. "I don't fancy your chances."

Vi shrugged. Eva was probably right, but she couldn't just sit here and do nothing. When she walked over to where their overseer was talking to one of the security guards, she was surprised to see that Mrs Johnson was almost white, and her usually unruffled nature had clearly taken a battering.

"Excuse me," Vi said, when there was a break in their conversation. "Mrs Johnson, is there any way I can find out about our friends from other sections, please?"

"You need to stay here for the time being. Major Tomlinson has brought in some of his soldiers from the barracks. They're still trying to get some of our workers out and make everything safe. I'm sure his men will finish their work soon."

From the anxiety on Mrs Johnson's face, Vi presumed there was some bad news they weren't being told yet, but she'd have to wait until someone was ready to speak officially. Mrs Johnson wasn't the sort of person who would talk without authorisation.

"Thank you." Vi turned and went back to Eva.

Another hour passed, and the girls simply sat where they were on the pavements, or stood in groups talking in hushed tones. Mrs Johnson had gone to talk to the men who had been checking names earlier. Vi was watching her every move. Eventually, Vi saw her nod, then head back to her group of workers.

Mrs Johnson clapped her hands to get their attention. "I'm pleased to say that all of our floor is accounted for. You may go home for the rest of the day, but should report for work as usual tomorrow. Unfortunately, at this stage, you cannot go to the lockers. If that presents a problem to any of you, then please wait to talk to me."

"How the hell are they going to clean that lot up for us to work tomorrow?" Eva asked, as Vi turned back to her.

Vi assumed that Eva wasn't expecting her to answer

that one. Even the army couldn't pull that off. She shook her head. "I need to get this hand sorted before I can do anything. What should we do about the others? We can't just leave them."

Eva nodded toward the security guards, who were encouraging those who had been released to leave the area. "You're going to have problems staying around here."

"I can't go home. What am I going to tell Tessie's mam? Goodness, I'm a coward."

Eva snorted. "You work in a munitions factory, and you think you're a coward. Look, come back to mine and we'll sort that hand. Maybe we can come back here afterward."

Walking away from Caulder and Harrison toward Eva's house, Vi had mixed feelings. She felt oddly as though she was deserting her friends by not waiting for news of their safety. At the same time, she had a feeling that she wanted to walk away from the factory itself and never go back. She wondered if, when the war was over, there would be jobs available back at the hat factory she'd worked at when she left school. Maybe she'd have to stay at Caulder and Harrison until then. The war couldn't go on forever, could it?

Eva's home was much like her own parents'; a back-to-back terrace with everyone in the one room downstairs. Being the middle of the day, all except Eva's mother were out.

"Oh, Eva." Mrs Podmore wrapped her daughter in a warm embrace, paying no heed to the dust and dirt covering Eva's overalls. "Thank God you're safe. I didn't know whether to come up to the factory or wait here for news." She stood back from her daughter and looked at Vi.

"Mam, you've met Vi before, haven't you?" Eva said.

Mrs Podmore reached out her hand to shake Vi's.

Vi held her hand in front of her, palm up. "Hello, Mrs Podmore. Sorry, I can't shake. That's why I've come. I got glass in my hand and need to borrow some tweezers, if you have some, please?"

"Oh, my. Yes, of course. You poor thing."

While Mrs Podmore went upstairs, Vi wondered quite what she'd make of the state of some of the others if she thought Vi's injuries deserved sympathy.

Shortly afterwards, Mrs Podmore returned with the tweezers and a strip of material to bandage the hand. While Vi sat on a chair, Eva's mam worked on her hand as tenderly as if it had been that of her own daughter, cleaning it up, applying iodine and bandaging it.

"There, that should do it." Mrs Podmore looked proud of her work. "Now, will you girls have something to eat while you're here?"

Eva shook her head. "Sorry, Mam, we need to get back. We're not sure if all the girls are out yet. We want to be there to make sure."

Mrs Podmore nodded, but looked very sad. "I said to your Aunty Mabel that I'd rather you found a nice domestic job. This war has a lot to answer for."

Vi remembered that Eva's uncle had been missing in action early in the war and now was presumed to have died. It must be hard for them not knowing what had happened to him.

Eva made to go toward the door.

"Don't you want to change out of your overalls while we're here?" Vi said to her friend.

"Into what exactly? My clothes are in my locker, except my Sunday best, and I can hardly wear those with all the dust and dirt around the factory." Eva shrugged. "Come on."

They took their leave of Mrs Podmore and headed back to the Caulder and Harrison factory. By the time they arrived, the whole road was cordoned off and they couldn't go anywhere close.

They went up and down the line which roped off the area, searching for any of the security men who might be able to tell them what was going on; there was no one they could ask.

"Bad business," Vi heard a man saying.

She turned to him. "I don't suppose you've heard any news. Is everyone out safely?"

He shook his head before answering. "They say there are at least a couple dead and a number of the injured have been taken to the main hospital."

Vi grabbed Eva's sleeve. "Come on."

"Where are we going?" Eva almost tripped over the man as Vi dragged her away.

"To the hospital, to see what they can tell us."

"Vi, stop. We can't go dressed like this. Wouldn't it be better to make sure they've not gone home safely, before going to the hospital?"

Vi laughed, almost with relief. "I didn't even think of that. Do you know where Beattie lives?"

Eva shook her head.

"Then let's find out about Tessie. I didn't want to worry Mrs Brown if Tessie wasn't home, but thinking about it, she'll be worried, anyway. She'll probably be glad to know we're trying to find something out. The rest of the team work in different buildings, so I'm guessing they're out safely."

"They're probably looking for Tessie and Beattie, same

as we are." Eva jogged along beside Vi.

As they approached Ivy Terrace, Tommy came running out of the house and wrapped his arms around her. "Mam, Mam."

Knowing she was all right, it hadn't occurred to her that Tommy would be worrying if he'd heard that something had happened. She lifted him up and hugged him tight. "I'm fine, love. What are you doing back from school at this time?"

"They sent us all home early."

Vi nodded. She didn't suppose many in the town would have settled after the explosions, wondering if everyone at the factory was safe. She turned to Eva. "Let me just take him inside and then we'll go next door."

When Vi went into the kitchen, her mother-in-law was there. "You needn't think you're coming in here in those overalls."

Before Vi had the chance to speak, Billy came through. "Mam! You know what's happened. The least you could do is say you're pleased that Vi's all right."

"Well, I am. But she still needn't think she's coming in like that. She's filthy."

Vi put Tommy down. "We were just going to see Mrs Brown to see if there's any news on Tessie. We're going up to the hospital if there isn't."

"Are you all right, love?" Billy ushered Tommy past him and went out through the back door with Vi.

Vi held up her bandaged hand. "Eva's mam did a great job of sorting this out. I told her she should have been a nurse. We're fine, just worried about the others. I'm not sure what I can do if Mam won't let me in like this. My clothes are in my locker and I can't fetch them."

"There must be something in the wardrobe you could

put on. I'll bring some things down so you can change when you get back." He kissed her cheek. "I'll wait here to see if there's any news on Tessie before I go in."

"There's an old skirt and blouse at the back of the wardrobe that would do. They'll be too big as I wore them when I was expecting Tommy, but I can tie the skirt up. Thanks, love." Vi kissed Billy and then went back to find Eva.

Steeling herself, Vi went to knock on Mrs Brown's back door.

"Vi, love."

"Hello, Mrs Brown. Is Tessie back?"

Mrs Brown looked her up and down and took in her appearance. "Oh, Lor', whatever's happened? I heard the noises, but I didn't think..." She reached behind for a kitchen chair and sat down heavily.

"We don't really know, but there's been an explosion in the section where Tessie works. We're trying to find out if she's all right."

Mrs Brown couldn't speak. The fear which was written across her face was plain for anyone to see.

Vi turned to Eva. "I'll make a pot of tea for Mrs Brown, then we'll get off up to the hospital to see what news there is." She turned back to Tessie's mam. "I'll come back as soon as I can. Perhaps I can ask Billy to come round and sit with you, or maybe his mam would come."

Once Vi had put the kettle on the stove, she left Eva with Mrs Brown and went to incur more wrath from Elsie Dobson by going into the house in her overalls again.

"Of course I will," Billy said when Vi asked him to go next door.

Elsie bustled past. "Don't be daft. It's a woman she needs at a time like this. You stay here."

Billy just looked at Vi and shrugged.

Billingbrook Infirmary was not somewhere Vi had been to before. "Do you have any idea where we go?"

Eva shrugged. "I suppose there'll be a desk somewhere; We can ask there."

The girls walked around the building until they found the main entrance. When they went inside, there was a lady sitting behind a desk in the foyer.

"Er, excuse me." Vi hated having to disturb someone who was obviously in the middle of something, but the woman hadn't looked up. Now that she did, it didn't make Vi feel any better. The woman oozed brisk, no-nonsense efficiency.

"We're trying to find out if Miss Tessie Brown or Miss Beattie Collins have been brought in," Vi said. Then added, "From the explosion at Caulder and Harrison."

"Are you family?"

Vi opened her mouth to say they were friends, although the woman could probably have worked out from their overalls that they were work colleagues. However, Eva elbowed her and came forward.

"Beattie's my sister."

"And I'm here on behalf of Tessie's mother," Vi added, which wasn't exactly a lie.

"Take a seat and I'll find out." The woman moved away from the desk to a small office with a window onto the corridor.

Eva nudged Vi and indicated with her head. "They've got one of those machines you talk to people on."

They watched as the woman picked up the handset and spoke just as though there was someone there.

As the woman returned to the desk, Vi tried to pretend

that she hadn't been staring.

"You're to wait here. Someone will come down to talk to you."

Vi tried to read from the woman's expression whether that was good or bad news, but it was hard to tell. "Thank you." She went back to the chairs.

A nurse walked briskly down the corridor. "Miss Collins, Mrs Brown?"

Eva didn't move, and Vi nudged her. She got up quickly. "Oh, yes. That's me."

Vi didn't correct the error on the names. It was easier just to go along with it, although, however bad she was looking from the explosion, she didn't think she could pass for Tessie's mother.

"Follow me."

They had to walk quickly to keep up with the nurse as they were taken to a side room. Vi tensed. The need for somewhere private didn't look good. She'd been expecting to be taken straight to Beattie and Tessie, not into an office.

It was only after they'd sat down that the nurse began. "I'm really sorry, Miss Collins, but your sister didn't make it."

The involuntary wail from both Vi and Eva could have left the nurse in no doubt about how close they were to Beattie, even if they weren't strictly blood relatives.

"And Miss Brown?" Vi asked, once she managed to compose herself. She held her breath as she waited for the reply.

"Miss Brown is stable."

Stable? What in God's name did stable mean? Vi could feel her heart racing.

The nurse went on after quite a pause. "She is not out of danger altogether. She lost a lot of blood, but we have her condition under control."

"Can I see her?" Vi was already on her feet and ready to seek out Tessie.

"Not today. We want to keep her quiet until she is completely out of danger."

"But I thought you said…"

Eva took Vi's arm. "We'd best go and tell Mam." She frowned at Vi.

Vi got the message, but there was no way they could break the news to Beattie's mam. The first problem was that they didn't even know where she lived. That would be something the factory would have to do. They needed to tell Mrs Brown that Tessie was at least alive; that would be easier, although the 'not out of danger' part might be better left unsaid.

Once they went out through the front doors of the hospital, Vi gulped down lungfuls of fresh air as she tried to digest what the nurse had said.

"Now what do we do?" Eva asked.

Vi could feel Eva shaking. "Honestly? I don't know. We start by telling Mrs Brown that Tessie is alive. I don't think there's anything we can do for Beattie's mam. I just hope she'll be told officially."

CHAPTER 9

Thursday 9ᵗʰ August 1917 - Big British Air Raids — 21 Large Ships Down - The Daily Mirror

By the time Vi had been over to see her own parents to show them she really was all right, it had been a late night. John wanted news of Tessie, and she was glad she could tell him that his girl was alive and being well cared for.

Today she was tired, and getting up for work was difficult. She didn't feel her usual anticipation of the day. Normally, she'd be looking forward to seeing the girls and having the opportunity for a kickabout in the yard at break time. Instead, she could only think of Beattie's family and whether they'd been told, and wonder how Tessie was doing.

As she dressed, she took a moment, sitting on the edge of the bed, to look at her pile of hat drawings from the back of the drawer. Making hats was so much nicer than working with explosives.

"What are you doing, love?"

Vi hadn't heard Billy come in. She must have been miles away. She put the papers back into a pile, hoping he hadn't seen. "Just getting ready."

Billy sat down next to her on the bed. "You should make some of them."

There was no use pretending that hadn't been what she was doing. She unfolded the pages again. "And where exactly am I going to find the things I need to make hats? I don't even have the material… or the time, for that matter."

Billy took one from the pile and looked at it closely. "You'd look good in this."

Vi took the drawing and held it at arm's length to have a good look. It would be fun to wear a hat she'd actually made. "What colour should I have?"

"Blue. You can't go wrong with a good navy."

"Oh, Billy, I know you're right, but I'd like to wear something bright and cheerful. I've had enough of how dour this war has made us all. If I asked Ena she'd say 'magenta', but I don't think that's really me." She gasped. "Here's me getting carried away and I need to go to work. I'll be running all the way if I'm not careful. It's a good job I'm wearing my overalls."

Dressing in her overalls was best; she didn't want spare clothes in the factory. If she was honest, she preferred the practicality they gave compared to the skirt she'd found in the wardrobe. Clothing was so much easier for men.

Billy was planning to accompany Mrs Brown on the bus to the hospital, in the hope she could see Tessie later. Their neighbour's relief that Tessie was alive was quite overwhelming. She thought again of Beattie's mam. She and Eva would visit the family, as soon as they could obtain an address from someone.

Mrs Johnson was standing at the factory gate, waiting for her section of workers to arrive. Vi looked up at the big clock on the central tower, wondering if she was late.

"I'm sorry…" Vi was slightly out of breath from running.

"No, Mrs Dobson, I'm sorry. There'll be no work until

the start of next week when all the mess has been cleared away and repairs done. It may mean extra hours when you come back as there's a big order to send out. That will help to compensate for the pay you'll lose this week. You may go to the lockers to collect your things, but you may not enter any of the corridors."

The woman didn't actually sound sorry. She sounded as though it was the thirtieth time she'd trotted out the line, and it probably was.

Vi nodded, then hesitated. "Beattie, that is Miss Beattie Collins... has someone told her family? Could you tell me where they live?"

"I only deal with the girls on our section. You'd need to talk to management." Mrs Johnson sounded more as though she didn't want to discuss it, but maybe Vi was being uncharitable. Perhaps she really didn't know.

"Mr Giffard..." Vi wasn't sure how to ask if she could go to his office but didn't get any further.

"You may not venture into any of the corridors, and that includes the management floor."

Vi sighed. She went to fetch her belongings from the locker and bumped into Clara.

"At least we can fit some practice in," Clara said as she took her own things out of her locker.

"I certainly don't feel much like it without Beattie and Tessie."

Clara looked at her and frowned. "What about them?"

"You don't know?" Vi sat down on one of the benches. "Tessie's still in hospital, and Beattie's..." She couldn't say the word, she just couldn't.

"Beattie's what?" Clara clearly hadn't understood.

Vi looked at her. "She's... she didn't..."

Clara stared; all colour drained from her face. "You

mean...?"

Vi nodded. They sat quietly until a guard came past. "Come along, girls. Collect your things and then leave the premises."

They walked in silence back toward the gate. "I'll see you Monday then," Clara said, giving Vi a weak smile.

Vi put her arm around the girl and hugged her. "Take care. I'll see you then." This was going to be hard for all of them.

When Vi returned to work the following week, her heart wasn't in it. "I'll be glad when Tessie comes out of hospital," she said to Eva at break, "but I wish there was something else we could all do for work."

"Don't be daft. Who'd pay us these sorts of wages?"

Vi knew Eva was right, but having Billy injured by the war was bad enough without taking a risk with her own life. "I did enjoy hat making, and if I say so myself, I was quite good at it when I wasn't just working on bowler hat brims."

"You can make hats?" Eva seemed surprised.

"You knew that's what I used to do."

"I thought it was like here where you just do part of the process. I mean, you wouldn't go away saying you could make shells, would you?"

Vi thought about it. "I really can make hats. When I started, I worked with a milliner who designed her own. I used to go home and draw pictures of the hats I'd like to make."

"Do it." Eva looked excited.

"How can I? I work here all hours. Besides, I don't have the materials to make them, and we don't exactly have any spare money."

Eva clearly wasn't giving up. "What about making a hat for me? I'd pay you, not too much, mind. I've been saving when I can. I could even pay you in advance so you could buy the things you need."

"Let me talk to Billy. I'd need some equipment if I was going to do it. Maybe he'll have some ideas."

Vi liked the idea of making hats, although she couldn't see how she could make enough to live on and leave the munitions factory. It was nice to have dreams, but sometimes that was all they could be. A bit like her dream of a big football tournament and their team winning. Dreams might be for her, but them coming true was for other people. She was just Violet Dobson, and what life had in store for her was hard work. She made her way back to her bench, but she couldn't get the thought of hats out of her mind.

"Nothing. Not a bloody word." Billy threw the paper down on the sideboard. "I have looked from cover to cover in every day's paper since the explosion. Apart from saying there'd been an accident on the first day, they've said nothing more about it. It makes it sound as though someone knocked over a bucket of water. That's an accident. Not a bloody great explosion that leaves people dead."

"We must have missed something." Vi took her coat off as she talked to Billy. "You know..." Vi stopped herself. Maybe it was best not to say.

"I know what?" Billy snapped in reply. "You can't leave it there."

Her and her big mouth. "When you were all fighting, when Stan died, the papers said we were winning and didn't mention any casualties."

Billy wheeled around, his face dark. "Didn't mention casualties? There were bodies everywhere; parts of bodies. Not just men, but horses, too. That was the worst. Poor innocent bloody horses. It wasn't even their war." He sat down on a chair and put his head in his hand. "It wasn't our war, either. God knows what we were fighting for, but we fought. We fought for King and Country, we fought because of bloody propaganda. And it's still bloody propaganda, them not telling you what's really happening, because they still need more poor sods like Stan." He stood up again, his anger palpable. "I'm going out."

Vi stood aside to let Billy pass. Her heart was racing from his outburst and she wanted to soothe him, but she'd learned by now that she couldn't help. She just bit her lip and watched him go. Nipper went running not far behind. Thank God for Nipper. Billy would probably walk around for a while, then go to the pub for a beer. He'd calm down with the quiet and space of the fresh air. He was a good man, and she knew he'd be back after just the one pint; he wasn't a big drinker even now. Nipper would keep an eye on him.

Billy was right, of course; so many lives lost and yet so little said. If Billy hadn't been there to see what happened himself, she probably wouldn't have believed there was another side to the story. It was so easy to believe what was printed and put in front of you.

When Vi and Eva eventually found an address for Beattie, they took some flowers to her parents. The curtains to the house were drawn and all was silent.

"Do you think we should just leave the flowers with a note?" Vi asked.

"I'm going to knock, but if no one answers then we'll just leave them." Eva reached up for the knocker but hesitated. "Do you think I should?"

Vi nodded. "I want to tell them how we all feel."

Eva let out a breath and rapped the knocker twice. They waited.

It was a man who answered the door. Vi thought she'd seen him at the football and assumed it was Beattie's dad, but the man looked nearer eighty than the forty she'd been expecting.

"Mr Collins?" Vi wasn't sure what to say as the man made no move to allow them in. He looked vacant and lost. She steeled herself. "We wanted to say how sorry we are about Beattie. She was our friend. We played together in the football team."

A look of recognition flickered across the man's face, but was gone almost as soon as it appeared.

Vi held out the flowers. It felt an awkward gesture. "We brought you these."

He looked at her, and then at Eva, and nodded slightly, but still didn't speak.

Vi tried to give a reassuring smile. "We'll come another time." She went to turn away but then had a thought and turned back. Beattie's dad was still standing in the open doorway. "If there's anything we can do to help..."

He nodded and this time stood back in preparation for closing the door.

"Goodbye, Mr Collins." Vi turned and followed Eva down the path, feeling an emptiness and wishing there was something more that she could say or do.

Vi thought a lot about the things Billy had said as she went to work that week. How could she spend her days making shells when she knew the devastation they were designed to cause? She tried hard to put it out of her head while she was working. She needed the job, and that was all there was to it. If only Tessie were around; at least then she'd have less time to dwell in her own thoughts as she walked to and from the factory.

It was Thursday before Tessie came out of hospital, and despite the lateness of the hour Vi went straight around to the Brown's house when she arrived back from work. "It's good to see you home. I couldn't have borne it if we'd lost you as well as Beattie." Vi hugged her friend.

"I was with her," Tessie said quietly. "We were at the same end of the bench when it happened. I had to identify her in the hospital." She looked down. "I want to visit her family when I'm well enough. Will you come with me?"

"Of course I will. I did go last week when we eventually found where they lived. It was awful. Mr Giffard has said that some of the money from the next football match can go to the family to help provide support. That's kind of him, isn't it?"

Tessie looked up with anger in her eyes. "Kind of them? Shouldn't the factory be doing that for the family anyway? The football funds don't belong to them; that doesn't cost them anything."

Vi was taken aback. "I hadn't thought about it like that."

"Well, I have. I've had plenty of time to think, lying in that hospital bed this last week. I received a letter saying they'd pay my wages while I was off as a 'special concession', as though any of this was my fault."

Vi began to understand. Billy's disability pension didn't cover most of their day-to-day costs, let alone the extra help he needed. "I'm sorry," she said to Tessie. "Will you still play football when you come back?"

"Oh, I want to play football all right. It's the factory I'm cross with, not the football. The other thing I've been thinking about is, what if this war doesn't stop? John will get his call-up papers next April. I don't want him to go and fight."

"I know." Vi couldn't give Tessie any reassurance. She understood. She didn't want her brother to join the army either.

"He came to see me earlier. He's promised he won't go until he has to." Tessie was biting her lip as she spoke.

"That's good, anyway." After the things Billy had told her, she really didn't want to think of John going through similar experiences. Vi wanted to change the subject. "Eva wants me to start making hats. I didn't feel much like going back to work at Caulder and Harrison after last week either." Vi was fiddling with her cuff. She wasn't used to voicing her dream as though it could be real.

Tessie's face lit up. "That would be lovely. I could work for you. What a time we could have."

Vi laughed. "I couldn't make enough money to feed us, never mind employ you as well."

"What does Billy say?" Tessie looked much brighter now the conversation had moved away from the factory and the war.

"I haven't even talked to him about the idea of making them, other than in my spare time. There's no point." Vi had spent a lot of time thinking during the last week, but could see no possibility of making any progress with her dream, even though Eva kept nagging her to make a hat for her.

"We should do it." Tessie gave a little jump of excitement. "Somehow, Vi, there must be a way we could do it."

Vi laughed. She'd almost forgotten what it was like to be young and still believe there was a way to do anything if you really tried; but then she'd never had Tessie's confidence. Maybe she should learn from the girl.

By the time of their match against a Bolton team in October, Tessie was fully recovered. You could almost hear the dying leaves rustling on the nearby trees as the crowd stood silently before the match, to honour and remember Beattie.

Afterward, as Vi wiped a tear from her eye, she said to the team, "Go out there and win this for Beattie. Not for the factory, we're doing this for Beattie."

The team cheered and, with renewed determination, Vi set off down the pitch.

They didn't win, they were held to a one-all draw, but Vi's team had their spirit back and were ready to face whichever opposition they could take on next. It was funny; the football boosted Vi's confidence, and she began to wonder if there might be a way she could earn a living out of making hats.

That Sunday was quiet, and once they'd come back from visiting her family, Tommy had fallen asleep exhausted, with Nipper curled up beside him. Billy was reading the paper, in between dozing off over the table it was resting on. For a brief time, no one needed anything from Vi. She went upstairs and opened the drawer she'd put her bundle of drawings in. She sat on the edge of the bed and looked at each sheet in turn. How fashions changed; even the width of hat brims wasn't a constant.

She hadn't added to the drawings for a while, but it

came back to her quickly enough. She sketched a tight-fitting hat with a ribbon garland, finishing with a flower at the side. She'd seen something similar in a fashion magazine in the library. It would look lovely on Eva if she could get the material to make it.

"What are you doing?"

Vi jumped and dropped some of the sheets of paper. She hadn't heard Billy come in. "Nothing important." She gathered up the drawings quickly.

Billy sat next to her. Nipper moved over to rest his head on Billy's leg.

"You missed some," Billy said, picking up a piece of paper which was sticking out from under the bed. "This one's really good." He studied the drawing of a wide-brimmed hat, one side of which was turned up, adorned by a large bow.

Vi could feel herself blushing. Although she'd shown some of them to Billy before, this felt different. She hadn't been thinking of making them then. "They're just ideas." She took a deep breath. "What would you think of me trying to make some of them?"

One by one, he went through the drawings, not saying anything.

"They aren't very good," Vi said, feeling anxious.

"Look at me."

She turned her face to his.

"Violet Dobson, I may not know a lot about drawing hats, and probably even less about making them, but I do know that these are very good."

She smiled and laughed. "Billy Dobson, I love you. You're really very kind." She reached out to take them back.

"Just tell me about them, please?" He'd closed his hand

around the pile of papers so she couldn't take them away.

She sighed. "It's just a silly dream. I'd love to design and make my own hats, but it's never going to happen. I haven't thought about it for a while, but Eva's trying to persuade me to make one for her. And I was wondering if there was any way I could do that."

"Why don't you?"

Billy was looking at her so intently that Vi almost wanted to turn away. It was as though he was looking right inside her; as though he would see through anything but the truth.

"I've always said that I can't afford to. I'd need materials and some basic equipment. And I'd need somewhere to work. I know we've got the money in the jar that we were saving toward our own home; I could use that and replace it, so I don't think that's actually the truth. Really, I think it's because I'm scared I'd fail. While it's only a dream, I don't have to find I can't do it." She looked away from his gaze.

Billy's reaction wasn't what she was expecting. He laughed. She looked back at him and frowned. "Are you laughing at me, Billy Dobson?"

"No, I'm laughing at me. I'm laughing at us."

Vi had no idea what he was talking about.

"I've got a confession to make."

Vi felt her chest squeeze and her breathing became shallow. She wasn't sure she wanted to hear anything that followed that expression.

CHAPTER 10

Sunday 21st October 1917 - Families Murdered in the Raid - Sunday Pictorial

Billy saw the look on Vi's face and wished he hadn't said it quite like that. "It's all right, don't worry. I've gone back to school." He laughed, feeling uncomfortable to be finally telling Vi. "Not school exactly, but adult learning, an adult school." He paused to watch how Vi might react. Her face seemed to flood with relief. "What did you think I was going to say?"

They both started laughing.

"Oh, I don't know, Billy. It was just how you said 'confession'." It took a while for their nervous laughter to stop and for Vi to continue. "So, what have you been learning? You can already read and write."

"Well, I could, write I mean. Obviously, I can still read, but with losing my right arm, I couldn't write very well anymore. What I was doing with Tommy helped, but it just wasn't enough. You said I should learn, and I have."

"That's great." Vi was smiling now and looking a lot less concerned.

"Hang on, I haven't finished. Anyway, the bloke there asked if I'd like to learn some other things. You know, arithmetic and stuff… accounting. I'd had to do some for my carpentry, and we learned some in the army, but I'd never really put it all together. I didn't have any confidence that I could do it." He felt embarrassed admitting it. He was used to doing manual work. Saying he'd learned to do office work was completely alien to him. He thought it made him sound like he was clever, and he really wasn't. "I had some opportunities in the army, and they helped me with things like concentration. It means sitting in a classroom hasn't been as hard as I thought it would be."

Vi was staring at him and he began to feel even more uncomfortable.

"How long have you been doing that?"

"A few months. It's easier than you'd think."

"Billy Dobson, you never cease to amaze me."

Vi stroked his face and he couldn't help but smile. "Anyway, if you did something with the hats, maybe I could do the business side." He felt sheepish for a moment. "I was actually wondering about it after I saw some of your drawings before. I talked to the man who's been teaching me, and we used the idea to help my learning." He took a sheet of paper out of the inside pocket of his jacket and opened it out. "Of course, I didn't know all the things you might need for hat making, but, well, this is what we put together." He handed her the sheet of figures and felt awkward. He hoped Vi would take it the right way and not think he was interfering.

Vi stopped with her hand mid-air. "You're serious, aren't you?"

He shrugged. "Maybe, though I still can't really see where we'd start."

Vi looked down at the page of numbers and shook her head. "I might be able to draw hats, but I don't have a clue what any of this means."

Billy smiled. "That's where I come in. I understand the

basics now. I'd still need some help, but I've got nothing else to do with my time. No one much wants a one-armed former soldier."

"I do." Vi put the papers down on the dressing table and kissed him.

Nipper, not wanting to be left out, tried to reach up and lick Billy's face at the same time.

"I think he's saying that he needs a job too," Vi said, lifting the dog down again and putting him on the bed where Tommy was still sleeping.

The more he thought about it, the more Billy liked the idea of having a business of their own. He wouldn't need to feel useless and compare himself to anyone else if he could work for himself. He wondered if there was any way to make it happen. People like them just didn't do those sorts of things.

Billy tried not to complain too much to Vi. For one thing, he didn't want anyone feeling sorry for him; he couldn't bear that. He hated the looks of pity he got when people realised he had a missing arm. People couldn't even see the leg, but he guessed they couldn't really miss his limp. Every day, he got up as though he was going to work. He strapped on the wooden leg; it took a while, but Vi seemed to have learned to let him struggle and not to mother him. He preferred to do it once Tommy was out of the way, so his bad language wasn't overheard by the lad. He invariably ended up swearing before he got the job done.

His stump often rubbed on the wood and was at best sore, or at worst painful. He'd come to see it as almost his punishment for being alive when so many men he'd known weren't. Somehow, in Billy's head, that made the pain bearable.

Much to his surprise, the scarring to his face had healed over time and was now much less obvious. At least people stared and pointed less often, which was something.

It was now only a few weeks to Christmas. They couldn't afford much, but Billy wanted to do something special for Vi. She put up with so much and he never really knew how to tell her how grateful he was. He couldn't get her hat idea out of his head, and wondered if there was something he could do about it, even as a hobby.

He didn't know anyone at Strywell & Sons, the hat factory where Vi used to work, and she hadn't kept in touch with her old workmates. The only option Billy could think of was to go to the factory itself and ask. He presumed there was no harm in doing that, so leaving Nipper at home, he made his way to their premises and followed a sign to the reception.

"Excuse me, but what happens to your offcuts?"

The woman at the reception desk looked confused. Billy could only assume that was not something she was used to being asked, or maybe he'd used the wrong term.

"I really don't know. Take a seat, Mr...?"

"Dobson."

"... Mr Dobson, and I'll get someone to come down to you."

Whilst he sat there, Billy looked around at the posters on the walls. He'd never really thought much about hats before he and Vi talked a few weeks ago. When Vi had worked here, he thought it was just a job, much the same as his had been. It just showed, however long you knew someone, there was so much you still had to find out.

He wondered how many people wore bowler hats. He certainly didn't see that many in Billingbrook; maybe it was men in the big cities rather than here. Everyone he knew wore a cap and nothing more. Looking at the four different pictures in one of the posters on the wall, he realised that even caps came in very different styles. He shook his head in wonder.

He was still miles away when someone coughed to attract his attention. He turned around suddenly and nearly overbalanced.

The woman caught his arm. "Please, Mr Dobson, do take a seat. I'm Mrs Prendergast." She guided him to the waiting area chairs. "Now, how can I help you?"

Billy could have sworn the name was familiar, but he was sure the woman Vi had talked of was a complete battle-axe. He thought it best not to mention Vi by name, just in case. Now that he came to ask, Billy felt foolish. "I was wondering what happened to all your offcuts of material. You know, the bits that are all the wrong shape to use."

"I know what an offcut is." Her lips twitched as she answered.

"Yes, sorry, I suppose you would." He took a deep breath. "I wondered if you ever sold your offcuts. I want to buy some material for my wife for Christmas, but, I can't afford…" At that point, Billy's pride got the better of him. "I'm sorry, I shouldn't have come to ask. Excuse me." He got up and made to go to the door.

"Mr Dobson, were you injured in the war?"

He bit his lip and turned around. "Yes, Mrs Prendergast, I was."

"Then I'd like to help. My son…" She waved a hand as she swallowed. "… he's out there now."

Billy nodded. "I'm sorry. I hope he returns home safely."

"If you come back tomorrow morning, I'll have

something ready for you. Will you be able to carry it?"

"I'll bring someone to help me. How much will it be?"

"See it as a contribution from Strywells."

"Thank you." Billy wondered if she'd be saying that if she remembered Vi, but he certainly wasn't going to ask.

The following day, Billy was very glad he'd asked Vi's dad to go with him to collect the bundle.

"I'd never have managed all this on my own. Thank you. Please, can I pay something toward it?"

"See it as a gift." Mrs Prendergast smiled.

"Thank you. I don't know what to say."

She touched his arm. "Thank you, Mr Dobson."

He thought she had a tear in her eye as she turned away, and he presumed she was thinking of her son.

"Can we get the bus?" Frank Tunnicliffe asked as he struggled out with the parcel.

"I think we'd better. No one would be happy to carry that home." Billy wouldn't have managed even with two good arms and legs.

"If this doesn't keep that girl of mine happy, then nothing will. You're a good lad, Billy. Thank you for taking care of her."

Billy had no idea what to say in response. "Where are we going to hide it?"

"Now there's a point. I'd take it back to our house, but there's nowhere for it to go; and besides, it's further from the bus stop."

Billy laughed. "I think we'd be best asking next door. Mrs Brown won't mind, and at least Vi won't find it there. As long as Tessie doesn't say anything, it'll be fine."

By the time the package was safely stowed in Mrs Brown's front room, Billy was exhausted. He'd have taken his leg off if the thought of putting it back on again hadn't been so daunting. Vi's dad had gone straight home, rather than taking Billy up on the offer of a cup of tea, so Billy was sitting on his own in the back room and must have drifted off to sleep.

He was woken by his mam. "You've got visitors. They're in the front room. Mind you leave it tidy, I've only just cleaned in there, so no taking that dog in."

"Who is it?" He didn't know anyone likely to call at the house.

"What do you think I am, your maid? You'll be wanting me to put the kettle on next." Elsie Dobson shook her head and turned toward the door with a disapproving air.

Billy struggled to his feet. "A cup of tea would be grand, mam. Thank you." He gave her a peck on the cheek and grinned. It always got him what he wanted. Nipper started to follow him, but Billy ordered the little chap to his bed and the dog dutifully went.

Elsie Dobson gave a resigned smile and shook her head. She went out of the room ahead of Billy and turned toward the kitchen. Billy went to the front room.

Once he opened the door, Billy frowned in confusion. A man, probably a little younger than his own father, but very much more smartly dressed and with a pocket-watch chain visible leading to the pocket of his waistcoat, was standing, rocking back and forth on the balls of his feet, in front of the fireplace. A woman was sitting demurely on the edge of the settee, beautifully dressed and with what to Billy looked like a set of pearls around her neck. If they hadn't been right in front of him, he'd have let out a low whistle. What in heaven's name were they doing in the front room of his parents' house and asking for him?

He felt his hand sweat and wiped it on his trousers. "Billy Dobson," he said, holding it out.

It always confused people that he was holding out his left hand and they invariably did a little hand dance, first putting out their right hand before taking it back quickly and looking embarrassed when they realised the reason for the change.

"How can I help you?" Billy wasn't sure if he should sit down or remain standing. There was something about this gentleman which radiated authority, and even though it was the Dobson household, Billy felt he should wait to take his lead from the man.

The woman was looking up at her husband, clearly expecting him to explain. She was clutching a handkerchief and had already used it to dab the corner of her eye before anything had been said.

When the man started speaking, he was much quieter and more gentle than Billy had been expecting. "You knew our son. We're Terence and Audrey Moore, David Moore's parents."

Billy screwed up his eyes in confusion.

It was Mrs Moore who chipped in. "He said you called him Davy."

Billy's eyes widened and he sat down heavily at the mention of Davy. He'd presumed the lad had been lost, but didn't know for certain. He nodded, unable to find any words.

"We wanted to say thank you. We'd have come sooner, but it's only been recently that Audrey has been able to bring herself to go through his personal belongings which the army sent back. It was too painful before."

Audrey Moore dabbed her eyes again.

Davy's father continued. "Audrey read his diary. That's how we found out how kind to him you'd been. We didn't want him to sign up. Even when there was call-up he wouldn't have needed to go. Our business is protected. He wasn't cut out for the army. We were very worried about him. We're glad there was someone to look out for him."

"I didn't do anything another man wouldn't have done." Billy felt embarrassed by the praise.

From the timing of his mother coming in with a tea tray, and the beaming smile on her face, Billy guessed she'd been listening at the door.

"He's a good lad, my Billy. He'd help anyone. And how does he come home as a result?"

"Mam, please. That's enough." His mother harrumphed and left the room.

Billy turned to Davy's parents. "I'm sorry. I'm sorry about Davy, er, David. I'm sorry for your loss. There was nothing I could have done to protect him. By rights, I should have died too. I don't know to this day how I didn't."

"Now come, lad, don't talk like that."

Billy found Davy's parents oddly easy to talk to and, over tea, he told them how hard it had been coming back, and the guilt he felt at being alive.

"Can you tell us anything about David's life in the army?" Mr Moore asked.

As hard as Billy found talking about the battlefield itself, he found he could tell them about some of the funny things that happened in the early days on the assault course; right up to finding out that Davy spoke German, and how he'd been on special missions as a result.

Billy had locked away almost everything about his time in the army, and it was a relief to open up a little. The time passed enjoyably, and before he knew it, Tommy came tumbling into the room, home from school.

"Tommy, I'd like you to meet Mr and Mrs Moore. They're the parents of a friend of mine."

To Billy's surprise, Tommy stood a little taller when he looked at them and politely went and offered his hand to shake. "Pleased to meet you."

Where did the boy get his manners? Billy wanted to laugh. They certainly hadn't come from him. He felt a rush of pride in the boy, and the Moores were clearly impressed.

"We were wondering," Mrs Moore said, "if it isn't too much trouble, whether you might all like to come to tea with us one Sunday, you and Mrs Dobson and young Tommy."

"That would be very nice, thank you. What do you think, Tommy?" Billy turned to his son, who nodded earnestly.

"Shall we say Sunday week at three o'clock?" Mrs Moore looked happier than she had all afternoon.

As Billy showed them out, he looked down at Tommy and thought how hard it must be to lose your only child. He put his hand on Tommy's shoulder as he watched the Moores leave.

CHAPTER 11

Dreams are the strangest things in life,
So fanciful, yet real;
Sometimes depicting scenes of strife;
In others they reveal,
Such happiness that were it not,
Some sign the spell was breaking,
That we were sleeping we'd forget,
And fancy we were waking.
I Knew That I Was Dreaming - Fred Albert & A J Birtchnell
1875

Sunday 2nd December 1917 - British Recapture Gonnelieu in All
Day Battle - Sunday Pictorial

"No playing outside now until we get back," Vi called to Tommy, who she'd just washed and made as tidy as possible. "Do I look all right?" She turned to Billy for his approval. Vi wasn't used to needing to look smart except for the occasions when they went to church, and that wasn't a common occurrence.

"You look lovely, but then you always do to me." Billy had a twinkle in his eye. "Maybe you should ask Mam."

Vi shook her head in despair. "She really doesn't need to be jealous of us going for tea with the Moores."

Billy laughed. "I think she probably wishes she'd been invited too. Especially with them living in one of those big houses. Do you think they'll mind us taking Nipper?"

"I don't suppose your mam would thank us for leaving him here, and there's not enough time to take him over to my mam and dad, so we have no choice. We'll tie him to the railings outside the Moores' house. He'll be happy enough knowing we're nearby." Vi paused, trying to think if there was anything she'd forgotten. Not that there was really anything she needed to do, but it felt like an important occasion and she was worrying about the details. "We'd best keep a close eye on Tommy while we're there. We don't want him breaking anything." She frowned. She had no idea how Tommy would behave somewhere like that. They'd never been terribly strict with him, but he wasn't a badly behaved child; at least not by their standards.

It was a dull afternoon as they set out to walk across Billingbrook to where Terence and Audrey Moore lived. It was a part of town that Vi didn't know very well and had never had cause to visit. She wished it was still properly light so she could see more of the beautiful houses they were passing with their bay windows, and some with electric lights. Most of the windows were shielded by heavy curtains, but one or two with the curtains open made it possible to see some of the grand interiors.

The Moores' house was a detached three-storey property, double-fronted with the door between two impressive bay windows. Vi wished she could stand and stare for a while, taking in the detail, but Audrey Moore must have been watching for them, as no sooner had they gone up the steps than the door was opened wide.

"Come in, come in," Mr Moore said, ushering Billy and Tommy forward.

Vi was still tying Nipper to the railings.

"Mrs Dobson, there's no need, really. Bring the dog in as well."

Vi looked up, a little surprised. Mr Moore was smiling warmly and beckoning for her and Nipper to join the others. Now she worried that Nipper wouldn't behave, never mind Tommy.

"Come through to the garden while it's still light enough," Mr Moore said to Tommy, and then looked at Billy, who nodded. Nipper followed behind, wagging his tail.

Vi sat down with Mrs Moore and wondered if conversation would be awkward. It might have been easier to follow the boys out to the garden. She sat and folded and unfolded her hands, not knowing what to say.

"We miss the noise and bustle of children," Mrs Moore said when the boys were out of hearing. "Terence misses having a son dreadfully. Some days I think he misses David even more than I do. We really wanted a big family. Losing the one child we had has been very difficult. Even though he'd been away at school for a while, the house seems quiet now. Having Tommy and Nipper running about will do us the world of good."

Vi watched Audrey dab the corners of her eyes.

Nipper chose that moment to come bounding back into the room and oddly went straight to Mrs Moore and nuzzled her legs. It was as though he sensed her distress and wanted to help. Audrey absentmindedly reached down and stroked Nipper's head.

As it turned out, Audrey was easy to talk to, and Vi told her about wanting a large family herself and the difficulties of living with Billy's parents. She even told her about Eva wanting her to make a hat and, of course, about the football.

Audrey Moore stared at her. "How wonderful. You actually play?"

Vi nodded.

"I've never so much as kicked a ball. I didn't think…"

Vi finished the sentence for her, "… that women could play?"

Audrey nodded. "I mean, well, I suppose there's no reason why we can't, it's just that I've never even thought about it." She paused, frowning. "Do you think I might be able to watch you?"

Vi broke into a broad smile. "I would like it very much if you did that." Vi was just talking about when their next match would be when the others came in to join them.

Tommy couldn't talk fast enough as he began telling his mam about all the things he'd seen in the garden. "There's trees you can climb and a treehouse and a pond with fish in it and a glass room where there are plants and…" He looked to his dad, apparently trying to remember his long list of items.

Mrs Moore was a natural with children, and once Tommy's excitement had died down she said, "Would you like to help me getting the tea things, Tommy?"

Vi watched astounded as Tommy nodded and followed her to the kitchen. A few minutes later he came back, carefully carrying a plate of cakes.

That evening, when they were on their way home, Tommy's first question was, "When can we go there again? I liked the cakes and the man said I can play in the treehouse if it's light when we go."

"It's a shame Davy's not here too, but then I guess they'd never have invited us if he was." Billy sighed. "Looking out for Davy helped me deal with being away from home. It was strange, really. He was a nice lad."

"Well," Vi said, "you can certainly see where he got that from."

They visited again just before Christmas, despite the tutting from Billy's mam as they were getting ready. Vi was looking forward to the visit this time, and wasn't disappointed.

"I was thinking," Mr Moore said. "This football match on Boxing Day, what would we need to do if we wanted to come? I've not watched a match since I was a boy and went with my own father."

"You'd be very welcome to come with us, if you don't mind standing on the terraces," Billy said. "I don't actually stand, if I'm honest. They always let us have a space at the front and I take the wheelchair. I find it's too long to be on my feet."

"If you really don't mind, I'd love to, but I think Audrey might prefer to be seated if that's possible." Mr Moore looked to his wife.

"Well..." Audrey appeared flustered. "I've never been to anything like that. I talked to Mrs Dobson about it last time they were here. Terence, do you think it would be appropriate?"

Vi opened her mouth to tell them there were a lot of women watching, but before she could say anything, she was astounded to see her son slip his hand into Mrs Moore's hand.

"Please come. I'll look after you," Tommy said, earnestly looking up at her.

Seeing the smile which broke across Mrs Moore's face, Vi was delighted by her boy's behaviour.

"Well," Mrs Moore said, "how can I turn down an offer like that?"

Early on Christmas morning, Tommy leaped from the bed, sending Nipper scurrying out of the way. "He's been!"

Vi laughed, watching the scene from the previous year replaying this Christmas. She looked across to Billy, who was entranced, watching his son. For Billy, seeing Tommy's wonder at finding his Christmas stocking was new, and Vi felt a sudden thrill at the pleasure of being able to enjoy it together. She climbed back into bed and snuggled up to Billy as they watched their son together.

"How did he get in?" Tommy asked. "Did you see him, Mam?"

"I was asleep long before he stopped by our terrace," Vi said. "Maybe your dad saw him?"

Tommy turned to his dad, who opened his eyes wide and shook his head in mock innocence.

Vi smiled. This was what life was supposed to be like; Christmas at home as a family. Her thoughts strayed to the thousands of families whose loved ones were still away fighting, or who had never come home, and she shuddered. She looked at Billy, who was now attaching his wooden leg, and thanked God that, even wounded as he was, he was one of the lucky ones.

Billy went downstairs and Tommy raced after him. Since the first day of helping Mrs Moore carrying the plate of cakes back from the kitchen, Tommy had begun helping his dad with things which needed to be carried. Vi presumed they had gone to make a cup of tea and would bring one upstairs for her. She was surprised by how long it was taking.

Eventually, she heard Tommy running back up the stairs, shouting, "There's presents downstairs too. You need to come, Mam. There's a big one for you."

"Me?" They'd never done much about presents for the

adults. They really couldn't afford to. A cup of tea in bed was as much as she'd been expecting. She put on her dressing gown and went downstairs.

Billy and Tommy were standing in the back room on either side of a large misshapen package, wrapped in brown paper. They looked at her expectantly.

"Open it, Mam," Tommy said.

Billy's parents hadn't come down yet and Vi wondered if she should wait for them, but it was nice to have just her little family. She looked at Billy, who was grinning broadly. He nodded.

Vi knelt down on the floor. Her hands were shaking as she undid the string. Then, gently, she unwrapped the paper. Piled up, and spilling out as soon as they were released, were pieces of cloth in all shapes, sizes and colours. For a moment, she forgot the others were there as she picked up a piece of bottle-green felt. She ran her hand over the softness of the fabric. As she looked through the pile, the smells of the hat factory came to her, and she was sent back to a time before the war. She sat on her heels and sighed, still holding the green felt to her cheek.

"What's it for, Mam?" Tommy asked, sounding confused, as Nipper ran off with a small piece of tweed.

She looked up at Billy, who had so much love in his eyes. "Thank you. How did you...?"

"Happy Christmas, Vi," Billy said, smiling at her.

Vi suddenly realised she hadn't answered Tommy. "Come." She beckoned for him to join her on the floor and then took some checked material from the pile. "I think a cap in this fabric would suit you, sir," she said to Tommy, holding it up to his head and laughing.

Tommy's eyes lit up. "Really? Would you make me one?"

Vi put all thoughts of getting up or of cooking Christmas dinner aside and went to find a pencil and paper. She sketched what a cap might look like for Tommy and then sorted through the material to find enough offcuts to put it together. As long as she was careful about how she sewed the joins, no one would know it hadn't been cut from a single piece of cloth. She also sorted out all the pieces of green felt and carefully folded them together. When she went to get dressed she put the felt at the back of the drawer, ready for when she could make them into the hat she'd promised to Eva.

Throughout the rest of Christmas Day, Vi couldn't stop thinking about what else she would need in order to make Eva's hat and Tommy's cap. Even when they went over to her family in the afternoon, she couldn't stop herself from talking about it.

"You should follow your dreams, love," Dad said as he played the accordion, a wistful look in his eye.

Vi wondered what dream her father hadn't been able to follow, and guessed it was tied up in the music.

"That's what I said, Mr Tunnicliffe," Tessie chipped in, as she sat in the corner of the room with John. "I want her to start selling them properly so we can leave the munitions factory and work together."

"You'll need something when this war's over," Dad said. "It won't go on forever."

"I want it over before our John's called up." Queenie Tunnicliffe came over and put a hand on Tessie's shoulder. They'd totally accepted Tessie into the family, and now Vi couldn't imagine life any other way.

"What time are we going tomorrow?" Tessie asked as they were walking home later that evening.

"I'd like to get there early, if Billy doesn't mind." Vi

looked across at her husband, who smiled his agreement. "I want a good warm up after all I've eaten today. I'm sure arranging a football match for Boxing Day is a bad idea. I could do with a long walk and a sleep."

The Boxing Day match was always popular, but this year it drew the biggest crowd the girls had played in front of yet. They were taking on a team from Manchester, and the away side brought a large number of fans with them which swelled the crowd. Seeing the Whittingham Road ground with so many spectators made Vi shiver with pleasure.

"Looks like we've hit the big time," Tessie said as they warmed up on the pitch. "I just hope I don't let you all down." She was still struggling with her fitness after the accident.

"You'll be fine," Vi reassured her. She was looking along the line of the terrace to see where her family was. When she saw them, she broke into a broad smile and nudged Tessie. "Look. Are my eyes deceiving me or is that Billy's mam with them?"

"Well, who'd have thought it? I thought she said she was happy staying warm at home. Do you think it's because that Davy's mam was coming too?" Tessie was smiling. "I'd love it if my mam could watch, but she can't get down here. It's too much for her."

There was no sign of them having overeaten when the whistle blew to start the game. The girls set about trying to score as though their lives depended on it. Both teams were on the attack and playing a very similar style of football, moving players into the opposition's penalty area at every opportunity.

"Are we leaving ourselves weak at the back?" Doris asked at half-time.

Vi gave it some thought. "No, the crowd's enjoying the way we're playing. You can hear it when they cheer us on. I know we're leading by a goal at the moment, but I think I'd rather lose than play football that no one enjoys watching. What do you think, girls?"

The cheer that went up told Vi all she needed to know. They were having fun, and entertaining the crowd was a big part of that. Vi led them out for the second half. "Let's show them how to play this game," Vi called to the others as the girls separated across the field.

As they came off the pitch at full time, Vi felt euphoric. Not only had they kept the crowd cheering by playing great football, but they'd won by three goals to two, with Vi having scored two of the home team's goals.

The family were all waiting for her when she came out of the changing rooms afterward.

"You were very good," Mrs Moore said. "If I were twenty years younger, I think I might rather like to play."

"You can play with me," Tommy said, taking her hand.

Billy's mam harrumphed. Clearly she was unhappy with the bond that Tommy had formed with Mrs Moore.

"You know he'd love you to play with him, Mam," Billy said to Elsie Dobson.

Vi had to stifle a laugh at the look his mam gave Billy.

Now that Christmas was out of the way, Vi really wanted to make some hats. Tommy had gone to bed, Elsie was knitting, and both Billy and Alf were reading newspapers.

She looked at some of the pieces of cloth which she'd spread out on her knees. "You know, what I'm really going to need are some hat blocks. We used to have all shapes and sizes at Strywells. I have most of the other things I need from altering and making clothes. I don't have a dolly, but I'm sure I can make do."

"What's a hat block?" Billy asked.

"It's a piece of wood in the shape I want the hat to be, so I can get the form right as I'm working." She sketched some basic shapes to show him.

Billy looked at them and then turned to his dad. "Do you have bits of wood lying around at the workshop that they wouldn't mind us using?"

Alf took his pipe out of his mouth and put it into the ashtray. He took the piece of paper and looked at it. "I dare say we do. I can ask. I could cut them roughly to the right shapes, but I probably can't use work time to finish them."

Billy frowned. "I still have my old toolkit. It hasn't been out since I came home. I couldn't see how I was going to do much with one hand, but I might be able to use my left just to do a bit of whittling and sand off some rough edges. Maybe we could make them between us."

Billy's dad nodded. "We can try."

Vi was delighted. Now all she needed to do was work out what she could use to make brims and stiffen them; then she could get started. She could at least cut the pieces of cloth ready to put Tommy's cap together.

Billy's dad was as good as his word, and over the next few weeks he and Billy set about making a few different hat blocks for Vi. Tired as she was when she came home from work, Vi found a few minutes every day either to do a little stitching or to put some design ideas together. Between working, playing football, spending time with Tommy and trying to make some hats, Vi had no time to spare at all, but she was happy. Even Billy seemed to be happier than he'd been since he came home. He became frustrated with the things he couldn't do every now and again, but who wouldn't? As his left hand became more adept at the work and he secured the block firmly with a vice, he began to make some very good blocks for her. Tommy loved to be around his dad when he was working; he learned how to use some of his dad's woodworking tools and helped where he could.

Vi only worked on the cap once Tommy was asleep. It wasn't just that she wanted it to be a surprise, but she knew that every five minutes he'd be asking when it would be finished, and she didn't want to rush what she was doing.

When Vi finally presented the cap to her son, his eyes widened. "For me?"

Vi's heart melted and she carefully placed it on his head. She knew he'd want to see what it looked like, so she took him through to the parlour and lifted him up to look in the mirror above the fireplace.

"I'm going to wear it all the time and never take it off," Tommy said as Vi put him down again. He went running out into the hall calling, "Look, Grandpa."

Vi smiled as he went. She hoped all her customers would be as happy as Tommy.

"Vi!" Eva gasped and covered her mouth when she unwrapped the green felt cloche hat that Vi presented her with in February.

"What do you think?" Vi was biting her lip anxiously. She hadn't uttered a word about it to Eva so that it could be a surprise.

Eva was crying. "I think it's the most beautiful piece of clothing I have ever had, and the style's ever so modern."

The other girls had gathered around.

"Where did you get it, Eva?"

Eva carefully put it on her head. Despite needing to be

a close-fitting style, Vi had estimated well and it was a perfect fit. "Vi made it."

"Never! Will you make me one?"

"How much do you charge?"

"I love the style."

Vi felt overwhelmed. Every girl around them in the factory wanted a hat made by her. She supposed many of them wouldn't be able to afford it, but that was up to them to decide. There wouldn't be enough hours to make all of them and she didn't have enough fabric, but she could make one or two to sell and use the money to buy more material.

"Can you make one for me to give to Mrs Moore?" Tommy asked.

Mrs Moore had been as good as her word and gone outside to play football with Tommy and Nipper on their last visit. He had quickly adopted her as an extra grandmother, and she certainly seemed happy with the arrangement.

"Oh, I don't know. She must be used to buying whatever hats she likes. She wouldn't want one of mine." Vi was terrified at the prospect of showing Mrs Moore her handiwork. It was one thing among her mates at work, but quite another to show them to someone used to the quality she must buy.

"Please, Mam?" Tommy wasn't going to give up on the idea easily. "She liked my cap."

"Yes, she did." Vi presumed Mrs Moore was just being nice when Tommy had shown it to her, but she wouldn't say that to Tommy.

"Please, Mam?"

Vi smiled and sighed. "All right. I'll do it." First, she

needed to find enough material that would be suitable. She wondered if she could afford to buy some to ensure the pieces would be an exact match.

CHAPTER 12

"Where else am I going to take the money from if I don't take it from there?" Vi slammed the jar back on the shelf.

"I don't know, love." Billy ran his hand through his hair. "It's just that no one seems to want to employ a one-armed soldier, and that's all we've got put by."

Vi's anger drained away. "I'm sorry. It was just with Tommy wanting to give a hat to Mrs Moore, I wanted it to be special."

"If you were making them to sell, I can see that it would be a good way to use the money; an investment. As it is, we just keep giving them away. We can't afford to. What's the sense in giving things away when we can't afford the things we need for ourselves?"

"Eva paid for hers." Vi had felt uncomfortable taking her money, but Eva had insisted.

"I know, love, but that wasn't as much as the material would have cost us if we'd had to buy it."

Vi knew that Billy was right, but she'd promised Tommy she'd make one for Mrs Moore. She lifted the parcel of fabrics onto the table and began to sort them out. Perhaps if she went through everything, she could find enough pieces that were a good match to make this one. Studying each piece calmed her, and she was quite enjoying herself until Elsie came in.

"You'll need to move all of that rubbish. I need to use the table."

Vi's frustration boiled over and she used her arm to brush all the sorted pieces onto the floor. "You won't let me use the parlour. This is the only bloody table I can work at. What am I supposed to do?" She didn't wait for an answer. Leaving Elsie chuntering behind her, Vi marched out of the room, picked up her coat and headed for the back door. She could hear Billy hobbling after her, but she didn't turn around.

"Vi, wait."

She carried on walking. She was patient; she did her best to support Billy and everyone around her, but there was only so much she could take. As she walked out into Victoria Street, Vi had no idea where she was going and just walked. She wanted to sell hats, of course she did; but how could she do that if she didn't have material, or somewhere to work?

As she wandered into the centre of Billingbrook, Vi looked in the shop windows. She stopped outside the greengrocer and read the cards in the window; not for anything in particular, just to see what people were offering.

Another woman stopped alongside her and did the same thing. Neither of them spoke, but out of the corner of her eye, Vi watched. The woman was well-dressed and was wearing what looked to Vi to be an expensive hat. Vi frowned. It had been nice when the girls at work asked for hats, but most of them couldn't afford to pay enough for Vi to get started. But what if she put a card in the shop window? If people were to pay her a deposit, which would be enough to buy the material, and then the balance when they received their hat, she wouldn't need to dip into savings.

She wasn't sure. She walked on along the road, but then turned back and watched the greengrocer's shop. Almost all the women passing, and some of the men, stopped to read the cards in the window.

Before she had time to change her mind, Vi went back to the greengrocer's. Inside, her hand was shaking as she asked if she might have a card to put in the window. Paying her halfpenny, Vi took the card over to the side to fill it in. She sketched a hat like the one she'd made for Eva and added the details she thought would be needed.

Once she'd handed over her completed card, with the assurance that it would be added to the others, Vi walked home. She planned to tell Billy what she'd done and hoped he would be willing to help her. If she received orders for even one or two hats, she could earn enough money to make one for Mrs Moore as well. If no one responded, she would need another plan. She'd give it a week and see what happened.

"I'm sorry," Billy said, even before she'd taken her coat off.

Vi turned around and reached out to him. "I am too." She didn't really know how to explain what she'd done. Then she had a thought. "Are you up to a walk?"

At the sound of the word 'walk', Nipper started barking, making them both laugh.

"I think he's answered for me." Billy took his coat from the peg and followed Vi back out to the road.

They didn't say much as they walked. Vi was on Billy's left so she could slip her arm through his, although, with him using his stick, that was still awkward.

It took much longer to get back to the greengrocer's

walking together than it had taken Vi on her own. When they arrived outside, Vi simply pointed to the card in the window and let Billy read it for himself.

When Billy finished reading, he kissed her on the cheek. "I'm proud of you, Vi. I'm also very glad you brought me. You've forgotten something."

Vi frowned and looked at the card. She'd included that she was offering to make bespoke hats. She'd explained that they would need to pay a deposit and the rest on delivery. She looked at the card again. "What's missing?"

"Violet Dobson, I love you. You haven't told them how they can contact you."

Vi gasped and put her hand to her mouth. Then she almost ran into the shop in her haste to correct the error.

By the end of the week, Vi was starting to doubt that anyone would respond to her advert. Every night she came in from work and checked for any letters or notes before going to take her things upstairs. On Saturday morning, she was surprised to hear the knocker on the front door. No one they knew came to the front of the house. She wiped her hands on her apron and opened the door.

A petite woman, with auburn hair and skin that was pale enough to grace any fine soap advert, was standing on the doorstep.

"Excuse me," she said in a confident but not overbearing voice. "I'm looking for Mrs Dobson, the milliner."

Being described as a milliner suddenly made Vi feel as though she were a complete fraud and that she ought to be apologising to this lady. It was only hearing Elsie coming out of the back room that brought Vi to her senses, before her mother-in-law decided to get involved.

"Yes." She held out her hand to the lady. "I'm Mrs Dobson, please would you come through?"

Knowing she was risking incurring Elsie's wrath, Vi showed the lady into the parlour and invited her to take a seat. Then, using the excuse of getting the lady a drink, Vi went into the hall to head Elsie off and to fetch her drawings.

For the next half an hour, Vi discussed hat styles and colours with Mrs Speedwell. The lady was due to attend an important wedding and felt hopeless choosing something that would suit her. By the time she left, Vi had sketched out a hat which Mrs Speedwell thought she would be delighted with, and happily left her deposit.

As soon as the lady had gone, Vi checked the clock. If she set off now, she'd have time to buy the material and still arrive at football practice on time.

"I'll tell you later," she called to Billy as she headed out.

The card in the greengrocer's window did bring her one other order, but it wasn't the start of the rush that deep down Vi had hoped for. What it gave was enough money to buy properly matching material for a hat for Mrs Moore, just as she'd promised Tommy. It was ready in time for their visit to the Moores' on Easter Sunday.

Just before they went into the house, Vi gave the brown paper parcel to Tommy.

"Now, remember what we said."

The boy nodded.

When Mrs Moore answered the door, before they'd even gone in, Tommy held up the parcel and said, "Happy Easter, Aunty Audrey."

The woman's face flushed pink and she bent down to

take the package from Tommy. "Well, thank you. I wasn't expecting this. How lovely." She looked up at first Billy and then Vi, as though she'd find an explanation for the surprise. Nipper didn't stand on ceremony and ran straight into the hallway.

"You'll have to open it before we can explain," Vi said as they stepped inside. "It was all Tommy's idea."

Mrs Moore nodded and took his hand with the one that wasn't holding the parcel. "I've got something to show you, but I'd like to open your present first, if I may?"

Tommy sat watching as Mrs Moore carefully unwrapped the peacock blue cloche hat.

"Oh, my." She seemed utterly speechless. "It's beautiful." She stood and looked in the mirror above the mantelpiece as she put it on. "Terence, come and see what Tommy has given me."

Mr Moore came through to the front room. It was obvious from his reaction that he thought it suited his wife; his words only confirmed what his face had already said. "You look beautiful, my darling. I shall need somewhere special to take you wearing that. What do you think?"

Once they were sitting down, Vi explained about her hat making hobby. "And it really was Tommy's idea. I made one for the girl I work with, and now all the others are asking me to make them. I'd love to, but there just isn't time, and I don't have all the material I'd need. What I've done to get started is have a card in a shop window." By the end, Vi had poured out the whole story, bringing Mr and Mrs Moore up to date.

Vi noticed that while she spoke, Mr Moore took a keen interest, and she felt flattered.

"What would you need to make more of them?" he asked.

"Well, material mostly. Billy and his dad have been making my hat blocks. I could do with a hatstand or two and a dolly. I've got most of the things I need." Vi was thinking through carefully. "If I bought the material, I'd need somewhere to keep it. Billy's mam would rather I didn't have my millinery things everywhere at home."

Mr Moore just nodded and seemed to be thinking. "How's your bookkeeping coming on, Billy?"

Realising he'd stopped asking about the hats, Vi went to help Mrs Moore with the tea.

"Terence is bringing me to the match again tomorrow," Mrs Moore said proudly.

Tommy pointed to himself and frowned.

"Yes, of course, how silly of me. It's Tommy who's taking both me and Mr Moore."

Tommy beamed at her.

"That reminds me, Tommy. I didn't realise it was your birthday this month. I'm sorry. We have something that you might like as a late birthday present, if your parents don't mind." Mrs Moore looked to Vi. "It belonged to our Davy. We'd saved it in case we had grandchildren and, well…" Her voice trailed off.

"Of course, that would be very kind of you." Vi wondered if it was going to be a teddy bear. They were becoming popular, but perhaps they weren't around when Davy was young, so it couldn't be.

Mrs Moore beckoned for Tommy to follow and called her husband as she went into the hall. "I think Mr Moore might need to help you."

Mr Moore grinned at Tommy as he came through. "Have you seen it yet?"

"We're just going now," Vi said.

They all went out of the back door to a shed in the

garden. Mr Moore opened the door and brought out an almost spotless bicycle.

Vi gasped. "But you can't possibly."

"I think we can," Mr Moore said with a twinkle in his eyes.

Vi nudged Tommy. "What do you say?"

Tommy simply stood there, unable to say anything. He looked first to his father and then back to Mr Moore. "For me?"

Vi was struggling not to cry, watching the rapturous look on Tommy's face.

"Here, let me help you." Mr Moore held out a hand to Tommy and the boy inched forward.

Tommy put his hand on the handlebars and stroked the bicycle, almost as though it were Nipper. They took the bicycle out into the road and Mr Moore held on to the back as Tommy tried to get his balance and turn the pedals. It took about half an hour before he could wobble a short distance, with Mr Moore giving a little gentle support.

Vi had never seen Mr Moore looking so happy, and as for Tommy, his grin couldn't have been broader.

They eventually went in for tea, totally against Tommy's wishes, but by then he could go a little way on his own and was ready to practise without help, although Nipper had the good sense to stay some distance away.

"Can I stay out here?" he asked.

"No, my darling, we need to keep an eye on you when you're on the bicycle for a little while longer," Vi said, hating to see the disappointment on his face.

"Of course," Mr Moore said when they were indoors, "I do like coming to watch you play football, Vi, but I've always been a supporter of the rugby league."

Vi didn't think it had ever been mentioned, and wasn't

really sure how the game was played.

"I was wondering if Billy and Tommy might like to come with me to watch a game sometime. Not that there are many taking place at the moment. As with the football, many of our lads have gone off to fight." He looked to Billy. "What do you say?"

Billy laughed. "If you don't mind me not knowing the first thing about the game, then I'd be happy to go. What do you think, Tommy?"

"Can I bring my bicycle?"

Everyone laughed. Vi guessed that until the novelty wore off, he'd probably think about little else.

Vi couldn't help feeling she'd been neglecting her football. She'd even missed a Saturday practice to finish the hat for Mrs Moore, and that wasn't like her. Using her spare time for hat making was all well and good, but there simply weren't enough hours in the day.

The Easter Monday match was a home game against a team travelling all the way from Leeds. It was a long time since Vi had felt so unprepared, and by half-time she knew it was showing in her game. She sat down on a bench away from the other girls. They were losing by two goals to nil, and she felt as though it was all her fault. A moment later, Tessie came over with Billy following.

"What's wrong, love?" he asked, sitting down next to her.

"I can't do everything. I'm not fit enough, and the team would be better without me." Vi couldn't even bring herself to turn to Billy.

Billy took her chin gently in his hand and made her look at him.

"Now listen to me. You aren't unfit. This is what's

going on in your head, nothing more. When Stan and I were in France, there was this one night. We had to go over to the enemy trench to see if it was clear. In the dark we were quite safe, but we didn't get back before it was light. Stan was caught on the barbed wire on the way back, and while I was trying to free him he caught a sniper bullet in the leg. The only way that Stan would get back alive was if I carried him the rest of the way, and did it fast, without being shot. If I'd thought about whether or not I could do it, then Stan wouldn't have been the only one who didn't come home. Sometimes you have to do something and not spend time thinking about it. You're a bloody good player, Violet Dobson, and right now you need to go out and carry your team home. It doesn't matter if you win or lose, but it does matter whether you play with confidence." He kissed her cheek and, without giving her time to answer, he got up and left the changing room.

Vi hadn't known that there'd been a time Billy saved Stan's life. He'd never told her the story before. War was very different from sport. That was life and death; this was just a game. She could see the point that Billy was making though. Sometimes it wasn't about questioning what you could do, it was about finding reserves and doing what needed to be done. She'd go out there and make Billy proud of her. She wished Stan had come home safely. The least she could do was go out and do her best. She stood up from the bench, squared her shoulders and took a couple of deep breaths.

"Right, girls," she shouted, and they quietened down and turned to her. "Are we going to let a team from Leeds beat us at our home ground?"

The girls chorused in reply, "No."

"Then who's going to come with me to score some

goals?" Vi marched toward the changing room door and, with whoops and hollers from the girls, they set out for the pitch.

Vi didn't think she'd run as much in a game as she did that afternoon. She moved up and down the pitch, spotting opportunities, making tackles, intercepting through balls, and bringing her own team into the game. After ten minutes, she saw an opening and passed the ball to Clara, who scored their first goal. Twenty minutes later, it was Tessie who left the Leeds defence behind to score the second Billingbrook goal.

At full time it was a two all draw. It wasn't the win Vi had wanted, but it was a better result than she'd feared. She hoped Billy would be proud.

CHAPTER 13

Saturday 11ᵗʰ May 1918 - Navy Throttles Ostend Harbour Entrance - The Daily Mirror

Billy headed to the back door to see what all the banging was about. Tessie was standing on the doorstep, her eyes red from crying. "What on earth's the matter? Vi's not here."

"Oh, Mr Dobson, it's not Vi I need to talk to, it's you. John's had his call-up papers."

Billy wasn't used to dealing with distressed women and wasn't really sure what to do. "Sit down and I'll make some tea." He put the kettle on the stove as he was thinking what to say.

"He's only just eighteen." Tessie picked up the cup he'd put in front of her. "If he passes his medical, he doesn't have to go straight away for training, does he?"

Billy certainly didn't want John to face what he'd been through. "I don't think so. They used to say lads who were called up wouldn't go overseas until they were nineteen, but I think it's a bit younger than that now. Either way, he won't have to go yet unless he offers."

"Will you talk to him? He looks up to you." Tessie turned toward him with doleful eyes.

Billy nodded. "I'll talk to him. When is his medical?"

"I'll be ever so grateful. It's Wednesday."

They were going to Vi's family the following day. As

long as Percy wasn't around he'd talk to John then. "Come on, lass. I'll do what I can. You'd best fetch your kit or you'll be late for football."

Tessie put her cup down and headed to the back door. "Thank you," she said, before going out into the yard.

Billy just hoped that John would listen to him.

Other than the occasional success, such as his talk with John, Billy was finding it hard to accept that his own achievements were so minor when compared to Vi's. Here she was making hats and captaining the football team. Who wanted to know that yesterday he managed to put his sock on straight at the first time of trying? He did feel proud of all Vi was doing, but he needed something for himself. He'd never realised before how much being a man was about providing for his family and doing something useful. Without it he was lost and, at times, angry with the frustration.

He'd nearly come to the end of his course at the adult school and it was time to find work, but who would employ a one-armed invalid when there were so many others to choose from? The man who'd been teaching him had suggested he train to be a teacher himself, but much as Tommy didn't see his injuries, other children could be cruel, and Billy didn't feel prepared for that.

For now, he would do everything he could to help with the football.

"£250, Vi, that's a great deal of money, and that was one match," Billy said as they walked to the Caulder and Harrison recreation ground a couple of weeks later.

"I know, but I don't think about that. I'd happily play even if we weren't raising money for the hospital. I just love playing."

Billy couldn't stop himself thinking about the money the team was raising. If it hadn't been for Billingbrook Hall military hospital, he wouldn't be capable of half the things he could do now. He hadn't added up the total from all the games, but it was a considerable sum.

"I am getting a bit old compared to the rest of the team." Vi sighed heavily.

This was the sort of thing that made Billy angry. What he'd give for the chance to take part. Being able to play wasn't about age. He tried not to show his annoyance; after all, how could Vi really understand? He calmed himself by thinking about how much he still enjoyed helping with the coaching, even if he couldn't run along the side of the pitch.

"Vi, you're twenty-five, you've got years ahead of you yet. At least, if you want to."

"Maybe another couple of seasons before I hang up my boots." Vi kissed Billy's cheek before heading to the changing rooms, and Billy went over to join Joe Wood.

Billy was surprised to see Mr Giffard coming across the field toward them. "What's this about then?" he asked Joe.

Joe shrugged. "He said to get everyone together, there's some big announcement. I just hope it's good news."

Edith was already on the pitch doing some stretches. "Maybe we've got new kit. These ones are starting to look old-fashioned." Edith tugged at the long shorts as she did a curtsy.

By now the rest of the team had come out and joined them.

"That would be good. I'm never going to find a boyfriend dressed like this." Eva pouted and everyone laughed.

Billy didn't say anything, but he guessed that until some of the lads came back from the war, Eva wasn't going to find a boyfriend, either with or without a change of kit. The way the war was going, he just hoped there'd be enough young men who came back.

Mr Giffard strode onto the pitch and the girls, together with Joe and Billy, gathered around. Once he'd clapped his hands together for the girls to be quiet, Mr Giffard said, "Now, ladies and gentlemen." He was making it sound very official. "I think I have some news that you've all been hoping for. It's taken a long time to arrange and get enough teams together to make it worthwhile, but from September, there will be the very first Women's Northern Football Cup. What do you say?"

The girls were jumping up and down and cheering. Then he held his hand out for them to be quiet again.

"We'll play our home matches at Billingbrook United. There will be sixteen teams in the cup, but I can tell you all about that later. The important thing is that we need to be in perfect shape so we can do our best."

Billy could have laughed at the suggestion of being in perfect shape, given that Mr Giffard seemed to be developing a rounder, fuller appearance almost every time they saw him.

After the practice, while the girls were changing, Mr Giffard stood at the edge of the pitch talking to Billy and Joe.

"Making all the arrangements for the matches is going to take some time. I think we'd be best to employ someone to help, just part-time anyway," Mr Giffard said.

"What would they need to do?" Joe asked. "My dad's after work."

"Well..." Mr Giffard rocked back slightly on his heels

as he was thinking. "I'll need someone with accounts training and who can write a good letter. He'd need to answer the phone…"

Joe laughed. "You may as well stop there, Dad's no accounts clerk. He can count, but that's probably about it."

Billy wished Joe hadn't interrupted. They were the sorts of things he'd been learning, though he'd never put any of it to the test. He wanted to ask for more details, but held back. He wasn't sure if his reluctance to put himself forward was because he couldn't face being employed out of pity, or maybe he was scared they wouldn't want his disabilities; they wouldn't want someone like him.

As he, Vi and Tessie walked home that day, all the girls could talk about was the cup, but Billy was still thinking about the job Mr Giffard had talked about.

"Which teams do you think we'll be playing against?" Tessie asked.

"Probably the ones we've been playing in recent months. What do you think, Billy?" Vi looked across to him.

"How should I know? It's not as though I'll be playing." He stopped walking and turned to go in the other direction. He needed some time on his own.

He limped away, leaving Tessie and Vi where they were.

A moment or two later he heard Vi calling, and the sound of her feet pounding the pavement as she came after him. "Billy, what's wrong?"

He leaned against the wall of the factory they were walking past. "I can't do this, Vi."

"Can't do what?" Vi frowned at him.

"I can't be just the man who tags along after his wife. I'm useless. I used to be a carpenter. Then I was a soldier.

Now I'm nothing." He wanted to scream and shout, but he had no idea what about, or at whom. He wanted to punch the wall, but he really couldn't afford to hurt his one good hand. Inwardly, he laughed at himself, even now rationalising the risk of punching the wall.

"Did something happen?"

The innocence of Vi's question made him want to laugh again. This wasn't about one thing, but how could he explain the hundreds of ways he felt a failure to the woman he loved? How could he explain that he felt less of a man than he'd been before?

After a long pause, he said, "I need a job."

"Didn't Mr Giffard come to find you?"

Billy looked up at Vi. "You put him up to it? Don't you think I can get one on my own?"

"No, silly. He asked us all if we knew anyone who might be suitable. I just said it would be worth him talking to you. I thought I saw him come over."

"Oh, he came over all right. I want a job that I get for myself, not a pity job because my wife's in the team." Billy balled his fist as he talked to Vi, trying desperately not to shout, but wanting to let all his frustration out.

Vi looked straight at him. "Billy, how did you get your carpentry apprenticeship when you left school?"

"It was with a bloke that Dad knew from the workshop, but what's that got to do with it?"

"How did I find out about the job at Caulder and Harrison?" Vi's voice was soft.

"Because Tessie worked there, but…" He suddenly began to see what Vi was driving at. "This is different. This would be because of pity."

Vi stood with her hands on her hips. "Now you listen to me, Billy Dobson, Mr Giffard can't afford to give you a job out of pity. He knows what you've done coaching the team. He's been impressed by that. If he gives you a job, it will be because he thinks you can do it and he's willing to give you a chance. If you just think anyone's only doing things for you out of pity, then you'll never do anything."

Billy wasn't used to Vi putting him in his place and he felt chastened. Was she right? Was he just talking himself out of it? He heard Stan's voice in his head as though his mate were right there with them. *'You silly sod, why pass up the chance of a job? What's the worst you can do?'*

"What do you think I should do?" he asked Vi. "I can't just go to his office and ask."

"Write a letter for me to take in. That way he can see your letter writing skills as well."

Billy nodded. It sounded a lot easier than going in person.

On Sunday, Billy felt in slightly better spirits. He'd already drafted the letter to Mr Giffard and would write it out properly later.

"How did your writing get so good?" Tommy asked, looking at what he was doing.

"Practice, Tommy, just like Mam and the football." Billy reached across and took Vi's hand. "Thank you."

"What for?" Vi looked confused.

Where could Billy start? "Mostly for never giving up on me."

He could see Vi blush. How beautiful she looked, and how much Billy wanted to take care of her. He sighed. He wasn't going to let himself become dispirited again today. "Are we ready?" He changed the subject abruptly and stood up. They were going over to Vi's parents. Recently they'd fallen into a routine where one Sunday they spent the afternoon with Vi's family and the next with the Moores. For Tommy especially, it was like having three lots of grandparents, and they all enjoyed it.

Today was to be spent with the Tunnicliffes, and Tessie was going with them.

Tessie said nothing about Billy walking off the day before, and carried on as though they were picking up the conversation where they'd left off.

"Which other teams d'you think will be in the cup?" Tessie asked.

"There's been a little in the papers about teams in other areas," Billy said, trying to remember where had been mentioned. "If it's the north of England, there could be teams from the other side of the country."

Tessie clapped her hands. "We might get to travel to all sorts of places."

As they neared the Tunnicliffe house, Tessie became suddenly serious. "I'm glad John didn't go straight for training, but I'm still scared he'll be called to fight eventually."

"I think you should make the most of the present and not think about it too much. He should still have a few months. Hopefully it will be over before that." Billy just hoped that John wasn't called away sooner

Billy liked going to Vi's parents' house; they always made him feel welcome. As Vi opened the door that Sunday, Billy let out a groan. Percy was there. Vi's sister Ena was all right, but why she'd ever married Percy Mayberry was beyond him. He steeled himself for whatever snide remarks he would face on this encounter.

"Still limping, I see." Percy reached out to shake Billy's missing right hand.

Rather than offer the other hand, Billy simply nodded

to him and moved to the other side of the room, to sit near Vi's dad, Frank.

"Are you all right, Billy, lad?" Frank Tunicliffe asked when he was comfortable.

Billy enjoyed talking to Frank, but there was only so much he wanted to say in Percy's hearing. He gave a weak smile. "Vi's football's going well."

"And mine," said Tessie, dropping down into the seat the other side of Billy. "There's going to be a cup and everything."

Having Tessie there definitely helped to take away the pressure from Percy. Billy held off talking about anything more personal, hoping Percy would leave sooner than they did. It didn't stop the jibes, but at least it gave the man less ammunition.

"From what Dad says, it looks like the fighting could be all over before our John has to go," Mam said over dinner.

"It might do him good to get in while he can," Percy said. "What do you think, Billy? Did it make a man of you?"

Billy gritted his teeth. Coming from a man who had found a bent doctor to sign papers preventing him being called up, Billy really couldn't stomach Percy's comments. "Let's hope it's all over soon. Quite enough harm has been caused."

Vi took Billy's letter when she went to work on Monday and all he could do was wait anxiously to see what Mr Giffard replied. Even by the time he went to the adult school that day, he'd talked himself into believing that he wouldn't be considered. The day dragged, and even the gentleman who'd been helping him, Mr Roberts, asked if everything was all right.

He was glad when his time was over and he was back in the fresh air on his way home. "It's probably for the best if I don't get it, Nipper. I'd never be able to take you with me."

The wait for Vi coming home was impossible.

"If you don't sit down, you'll wear out what's left of the carpet," Mam said as Billy did another circuit of the back room.

He clenched his hand and bit back the urge to snap. Instead he went out into the kitchen and leaned against the sink, waiting for Vi to come in.

The minute he heard the back gate he went to open the door. "Well?"

Vi looked startled and he stepped back to let her enter.

"I don't know anything."

"What do you mean?" Billy wanted to shout at her. "Didn't you give him the letter?"

Vi flinched from his words and frowned. "Of course I did. I went before I started work. I just haven't heard back from him, that's all."

Billy slammed his fist against the wall. "I'm going out." He went through the back door without another word, Nipper following at his heels.

His studying was coming to an end, and he had to find work. He'd go mad if he didn't. Why had he ever bloody well signed up in the first place? He was just another piece of debris, brushed aside and useless. He'd have thought, with so many away fighting, someone would have work for him. If the war ended and the whole army returned, he'd have no chance.

It was late by the time he went home, and both Vi and Tommy were asleep. He didn't want to wake them trying to wriggle into the middle of the bed; it wasn't that easy for him to do, so he went back downstairs and settled in a chair. Two hours later he woke, screaming. He was sitting, leaning against the side of a trench. Shells were landing around him and the noise was unbearable. "Stan, Stan." The darkness was thick and unbroken. There were no flashes. He heard a noise and started. A faint glow came into the room as the door was opened.

"Billy! Billy!"

Billy could feel the sweat dripping down his forehead as he slowly gathered his senses. "Vi?"

She came over and knelt down beside him. "It's all right. You're safe."

Billy felt his shoulders drop slightly as the tension left his body. Only then did Vi put her arms around him. She no longer risked holding him until he clearly knew where he was. He'd fought her off several times before.

"They're back," he said simply. He'd had a few weeks with virtually no nightmares, and he thought things were improving.

"It's all right." Vi rocked him gently. "We'll be fine."

But it wasn't all right, not to Billy. The way things looked now, it might never be all right.

CHAPTER 14

Tuesday 11th June 1918 - Further Foe Gain After Terrific Fighting - The Daily Mirror

Over the next few days, it was obvious to Vi how disheartened Billy had become and how his mood had darkened. He'd been better able to deal with his nightmares when he felt his days were so positive; now they left him depressed, and he seemed to be disappearing into a world where he was harder for her to reach. She was surprised there had been no reply from Mr Giffard, but she wasn't really sure what to do. "Something will turn up, love."

"What use am I, when there are so many women willing to work now? Don't get me wrong, I'm glad you're working, we need the money. But I'm just scrap."

Vi didn't know what to say. "Have you thought of asking Mr Moore?"

Billy slammed his fist on the table. "I can't ask him to pay me wages for a job I can't do, just because I knew his son."

Vi decided not to say anything further. She'd only end up making it worse. There were many men in Billy's position; she'd heard girls at work talking. Some seemed to be out all hours drinking, and Vi didn't want that. This was her wonderful, mild, Billy. She wanted him to stay that way.

Vi wondered about going to talk to the matron at the hospital. She must have experience of this. She might at least know how to handle his mood swings. If Billy found out she'd done that, though, he really wouldn't be happy. Perhaps she'd be better talking to Mrs Moore. She was a practical woman. She might at least have some ideas that would help. The only problem was, that with all the hours Vi was working, there was no time when she could go without Billy knowing.

"No practice today, girls," Joe Wood said to them at their morning break on Wednesday. "The sports ground's not available. Sorry."

Vi's mind raced. If they weren't going to practice at such short notice, maybe she could ask for a couple of hours off to see Mrs Moore. She wasn't sure if she should ask Mrs Johnson, or if she might have more luck going to Mr Giffard's office to ask for permission. If she did that, there was a risk Mrs Johnson wouldn't be impressed. She sighed.

"Cheer up, lass," Joe said. "It's only today. You'll be back playing on Saturday."

"It wasn't that. I was just thinking…" She trailed off, but then wondered if Joe could help. "I'm worried about Billy." She explained about the retraining Billy had done, and how difficult he was finding getting a job.

Joe turned visibly pale. "Oh, Vi, I'm so sorry. I'd completely forgotten last week that I was supposed to ask you to see Mr Giffard. It never dawned on me it was about anything other than the football, but it could be about the job he was talking about, and I simply forgot."

"What did he say?" Vi could barely stand still as she asked.

"It was Mrs Simpson who asked me, so not much

really."

Vi looked across at the clock; break was almost over. She'd have to wait until lunchtime, but maybe Mr Giffard wouldn't be there then. The decision was made for her as Eva came over to return to their benches. There was always after lunch when they were supposed to be at football; somehow being back to her bench late then didn't seem so bad, at least not to Vi.

"Vi, what are you doing?"

Vi looked up suddenly, it wasn't like Eva to risk talking while they were working. She looked at the shell case she was packing and realised that she wasn't concentrating. She'd had the same shell case in front of her for the last few minutes. Thankfully there was no sign of Mrs Johnson. "Thanks, Eva." She pulled herself together.

The lunchtime bell couldn't come soon enough. When it finally sounded, Vi went to clean up so she could head to the management corridor.

By the time Vi reached the outer office where Mrs Simpson normally sat, it was empty. Vi knocked in case Mrs Simpson was around somewhere, but she didn't hold out much hope.

It was Mr Giffard's voice that replied, "Come."

She felt suddenly flustered as she went through the outer office to his door.

"I... that is... Mr Wood said you wanted to see me."

"Ah, Mrs Dobson, do come in. I was starting to think you were avoiding me."

"I'm sorry, he only gave me the message this morning." She suddenly felt the need to protect Joe. "I hadn't seen him for a few days. I..."

"Not to worry." Mr Giffard dismissed the need for explanation with a wave of his hand. "I wanted a word about Mr Dobson. I'm afraid by the time I received his letter I'd already sorted out how we'd do the administration for the football."

Vi felt her shoulders slump. She'd presumed that had been what he wanted to discuss.

Mr Giffard continued, "However, there are other vacancies in the factory."

Vi frowned and felt awkward. "But he couldn't make shells."

Mr Giffard laughed. "There are jobs here other than making shells. Someone has to do the accounts and process the invoices."

Vi looked up for the first time. It had never occurred to her that in a place this size there were lots of different jobs. Obviously she knew there was management, but apart from that she only ever mixed with the other girls who worked on the factory floor, doing the same things she was doing. "I didn't know."

"Why should you? But someone has to pay you all each week."

Mr Giffard was smiling warmly, and Vi felt herself begin to relax.

"I've been impressed with the work your husband's done helping the football team. I think he could be a real asset to the company."

It had never occurred to Vi that Mr Giffard would have even noticed Billy's involvement. "Thank you."

"If he can report to the personnel office, we'll give him a try. Thank you, Mrs Dobson." Mr Giffard stood up from his desk, and Vi realised her interview was at an end.

As she headed back outside, Vi couldn't stop smiling. However, she'd seen Billy's temper when he thought people were doing him a favour, and she didn't want to make him angry. This came about because he wrote to Mr Giffard, not from something she'd done. Now she just needed Billy to believe that. She wished Mr Giffard could have written to Billy, rather than gone through her.

That evening, Vi looked into the back room before going upstairs. "I'm home." Even she could hear that her voice sounded a little false, but she didn't know what to say to get some time with Billy on his own.

"Is everything all right, love?" Unusually, it was Alf who looked up at her concerned.

"Fine thanks, Dad. I just need to talk to Billy if he can spare a minute."

"You've not lost that job of yours, have you?" Elsie didn't even raise her eyes from the sock she was darning as she asked.

Vi sighed. "No, Mam. I have not lost my job." She shot a look in Billy's direction and then toward the door. She headed upstairs, and hoped Billy would follow. As she went into the bedroom, she suddenly thought that if Billy got upset then doing so where Tommy was asleep might not be such a good idea. She really wished they could move into a home of their own, but for now that was just a pipe dream.

She was still taking her coat off when Billy came up. It made her jump when he opened the bedroom door.

"Are you all right?" Billy looked worried.

Vi fumbled putting the coat on its hanger. "I'm fine."

"You don't look it." Billy came over to her and sat on the edge of the bed.

Vi sat down next to him, folding and unfolding her hands in her lap. "Mr Giffard says if you go to the personnel office there's a job for you at Caulder and Harrison." She gripped her hands tight as she waited for a reaction.

"Oh?" Billy's reply sounded cautious. "Doing what?"

"I don't know." That was definitely true. Vi had absolutely no idea about accounts or personnel, or any of the other activities. "If you go to see them, you could ask." Vi held her breath to see what would come next.

"This isn't the football job then. I guess I wasn't good enough for that. They're not going to want a broken old soldier like me. There's no point."

Vi sighed. Broken Billy was almost harder to deal with than angry Billy. She tried to think carefully before she replied. "It isn't that. Mr Giffard had already sorted that out before he got your letter."

Billy didn't reply. He simply pushed himself up from the bed and walked out of the bedroom. Vi kissed Tommy and then followed Billy down. She didn't know what to do next. She couldn't push the point.

As she passed the back room to go to the kitchen, she heard Alf's voice and saw a glimpse of how he must have coped with Billy's mam all these years.

"That's enough of that, Billy, lad. You've sat around here quite long enough feeling sorry for yourself. I didn't bring you up to give up at the first problem, and I don't expect you to give up now. You take yourself up there tomorrow and make enquiries."

Vi could have hugged her father-in-law. Billy never argued with his dad, and this time was no exception. He said nothing, and Vi crossed her fingers that the following day he'd do exactly what his father had instructed him. She wouldn't ask. She wouldn't say a word. She'd just wait to see what happened. That was going to be hard, but it was her only option.

"Are you all right?" Eva asked at break the following day.

"I'm fine." Vi frowned. "Why?" She really didn't want to say anything about Billy to the others.

"You seem very twitchy for someone who's fine. You were odd yesterday as well." Eva looked her up and down as though trying to weigh up if she was being honest.

Vi forced a smile. "Really, I'm fine."

Eva gave her a look, which Vi knew meant she wasn't buying it. Hopefully she could explain soon.

If she'd been on her own, Vi would have run home that evening. As she and Tessie reached Ivy Terrace, her heart was racing. She said goodnight to her friend, and went in to find Billy.

"They've gone for a walk," Elsie said to her as soon as she poked her head into the sitting room. "And before you say a word, it's no good asking me. No one around here tells me anything."

Vi went upstairs to check on Tommy, who was curled up with his arms around Nipper.

Her heart sank thinking about Billy; surely it could only mean it wasn't good news. She looked out of the window, but there was no sign of him. She sighed.

It was another hour before the two men returned. Thanks to Elsie, there was no need for Vi to ask any questions.

"And where have you been, Alf Dobson?"

"Can't a man buy his son a drink once in a while?" Alf had a twinkle in his eye and looked to his son. "Billy's had some good news and I wanted to share it with him."

"Billy?" Vi clapped her hands together.

Billy looked almost shy as he said, "I've been taken on for a trial period. I shall be working with the purchase ledger as a junior clerk. It shouldn't be too difficult, unless my missing arm holds me back." He gave a nervous laugh, as though intending it as a joke.

"That's wonderful." Vi went over and kissed him, but felt him tense slightly as she did. "When do you start?"

"Tomorrow. The hours aren't as long as yours, but the pay's not too bad. It's better than sitting here, that's for sure."

Vi couldn't work out why Billy didn't seem happier. He said no more about it until they went to bed.

Billy spoke in a quiet and sad tone when he said, "This is your doing, isn't it, Vi?"

Vi was worried that it wouldn't take much for Billy to walk away from this. His bloody pride would get in the way, even if the job was on his own merit. "They wouldn't give you the job if they didn't think you could do it." She thought she'd better stop before she said too much. At least with him not starting until nine o'clock, they wouldn't all be walking to work together, so it should mean there was less chance for her to put her foot in it, or Tessie for that matter.

He didn't cuddle up to her when they got into bed that night, and she sighed, hoping that once he started it might give him some of his old confidence.

For the first few days, Billy was so tired when he came home that he was already asleep when Vi came in.

"How's he doing, Dad?" she asked Alf toward the end of the week.

"It's hard to know, love. He's not said much. Give him a while. I don't think the time of year helps." Alf Dobson took a long draw on his pipe.

"I'd have thought the summer was the best time to be getting used to walking all that way." Elsie picked up her knitting and looked at where she was shaping a sleeve. "It would be better if he'd take that bloody dog with him."

Alf drew on his pipe again and then folded his paper. "I don't suppose you've thought about the fact that it will be two years on Monday since Stan died."

Vi gasped. Once she'd realised Billy was alive, she'd put all thoughts of 1st July 1916 out of her head; but that would be something Billy would never be able to do. It was hard to know whether to say anything to him or not. It wasn't as though there was a grave they could lay flowers on.

As the summer wore on, Billy's mood began to lift. When Caulder and Harrison made his job permanent a month after starting, he stopped saying he wouldn't be there if it hadn't been for Vi, and began to accept he was worthy of the job. He even apologised for thinking it had been her doing.

Vi knew things were really looking up when he said, "You remember we used to dream of having a home of our own?"

She laughed. "Oh, I remember all right."

"Well, I reckon if we keep saving for another two months, we might have enough. Look..." Billy pushed a piece of paper over to her. "I've been working out what we'd need."

Vi had been so happy to be able to buy new shoes for Tommy, ones that actually fitted and didn't have holes, that she hadn't really thought about what else they could do. She looked at the piece of paper, although it didn't really mean much to her.

"It would just be a small place, mind." He was looking to her for a reaction.

"Mam and Dad have been happy enough in their house, and I don't see why we couldn't be happy in somewhere like that. Although…" She paused, wondering whether she should say it or not. "I do like that we don't have to share a privy with half the road."

Billy laughed. "Yes, it would be nice to have our own. We'll have to see what we can do. You're still earning more because of the hours you work, but at least I'm bringing some in. They've said I might be able to move into a better role if I keep doing well."

Vi looked at him and broke into a smile. "That's wonderful. Oh, Billy, I do hope this is the beginning of things starting to improve. If only this wretched war would end."

With the long summer evenings and warm August days, Vi wished she didn't work the hours she did. At least Billy finished earlier and was able to spend time with Tommy and Nipper. The boy was growing so fast. He still loved the bicycle Mr and Mrs Moore had given him, although the rate he was going, that would be too small for him before long.

She loved her Wednesdays, when she had football in the late afternoon and both Billy and Tommy would come to join them. There were only three weeks to the first cup match, and Vi already felt excited. They'd played well enough in their games the previous year, and she knew the girls took it more seriously than many of the teams. If she could lead them through the season and lift the cup at the end, she thought she'd probably be the happiest person alive.

"Right, girls, you've drawn Bolton in the first round. Unless they've changed their team, that's a match you should win." Mr Giffard was addressing them at the end of practice. "It's an away match, so the crowd will be more on their side."

Vi groaned. She loved hearing the crowds cheering them on. Their supporters even knew the players' names now and would shout encouragement to individual girls. Gone were the days when seeing women's football was about the novelty and the spectacle; now, for many who came to watch, it was all about the game. Some of the girls still courted wolf-whistles from the crowd, but who could blame them? It wasn't as though there were many young men around for them to walk out with. Vi couldn't begrudge them the bit of attention the football brought.

The three weeks before the game passed quickly, and by match day they were all feeling anxious.

"Where's Sarah?" Joe asked as they met up to be driven to Bolton.

Before anyone could answer, Sarah came running around the corner of the road. "Sorry I'm late, Mam's got the flu, I had to help with the others. Dad says he'll be all right with them for the afternoon."

Vi could see how tired Sarah looked, and hoped she was fit to play.

The Bolton team seemed as excited about the cup as Billingbrook, and the crowd were definitely on Bolton's side.

"Shame we couldn't have brought more of our supporters," Clara said as they warmed up on the pitch.

"We just have to concentrate on the game and not listen to the crowd," Vi said, trying to calm her own nerves with some deep breathing. At least Billy was there on the sideline, which she always appreciated.

The play seemed fairly even in the first half. Both teams had opportunities and shots on goal, but the goalkeepers on either side worked hard, and by the time they went in at half-time there was still no score.

"Come on, girls, you can still win this." Joe Wood was as encouraging as ever.

"Are you all right, Sarah?" Vi asked. "When I passed the ball to you, you seemed miles away."

"Sorry, I was worrying about Mam. She was really poorly when I left and, you know, well, you read things in the papers." Sarah was chewing her bottom lip.

Vi put her arm around the girl. "There's nothing you can do now until you go home. Just think how proud she'll be if you take her some good news. It would brighten her up if you win."

Sarah nodded, but said nothing.

As they walked out onto the pitch for the second half, Sarah gave Vi a little nod and Vi smiled. She could see the determination in the girl's eyes and knew she'd give it all she'd got.

The second half progressed and there had still been no goals, but it was obvious to Vi that her own team had the better level of fitness. She was grateful for how much practice they'd all put in.

When the ball arrived at Vi's feet, she needed to pass it before the Bolton player was able to tackle. She looked across the field and there was Sarah. This time she was alert and focussed on Vi. Vi kicked the ball across to her and sent up a silent prayer.

As Vi continued to run up the field to give support if she were needed, Sarah was away with the ball, and when she was a reasonable distance from the goal she aimed an almighty kick, sending the ball past the goalkeeper and into the net.

"Thank you," Vi muttered to whoever had taken on

board her earlier prayer.

There were still another ten minutes of the game, and they needed to hold their lead. Another goal would be a welcome addition, but their score now was enough to take them through. The girls didn't let up, and as the final whistle blew Vi let out a long sigh of relief. They were on their way into the next round.

CHAPTER 15

Tuesday 1ˢᵗ October 1918 - Bulgaria's Unconditional Surrender Confirmed - The Daily Mirror

"Where's Sarah?" Eva asked at break on Monday, when they'd all gone down to the yard for some fresh air and a kickabout against the men.

"It's not her mam, is it?" Vi asked.

Florrie came to join them. "Haven't you heard? Sarah went down with the flu yesterday. It's a wonder she played at all on Saturday."

"No! Will she be all right? You don't think she'll have given it to the rest of us, do you? Mind you, it's a good job she did play." Clara shook her head. "We'd never have won without her."

"There's a few in her section gone down with it," Florrie said. "It's everywhere. Uncle Anthony says he's already been asked to do two funerals for people who've died from it."

"Let's hope she's better quickly. She should be all right, shouldn't she, being so young?"

Their closeness was one of the team's strengths. Vi saw them more as sisters than friends, and they all looked out for each other. Their next cup match was in three weeks, and they were going to need a strong team.

Vi wished they had more spare players, but the company would only pay the wages of a small number, and the other girls couldn't afford to lose pay. Some of them joined in the Saturday practice sessions, but with them only training once a week they were not as fit as the rest of the team.

Being captain, Vi spent a lot of time thinking about the team and how to get the best out of the girls. If Sarah couldn't play, they'd need to move Clara to play on the left again; she'd done that in the early days, so it wouldn't be new to her.

On her way home that night, Vi ran her thoughts past Tessie. Tessie was a good solid player, but she could never see much of the team strategy. It didn't matter though, as Vi found just saying her thoughts out loud helped.

She said goodnight to Tessie at the end of the passage between the houses and went in to the Dobsons' house. She was surprised to find Billy waiting for her in the kitchen.

"I heard you coming in. Close your eyes."

Vi wasn't used to being greeted in this way and really just wanted to get her shoes off. She closed her eyes anyway.

"Now open them."

Vi could hear the happiness in Billy's voice. She opened her eyes to see him holding out a bunch of flowers.

"Billy, they're lovely, but we can't afford to go wasting money on flowers."

He was grinning broadly. "Oh yes we can. They've moved me into the wages office and increased my pay."

"Oh, Billy." Vi wrapped her arms around him, still clutching the flowers. She gave him a big kiss. "That's wonderful news. Here, I'd best get these in water."

"It means we can start looking for a house." The smile on Billy's face couldn't have been wider.

"We can?"

Billy nodded to her.

"Have you told your mam and dad?" She lifted a vase down from the shelf as she asked. It wasn't used often and needed rinsing out to get rid of the dust.

"I've told them about the job…" He trailed off.

"But not about us moving?" Vi finished for him. "Maybe we should find somewhere first. Mind you, if we start asking around they'll soon find out."

"Let me wait and tell them at the weekend, when we're both around and not so tired."

Vi nodded. They'd need to have their wits about them if they were to deal with breaking news like that to Billy's mam. Elsie wasn't going to take it well that her little boy wasn't going to be where she could look after him.

"And how's Dad going to afford to retire if you're not paying the bills?" Elsie puffed her cheeks and let out a heavy breath, as though she could blow the idea away. "I expect this is all her idea, isn't it? Too used to living in the cheap end of town, doesn't know when she's onto a good thing. Now she's taking you away from us, and after we took her in."

"Mam!" Billy looked anxiously from his mother to Vi.

Vi wished she'd let Billy break the news to his parents on his own and hadn't said she'd be there. Still, she was used to the insults about her upbringing. There was a time they would have bothered her, but now she just saw the incredibly sad woman that Billy's mam was. She'd probably be the same if she'd been through all those miscarriages. The worst of it was that Elsie was missing out on so much that she could be enjoying. When Vi thought about this house compared with the chatter and happy voices of her own family home, she realised there was little point reacting to Elsie's comments. She'd do her best to reassure her mother-in-law if she could.

"We will still visit, and you'll always be able to come to our house." Vi looked across to Billy, hoping he would add something to what she'd said, but his face was stony.

Elsie ignored Vi's contribution to the discussion. "Say something, Alf."

Alf sighed and lowered his paper. "I hope you'll both be very happy wherever you end up. You know you'll always be welcome here when you do visit."

Elsie scowled at him, and Alf simply raised his newspaper again and carried on reading as though nothing had happened.

"At least if you move out I won't have to put up with that dog leaving his hair everywhere and scratching at the door." Elsie made a point of removing some dog hair from the arm of the chair.

Vi looked down at Nipper, who was lying on Billy's foot, and couldn't see how anyone could object to the little chap. He had his naughty side, the same as any dog, but he was never really bad; except maybe the time he'd eaten one of Elsie's best shoes. That hadn't been a good day. Now that she thought about it, when Nipper did misbehave it was almost always Elsie who was on the receiving end.

Billy had already started looking in the local newspaper and asking around about places to rent.

"Don't you think we should give it just a few weeks, to make sure your new job seems all right?" Vi couldn't believe she was being the voice of reason, when she really wanted to pack her bags there and then and move out. It was just a niggle though. With the war and everything else, she realised it was a big step to take on all the costs of a place of their own. "I know I'm bringing in good money, but it's still only a woman's wage."

"I meant to ask you about that," Billy said. "Do you know who Mr Albert Fuller is at work?"

"Bert? Yes, he works further down the benches on our section. It's hard not to know him, he's one of the only men on our floor." Vi looked at him and frowned. "Why?"

"What job does he do?" Billy asked, still giving nothing away.

"Same as me and the other girls. What is it, Billy?"

"I shouldn't be saying this." Billy ran his hand through his hair. "It was just that, although he's listed in the ledgers with the rest of you in your section, he's paid more per hour. I just wondered if he was doing a different job."

"Don't be daft. He does exactly the same as the rest of us. I suppose he's got a family to support." Vi knew the women were paid less, she'd realised that since the start; it was even in the job adverts.

"You'd have had a family to support if I hadn't come back."

He said no more, but it was enough to make Vi think.

Sarah still wasn't back at work the following week, and now Edith was off with flu as well.

"D'you think we'll all get it?" Clara asked.

"It can't be that bad, can it?" Eva stopped what she was doing and frowned.

"I wouldn't bank on it." With only two weeks until the cup match, Vi was beginning to worry. They were now missing both their goalkeeper and a good midfield player; it was going to be hard to beat the Calderley girls like that.

She couldn't bring herself to hope the Calderley team wouldn't be at full strength. From what the newspaper was saying, she wouldn't wish this flu on her worst enemy.

"Maybe the match will be postponed if too many of the players are ill," Billy said, trying to cheer her up.

"That presumes all this flu will be over soon and we'd be able to play the matches then. It just seems to be getting worse. Maybe you could ask Mr Giffard what he thinks." Vi was happy for it to be Billy who now went to the management corridor rather than herself. He looked more suitable in his pressed and starched shirt than she did in her overalls. It helped that he wasn't scared of Mrs Simpson; in fact, she seemed to have taken quite a shine to him.

"There are still enough girls to make a team, aren't there?" Billy asked.

"Just about, as long as we don't lose anyone else. We'll manage two substitutes, but that will be everyone." Vi sighed. She had never won anything in her life before, not even a Sunday School prize. She came from a family who didn't win things. She was desperate to change that by winning the cup, but no one could have anticipated this was going to happen.

When Vi went down to the yard for morning break four days before the match, she was delighted to see Sarah coming from her section.

"You're back." Then Vi looked at her closely. "Are you all right?"

Sarah shook her head. "I'm going to struggle to get through the day, but we need the money. I'm really sorry, Vi. I hate letting the girls down, but I'm just not going to be able to play yet."

Vi felt her heart sink. "You shouldn't really be here at all, should you? I don't mean to be unkind, but you don't look as though you could run the length of the yard, never mind a football pitch. Here, come and sit down."

Sarah didn't argue as Vi took her over to a bench. "Are your family all right?"

A tear dripped down Sarah's cheek. "Nan's bad, but it's my brother I'm really worried about. One minute he seemed fine, and then the next... I should have stayed to look after him, but I had to come back to work."

Vi could see the sadness in Sarah's eyes and how much weight she'd lost. She just wished there was something she could do to help.

"I'm sorry," Sarah said again.

Poor Sarah would be struggling even to lift the shell cases she was working on; there was no way she'd be playing football for some time.

"Don't be daft, the football's not as important as your family or your health. We'll manage." Vi tried to smile. This wasn't Sarah's fault; the girl shouldn't be feeling guilty. Vi tried to remind herself that football was only a game, but the match against Calderley was important to her, whatever she said. She still felt they had a score to settle after the Calderley team had got away with an appalling foul on Vi the first time the two teams met. "Edith's still off and now Florrie's gone home. I'm hoping the game will be called off. If we could delay the match, maybe you could play then."

By the time the Billingbrook girls stepped out onto the field that Saturday, whilst they'd managed to pull together a full team, there were no substitutes on their bench. The

Calderley team hadn't been hit as hard by the flu, and they were at full strength. Vi's heart sank. She knew it was down to her as captain to instil some confidence into her own team, especially those who weren't as used to playing. She forced herself to smile and hoped they wouldn't realise how hard she was finding it.

"We can do this, girls. We just stick to the plan and play our best." She hoped they couldn't see she was crossing her fingers.

For the first half, Vi's team managed to hold the Calderley girls back. It was hard work. Calderley were definitely the stronger side, and Vi feared that her own team would flag long before the final whistle. She had worked so hard she could have cried by the time they went in at half-time.

Just before they were due to go back out, Vi was surprised when Billy came to the changing room.

"I know it's normally Vi as your captain, or Joe who'd give you all some encouragement at half-time, but I just wanted to come and say you're doing a great job." He took a deep breath. "Look at me; one arm, one leg, but thanks to Vi, I've not given up. You shouldn't give up either. You can still win this."

Vi smiled her first real smile of the day. She hugged him. "Thanks, love. You're right." She turned back to the team. "Come on, girls, let's get back out there."

If they'd worked hard in the first half, that was nothing to how fired up they were when they returned to the pitch. Whatever they did and however much they covered the ground and found space, none of Vi's team could find a breakthrough. As she caught her breath, Vi realised she had no idea what would happen if they were drawing at full time. No one had told the team what the rules for the cup games would be. Someone needed to come out as winner and go through to the next round. She was still wondering when Eva was brought down with such force by one of the Calderley players that she had to be carried from the pitch. Despite the very obvious nature of the foul, exactly as had happened the first time the Billingbrook girls played Calderley, the referee had apparently not seen what had taken place. Vi was furious. She tried protesting, but was threatened with being sent off if she continued.

From that point on, very little went Billingbrook's way. When the final whistle blew, with it went Vi's cup dreams for another year.

"I'm sorry, love," Billy said as they left the stadium. "The girls did their best."

Vi knew he was right, but it did little to help the disappointment.

As October drew to a close, Vi had little time to think about football. So many of the workers were off with the flu that those of them left on the shifts were working longer hours. The mood was sombre. After the number who'd died fighting in the war, it seemed especially harsh that so many were now dying at home too. Sarah's brother would have been called up in a few weeks, but he was one of the many who died from the growing epidemic of influenza. Everyone seemed to know someone who had been taken by the illness, and many of those who'd lost their lives were young, just like her or Billy. There was an air of despair as they all wondered who would be next. Vi worried about all her siblings, as well as the girls on the team.

They were still allowed to practise for a couple of hours on a Wednesday afternoon, and that had the added benefit of meaning Vi rarely worked extra hours that day. It was a nice respite in the middle of the week.

One Wednesday early in November, as she came through the door of Ivy Terrace, Billy greeted her with excitement. "I've found a house to rent that I think we can afford."

This was just the news Vi needed. "Where? Can we go to see it?"

"The people there now are moving out at the end of November. If we like it, we could be in by Christmas." Billy handed her a slip of paper with an address a few streets away. "We can have a look on Sunday."

All Vi could think about, as she worked on Thursday, was that in a few short weeks, she, Billy and Tommy would have a home of their own. She even started to think about what material she might have spare which could be used to make curtains. She'd take a tape measure when they went on Sunday.

She was still thinking about the curtains when she left work. Tessie was usually by the gate before she was, but tonight there was no sign of her. Vi looked around for someone who worked in Tessie's section. She sighed; there was no one. She went over to the gatekeeper.

"Sorry to bother you, but do you know if Miss Tessie Brown has already left?"

"Is she a visitor?"

"No, she works here." Vi was still looking around as she spoke.

"Sorry, love, I only have records of visitors. You'd need to check with her section."

"Thank you." Vi looked at the clock. It was ten minutes after she expected to see Tessie. She sighed, then had a thought. "Can I leave a message with you in case she comes out late and can't find me?"

"Well, I shouldn't really." Then the gatekeeper smiled and nodded.

"Thank you," Vi said. "Please, if she asks, can you tell her that Mrs Dobson has gone? Mrs Violet Dobson."

When Vi reached Ivy Terrace she knocked on the back door of the Browns' house before going home. It was Mrs Brown who came to the door.

"She's come home with a right fever."

"Oh, Mrs Brown, I do hope she'll be all right. Please give her my love." Then Vi went into her own home, worrying about Tessie.

CHAPTER 16

When this lousy war is over, no more soldiering for me,
When I get my civvy clothes on, oh how happy I shall be.
No more church parades on Sunday, no more putting in
for leave,
I will miss the Sergeant-Major,
How he'll miss me how he'll grieve.
*(Anonymous - sung to the tune of What a Friend we have in
Jesus)*

*Friday 8th November 1918 - Beginning of the End of German
Militarism - The Daily Mirror*

Walking to work on her own that Friday felt odd to Vi. She
hadn't had to do that since Tessie's accident. It would be
at least a few days before Tessie would be back. Vi just
hoped she'd be all right. Then she thought of Sarah's
brother and shivered. The papers seemed to be reporting
more deaths from the flu than they were from the war.
After the trauma of losing so many loved ones over the last
four years, it just seemed so unfair. Even the Government
had given extra advice about washing hands and being
careful not to be too close to other people, though that was
easier said than done when you worked in a large factory.
She tried to put it out of her mind. Her own section of the
factory seemed to be all right, at least for now.

Whilst she was at work it was easier not to think, but

walking — her mind wandered. The dull November days were sitting heavily on Billingbrook. When it was supposed to be light the fog never seemed to lift, and with the constant grey, Vi was finding it hard to smile. She kept reminding herself about the house they were going to see on Sunday, and the new start that might present. She hoped there'd be a corner of a room she could use for hat making and give it another go. If she could start selling them, then maybe she could leave factory work behind. Now Billy was working perhaps they could try that, although they would need her wages to help with the rent.

Many of the girls were either sick or nursing relatives and, as they didn't have a game coming up, football practice was cancelled for a couple of weeks. It was probably for the best, but the lack of football was another thing affecting Vi's mood. She'd worked the Saturday morning shift, to help with the factory being so short-handed because of the flu. Now she planned to spend the afternoon sorting through material, to see which left over pieces were large enough to make curtains.

"Have you heard the news?" Billy called when Vi came into the kitchen.

"What news?" For a horrible moment, she thought it might be Tessie, but then she looked at Billy and realised he was smiling.

"The Government is hoping there's going to be an end to the war. It was in the paper."

"We've been hoping for an end to this bloody war for four years." Vi sighed. "I do hope they're right. I don't want to see John going away, and I can do without the rationing and shortages getting worse than they are now." Then she stopped. "D'you think I'll still have a job if it finishes?"

"I suppose we'll still need weapons, just in case, and then I suppose the factory can go back to making whatever it did before the war. It used to do other engineering." Billy sounded optimistic. "I'm hoping that means my job would carry on at least."

Vi nodded. Perhaps with an end to the war, and a new home, things were really looking up. She tried to smile, but there were too many things niggling away at her to trust what the papers were saying.

Vi couldn't sleep that night. She'd wanted a home of their own for so long. Now she didn't want to let herself believe it was happening at last, as she couldn't face the disappointment if it didn't. She was worried about Tommy too. He seemed excited, but Vi wondered if there'd be as big a yard for him to play in, or whether he'd end up spending more time out in the street. She was also unsure how quickly he'd get used to having a room of his own, but then Nipper would help with that one.

"I just want to pick up the Sunday newspaper on the way; see what's happening," Billy said.

It took them ages in the newsagent's, not because of a queue but because of the speculation about the war. Vi could hear snippets of the conversations as she stayed outside, so Tommy could play in the street while they waited. The headlines on the boards read 'Kaiser Abdicates' on one, and 'Huns' White Flag at Front' on the other.

"It's not all over yet," Billy said as he came out carrying the Sunday Pictorial. "But it sounds as though it might be by tomorrow. I wonder when we'll hear."

"I hope you're right." Vi took the paper and put it into her bag, so that Billy's hand was free to use his stick.

The house they were viewing was in the middle of a

terraced row, smaller than Billy's parents' house, but still two rooms upstairs and two down.

"You can have your own bedroom," Vi said to Tommy. He did look a little uncertain about the prospect, until she said, "With Nipper, of course."

To Vi's relief the house had its own privy, and a small but useable yard at the back. It was enough to be able to take Nipper out into, if nothing else. It wasn't as clean as the Dobsons' house, but she could soon have that sorted. She looked at the other terraces nearby; most of them appeared well looked after. Their steps were neatly polished, and she nodded with approval.

"What do you think, love?" Billy asked.

"It will be perfect when I get it all straight." She looked out of the front window at the view of the street. The walk to work would be about the same, and she might even be able to meet up with Tessie on the way.

"I'll write to the landlord and say we'd like to take it, then."

Vi thought Billy seemed to be standing taller as he spoke. It clearly meant a lot to him. A flicker of a smile began to play on Vi's face, as she started to trust that this might finally be happening.

As soon as they got home, Billy sat down and wrote a letter to the landlord, asking what they needed to do in order to go ahead with renting number 11 Osbald Terrace from the first of December.

"I can post the letter on my way to work in the morning and then we just need to pay the deposit, I presume." Billy was doing his best to hide his excitement, as Elsie was clearly very unhappy. It made Vi laugh watching him trying to look serious, but with his lips twitching into a grin every time he forgot himself.

Tessie was still not back at work on Monday. However much she was missing her, Vi knew it was best not to go next door whilst they had flu in the house. All the Government advice seemed to be to stay away from those who were already ill. Vi wondered how her friend was, and was keen to tell her all about the house she and Billy would be moving to.

Not long after the girls came back from break that morning, the klaxon sounded. Vi was working hard at her bench, concentrating on what she was doing.

"That shouldn't be going now. We'd best get down," Vi shouted to Eva and began crawling under the bench as they had when there'd been explosions. "What time is it?" she asked when Eva joined her. She looked at the clock on the far wall behind Eva. The klaxon was still sounding. "It's eleven o'clock, just gone."

"I can't think with that thing going." Eva had to shout to make herself heard.

Vi watched Mrs Johnson look out of the window and then come bustling from her office. This time she wasn't looking drawn and serious. She was smiling, something the girls didn't see often. Mrs Johnson clapped her hands. There was no point in her shouting, she wouldn't have been heard. She indicated for the girls to leave their benches and follow her outside. This time there was no fear or alarm, but no one could hear each other over the siren.

In the yard and out into the street, there were people everywhere. They'd come out of their houses, out of the offices, the factories, and wherever they had been. The cheering could only mean one thing. Four years of war were finally over.

Vi gasped and grabbed Eva's arm. "Does this mean

what I think it does?" She left Eva and ran to look for Billy amongst the crowd. Even the dull November day couldn't temper the sheer joy and exuberance of everyone on the streets around her. News was spreading rapidly that the armistice had been signed, and the mood of celebration grew.

Vi finally found Billy. "I know that this isn't appropriate behaviour, and Mrs Johnson will be after me, but I love you, Billy Dobson." She wrapped her arms around him and kissed him passionately.

"I can't help wishing Stan and Davy had made it through to see today," Billy said with tears in his eyes.

Vi hugged him closer. "I know."

People around them were dancing and laughing as though it were a summer fair. Vi just wished Tessie was there too, so they could celebrate together. She couldn't wait to go over to see her own family. Thank goodness that John wasn't going to have to fight.

Eventually the shift all went back to work, but for once Mrs Johnson didn't stop the flow of chatter, and it was a lighter atmosphere than they were used to as they worked. Vi wondered what would happen to the shells they were making if the fighting had finally stopped.

When she went home that evening, she was still singing to herself. "Had you heard before Billy came home?" Vi asked Elsie who was in the kitchen.

"Heard? Of course we'd heard. Dad had me outside dancing in the street. Even Tessie came out, though she did look awfully pale when I hugged her."

The thought of Elsie dancing made Vi wonder if her mother-in-law had helped herself to a medicinal tot of brandy to celebrate. She really couldn't imagine either that or her hugging Tessie. It made her wish they could have been part of the celebrations at home as well as at work. She wondered if her own parents were partying as well. She looked at the clock; she couldn't wait to see them. "I'm going to Mam and Dad's," she called to Billy. "Will you come?"

As they walked across Billingbrook, there were still people out on the streets celebrating. There was singing coming from doorways and windows of houses, as well as bars. Long before they reached the Tunnicliffe house, Vi could hear the sound of her dad's accordion as he played reels and jigs, as well as some of the music hall favourites. As they approached the house, a chorus of *'It's a long way to Tipperary'* came out on the night air.

Before they went in to join the crush of friends, neighbours and family, Billy turned to Vi. "I don't ever want to forget all those who didn't come home, but tonight let's celebrate the end of this bloody war.

Waiting for the reply from the landlord was the longest wait Vi could remember. She presumed they would hear back by Wednesday at the latest, but nothing had arrived.

"Do you think he's found someone else?" she asked Billy when they went to bed that night.

Billy sighed. "There'll be so many coming back from the war now. I suppose he might think he can charge more for it."

Vi couldn't sleep for thinking about the little house which might be theirs. She'd set her heart on it; there was enough space in the front room for hat making. She'd keep it tidy of course, in case they had visitors, but it would be a shame for it not to be used at other times.

There was still no sign of Tessie returning to work. From what Vi knew, Tessie seemed to be through the

177

worst, thank God, but the flu had left her pretty weak. Maybe she'd be well enough after the weekend. The poor girl really couldn't afford not to be paid.

By the time Vi walked home on Friday, she'd made up her mind that if there was no letter from the landlord waiting at home that day, then they probably hadn't got the house. She was determined not to show just how much she cared. It was hard for Billy. Even though he was excited, his loyalties were always slightly split. He hated feeling he was letting his parents down, after all they'd done, and she could understand that. They'd help where they could; they wouldn't be far away. She was still thinking about the house as she went in through the back gate.

Billy's face was stricken as he met her at the kitchen door. "Thank God you're home."

She dropped her bag down and quickly unpinned her hat. "Whatever is it? Is there something wrong with Tommy?"

Billy gulped and shook his head. "It's Mam. She's got the fever and she seems really sick. I don't know what to do. Dad's with her."

Vi's thoughts started racing. "Now listen to me, Billy, make sure she's having plenty to drink. Get a damp cloth and gently sponge her forehead. I'm taking Tommy out of here. I want him somewhere he won't risk catching it. I'll take him to Mam and Dad's."

"Don't be long. We need you here."

Vi couldn't help thinking that Billy looked wretched. However difficult his mam could be, Vi knew how much Billy loved her, and, in his mam's softer moments, even Vi had seen a completely different side to her. Her mind was racing, thinking of what bits and pieces she might need to

178

take for Tommy. She took some money from the jar so she could at least cover the cost of his food. She knew her parents would welcome him, but it wouldn't be easy for them.

She was already fastening her coat as she asked, "Where is Tommy?"

"He's out on his bike in the street."

"At this time?" Vi was horrified. What would the neighbours think?

"I thought it best to have him out of the way. I thought Mam might be better without his noise."

"It's not his noise I'm worried about," Vi grumbled under her breath as she went out into the night.

She was grateful that Tommy circled around past the house on his bike just as she was coming out of the passageway. "Tommy," she called quietly.

He stopped.

"We're going to Nan and Granddad's. You can bring your bike."

Without any question Tommy started cycling toward his grandparents' house, looping back at intervals to check Vi was still there.

Vi's feet were already aching after a long day, and all she really wanted to do was sit down.

"Oh, Vi." Her mam looked flustered as she went in. "Whatever are you doing here at this time of night?"

"Billy's mam's got the flu. I thought it best for Tommy to stay somewhere safe, out of the way."

"Then I wouldn't bring him here, lass. Both John and Lizzie have got it. Ena's here to help me nurse them. I've just come down for some tea."

Vi stopped exactly where she was. Tommy would be worse off here than at home. She nodded. "Ok, Mam, give them my love and Dad. I'll take Tommy home."

She set off back along the street with Tommy still happily cycling around on his bike and Nipper running behind. It was a wonder Tommy was still awake at this hour. That bike had been such a blessing. Then she had a thought. Tommy loved all the time they spent with Mr and Mrs Moore. Perhaps they could help. "Tommy, how would you feel about going to stay with Aunty Audrey and Uncle Terence for a few days?"

"Can I?" The boy's face lit up.

"Maybe," she said. "Only if they say it's all right."

It was already nine-thirty in the evening by the time they approached the Moores' house. Vi was very glad to see there was a light on in a downstairs room. Tommy leaned his bike against the railings and they went up the steps to the door. Taking a deep breath, Vi knocked hard with the knocker, hoping they'd hear and be prepared to answer even though it was late.

She heard the heavy steps of Mr Moore coming to the door and the lock being turned. Then he opened it and peered out.

"Vi, love, whatever's wrong? Come in." He called through to his wife and indicated for Vi and Tommy to go straight through.

Vi explained why they were there.

"Of course we'll have him," Mrs Moore said. "He'll be safe and happy here. You'd best take your bike around to the shed, Tommy. Mr Moore will open the gate."

Once Tommy had gone with Mr Moore, Mrs Moore continued, "You know, he can stay here as long as you need, and Nipper too. If Nipper's here, he'll feel more settled. What about you?"

Vi sighed. "I need to go home to help." She was grateful

for the offer of a cup of tea before she went, but as soon as Tommy was settled she set off home.

By the time Vi arrived back at Ivy Terrace it was way past eleven. All she wanted to do was go to bed. She needed to be at work by eight o' clock the following morning.

As she went upstairs, she realised she hadn't eaten. That would have to wait. Billy came out of his parents' bedroom as she got to the landing.

"It looks like Dad's going down with it too."

"Oh, Billy. What are we going to do?"

Billy shrugged. "I can just about manage if you go to bed. At least with tomorrow being Saturday I'm not working."

"Call me if you need me." Vi kissed him and then ran her hand down his face. She didn't know what to say. She just prayed that Billy wouldn't go down with it as well.

Vi was so tired that she slept soundly, despite the worry, but woke early. She hoped the fact that Billy hadn't called her was good news. There was no sound from his parents' room and she assumed he was probably asleep in the chair beside their bed.

She made as little noise as she could getting ready for work and, as she ate some toast, she made a tray of tea and took it up. She knocked on the door until Billy responded. "I'll leave the tray on the shelf here. Is everything all right?"

Billy came to the door. He looked exhausted. "Mam's bad, but I don't think Dad's quite as ill. Can you see if Mrs Brown could come round later?"

Vi nodded. She felt guilty going out and leaving him, but she didn't have much choice. She went next door before setting off for the factory. Mrs Brown was still in her dressing gown and curlers, but said she'd be happy to go in for an hour or two once she was dressed.

As Vi walked away from Ivy Terrace, she suddenly realised that she hadn't asked how Tessie was, nor had she checked to see if there had been any post.

CHAPTER 17

Billy sat in the chair watching his mam and dad. He'd have paced the room if it were large enough, and if it wouldn't have caused them distress. He knew next to nothing about caring for the sick, but there was no alternative. He told himself he was fighting another battle; this might not be France, but the enemy here was just as deadly. It made him think of Stan and all the things he'd never realised his mate had had to learn for himself growing up, because there had been no one else to do it for him. He looked at his own mother. However difficult she could be, no one could have loved him more than she did, and no one could have worked so hard to take care of him when he was a child.

Billy rinsed the flannel in the bowl and went to mop his mam's forehead. She had to pull through this. There was so much he still wanted to say to her; so much he wanted to thank her for. Oddly, it struck him that more than anything, he wanted to get to know who she really was. Of course she was his mother, but he knew precious little about the person underneath. He wanted to know about the girl his father had fallen in love with, and the woman it was clear Dad still loved.

Billy felt a tear roll down his cheek.

"Billy, lad." Alf's voice was quiet and croaky.

183

Billy got up to go to Dad's side of the bed, so he could hear him properly.

"I'm here, Dad."

"How is she?"

Billy heaved a long breath. "I don't know. She's still in the grip of the fever, and I just don't know what more to do."

"You're doing your best, Billy, lad. That's all we can ask for." His dad's eyes closed again almost before he'd finished speaking and he relapsed into slumber.

Returning to the chair for a few minutes of sleep himself, Billy was reminded of being in the trenches, sleeping anywhere, whenever you got a moment. Thank God the bloody war was over, but how many lives had been lost? And now this is what families were facing. He looked across at his parents. It might just be that he was wishing for it, but he thought his mam looked a little easier. He closed his eyes and found sleep.

Billy woke with a start when he heard knocking. He looked across to the bed, thinking one of his parents must need him. His father was asleep, and his mother was still tossing and sweating. As his heart began to settle, he heard Mrs Brown's voice calling as she came up the stairs.

"It's only me. I thought I'd best let myself in."

Billy got up and went to the bedroom door. "Thank you," he said, feeling a wave of relief that she was there.

"Now, what's to do?" She stood in the doorway and assessed the room. Her voice was kind as she asked, "Have you got any water into her?"

Billy sighed. "I've tried holding a glass to her lips, but she's just not taking it."

Mrs Brown nodded. "We'll need a clean bowl and

another flannel."

Billy made to go toward the stairs.

"No, lad, you stay here. Let me do the running around."

Billy almost smiled. The choice was a badly arthritic woman, or a one-legged soldier. What a pair they made. "Thank you." He directed Mrs Brown to where she'd find the things she'd need, although he wasn't completely certain, and said she might need to rummage for the flannel.

When he went back into the bedroom, his dad was awake. Billy helped him to sit up a little.

"I'll fetch you some tea when Mrs Brown comes back."

"How is she?"

Billy knew his dad wasn't asking about Mrs Brown. He shrugged and grimaced slightly. "I don't know, Dad. I'm hoping now Mrs Brown's here she'll have more idea what to do."

His dad nodded.

When Mrs Brown returned, she sat on the edge of the bed by Elsie and tried to drip water from the flannel onto her lips. Drip by drip she let the water fall, for Elsie to swallow reflexively. The amount his mam was sweating, Billy couldn't help thinking it was going to take a lot more than drips to give her the fluids she needed. He said nothing, but went down to the kitchen to make tea for his dad.

Despite it being a cold day, Billy opened the back door and went outside. He wanted to breathe the chill in the air and feel alive. He wished Tommy and Nipper were in the house, instead of having gone to the Moores'. He wanted to hear laughter, shouting and barking. Most of all, he wanted to hear his mam's reprimands as they all got under her feet.

The kettle began to whistle, and he went back in. For now, the kettle was the happiest sound he'd hear.

As long as he placed them in the middle of the tray, Billy had mastered carrying several cups with only his left hand. He made drinks for his dad, Mrs Brown and himself. He wondered about adding a cup for his mam, but thought it unlikely they could get her to drink it. He could always come back down for another.

He waited on the landing for Mrs Brown to open the door, and as she did, he heard his mother's voice. "At last! Does that mean the fever's broken?" Billy felt a flood of relief.

"Unless you know the whereabouts of her mother and why she isn't here to pick her daughter up, then I wouldn't hold your hopes up." Mrs Brown shook her head and sighed. "She's not with us at the moment, that much is certain."

Billy tensed again.

"If you can help your dad out of bed, I think it would be for the best. She's thrashing about rather a lot, and he's going to get hurt." Mrs Brown took the tray so that Billy could go to his father.

"He'll want to stay near Mam, but I'll try to sit him in the chair."

Billy went around the bed to his father's side. His dad was dozing again, but as Elsie flung her arm wildly across the bed, he woke with a start.

"It's all right, Dad. We're going to get you into the chair. I'll bring the blankets in from mine and Vi's bed for you." With his good arm, Billy hooked under Dad's shoulder and took much of his weight as he got to his feet. He was shocked how weak Dad seemed, when he'd been ill for such a comparatively short time. Billy waited whilst his dad pushed his feet into his slippers, and then supported him as he went over to the chair.

Mrs Brown raised her eyebrows to Billy when he looked at her. It was clear she was as concerned as he was. He passed some tea to his dad and then left the room to fetch the blankets. He heard Mam call out again as he went and shuddered. Perhaps Dad would be better off in his and Vi's room, but he supposed he'd want to stay close to Mam however hard that was.

"You get some rest, Billy," Mrs Brown said when he went back in. "I'm all right here for an hour or two. You need to look after yourself as well."

Billy nodded. "Can I fetch you anything first?"

She shook her head and Billy went back to his bedroom. Having given the covers to Dad, there was nothing for him to get under. He sighed and began unstrapping his leg. He heard Mam thrashing about next door and wondered if that would keep him awake, but that was his last thought for a while.

Billy was woken by tapping on his door and a voice calling, "Billy, love, I want to bring some broth for your dad to eat. Can you sit with your mam until I come back?"

"Give me a minute, Mrs Brown. I just need to sort my leg out." He rubbed his eyes to rid them of sleep and moved to the side of the bed. He must have slept for a couple of hours, at a guess. Hopefully it meant Vi would be home soon too.

There seemed to be no change in Mam when he went in, but Dad seemed more alert, and he took the fact that he wanted something to eat as a good sign.

"She seems to come and go a bit," Dad said as Billy sat

on the edge of the bed. "She's quieter at the moment."

As his mam thrashed about in the bed, Billy wiped away the sweat and then tried to drip water onto Mam's lips, as Mrs Brown had been doing. If this was quieter, he guessed that overall she must be worse. He sent up a silent prayer for his fighter of a mother to have enough strength to win this battle as well.

CHAPTER 18

Saturday 16th November 1918 - Beatty Meets German Naval Envoys at Se' - The Daily Mirror

When Vi arrived home that Saturday lunchtime, it was Mrs Brown who met her in the kitchen. "It's a bad business." She shook her head. "Elsie's delirious. It's hard to know what to do for her. Mrs Fairclough says there's no doctors to be had for love nor money. If that fever doesn't break soon…"

Vi stood open-mouthed as she listened to Mrs Brown. She pulled herself together. "Where's Billy? How's his dad? We could use our savings for the doctor if we can find one."

Mrs Brown patted Vi's hand. "There's not a right lot they can do if they come out, love. Save your money. There's nothing they can give her, and they'll only tell you to get water into her, same as I've been doing all morning. Billy's sitting with them. His dad's not so bad. I'm hoping he'll be fine."

"If you've been here all morning, does that mean Tessie's better?" Vi bit her lip, waiting for Mrs Brown to reply.

"She's going on nicely, love. She's well enough to make herself a cup of tea and is sitting in a chair downstairs now." Mrs Brown looked at the clock. "I'd best get back to make her something to eat."

"Give her my love. I've missed her," Vi said, as Mrs Brown went out of the back door.

With Alf in the chair, there was only space for one of them to sit in the room with Billy's mam. She was thrashing so much that sitting on the bed wasn't great. Besides, the more time they spent in the room, the higher the chance that they'd go down with it as well, but one of them needed to be there to tend to her. If they didn't give her some fluids, things were going to be a whole lot worse.

"Why don't you stay downstairs, love?" Billy said. "We need at least one of us fit for work next week, and I can't see Dad being up to it."

"I know that, but I want to help. Mam was there for me when I really needed her... when I lost the baby, and I want to be there for her now."

Billy nodded.

Over the next couple of hours they took turns at Elsie's bedside.

Around five that afternoon, just after Vi had taken over for a shift, Elsie started struggling for breath. "Billy," Vi called from the doorway. She could hear his uneven tread hurrying back up the stairs.

His face was ashen as he looked at his mother. "What can we do?"

Alf could only look at Vi, beseeching her to help. At intervals he coughed, but then fell back against the chair.

Vi shook her head. "Pray is the only thing I can think of to do now." She knelt down by the side of the bed and put her hands together. The only prayer she really knew was the Lord's Prayer, and she said it with more determination than she ever had done before. When she finished and looked up, Elsie had stopped struggling for breath. She had stopped breathing at all.

Vi stared in horror as silence descended on the room. This couldn't be happening. She reached across to mop Elsie's brow again. Surely she'd breathe, and everything would be fine.

"Vi, love." Billy's voice was barely a croak. "She's gone."

Vi put the cloth in the bowl and got to her feet. Alf was staring blankly, as though not really registering what was happening. She clung to Billy. He was shaking, or at least she thought he was. It might be her; she couldn't tell.

"Your dad," Vi said, "he needs you. I'll sort out arrangements. I'm sorry. At least she's at peace."

Billy nodded mutely, his face contorted with anguish. Vi watched as Billy went to his father's side. He sat on the end of the bed and took his father's hand in his. Then she left the room. She needed to see the undertaker and only hoped they weren't too busy to come soon. Having Elsie lying there wasn't going to do any of them any good. They'd probably have to move her to the parlour, so that Dad could use the bed.

Vi felt sick as she put on her coat and hat to go out. She'd only gone into the back yard when she heard Mrs Brown calling her. Mrs Brown was standing in her own kitchen doorway.

Vi's face must have said everything.

"Oh, Vi, love." Mrs Brown came out and wrapped Vi in her arms.

In the warmth of the embrace Vi let out a heaving sob. "I thought she'd be safe being older. I thought it was just young people it was taking. All the things I never said."

"Shh. Don't fret, love. You weren't to know." Mrs Brown held Vi so she could look into her face. "She might not have shown it to you, but Elsie was so proud of you."

"Me?" Vi was genuinely surprised. "I thought I was just an inconvenience."

Mrs Brown shook her head. "Oh, love. Elsie was never one to show her feelings. She had times in her life when her feelings overwhelmed her, and she'd learned to shut them away. But you should have heard her telling me about the things you were doing."

"You knew about her miscarriages?" Vi was struggling to assemble her thoughts.

"Of course I did, love. We've been through a lot together over the years, me and Elsie."

"I never knew."

"Would you like me to go over and lay her out? It will be best for Alf if it's done soon. Make her look presentable."

"Thank you. Yes, please. I'm sure both Dad and Billy would be glad of that." Vi wiped the tears from her eyes and sighed heavily. "Thank you."

As Vi walked into Billingbrook toward the undertaker, her mind went over and over the things Mrs Brown had said. She wished she'd known, but it was too late for thoughts like that now. Poor Elsie, how hard it must have been for her. Poor Alf now, too. She could understand a little more why he'd loved her so much. He knew the woman underneath, and not just the one that Vi saw most of the time.

With everything that had happened in the last few days, all thoughts of the landlord's letter had gone out of Vi's mind. It was only when Billy picked it up off the side that she remembered. She watched him opening the envelope, but felt none of the excitement of a week ago.

"It came in Friday's post, I think," Billy said, sounding distant. "I suppose I'd best write to say we won't be taking it."

Vi sighed. "No, we can't. Not just now." She turned back to where she was making a light meal for Billy's dad, who was over the worst of the illness, though at the beginning of grieving for his wife.

"We can't leave Dad on his own. He'll need us here."

Vi nodded slowly. Of course it would have been wrong to go now, but the reality of the situation started dawning on her for the first time. With Elsie gone, someone was going to have to look after Alf, not just for the next few weeks or months. They couldn't just leave him on his own, not after all he and Elsie had done for them. Her dreams of a home of their own needed to be put aside, at least for the time being. "I should go over and see Mrs Moore and tell her what's happened; see if she can keep Tommy for a few more days."

That week, Mrs Brown took charge of looking after Alf while Vi went to work. Billy didn't go in on the Monday as he made arrangements for his mother's burial, but needed to be back on the Tuesday. By Saturday, Alf was finally up and dressed, but nowhere near ready to return to work.

"Some of the girls are leaving the factory, now their men are starting to come back from the war," Vi said as she prepared lunch for the three of them. "We've been told they won't be replaced, as there are fewer orders for shells. There's no overtime now either. It's probably a good job, as I'll have more work to do here."

She would be able to organise the house her own way, but it felt very odd not having Elsie looking over her shoulder and complaining.

"Probably means I'll have less to do in the wages office too. I just hope they still need me."

"Someone has to pay the employees who are still working. Let's hope it's you."

Once she'd cleared away, Vi put on her coat. "I'll fetch Tommy home. It'll give you a bit of time with your dad."

"Thanks, love," Billy said, and went through to where his father was sitting in the back room.

"He's been no more bother than David was at that age," Mrs Moore said when she opened the door to Vi.

Nipper hurled himself at Vi in his excitement at seeing her, and Tommy wasn't far behind.

"You will stay for some tea, won't you?" Mrs Moore held the door wide for Vi to go in. "You look like you need it."

Vi had hoped she wasn't looking too bad, but she did rather feel as though she was carrying the weight of the world. As she'd walked over to the Moores' house she'd been worrying about what would happen if she lost her job. She followed Mrs Moore into the front room and sat down. While Mrs Moore went to make tea, Vi sat with her son. She wanted to let him tell her about everything he'd been doing, but she felt heavy with the need to break the news about his grandma to him.

She'd thought about all the wording she could have used, about Grandma going to Heaven to be with Jesus, but it wouldn't have meant much to Tommy, so she settled on something he would understand for its simplicity. "Come here, Tommy, love." She wrapped her arm around her son as she began. "You know that Grandma had the flu? Well, she became much more ill after you came here."

She paused whilst what she'd said so far sank in. "I've got some bad news for you. Grandma isn't going to get better. She died from the flu."

Tommy stared at her. Vi didn't know whether to speak or wait for what he said next. She drew him in closer as his eyes filled with tears.

"Is Grandpa all right?"

"He's getting better, but it will take a while."

Tommy nodded seriously, a tear dripping down onto Vi's hand.

"I'll have to love Grandpa enough for both of them now," Tommy said as he turned his head into her shoulder.

Vi thought about the simple words of her child, and realised that was exactly what she needed to do too.

When Mrs Moore returned, she looked at Vi and raised an eyebrow in question. Vi nodded sadly and mouthed 'Billy's mam'. The older woman acknowledged that she'd understood that Vi had told her son.

Eventually Tommy pulled away from his mother and gave a loud sniff, before, to Vi's embarrassment, wiping his nose on the sleeve of his jumper.

Unashamed, he turned to Mrs Moore and asked, "Can I take Nipper out into the garden?"

Mrs Moore nodded. "We'll come and see what you're up to in a little while." She turned back to Vi once he'd gone. "Now, my dear, why don't you tell me what's troubling you? This looks to me as though it's about more than Mrs Dobson."

Vi blinked. How could Mrs Moore tell that so easily? Vi needed someone to talk to and was grateful for the opportunity. She hadn't organised her thoughts expecting to lay them out before anyone, so they came tumbling out like spare balls of wool from the hall cupboard, seemingly rolling in all directions.

"I wish I'd understood Billy's mam better. If she'd let me get close, I could have been more of a support for her. It would have made loving her easier."

"It must have been hard for her having so much bottled up, especially when Mr Dobson was away." Mrs Moore moved to sit next to Vi and patted her hand. "You can't blame yourself. And you can't stay to look after Mr Dobson just because you feel guilty."

Vi looked up sharply. "I didn't say…"

"No, that's not what you said. I know that. But I think that's a little of what you're feeling." Mrs Moore looked at Vi as though she could see every last thought.

"I don't mind living with Billy's dad; he's going to need us at least for a while. It's just that I'd got such hopes of making hats, and maybe even having my own little business. In case I lose my job as much as anything."

"And why can't you still do that at Ivy Terrace?"

"There won't be the room. We've said that Dad will have the back room as a sitting room, where he can be on his own if he wants to be. It means we've only got the front for everything else. I can't take up part of that with my hat making. Even if I did leave things out, they'd end up with dog hair and all sorts." Vi didn't want to sound negative. She tried to think of a way she could make it work, but it just wasn't possible.

"What if you were to use one of the spare bedrooms here? We've got a couple which are never used. I've hardly set foot in them in years."

Mrs Moore's look was a mixture of encouragement and sadness. Vi opened her mouth to reply, but just sat there feeling stunned. She could think of no reason it wouldn't work, if Mrs Moore really meant it, except she'd be out of the house when she was working on them.

"I... I... I don't know what to say. It would be perfect, as long as I came at times that suited you, and I could find someone to look after Tommy."

Mrs Moore looked serious for a moment. "You know you can bring Tommy with you at any time. Terence and I love having him around."

Tommy had come bursting in from the garden with Nipper at his heels just as Mrs Moore was saying that. "Can I stay again?" Tommy asked Vi eagerly.

"I don't know about stay, but if Mrs Moore really doesn't mind, I think we might be here rather more than we have been." Vi looked up at Mrs Moore, who had a beaming smile, as though she was the one being done the favour.

"Could we just sort one thing out first?"

Vi stiffened. For a moment she wondered if she'd misunderstood and would need to pay rent for the room.

"Will you please stop calling me Mrs Moore and start calling me Audrey?"

Vi laughed with relief. "I think I can manage that."

They discussed the details of how Vi making hats there could work, and then Audrey showed her the bedroom at the back of the house which she could set up exactly as she pleased. Vi could have wept with joy when she saw the bright clean room. It had a large window with sunlight flooding in and looked out onto the garden. Vi couldn't imagine anywhere nicer.

As they walked home, Vi's mind was a cascade of ideas of what she needed to do, while Tommy busily told her about climbing trees in the garden and how much he liked having a room all to himself and Nipper. She paused from her own planning and wondered how she was going to break the news to him that they wouldn't be moving to their own home now.

Billy's mam's funeral was on the Tuesday. They'd had to wait until the funeral directors were available. There'd been so many deaths in the preceding weeks, as well as some of the grave diggers being themselves ill with flu. It was a sombre affair, but Reverend Smith conducted a lovely service, and Vi was grateful that he spoke as though he'd known Elsie. Alf sat through the service, his inability to stand caused as much by illness as grief; the poor man looked like a shadow. All Vi could think, as she held Billy's hand, was how much she wished Elsie had opened up, and not been so distant. How much love could Vi have given her if she'd felt more accepted as a daughter? It weighed heavily on her that it was too late to put right. Life without Elsie was going to be hard to adjust to.

Over the next few weeks, numbers of workers at the factory reduced steadily. Where jobs became available, it was the men who'd come back from the war who filled them. The whole character of the shifts was changing, and the camaraderie that Vi had enjoyed so much had gone. Nothing was said about the football team restarting, but as so many of the girls had left, Vi couldn't see there were any options. At least Tessie was still there, and she was grateful for that.

"Why don't you talk to Mr Giffard, love?" Billy said, when she told him how much she was missing playing. "He might be happy to continue the women's team."

"Will you talk to him?" She looked pleadingly at Billy, who smiled back.

To Vi's surprise, Mr Giffard was supportive of the idea, and Vi wrote to the girls who'd left the factory to see if they'd be interested in re-forming the team. They wouldn't be paid for practice time during a shift, so they'd only be able to train on a Saturday, or maybe in an evening now the hours weren't so long, but they could use the Caulder and Harrison sports ground for practice, and they could continue to play in the factory team colours. Vi was pleased that it meant they could go on raising money for the hospital. That need had certainly not come to an end.

Most of the old team agreed to play, and in February they started practising again, with their first match planned for Easter. All that was different was that they wouldn't work together; that and the fact that they no longer had a coach.

"What are we going to do?" Vi asked Billy. He couldn't very well do all the coaching, with him not being able to run along the pitch.

Billy grinned. "If I've got an idea about it, would you be all right with that?"

Vi nodded, frowning. Who could Billy possibly have in mind?

"Come with me," he said.

Vi followed Billy into the sitting room where Alf was slumped in a chair, looking far older than his sixty years. Other than go to work, he'd done virtually nothing since Elsie died a few months previously.

"Before you met Mam, I know you played football, but you've never told me who for," Billy said to his dad.

Alf's face changed in an instant. "I always promised your mam I'd never talk about it, but now she's gone, I don't see any harm in telling you. I played for Billingbrook United's reserve team."

Billy's mouth dropped open. Vi didn't think she'd ever seen him so shocked.

"You did what? Why couldn't you tell me?"

Alf looked years younger with a boyish smile. "She made me choose, your mam. It was either her or Doris Earnshaw. Doris was the team manager's daughter. If I chose Doris, I'd stay with the football, but if I chose your mam, the football had to go. There was no contest. Oh, I loved my football; I never stopped wanting to play. But your mam was a wonderful woman, and I'd have done anything for her."

Vi could think of so many questions she'd like to ask. How had Alf not said anything the times she'd played at Whittingham Road? It also helped to explain why Elsie had been so against the idea of her playing, and had struggled with the idea of going to the ground to watch the games. Vi was miles away thinking, and suddenly realised that Billy was talking again.

"In which case, Dad, you might just be able to help us with a little problem. You see," Billy continued, "we don't have anyone to help me coaching the women's football team anymore. Joe, the man who used to do it, he left Caulder and Harrison and moved to another job. I can't run, but neither Vi nor me want to give up." He paused and looked at Vi, who began to understand where this was going.

"Dad," Vi said gently, "you always tell us what Billingbrook does wrong when you read about their matches. You obviously still care about the game."

"Would you at least come with me to the next training session and tell me what you'd ask the girls to do?" Billy said to his dad.

"I promised your mam." Alf looked away and reached

for his pipe.

Vi sighed. They wouldn't get any further talking to Alf now, so they left him to his pipe and went back to the other room.

CHAPTER 19

Saturday 15th February 1919 - League of Nations Draft Before Congress - The Daily Mirror

By Saturday, Alf had said nothing more about the football. He wasn't a man to be pushed, and Vi wondered what the team was going to do for a coach. As they hadn't come up with any other ideas, she could see nothing else for it but for her to try, even though she didn't have the experience they needed. She wondered if her own father could help again, but he was still working long hours and could never be sure he'd be free.

"Where are you going, Grandpa?" Tommy asked as Alf put on his coat to go out.

"Just up to the cemetery, lad, same as I often do."

"Are you going to talk to Grandma? I talk to her sometimes too."

"Yes, in a way, I suppose I am. I just wanted to be with her really." Alf made to go toward the door.

"Can I come and talk to Grandma?" Tommy went and slipped his hand into Alf's.

Alf looked around, surprised. "Well, if that's all right with your mam and dad, I don't see why not." He looked from Billy to Vi and back again.

"We're on our way to football practice, so perhaps you could bring him there when you've finished," Vi said, passing Tommy's coat down from the peg.

Vi was pleased to see they had a full complement of girls when they arrived at the Caulder and Harrison recreation ground. Some of them hadn't seen each other for a couple of months, so there was a fair amount of catching up to do before the girls were ready to settle down and play football.

"We don't have a proper coach at the moment," Vi shouted over the hubbub of the talking. "Billy and I will try to keep things going until we can find someone suitable. If any of you know anyone we can talk to, then please let us know."

Vi split the girls into two teams so they could have a knock about and get back into playing. It was amazing how much fitness they'd lost in a short time. The girls who'd left the munitions factory were in general doing work which was not as physically demanding, and that didn't help. They played for half an hour, then Vi gathered the girls around so that Billy could make comments from the observations he'd made.

"Maggie, I want to see you moving up the field more, Doris can help out Edith at the back. Annie, you need to be quicker at passing the ball. If you keep it that long, you'll be tackled long before you pass it to another of our own team."

As Billy carried on running through the points he'd noted, Vi looked around to see if Tommy had joined them yet. He was there, on the sideline, holding his grandpa's hand and watching what was happening. She waved to them and turned back to listen to Billy.

As they walked home that afternoon they were all quiet, apart from Tommy, who made up for the others by giving a running commentary on his earlier visit to the cemetery with Alf.

"I think it's easier talking to Grandma there than it is when I'm on my own. I told her you were playing football again and about school. I told her about the tree-house in Aunty Audrey's garden too." Eventually Tommy decided to run the rest of the way home, with Nipper barking madly.

The adults walked in silence for a while before Alf said, "What we need to do, is move Clara to the other side of the field. She's a natural with her left foot."

Vi turned to Billy and smiled. Of course, what Alf was saying was a good point that no one else had thought about, but more importantly, Alf was getting involved; it looked as though they'd found their coach. It might just help him to cope with the loss of Elsie.

As life began to settle into a new normal, Vi put out of her mind the idea of having their own home and did her best to make the most of sharing with Billy's dad. They'd made the front room into both the dining room and a room which Billy, Vi and Tommy could use, while Alf had the back room as a place he could find peace and quiet for his pipe and reading. Most of the time it worked well. They didn't have many visitors, so the lack of a room kept for best didn't matter to them.

"We'd have to move in with Mam if John and I got married," Tessie said one day as they walked to work.

Vi stopped walking. "Has he asked you?"

"No, silly." Tessie grinned. "But I'm hoping he will."

Vi wondered if her brother had any idea what Tessie was thinking. She knew how much slower men were to catch on to ideas like marriage. She wondered if she should drop a hint to him, but maybe she should just leave them to it.

"Ena says being married isn't everything."

"Ena? My sister Ena? When did you see her?" Vi couldn't help but think this was a morning full of surprises.

"She was at your mam and dad's when I saw John on Tuesday. Said if she didn't get out of the house, she didn't know what she'd do." Tessie grimaced.

Vi did worry for her sister, but except on the Sundays when they were all at her parents' for lunch, she never saw her.

Vi set up her hat making in the room which the Moores were allowing her to use, and, whilst it gave her everything she needed, she had little time to go across town to work there. She went straight from work some days, as the shifts were now shorter; at least it gave her an hour or two to work on her designs. She hoped that if she had a selection of hats to show to customers, they'd have a better idea of the quality of her work. It meant every penny from the ones she'd sold so far went into buying material, but as they weren't looking to move out from living with Alf, Billy agreed it was the best thing to do.

"You look tired, love," Billy said to her when she went home that evening.

Vi sighed. "I'm struggling to do everything. I wish I could leave the factory and just make hats, but I can't see that ever being possible."

Billy looked sad. "And I wish I could help you more here. If I could start the dinner for when you came home, it would be easier." He held up his one hand and she knew what he was thinking.

"Maybe when Tommy's a bit older he could help you." She kissed him and went to take her coat upstairs, before heading back to the kitchen. She was tired. He was right, but she didn't want to give up either the football or the hat making; they were the things she enjoyed. She could live with staying here at Ivy Terrace, but even then, they couldn't afford for her to give up work. The biggest problem was the lack of a bedroom for Tommy; now that he was eight years old, he was getting too big to share easily with Vi and Billy. They'd managed to move things around in their room so that he could have a small bed of his own, but with only two rooms upstairs, there was very little they could do beyond that.

As there were no league fixtures for the men's teams that season, it was still fairly easy to sell tickets for the women's matches, and to find dates that they could use the Billingbrook United ground to play. It was also relatively dry that Easter weekend, and in addition to the tickets they'd sold in advance many people turned up to buy tickets on the day. When Vi stepped out onto the pitch and looked around the stadium, the old feeling of excitement returned. Vi's father was with Mr and Mrs Moore in the stand. However, because Tommy had attended all the team practices, with the whole family being involved, he had become the team's mascot. He had his own kit, with white shorts and a shirt with broad black and white stripes, just like the rest of the team, which he wore with great pride. Vi couldn't help smiling as she saw him.

Their new team formation and positions worked. Despite being a little rusty, they beat a team from Bradford by four goals to nil, and as the match whistle blew, no one seemed happier than Alf. He was already talking excitedly about what other matches they could arrange.

"What are we going to do if the factory stops supporting the team?" Billy asked as they packed up.

"Why would they do that?" Vi presumed that as they were happy with the girls working in different places, it wouldn't be a problem.

"They don't receive as much publicity from it now the war's over. They've started making motor car engine parts too, so I guess they're looking beyond the munitions work."

"What about our jobs?" Tessie asked.

Billy shrugged. "I don't know. At the very least I suspect there'll be some changes."

At home, Alf said to Vi, "Have you got a minute, love?"

Vi frowned. "Yes, of course. Shall I get Billy?"

He hesitated. "No, I'd like to run an idea past you first. I can talk to Billy about it if you're happy."

Vi followed Billy's Dad into the back room and sat down.

"I've been thinking about the problem of what we do if the factory stops backing the football team. And I've had an idea."

"Oh, Dad, what? I still love playing and I really don't want to stop." Vi was fidgeting with the sleeve of her dress, waiting for Alf to explain.

"I wondered about seeing if I could call in some favours from my playing days. It's a very long time ago now, but there are still one or two people I know from back then. What if you could officially be part of Billingbrook United?"

Vi's eyes widened. "Do you think they'd agree?"

"Well, I can't say, love, but it's got to be worth a try." He picked up his pipe and began to fill it.

"Yes, oh yes, please ask." Vi wished she could go to see Tessie and tell her, but perhaps she shouldn't say anything, at least until Alf had a reply.

Over the next few weeks, as the team trained regularly together, the old camaraderie returned.

"This is what I missed," Clara said as they all packed up their kit after a home game against Bury in June. "I do wish Florrie and Beattie were part of it, but I'm grateful so many of the old crowd are still here."

They were all laughing and joking as they went back out carrying their kit bags. Alf was waiting for them on the edge of the pitch and called them over.

"Before you go, girls, we've got some news for you." He looked across to Vi, who nodded that he should go ahead. He held up his hand to call for complete silence. "I'd just like to wait… ah, here they are."

Two men wearing three-piece suits, were walking across from the other side of the pitch to join Alf. He called the girls together and then raised his voice. "As you all know, we've been working on an idea over the last few weeks." He looked across to Vi and Billy before continuing. "Billy's spoken to Mr Giffard at Caulder and Harrison, and he is in complete agreement." He paused and looked around.

Vi wanted him to hurry up and tell the others before she burst with the excitement.

Alf broke into a broad smile. "These gentlemen are Mr Clifford and Mr Thomas. They're directors here at Billingbrook United." The two men nodded to the women. "They have agreed that from this summer, the team that was formerly known as the Caulder and Harrison team can become the Billingbrook United Women's Team."

Vi didn't think Alf could have looked more proud if he was captaining the team himself. If anything, he looked even more excited than she felt, and that was saying something.

"Did I hear that right?" Tessie asked her, looking somewhat dazed.

Vi nodded.

"You wait until I tell John." Tessie started dancing a little jig.

"Before I get as excited as I think I'm about to, please can I just check that I've understood this correctly. Are you saying that we are all now the Billingbrook United Women's Team? We all still have places in the team, exactly as we were?" Edith was wide-eyed as she waited for an answer.

The two men in suits were smiling now and nodded their assent.

"And are Alf and Billy still going to be our coaches? And Tommy our mascot?" Eva asked.

Mr Clifford, who looked to be a very kindly and jovial man, laughed in a very genial manner. "Yes, madam, nothing else will change. You will have new kit to reflect your new team name, and we will help in arranging your matches instead of Mr Giffard. You will still have some of your training at the Caulder and Harrison recreation ground, although you may also have some of it here. We're hoping there'll be a women's league to run alongside the men's league next season."

As fast as he answered one question, the girls thought of others. "Will we still be raising money for the hospital?"

It was Mr Thomas who answered this one. He looked more serious than Mr Clifford, but not unfriendly. "We will be making an appropriate donation to the hospital from the gate money of all the women's matches."

It didn't sound quite the same as giving all the money, but it sounded fair. They'd have costs to take out first, she presumed. She stepped forward and tentatively offered her hand to first Mr Clifford, "Thank you," and then moved on to Mr Thomas.

After that, the girls all began talking at once. They were now an official football team, and it no longer mattered where they all worked.

CHAPTER 20

Monday 23rd June 1919 - 'Germany Says "Yes" But With Two Reservations' - The Daily Mirror

Vi cut around the small piece from the *Billingbrook Mercury*. She felt a thrill seeing it there in black and white. Their football team was now part of Billingbrook United. "I thought I'd take this over to show my dad, just in case he didn't see it in the news pages," she said to Billy on the Monday evening. "Perhaps we could all go when I finish work tomorrow. I'll leave something ready for your dad's tea, and we can eat when we come back."

Tommy was becoming far more independent and cycled to his maternal grandparents straight after school each day. He and Bobby were still close, despite being in different schools. By the time Vi and Billy arrived, the boys were out in the street playing football with other children from along the road.

"You should join in," Billy said, grinning at Vi. "They'd be chuffed to be playing with a Billingbrook United player."

"Even if that player's a woman?" Vi laughed.

It wouldn't have been the first time she'd been roped in to playing with the children, but not today. "I want to see the look on Dad's face when I tell him the news."

"Vi, love. Billy." Queenie Tunicliffe stood up to welcome her daughter and son-in-law. "We were just having a little tipple in celebration. Come and join us." There was a small bottle of brandy on the table and Queenie went to fetch more glasses.

"Oh." Vi was taken aback. "You've already heard."

Queenie frowned. "Yes, Ena came and told us herself. They're over the moon. She says if it's a girl, she wants to call it Queenie after me. Isn't that lovely?"

"Yes." Vi's mouth was moving mechanically as her brain caught up. They were celebrating her sister Ena expecting a baby. She slipped the cutting about the football into her pocket. Today wasn't the day to share that. At least she could tell Mr and Mrs Moore when they went over to see them on Sunday.

She raised her glass to Ena and hoped Percy would be happy about the news. She was pleased for her sister, and the idea of being an aunt was lovely. It did remind her how much she'd like another child, but she tried to put that out of her mind.

Billy squeezed her hand. They'd tried for a baby since he'd been back, though that was easier said than done, both with his injuries and sharing a room with Tommy; but they'd had no success, and she suspected now that their chance had gone. She would have to make the most of having nieces and nephews. At least Tommy had her youngest brother, Bobby, to grow up with.

Later that week, Billy was reading the newspaper. "It's no wonder Caulder and Harrison were ready for the team to transfer." He looked up at Vi. "It doesn't look good for you girls keeping your jobs at the factory."

Vi frowned. "Why ever not? We do a good job."

"There's been a law passed making factories give soldiers their old jobs back." He ran a finger down the column to find his place. "The 'Restoration of Pre-war Practices Act' it says it's called. Gives them two months. Your job might be all right, but we shouldn't bank on it."

Vi snorted. She was still putting what money she could away in the jar. Now that Alf was more settled, she was hoping they could all move to a three-bedroom house. She'd tried broaching it with Billy, but he didn't want to suggest it to his dad just yet. If she lost her job there'd be no hope of that happening, especially with Alf's job looking precarious.

Thank goodness the football provided an escape, just as much as it always had. Under Alf's direction, and the banner of Billingbrook United, the girls practised hard ready for the games which would start again in September. There was still no league in place, but the cup had been restarted, and this year Vi was determined they would win.

Nothing was said at the factory about any changes, and Vi began to hope that her job would be safe; but then at the start of August she was called into Mrs Johnson's office and her heart sank. She would leave at the end of the week. As she came out, Eva was called in.

Vi went back to her bench, but she really didn't feel much like working now. Despite the danger of the work, and what the shells were then used for, she'd enjoyed her time at Caulder and Harrison. She knew demand for munitions had dropped and the factory had little choice in the matter; of course she understood too that returning soldiers needed work, but she still resented the fact that women, who had given so much during the war, counted for nothing.

"Perhaps I should be looking for something else too," Tessie said as they walked home that evening. "No one's said my job's going, but I guess it could be. It won't be the same without you there, anyway."

Vi linked her arm through Tessie's. They'd become so close over the years they'd walked to and from work together, and from playing football. She wouldn't lose that, whatever happened. She suspected it wouldn't be too long before Tessie would be part of the family, which was a comfort to her.

"Maybe another job will turn up," Vi said, but without feeling a great deal of hope. "Still, let's look for the positives, maybe my hair will go back to its old colour. I can hardly remember what that was." They laughed.

When they went to see Mr and Mrs Moore that weekend, Vi poured out the story of losing her job. Both Audrey and Terence listened intently.

"I shall have to start looking for work, although I'm not altogether sure where to begin. There seem to be ten men looking at every job. I think we women are just supposed to retreat quietly home," Vi said.

"Why don't you try to earn a living from making hats?" Terence asked.

Vi saw a sudden picture in her head of how nice it would be to design and make hats all the time; but maybe it was just another of those dreams that could never happen, along with the big family and winning the football cup. She gave a weak smile.

"What's stopping you?" Terence didn't want to leave the subject behind.

Vi thought about it. "I don't really know. What if no one wants to buy them?"

"Oh, you silly girl." Audrey was shaking her head. "You really have no idea how good the hats you've made are." She stood up and went over to the bureau, then returned with a piece of paper. "I didn't want to push you, but I've kept a list of the people who have seen the hat you made for me and asked where I bought it from. I don't suppose they would all be ready to buy a new hat, but I think many of them would. I do meet all sorts of ladies through the different organisations I'm part of."

Vi gasped as she looked down the list.

"And you'd need to advertise. I'm sure Billy could do your accounts and I could give some advice on the business side." Terence was looking pleased with himself.

"What about people coming for fittings? I can't very well bring them into your house." Vi had so many ideas running around inside her head, she was having difficulty getting them into any order.

Audrey smiled. "The ones on this list would all be welcome here. That might give you enough business to make the next step and rent some premises; a little shop somewhere."

Vi gasped. "Me? Own a shop?"

Billy's face lit up. "Rent rather than own, but we could sell other things too. What about material for curtains and dressmaking?"

"A milliner and haberdasher." Vi could picture it, almost as though it were real. Then her shoulders sagged. "People like me just don't do things like that."

"We could try," Billy said, getting up and walking across to where Terence Moore was standing. "Sir, if we did, would you really be willing to help us? I don't mean with money," he added hastily. "I wouldn't want that. I mean with advice. I know I've been studying, but there's a lot I don't know."

"It would be my pleasure."

"Do you really think I could do this?" Vi asked Billy as they walked home that afternoon.

"Well, you'll be the one making the hats, but we'll do the rest of it together. We're not going to know unless we try. We have the money we put by in the jar, that can keep us going for a while. As long as you pay for any new material and equipment with money you make from selling hats, then we'll be fine, at least while Dad still has work. We'll have to stay living at Ivy Terrace though."

Vi listened carefully to what Billy was saying. She hadn't thought they'd be moving just yet, and if it meant she could follow her dream of making hats, then she would willingly cope with that.

If she was going to make a success of hat making, Vi decided that from day one she had to treat it in the same way as her job at the factory: starting at eight o'clock and working until five, with breaks at the same time she was already used to. She could always change things later, but for now she needed the same discipline and routine. Arriving at the Moores' house on her first Monday morning, Vi was taken aback to find Mr Moore waiting for her to arrive.

"I'd like to show you something, but I need you to bring Billy and Mr Dobson as well. When could you all be free?"

"If they come straight from work, five thirty in the afternoon tomorrow." Vi looked to Audrey for a clue what this was about, but Audrey just smiled and nodded in a manner that made clear she wouldn't break the secret.

Vi spent most of that day writing short notes of introduction to the women on Audrey's list, saying she was now in business and would be very happy to discuss their millinery requirements with them at their earliest convenience. It wasn't until she was back home that evening that she had time to speculate about what Terence could need all three of them for.

"You don't suppose he's going to offer you a job, do you?" Billy said.

Vi shrugged. "I don't know. I don't really know what his company does. Besides, he's the one encouraging me to start making hats, and he wouldn't need your dad if it was a factory job he was thinking of."

"No, you're right. I know their work was protected during the war, but it wasn't munitions. Besides, hat making is a great idea. You can do anything if you put your mind to it."

Billy gave her a sloppy kiss, which made Vi laugh. It was good to have someone who had so much faith in her, even if she didn't really believe it was true.

On the Tuesday when Alf and Billy arrived at the Moores' house, Tommy was more than happy to stay with Nipper and Mrs Moore while the others went with Terence. They set off toward the centre of Billingbrook, passing only general conversation as they walked. Thinking they were going to Terence's factory, it occurred to Vi how little he talked about his work when they visited. She'd never liked to ask too much; she didn't really know what to ask. The factory's red brick building came into view with its large sign reading 'T Moore & Son'. The sign must be a daily reminder of losing his only son.

"It's not my factory I want to show you. Follow me." Terence Moore was grinning now, like a child with a new toy.

Vi frowned. If it wasn't the factory, then she was right, it couldn't be a job. She felt a mixture of disappointment mixed with relief that she could continue with the hat making.

Just how close the factory was to the town centre became apparent when they turned the corner into a large courtyard, off a lane behind St Michael's Church. The church's bell tower stood tall compared to the surroundings and provided a key landmark to the town.

"What do you think?" Terence asked, stopping suddenly and turning to them.

Billy looked at Vi. She could tell from the lost look in his eyes that he had no more idea than she did. She was expected to say something, but she really didn't know what. She opened her mouth, hoping something would come to her, but was saved by Terence suddenly laughing nervously.

"Oh," he said, "I'm so sorry. I've been thinking about this so much that I'd actually forgotten I hadn't explained the idea."

Vi let out a breath of relief. "Why don't you tell us now?"

He grinned and took a key out of his pocket. "Follow me."

They walked across the courtyard to a little row of shops. There was a boot and shoe shop and a gentleman's outfitters. Further along there was a rather nice grocers' showing all sorts of foods that Vi had only ever heard of, a bookshop, and one very run down shop with a faded sign in the window saying 'new business opening soon'. Mr Moore walked straight to the empty unit and put the key into the lock. He opened the door and then stood back, inviting them to enter.

The space at the front would have been reasonably bright, had the window not been in need of a good clean. The shop window was large and the whole row seemed to face south.

"This row was part of the site when I bought the factory. They were all run down then and needed work. I didn't have any use for shops, so I sold them. This one has never been updated. It was taken on by a gentleman a few years ago, but he went away to fight shortly afterwards and..." Terence didn't finish the sentence. "Anyway, after we talked on Sunday, I thought I'd come to see if this one was still empty, and then I went to speak to the landlord. There's no living accommodation to speak of, but it's in a good location, and there's enough space to work and store stock, as well as the shop itself. Given what the other shops are, I thought a milliner's might fit quite nicely. What do you think?" Terence was still looking like an eager child as he waited for their reply.

Vi couldn't speak. She opened her mouth and closed it again. She looked at Billy. She did a slow turn, taking in every detail of the shop. Then she swallowed hard. "Oh, Terence, it's beautiful, but we couldn't afford the rent. It might take some time before I could make any money and..." She looked to Billy to continue. Her own emotions were taking over, and she just couldn't get out any other words.

"It's been empty for several years. The other tenants have been complaining to the landlord that he needs to do something about it. He says if you can do it up at your own expense, then you can have the first month free to do the work and the next six months at half rent to get you up and running." He turned to Billy. "What do you say?"

Billy looked to Vi, smiling. "What do you think, love?"

Vi felt tears pricking the corners of her eyes. "We'd need stock, and a worktable, and..."

Terence held up his hand to stop her. He took a sheet

of paper out of his pocket. "You told me some time ago the sorts of things you'd need. I costed them up then." He passed the paper to Billy.

Vi couldn't believe that this was happening. Her head was spinning as she began to think of the possibilities. "Do you think we can?" she asked Billy, but she didn't need his words; his grin told her all she needed to know. She looked at Alf. "What do you think? It could only happen if you could do the work to get this place in shape."

Alf didn't reply. He walked around the interior of the shop, casting his eyes from one end to the other and then back again. Once he'd done that, he went out to the front and looked back at the empty premise. He took out his pipe and, although he didn't light it, he put it in his mouth as he paced back and forth.

Vi held her breath, waiting for what he'd say.

Eventually Alf came back in. "There are some things I won't be the best person to do, but I can certainly get it into shape for you."

Vi turned back to Terence. "Thank you." She went over to him and kissed his cheek.

The older man's eyes sparkled and he reddened slightly. "I haven't done anything, really. It will be down to you, young lady."

Vi took off her coat. "Now I'm here, I may as well work out exactly what we need to do."

"Tomorrow will be fine for that," Terence said, gently taking her arm. "Audrey has some supper prepared for us all to celebrate. We rather hoped you'd say yes."

CHAPTER 21

If I go to the op'ra house, in the op'ra season
There's someone sure to shout at me without the slightest
reason
If I go to a concert hall to have a jolly spree
There's someone in the party who is sure to shout at me

CHORUS
"Where did you get that hat? Where did you get that tile?
Isn't it a nobby one, and just the proper style?
I should like to have one just the same as that!"
Where'er I go, they shout "Hello! Where did you get that
hat?"
Where Did You Get That Hat ? - Joseph J. Sullivan, 1888

*Tuesday 12th August 1919 - Lenin's Part in the Soviet Plot in
London - The Daily Mirror*

"I can run errands with Nipper," Tommy said as they
began talking about the shop that evening.

"Hats and Haberdashery — what do you think?" Vi
asked, looking at them all eagerly.

"You mean what we sell?" Billy frowned.

Vi was delighted that Billy was seeing it as his business
as much as hers. "Well, yes, but the shop name too."

"Hats and Haberdashery." He repeated what she'd
said as though rolling the idea around. Then nodded.

"What do you think, Dad?"

Alf looked wistful as he replied. "I think your mam would have thought it was a lovely idea. If she'd been alive today…" He trailed off.

Vi wondered what he was thinking, but decided it might be best to change the focus so he didn't feel uncomfortable. "Do you think we'll manage until the shop's up and running? I mean for money."

"It could take you a few weeks to set up, and even longer to start making any profit. I'll work out some figures later. We'll be all right, Vi. One way or another, we'll be all right."

Billy spoke with more confidence than Vi was feeling. There was a big difference between dreaming of doing something and actually seeing if you could manage it.

Over the next few weeks they all worked tirelessly to prepare for the opening of Hats and Haberdashery. Vi was trying to work out what stock she needed, and was making display hats so her customers could see some of the styles she could offer to them. She was also working on the orders that were coming in from Audrey's friends, who in turn were referring their own friends to her. Vi's plan was to continue to make the hats to order, so that each one would be a perfect fit. Maybe later she'd have some standard designs that she could sell when people came in.

Billy was just as busy. Terence was guiding him on exactly what he needed to do, and Billy seemed to be thoroughly enjoying continuing to learn. When he wasn't at work he was costing up the things Vi wanted to order, and carefully filling in ledgers with what had been spent so far.

Even Tommy was as good as his word, and set off regularly with Nipper to deliver messages for Vi, both to her new clients and to place orders for the shop.

Billy's dad was working short hours at the cartwright. Demand for carriages had reduced rapidly now that more people had motor cars. It gave him the opportunity to do all the carpentry they needed and make the shop look as good as any of the others in the courtyard. "I was thinking," he said one day, as he was taking a break from putting in some shelving. "You're never too old to do something new. Carts might have had their day, but maybe I could do something working with motor vehicles instead - as a driver, or maybe I could learn to be a mechanic. I said it before when Burt let me try his Morris Oxford. I've watched all that you and Billy have done to start in new directions; maybe it's my turn."

At night, it was Vi rather than Billy who was waking. She would suddenly think of something else which needed to be done, and was worrying about whether the things she'd already done were good enough. By contrast, Billy seemed to be sleeping soundly.

"Are you ready, Vi?" Tessie called to her at the back door of Ivy Terrace.

Vi looked up at the clock and gasped. "Oh my, is that the time?" She hurried out of the front room and closed the door to stop Nipper going in. "I'll get my bag."

"It's not like you to nearly miss practice. I'm surprised Billy and Alf didn't say," Tessie said as they walked to the football ground.

"The boys must have left and not told me. At least it is only practice. Start to worry if I miss a match. We'll be moving my work room from Mr and Mrs Moore's house to the shop in the next few days, and I was just making sure I hadn't forgotten anything that would need doing."

"Put me and John down to help. He's very good at carrying things." Tessie blushed.

"When are you two going to tie the knot?" Vi had been wondering for a while.

Tessie looked serious. "It's not that we haven't talked about it, but we'd have nowhere to live. He's worried about your mam and dad if he moves out, and I'm worried about Mam."

"Couldn't he move in with you and your mam? I know that doesn't help with my parents, but you want to be together, don't you?"

"He's not actually asked me properly yet, and he'd need to ask mam's permission first." Tessie sighed.

Football was still Vi's one relaxation, and her enthusiasm remained just as strong. Each season that went by left her wanting to win the cup more than ever. This year there would be twenty-four teams competing. Women everywhere wanted to play football, and it didn't seem quite so unacceptable as it had only a few years before. Billingbrook had a bye in the opening round and wouldn't play their first match until November, the week before the opening of Hats and Haberdashery. Vi suspected that was going to be a nerve-racking time.

Alf managed to arrange a match against a Manchester team, in the absence of a cup match in October. Billingbrook only managed a draw, and Vi began to doubt that they would be a strong enough team to lift the cup. The Manchester team seemed to be filled with girls at least ten years younger than Vi.

"Perhaps I'm not keeping my fitness up with everything else I'm trying to do," Vi said that evening.

"Maybe you need a younger player."

"Your mind might not be on things with the shop taking so much time, but you're still the best player we have." Alf spoke as sternly to her as he ever had. "So don't you go getting ideas of giving up. Besides, what would be the point of me and Billy coaching the team if you weren't in it?"

Vi resisted pointing out that they enjoyed the excitement and would probably continue with or without her. She tried to think about what was missing from her own game. Was it that she wasn't so fit? The only thing she could think of was that the girls didn't feel quite as close as they had when they'd all worked together. Then it really had been all for one and one for all. She wondered if there was something more they could do to improve their teamwork. There just wasn't time for everything at the moment. They could at least try returning to practising twice a week. She could suggest that.

By the time of their first cup match against Stockport, the girls had fitted in a couple more sessions of practice. It was hard though. It was dark by the time they all finished work, and no one would give them afternoons off now to play football. Instead they had short sessions on Sunday mornings, although some of the girls couldn't attend due to church involvement with their families; and almost all of them had family commitments on a Sunday afternoon. Even the suggestion of playing football on a Sunday was frowned upon, but they kept quiet about the morning sessions, and played them at the Whittingham Road ground so they were out of sight.

When it came to their cup tie, they were up against a team they hadn't played before, so it was difficult to know what to expect.

"We can do this," Vi said as they went out onto the pitch at the Stockport ground. Showing her own confidence seemed to help some of the younger players. It didn't matter whether she was completely convinced, as long as she sounded that way to them. She led the team out with Tommy ahead of her, still proud to be their mascot.

The girls played more as a team than they had for a while, passing the ball between the players and finding space to keep the game moving. When the full time whistle blew, they had beaten the Stockport girls by four goals to nil.

As the captain of the losing side congratulated Vi, she said, "To be honest, our hearts weren't in it. The team's being disbanded. The factory has already laid most of us off."

"I'm sorry." Vi shook the girl's hand. "I was laid off a couple of months ago. I'm setting up my own hat shop now. It opens next week."

"Really?" The Stockport captain's eyes were wide. "Good luck."

"Thanks." Vi laughed. "I feel like I need it. It's near St Michael's Church. If you ever come to Billingbrook, you'll have to come and see."

The girl smiled. "I've never been out of Stockport except for the football, but you never know."

It would be another month before the quarter-finals of the cup. The Billingbrook team needed to practice hard, but Vi's time would have to go into the business first. It suddenly occurred to her that she'd need someone to cover the shop when she was away at the games, and so she could attend practice as well. This was going to be harder than she'd imagined. Then she thought about her sister,

Ena. She could do with something to keep her going until the baby arrived; maybe she could help.

Vi loved the window display that she'd put together for the opening of Hats and Haberdashery. She'd made a cloche hat in peacock blue, as well as a wide-brimmed hat in autumn colours, with a grouping of small flowers in decoration. She'd also made a cap and a bowler hat, to ensure it was clear there was something for everyone. Behind the hats, Vi draped some of the material they offered for sale. She would use any ends of rolls to make clothing for the family. If they started doing well enough, maybe she could buy lengths of her favourite cloths, instead of having to hope there were unsaleable offcuts at the ends of the reels. There were so many to choose from, it was hard to know which she liked best.

She'd managed to buy a mannequin to style some of the cloth around, and had enjoyed fashioning the dress using only tacks and pins to hold it in place.

She went out into the courtyard to look at the final effect.

"I should get you doing my window. Have you been doing it long?"

Vi turned to see a gentleman rather older than herself wearing a leather apron over his clothes. "I'm sorry, I didn't see you there. No, I'm new to it all, actually."

The man held out his hand. "Mr Stibbins. Stibbins Boots and Shoes."

Vi shook his hand. "Mrs Dobson, pleased to meet you."

"With a display like that, you should get the customers in. Opening this Saturday, I see. To be honest, things have been a bit quiet since the war; not so much money about. But you'll get the trade in the run up to Christmas, so that should help."

On the morning of the opening, Vi was awake long before she needed to be. She tried to get up without waking Billy or Tommy. It was hard to find the things she needed in the dark. She gave a start when she felt Nipper brush against her bare foot and had to stifle a laugh. Tommy stirred, but she suspected she could have led a marching band through the room without waking Billy.

Nipper followed her downstairs and she let him out into the yard. As she filled the kettle and prepared breakfast for the others, every few minutes she'd think of something she needed to do and have to write it down. She just wished Billy could be there for the first day, but he'd come to the shop after work. It was the best he could manage. Terence and Audrey had promised to come for the opening, and Alf would be there. She hoped her own parents would come too, but that would be after her dad finished for the day at the mill.

The kettle was just boiling when there was a knock at the back door.

"I wanted to wish you good luck," Tessie said, giving Vi a hug. "And Mam said to give you this." Tessie handed Vi a horseshoe, with white ribbon tied around it. "She said you should hang it above the door, but make sure you put it the right way up."

Vi smiled. She'd never had Mrs Brown down as being superstitious, but any luck she could find would be very welcome.

Hats and Haberdashery wasn't opening until ten o'clock, but by eight Vi had said goodbye to the others and was heading for the shop. She'd checked her bag several times to make sure she had everything. If there was anything else she needed now, it was too late.

They were having a little ceremony for the opening and had invited the newspaper to come. Vi wouldn't have thought of it, but Terence said it was a good way for people to hear about the shop, especially as she was the captain of the football team. He thought it would make a good story. Vi drew the line when he suggested asking the mayor to cut the ribbon. She was already too nervous about the whole event, and would have felt completely overwhelmed by so much formality.

St Michael's bell tolled the hour and Terence Moore stepped forward and cleared his throat. "It is my very great honour to formally open Hats and Haberdashery for business. We wish Vi and the business every success."

The little crowd, which included a reporter, together with the proprietors of all the neighbouring shops, family and friends, and even one or two passersby, shouted hooray and applauded.

Terence stepped back, allowing Vi to be the first person to enter the shop. She did one little twirl when she went in, trying to capture the image of this moment in her mind forever, and then went to fetch the tray of fruit punch drinks which Audrey had made, to pass around to those who joined the celebration.

By the time Billy called in later, Vi was about ready to close the shop.

"How's it gone, love?"

Vi grimaced. "One zipper, half a dozen buttons and three yards of muslin. Oh, and a blister on my little toe."

He kissed her nose. "It's a start. We always knew it would take time before people start to know you're here. We need someone famous wearing one of your hats."

Vi laughed. Of course, it was an excellent idea, but it was never going to happen.

"Have you seen this?" Ena handed her sister the newspaper as soon as she arrived at the store on the Saturday lunchtime.

Vi's hands were trembling too much to hold the paper, so she placed it on the counter. As she read the report in the *Billingbrook Mercury* she grinned. The paper really had done her proud with what they'd written about the shop. *"'The place to go for the latest fashions in hats'.* Oh, Ena, do you think it will bring people in?"

"You'll soon find out." Ena rubbed her hand across her expanded waistline. "I'm glad there's a chair for me for the afternoon. I don't think I could stand on these legs for more than about twenty minutes."

"And you will be all right? I won't be gone too long." Vi went to pick up her football kit bag from the back of the shop.

"You've been through everything. I know how the till works, and you've shown me all the prices. Even I can manage that. The baby's not due for another four weeks. I'll be fine."

Vi knew it was an extravagance to pay Ena to cover the shop so she could attend the practice, but Billy and Terence had both insisted that she shouldn't stop playing. Besides, she often wished she could help Ena out. Ena's husband Percy earned so little, and they had his elderly father to care for, as well as Ena's no-good brother-in-law.

Vi gave her sister a quick kiss before she left. "I'll be back as soon as I can."

CHAPTER 22

Saturday 29th November 1919 - Lady Astor's Triumph: England's First Woman M.P. - The Daily Mirror

"I'll see you at home," Vi said to Billy at the end of football practice. "I just want to make sure everything's locked up."

"Ena will have done everything, won't she?" Billy grinned at her. "But I guess it's more than that. You probably want to know if she's sold anything and can't wait until we see her at your mam and dad's tomorrow."

Vi felt sheepish. Billy knew her so well. "I said I'd go in." She kissed his cheek and headed toward the shop.

As it turned out, Ena had sold very little since Vi left her, and the takings from the first few days were disappointing.

"One lady said she might come back in to see you next week to discuss a hat design, so it might not be too bad." Ena sounded encouraging as she got up from the stool where she'd been waiting for Vi. "I've really enjoyed being out of the house. I can work next week if you want me to."

"Unless you're incapacitated," Vi said, looking at Ena with a raised eyebrow. Babies could easily come early, and she didn't want Ena going into labour in the shop.

As it turned out, Ena and Percy weren't at the Tunnicliffe house on Sunday lunchtime.

"She came in on her way home from the shop and said

they wouldn't be coming," Mam said. "Beats me why they changed their minds. You'd think at her stage she'd be glad of someone else doing the cooking."

"I don't much mind not seeing Percy." Vi grimaced. She hoped the baby would take after its mother and not its father.

As they talked after lunch, Dad sat and quietly played his accordion. It was a lovely sound to have in the background, and Vi found herself swaying, losing herself in the music. If she'd closed her eyes, she could have been asleep in moments. It felt as though it was the first time she'd sat down properly for days.

Although Monday in the shop was quiet, business began to pick up a little after that, and with it Vi's spirits lifted. When she arrived home on Thursday she said to Billy, "Ena's never going to manage on Saturday for me to go to Preston for our cup match. I can't see what I can do, except not play. I certainly don't want to close the shop when we're only just getting started." She took her shoes off and rubbed her tired feet. The situation seemed impossible.

"Why don't you ask Audrey?" Billy was working on another hat block for the shop as they talked.

"Mrs Moore? She'd never want to work in a shop, would she?" Vi hadn't thought about Audrey when it came to working. "Audrey doesn't need to work. She seems quite happy with the charitable events she attends, and sometimes helps to organise."

"Ask her." Billy was quite insistent. "Just because someone doesn't have to work, doesn't mean they don't want to."

Vi thought about what Billy said. She found working and earning her own living very satisfying, but there had never been an alternative. She didn't know how she'd feel if they had enough money without her working.

When she closed for lunch that Friday she walked to the Moores' house. She hated to bother them when they were likely to be eating, and her hands felt clammy as she knocked on the door.

By the time Audrey answered, Vi had almost talked herself out of asking.

"Come in, come in. I've not put lunch out yet, there's enough for three if you want to join us."

Vi marvelled at how welcoming and unruffled the older woman seemed. "I won't stay long. I need to get back. It's just..." Oh, how on earth was she going to ask this? "... I'm struggling to find cover for the shop tomorrow. We're supposed to be playing away at Preston and I think I'm going to have to drop out. Billy suggested..."

Vi got no further before Audrey butted in. "I'll do it."

Her eagerness took Vi by surprise. "I was going to ask you, but I realise what an imposition it is."

"Nonsense. I'd love to do it. I've been watching you all having fun and feeling a little left out. I'd love to help. Would it be all right for me to come in this afternoon, so I can see what to do while you're there?"

"Yes, yes, of course. Thank you. Ena will be there tomorrow, but the baby is due in three weeks and she's getting very tired."

"I shall enjoy getting to know your sister a little better," Audrey replied as Vi said farewell.

Vi hadn't been back at the shop for long when Audrey came in to join her. "Now, tell me everything," she said, before even finishing taking off her hat and coat.

They were just going through what materials were for

sale, and how to cut the cloth, when the bell rang and a customer came in.

"Good afternoon, madam. Welcome to Hats and Haberdashery, how may we be of service?"

Audrey had gently escorted the lady further into the shop without a moment's pause, and Vi could only admire her manner. It occurred to Vi that Audrey was more familiar with going into higher class shops than she was, and whilst she needed to teach Audrey about the things they were selling, there might be just as much that she could learn from the older woman. That feeling only increased when the lady was sent away satisfied, having made several purchases and having booked an appointment with Vi for the following Tuesday to discuss hats. She wanted to bring the dress into the shop that she planned to wear the hat with, so that Vi could design something to go with it perfectly.

The afternoon passed quickly, and business was brisk. Now Vi needed to turn her attention to the following day's football match.

Of all the days for Edith to be ill, it had to be the day of the quarter-finals. Vi was thinking through how best they could cover things on the field.

"Why don't you go in goal, Vi? You're better than the others," Alf said, taking charge of the situation.

Vi froze. It was one thing being up front and not always scoring a goal, but letting the opposition goals into the net would feel like everything was her fault if they lost. She told herself not to be so stupid. They had perfectly good defenders in the team. She would certainly show her appreciation of Edith when the girl came back.

The Billingbrook team's game didn't flow as it would if

they'd all played in their usual positions. The first time that Preston worked their way down the field and past the last of the Billingbrook defenders before the goal, Vi could feel her heart pounding. She was all that stood between the ball and the net. Trying to remember everything Alf had taught her, and all the things Edith did so well, she didn't let her focus waver. As she watched the Preston player, Vi was alert to where the girl's other teammates were, and whether she was likely to pass the ball. As the girl swung her leg back, Vi was prepared, and tried to balance her weight so she could shift in whichever direction the ball went.

As the ball flew through the air, Vi moved almost without registering what she was doing and caught the ball in the top right hand corner, then drew it into herself. That one hadn't crossed the line.

However hard Vi had tried, when the final whistle blew the score was four goals to Preston and only two for Billingbrook. She had to admit it could have been an awful lot worse, and she did feel they'd been outclassed by the other team. She tried to look on the bright side; being out of the cup would mean she could concentrate on the shop for a while.

"Do you think I should stop playing?" she asked Tessie as they all set off home. "I'm going to need to devote more time to the shop."

"Don't you dare. I'd stop too if you did, and then where would we be?"

Tessie's reply made Vi laugh. The girl was eighteen now, and at some point, if she and John married, there'd be children to think about, and Tessie wouldn't be able to play while she was expecting. They'd lost Florrie from the team; she found herself a young man who didn't want

235

other men seeing Florrie dressed as she was on the football pitch, and that had been that - four years enjoying playing the game brought to an abrupt halt. At least John wouldn't be like that with Tessie.

"I'll arrange other games," Alf said, trying to cheer them all up as they travelled back to Billingbrook. "And we can lift the cup next year."

It was past closing time, and she'd left Audrey with a key, in case Ena had to leave early, but Vi still went to the shop to check all was well. She then called at the Moores' house on her way home.

Audrey's face was beaming. "I've had a lovely day. I did send your Ena home, I hope you don't mind, but the poor lamb was exhausted. I'd be very happy to help again. I rather enjoyed myself."

Over the next few weeks, Audrey covered the shop for a couple of hours on the Saturdays when Vi had football practice, and occasionally for longer if she had a match. Business picked up through December, and Audrey's worth was more than proved with a certain class of client that she could relate to more easily than Vi was able to.

"I'll pop in on Tuesday if that's all right?" Audrey said to Vi, when they were locking up a week before Christmas. "Major Tomlinson's wife should be coming in. I suggested she should, and I'd rather like to show her around."

Vi smiled. "Of course." She'd never thought that behind the scenes Audrey might be telling all her friends and acquaintances about the shop. No wonder they were building up a steady stream of customers wanting to have hats made. When Tommy had wanted to give Audrey a hat for Easter, Vi would never have guessed where it would all lead.

On the Thursday before Christmas, when Vi had just

served up their meal in the evening, she heard the side gate and the sounds of laughter. John and Tessie called at the back door and came straight in, slightly out of breath.

"Mam thought you'd want to know, Ena had the baby this afternoon." John panted as he got the words out.

"It's a girl," Tessie added. "Oh, Vi, she's beautiful."

Vi felt torn. She was longing to see the new baby and find out how Ena was doing, but at the same time she felt such pangs of longing for another child of her own that she was finding it difficult. She chided herself that she already had Tommy, and she should be pleased for Ena. "I'll go over tomorrow as soon as we close up. Are they both all right?"

Tessie nodded. "Ena says it wasn't as bad as everyone had told her. Mind you, little Queenie's ever so small."

"Was Percy there when you went?" Knowing he didn't usually like visitors, Vi wondered how he'd react to them all going.

John snorted. "He'd gone to wet the baby's head. Don't suppose he'll be going home sober."

Vi sighed. Poor Ena, perhaps it was good she'd have little Queenie to brighten her life.

Christmas Eve was a Wednesday, and as that was half-day closing Vi shut the shop at midday and breathed a sigh of relief. Two and a half days without working. It felt such a luxury. She had hat orders to fulfil, but she'd decided they would wait. In any case, the family wouldn't have much time to spare in those days, especially with their usual Boxing Day football match to fit in.

The first event was for them all to go to Terence and Audrey's house that afternoon. Terence had been insistent that they needed to arrive before dark. Vi went home for lunch and then, together with Billy, Tommy, and Nipper, they set off.

Terence Moore could not stand still when they arrived. He rubbed his hands together. "I have something to show you, and then a surprise. To begin with I want to show you what Audrey and I have bought for ourselves." He led the way without another word and clearly assumed they would all follow.

They went through a hall to the side of the house and an exit which Vi wasn't familiar with. On the road beyond the side gate stood a gleaming motor car. Tommy gasped and ran over to it.

"What do you think?" Terence asked, looking just as happy as any child who had been bought a new toy.

Tommy was happy to speak for them. "Can I go in it? Will you take me for a drive?"

"I was rather hoping you might all like to come. I'm still getting used to it, but if you don't mind that, I thought I could take you out for a few minutes." Terence was grinning broadly.

"You mind you keep your hands off the windows," Vi said to Tommy, checking his hands were clean.

Terence opened the rear door and the three of them and Nipper squeezed in. There wasn't a huge amount of room, but there was enough. Vi ran her hand over the finely-stitched green leather seats and let out a sigh.

Audrey sat in the front, and once he'd cranked the engine Terence followed.

"Just think how much easier it would be to get about with one of these," Billy said quietly to Vi.

Terence had clearly heard despite the engine noise. "One day, everyone will have one, you mark my words."

Billy laughed. "I can't see that being likely."

They only drove around Billingbrook, but by the time they returned, Vi couldn't stop smiling, and it was obvious both Billy and Tommy were entranced.

"Now," Terence said, once he'd parked and they'd all got out, "it's time for the surprise."

Audrey took over. "I know that with how much you've grown, Tommy, you're finding David's old bicycle a little small." She took hold of his hand. "Follow me."

They went back into the garden and a large bicycle-shaped parcel wrapped in brown paper was leaning against the wall.

"I know it's not Christmas Day yet, but I'm sure your mam and dad won't mind you opening it."

As they all watched and Nipper barked, Tommy took the wrapping paper off a brand-new bicycle. Vi gasped.

"For me?" Tommy looked at Mrs Moore, as though his eyes were about to come right out of his face, they were so wide.

She nodded to him. Terence went and stood by his wife's side and slipped his hand into hers.

Tommy ran his hand over the bicycle, much as Vi had done with the leather seats, and she smiled watching him. Then he went over to Mr and Mrs Moore and flung his arms first around one and then the other. "Thank you," he said, in a voice that sounded as breathless as he looked.

"Can I go out on it now?" he asked.

Terence Moore looked at Vi and Billy. "Tommy doesn't need to be here for the other surprise, so if your parents don't mind…"

"Go on, but be careful and don't go anywhere near Uncle Terence's car," Vi said, seeing the look of wonder on her son's face as she watched him cycle off. "You shouldn't have," she said to Audrey once Tommy had gone.

Terence looked concerned. "I hope you don't mind. It's just, well, we don't have anyone else to buy something for, and…" He didn't finish the sentence.

Billy coughed to clear his throat. "No, we don't mind. We're very grateful."

Vi couldn't find the words to say how wonderful it was. She opened her mouth, but felt too overwhelmed to speak.

Once they were back inside and comfortably seated, Terence went and stood with his back to the fire. "That brings me to another matter. Maybe now isn't the right time to talk about it, but once I've put my mind to something I like to get on with it. I've seen all the work you've done setting up the accounts and sorting the purchasing for the shop, Billy. I don't mind telling you I've been impressed. I've given this a great deal of serious thought, and I need a man like you in my company. I'd like you to come and work with me at T Moore & Son."

Billy looked stunned. "In the wages department?"

Terence laughed. "No. I want you to be my assistant."

Vi didn't think she could have heard right. She looked first at Billy, whose mouth was moving, but with no sound; then she looked at Terence, who was grinning broadly and looking to Billy for a response.

Vi nudged Billy's leg, then realised it was his wooden one and he probably hadn't felt it.

Billy was shaking his head, and for a moment Vi thought he was saying no.

Finally he spoke. "I… I don't know what to say. It would be an honour, although I don't know the first thing about your business. I may not be much use to you."

"I'll be the judge of that." Terence shook hands with Billy. "You'll have to give notice at Caulder and Harrison first, of course. Shall we say you'll start on the first of February? We can talk about your salary, but I'm sure you won't be disappointed."

"Thank you." Billy looked as though he was in a trance for the next couple of hours until they went home.

"Who'd have thought?" he said, as he and Vi walked. "It looks as though 1920 might just be our year."

The following day, as they were heading to visit Vi's family after Christmas lunch, she said, "If we moved, maybe we could invite everyone to us for Christmas." There simply wouldn't be enough room at her parents' house, and where she and Billy lived now still didn't feel like their home.

"I'll talk to Dad, see how he feels," Billy said quietly.

Vi wanted to put her foot down and make clear they had to move. They would be the ones paying, and they really did need another bedroom, but she gritted her teeth and said nothing. After all, when she looked at the family crammed in to her sister Ena's house she should be more grateful.

They all squeezed into her parents' room for a cup of tea and to exchange small gifts. Ena was there with little Queenie. It was the first time Vi had seen her, although she'd tried to visit the previous week and been greeted by Percy saying Ena was resting and didn't want visitors.

"She's beautiful." Vi turned her face down after she'd said it. She didn't want Ena to see her cry.

Ena beamed. "I'd still like to help in the shop once she's old enough for me to leave, if that's all right. We need the money, and I need to get out of the house." She laughed awkwardly.

Vi frowned, wondering just how hard things might be

for Ena.

"Mam says she'll look after Queenie for me," Ena added, picking up her daughter as she did.

Vi nodded. Looking at Ena holding little Queenie, she just couldn't find any words to say.

CHAPTER 23

Thursday 1st January 1920 - Notabilities Whom The King "Delights to Honour" - The Daily Mirror

Billy was happy to have Christmas out of the way. For one thing, he was glad to see the back of Percy Mayberry for a while. He knew the man goaded him deliberately, but he couldn't stop himself rising to the bait. When Percy said only idiots joined up, Billy's temper always flared. It wasn't as though the man ever did an honest day's work.

So much had been happening at once, and Billy needed time to think. As soon as he had the opportunity to be on his own, he took Nipper for a long walk. He would have gone down to the river, but at this time of year, with the mud, he couldn't be sure of his footing if he was alone. Instead he walked through the streets to where Stan had lived. How he missed Stan at times like this. Stan would have told him to stop being a silly sod, for finding it hard watching all of Vi's success when he felt so useless. He could hear his mate's voice telling him how lucky he was to have a girl like Vi, and that he should make the most of it.

Billy looked at the house that had been Stan's mam's. They really hadn't had much, but Stan rarely complained. What would his mate make of Billy now, having an office job? He still felt his job at Caulder and Harrison had been a pity appointment, whatever anyone said to the contrary, although he hoped his promotions had been genuine. Now there was the job that Terence was offering; perhaps that was just the same.

He went and leaned against the railings at the end of the road, looking down onto the railway embankment. Life had seemed so simple when they were children, or at least his had. He knew much more about Stan's life now than he had back then. They first met when Stan stole food because he was so hungry. Billy had never known life like that. He'd never known how it felt to have to darn his own socks as a child, or go barefoot. And he'd never known how to be grateful for the things life did give him.

What if Stan had refused the sandwich Billy gave him in place of the food he'd been stealing? For one thing they'd never have been friends, but had Billy done that out of pity? He supposed he had in a way, but that wasn't how he'd felt. He'd been sharing the good things he had with someone who needed them. It had made him feel good, as well as helping Stan. He shook his head; if only he didn't keep letting his own pride get in the way. Perhaps it was time to stop feeling sorry for himself. Stan never had, and he'd had a lot to feel sorry for himself about. Then, with a sudden pang, Billy thought of Davy. He had been Terence and Audrey's only child; they must miss him dreadfully.

He looked down at Nipper, who was happily rolling in the gutter, and smiled. To Billy it was dirt, but to Nipper that was paradise. That was the attitude he needed. Make the most of whatever was on offer and find a use for it. Well, he couldn't guarantee changing how he felt overnight, but he'd take the job that Terence was offering as a first step and see how he got on.

When he arrived home, he went straight to the drawer and took out some paper. Before there was any risk of changing his mind, he wanted to write his letter of resignation to Caulder and Harrison, so that he could hand it in the following day. It felt like a big step. He'd never resigned from a job before, although he supposed he had when he left his carpentry work to join the army, but that felt different.

Vi came in while he was writing, but said nothing. He'd tell her he'd gone ahead when he came home the following day. He was scared that if he talked about it now, he might just slip back into his negative thoughts.

He was in the accounts office on time the following morning, having already been to the personnel office. He was just settling into work when the accounts manager came over to him.

"Mr Dobson, might I have a word?"

Billy felt like a wild animal that had been cornered. It was an odd feeling. He stumbled as he got to his feet and only just stopped himself falling. If they needed any proof he wasn't fit for the job, they had it right there.

He followed Mr Everly to his office.

"Sit down, Mr Dobson."

Billy sat on the edge of the chair and waited.

Mr Everly had Billy's resignation letter in front of him. "You've been a good worker, Mr Dobson. I don't mind telling you, I'll be very sorry to see you go. Now, I've already spoken to Mr Giffard and we were wondering if you would consider staying if we were to give you a rise."

While Mr Everly talked about his future opportunities at Caulder and Harrison, Billy simply sat there feeling stunned. They wanted him to stay. This wasn't about pitying him. They didn't have to say any of this.

"It's very kind of you, Mr Everly, and I won't say that I'm not flattered. It's just, I've been offered a better position, and I'd really like to take that up."

He even felt taller as he left Mr Everly's office. He'd never thought for a moment that they might want to keep him.

Going to work for T Moore & Son felt like a new start. No one had asked Terence to take him on. This was not because he was unemployed and in need. This was because of his own skills, and he intended to make the most of it. The strangest thing would be moving to being paid monthly instead of weekly, but if he could manage the accounts for the shop then he could certainly do that for their home. He'd even been to the Post Office to open a savings account.

Billy had always been neatly turned out since working in the accounts office of Caulder and Harrison, but to say that his suit had seen better days would be understating the situation. He went to see the outfitters which neighboured Vi's shop and agreed to them making him a suit which he could pay for over the next few months. Vi had been cross and said she could have made it, but with the orders they had for hats she was already working all hours. It was important to him to look the part from day one. He supposed there would be men who'd worked at the factory for a long time who'd resent the newcomer, and he didn't want to give them more grounds than necessary to laugh at him.

"I'll take you around the factory and introduce you to everyone you need to know," Terence said to him on his first day in February.

The machine shop was very noisy and it was difficult to talk as they walked through. Billy looked closely at what the men were doing and frowned. Some of it didn't look so very different from the woodwork he used to do, but with metal rather than wood.

"As I explained, we make machine tools. It's highly skilled work. What we produce is used to make a wide range of finished products, even cars," Terence explained as they went from one part of the factory to the other. His eyes twinkled as he said it. "The finished products can only ever be as good as the tools they use enable them to be. We have to be the best of the best." They carried on into the next machine room and conversation had to stop again.

Billy had his own office, which neighboured that of Terence. He sat at his desk later in the day and shook his head. He wanted to capture this moment in his mind forever. It felt good. He was going to work as hard as any man could, to learn this business and be useful. He was impressed by what he'd seen, and wanted to do it justice.

Each evening whilst Vi sat working on a hat and Nipper sat by his chair, he entertained both Vi and Tommy with stories such as having to use the telephone and how you placed a call through the operator. He told them about the machines and what they made, and how he needed to work out how they might be more efficient and have less waste. Tommy hung on every word.

It felt much easier to be pleased for Vi now he didn't feel so worthless.

"What do you think of me taking someone on full time?" Vi asked him one evening as they talked. "We've been running for a few months now and we have a very long order book. I need to teach someone else to make the hats with me, and maybe serve in the shop too."

Billy had been thinking about that himself. The accounts were looking better than they could have hoped for, and Vi never had a moment to herself. "Did you have anyone in mind?" He thought he knew the answer. Vi would want someone she could trust.

She nodded.

He thought she was about to suggest her sister, and he was apprehensive about that as a possibility.

"Tessie," she said firmly. "I always used to say she could work with me if I ever fulfilled my dream."

Billy blinked with relief. Tessie was a good girl, steady and reliable. She'd managed to stay on at Caulder and Harrison, but he didn't doubt she'd be happy to leave. "You need to be realistic on what you can pay her and the number of hours. You may not be able to do much more than match what she's earning now." He thought carefully and sighed. "Then there's the football. If you're both still playing..." He left the sentence hanging. Vi would see for herself that could be difficult.

Vi smiled and looked a little guilty. "Audrey says she's happy to keep looking after things, and there is always Ena."

Billy stiffened. He still didn't want to say anything to Vi, but he'd noticed small discrepancies on the till every time Ena worked. He hoped it was just errors, but he wasn't completely convinced. "I think Tessie would be good." He needed to work out what was happening with Ena, but now wasn't the time to raise that.

"Billy," Terence said one morning, "I want you to go to London for me on Thursday, to represent the company in a meeting."

Billy sat stock still, wondering if he'd heard right.

"You'll go by train from Billingbrook; you may need to stay overnight and come back on Friday. Mr Wetherby will make all the arrangements for you. I'll brief you on what's needed before you go."

Billy didn't know what to think. Terence had such confidence that he could do this. Perhaps he was right. But London? The thought of travelling all that way on the train on his own was both exciting and terrifying. At least when he travelled with the army there had been a whole group of men. He stopped for a minute and thought about Stan and Davy. In a strange way, he was living the life that should have been Davy's. He wondered how differently the lad would have done things and hoped that Terence didn't think about the comparison too often. It must be hard for him. If Billy were ever to lose Tommy, he didn't think it was something he'd ever recover from.

Billy could hardly wait to see the look on Vi's face when he told her he'd be going to London. He wished he could take her with him, but maybe he could at least bring back some memento.

When she came in from the shop, she seemed to have more than normal to talk about, and Billy sat quietly until she'd finished. He wanted her undivided attention for this piece of news.

"What are you grinning for? Did I say something funny?" she asked eventually.

Billy could contain himself no longer. "What would you say if I told you I have to go to London this week?"

The colour drained from Vi's face. That wasn't the reaction he was expecting. He got up and went to her and ran his hand down her cheek. "Hey, what's wrong?"

There were tears in the corners of Vi's eyes and Billy frowned.

Vi took out her handkerchief and waved it wildly as she sniffed. "Oh, I'm being silly really. It's just that the last time you went away it was to go to war, and look what happened that time. I thought I was never going to see you again."

None of that had occurred to Billy. "Come here," he said, pulling her to him. "I'm only going for two days. I'll be back on Friday. It'll be fine." He kissed her and she looked at him with watery eyes.

"I love you, Billy Dobson."

"And I love you. Now, sit down and let me tell you what I have to do."

Before he boarded the train, Billy bought the day's newspaper to read as he travelled. One of the stories caught his eye. It wasn't the fact that there were so many women still unemployed, who were trained for nothing other than munitions work; that was unsurprising, given how many returning soldiers still had to find work. What made him shake his head was some Dame saying women should do domestic work and, whilst there were roles for servants, they shouldn't complain. He wondered what Vi would say if she saw the report. He supposed the woman was struggling to find servants herself. She probably meant well, but perhaps she should meet the likes of Vi.

The meeting he needed to attend was at the offices of a London lawyer and involved a large order which was being placed with T Moore & Son. Billy found the deference with which he was treated strange. He felt like an impostor and had to hide his occasional smiles, and the feeling he wanted them to call him Billy rather than Mr Dobson. They would have expected William rather than Billy, he supposed; but he'd never been William, not even when he was christened.

He stayed in a hotel near Euston station and, feeling he'd had more excitement for one day than he could reasonably handle, had a quiet meal in the hotel before retiring to bed. He did want to look at the city itself, but it all felt wrong without Vi. He wondered if they would ever be able to go there together. Thankfully, the hotel offered postcards which could be used by guests to send messages. He took two as gifts for Vi and Tommy.

When he arrived home that Friday, he couldn't wait to tell the rest of the family about his travels. He was barely through the door when he saw his father looking happier than he'd seen him for a very long time. "What's up, Dad?"

"Not until Vi's here too. I want to tell you both at the same time."

This wasn't like his dad at all. Billy's thoughts of London went from his mind, and he began to wonder what could make Alf so agitated.

"Vi," Billy called upstairs, presuming she was there.

"She's next door, talking to Tessie, I think," Dad said, going into his sitting room. "Bring her in as soon as she's back."

Nipper started barking before Vi was through their own gate. Billy opened the kitchen door for her. She ran the last few steps and wrapped her arms around him.

Billy grinned. "I take it you missed me then?"

"No," she said, laughing. "Well, maybe just a little bit. Tessie can start on Tuesday, after the bank holiday. How did you get on?"

"I rather think that's going to have to wait. Dad wants to talk to us. You don't suppose he's met someone, do you?" Billy frowned. It was the only thought he'd come up with, however unlikely it might sound.

"Your dad, meet someone else? I doubt that very much. He still worships your mam, God rest her soul. We'd best find out what he's up to."

Alf was smoking his pipe when they went in. He wafted some of the smoke away with his hand so he could see them better.

Once Vi and Billy were comfortable, it was Vi who Alf turned to. "I probably should have waited until the whole team was together to say something, but the Club has received a letter inviting you all to play some matches against women's teams in France, and to visit some of the Billingbrook regiment war graves. All part of this so called 'entente' that's going on."

Billy looked at Vi who was blinking rapidly. He wondered how many of them would be able to go. Of course, the football was important, but more than anything, he wanted Terence and Audrey Moore to travel with him, and he wanted to lay flowers on the graves of Stan and Davy, if they had specific graves. He couldn't speak. He could feel the tears rolling down his cheeks as he remembered his dear friends and what they'd all endured.

"Do they say when?" Vi asked eventually, her voice sounding a little shaky.

"No, love," Alf said. "I think we can suggest when it would work. I was thinking, if it was Wakes week, being the factory holiday, the factories would be shut, so it would be easier for the girls."

Billy's mind was racing. On that basis it might all be possible. They could do this. Perhaps they could all go to France. He didn't know how he'd feel about it, but maybe it would be good, and would help him to lay some of the ghosts to rest.

"Wouldn't it cost a lot of money?" Vi asked.

Alf drew on his pipe. "I daresay it would, but the Club says all the team's costs would be covered from the ticket money for the games you play. Anything over would go to charity. All the girls would need is a little bit of pocket money."

"Would you close the shop?" Billy asked Vi.

"I don't know. Maybe Audrey could run it."

Billy shook his head. He was quite firm when he said, "No, I think Terence and Audrey need to come with us. Davy…" But he couldn't say anymore.

Vi nodded and put her hand on his. "I'm sorry, I hadn't even begun to think about that. I was thinking of the football. This is going to be hard. Maybe Ena could do it."

Billy looked up sharply. That didn't sound like a good idea to him. He had no choice now but to talk to Vi about his suspicions.

CHAPTER 24

But when ye come, and all the flowers are dying,
If I am dead, as dead I well may be,
Ye'll come and find the place where I am lying,
And kneel and say an Avè there for me.
And I shall hear, though soft you tread above me,
And all my grave will warmer, sweeter be,
For you will bend and tell me that you love me,
And I shall sleep in peace until you come to me!
Danny Boy - Frederic E Weatherly 1913

Friday 21ˢᵗ May 1920 - Britain's Homage to Ypres: Pictures By Aeroplane - The Daily Mirror

"How dare you say that about my sister?" Vi didn't think she'd ever felt so angry with Billy. "My sister is not a thief."

"I'm just trying to explain that the times she's worked, the till has always been short. It never balances. Maybe she doesn't write things down properly and makes mistakes. I think there's stock missing too. Look, love, I'm just saying that if you're going to leave her in charge, you need to make sure she can do the job."

Vi didn't want Tommy to hear her shouting, so tried to keep her voice down. "Whatever you might think of Percy, you can't just assume that means Ena would do anything wrong. She's my sister. She's family. Families don't do things like that to each other." It was no good, she couldn't stay in the same room as Billy a moment longer. She went out to the kitchen and put her hands on the sink, as she took some deep breaths to calm herself down. He couldn't be right, could he? Vi wasn't absolutely sure she was angry with Billy. He'd told her a while ago that he had concerns, and she'd gone through everything again with Ena to make sure she'd understood. But what if he was right? What if she was taking money from the till, and taking stock too? Vi shook her head. She knew Ena. Her sister wouldn't do that. Besides, who else could she ask to manage the shop if Audrey was coming to France with them?

Vi kept out of Billy's way for a while, but she couldn't stay angry with him for long. She knew he just wanted what was best for her and the shop. When she went to bed he'd already gone up. She wasn't sure if he was asleep, but she snuggled in to his chest and whispered, "I'm sorry."

He nuzzled into her neck and whispered back, "I am too, love."

As Vi walked to work the following morning, she tried to think about what she could say to Ena. She couldn't ask her outright if there were a problem. Perhaps if she just went through everything again before they went to France, that should clear up any misunderstandings. She put the thought out of her mind. Besides, she needed to start thinking about the team going to France. Alf would tell the others that afternoon. She hoped all the girls would be able to travel, but that might not be possible.

The morning passed quickly and Billy came into the shop to walk with her to practice. He was sitting on a stool at the back waiting for her to be ready. He seemed quiet, and she wondered if he was still considering what to do about Ena.

"What are you thinking, love?" she asked.

"Me?" he said, looking up.

"Well, there's no one else here right now, so unless I've started talking to myself." She rested her hand on his shoulder.

He looked at her and she was surprised to see the tears in his eyes. As she was about to sit on the neighbouring stool, the shop bell rang and she cursed quietly.

Vi put on her shop face and went through to serve her customer. By the time she'd finished and returned to the back of the shop, she found a note from Billy. *'Wanted some fresh air. Will see you at football.'* She sighed heavily. Surely from how he'd reacted, this wasn't about Ena.

When Alf made his announcement, all the girls started talking at once.

"You mean someone else pays and we get to travel?"

"When will it be?"

"I won't be able to leave my granddad on his own for a week."

"Is it just us?"

"One at a time, please." Alf was gentle but firm as he tried to call them all to order.

This time the girls raised their hands with the questions they wanted to ask, and Alf did his best to cover what he could, and made a note of the things they'd need to find out.

"I've never been away from home, me mam'll worry. Where will we be staying?" Clara asked.

"I might be able to come if it's holiday week," Doris said, "but I'll need to make sure everything's covered at home first."

Although it was readily agreed that the holiday week at the end of July was definitely the best option, the girls who cared for elderly relatives or young children needed to see what they could put in place before committing.

"We need to work out if we've got a full team," Alf said as they walked home afterwards. "If they all tell us by next week, that should be enough time."

"Could we borrow players from somewhere else if we're short?" Billy asked.

"It's a thought," Alf said. "Let's see who can come first."

Alf seemed to be enjoying what was happening so much that Vi thought it might be a good time to talk to him about moving. If only Billy didn't seem so low.

That night, Vi was woken by Billy's screams. She came to with a start and wondered what was happening. It was a long time since he'd had nightmares like this, and until she was fully awake her first thought was that they were being burgled, but then she realised Billy wasn't likely to scream for that; he'd be up and trying to defend them, although with his leg that would be hard. Billy was still screaming and wasn't awake. Now Tommy was crying and Vi felt torn.

"Take Nipper downstairs, Tommy, and if the stove is still hot, put the kettle on. I'll come down soon."

Her tone must have been firm, as without question, and still sobbing, he headed for the door in the dark. Thankfully, Vi heard Billy's dad getting up, so knew that Alf would look after Tommy. With her hands trembling she tried to light the little lamp by the side of the bed. She needed to wake Billy, but she wanted the room to be light first. She'd learned a long time ago that if he was woken in the dark, he could lash out before he knew what was happening.

When Billy woke, he was sweating and panting. Vi used the same tone of voice that she'd used with Tommy, at least until Billy was fully conscious. "You're all right, Billy. You're at home in Ivy Terrace. You're safe. Now sit up and take a few deep breaths."

Vi gave him time to register his surroundings and sit up against the headboard.

"Oh, Vi. I was back there. We were in the trenches and the shells were falling all around us." He was shaking as he talked.

"You don't have to come on the trip to France if it would be better not to." Vi was quiet for a moment and then reached a decision. "I won't go either. I'll stay here with you and Tommy."

Billy's breathing had calmed, and he shook his head. "That's not what I want. I have to go. I need to see Stan and Davy's graves and say farewell. I have to be there for Terence and Audrey, presuming they come. I'm just glad that Wakes week in Billingbrook is the end of the month and not…"

He didn't finish the sentence, but Vi understood. In his mind, Billy was reliving those final days at the end of June and beginning of July in 1916. She wondered if the nightmares would continue from now until then. Getting through more than a month of that would be difficult for all of them.

Once Billy was calm, Vi went down to see Tommy. "I'm sorry, love," she said, wrapping her arms around him. "Dad will be all right again soon."

"Can Nipper and me sleep down here?" Tommy asked.

Vi hadn't the heart to say anything other than yes. It was hard for him to see the state his Dad was in. "I'll get you some blankets and a pillow," she said, kissing him on the forehead.

It was their Sunday to go to the Moores' house for tea.

"I'll talk to them about France, if that's all right with you," Billy said, as he and Vi walked and Tommy cycled across Billingbrook. "Maybe Tommy could play outside while I do. He's had enough grief for one day."

Vi nodded. She could see the sense in what Billy was saying.

Terence and Audrey were very quiet as Billy told them what was planned. Audrey dabbed the corners of her eyes.

"We heard from the War Office telling us where David's buried, you know," Terence said after a while. "We'd already said we'd like to go and say a goodbye at his grave."

Billy nodded. "I don't know about Stan. I need to find out. It's going to be hard for all of us."

"Hard, but it is what we want to do. Need to do," Terence corrected himself, holding tight to his wife's free hand.

Terence turned to Vi. "Being holiday week, there's very little we can't arrange at the factory for it to be possible for both Billy and me to be away. How will you cover the shop? Will you close?"

Vi shook her head. "I thought Ena could look after things. Little Queenie will be seven months old; Mam will be happy to look after her I should think."

Billy was frowning, but Vi was sure that some retraining for Ena would soon sort any problems.

"Mam and Dad might have a bit of a full house though. I was going to ask if Tommy could stay there too. I can't really take him with us. For one thing it could be very difficult, and for another it doesn't seem fair on the other girls who have arrangements to make." Vi sighed. This was harder than she'd first thought.

On Saturday 24th July, the team, and one or two others who were accompanying them, including the Moores and a representative from Billingbrook United, gathered at Billingbrook station in plenty of time to catch their early train to London, and then on to the coast. Vi was still thinking of things she'd meant to say to Ena in preparation for her looking after the shop.

Billy rested his hand on her arm. "Just forget the shop for a week. There's no more you can do."

Vi laughed. How on earth had he known what she was thinking?

As the train sped through the English countryside, the girls were by turns excited and anxious. Not one of them had been away from home before, and they had no idea what to expect.

"You see all sorts in the newspapers," Tessie said. "Will we be safe going across London?"

Billy laughed. "I was all right on my own, and it's not as though I could have run very fast. I'm sure we'll be fine travelling as a group."

Tessie seemed mollified, but her concerns were not helped by the girls sharing all sorts of stories they'd heard, of everything from flashers to kidnapping, although none of them knew any reliable sources of the information.

Terence and Audrey were paying for their own trip, but were travelling in the same carriage with the rest of the party. Vi could see how uncomfortable Audrey looked, being squeezed in as they were. It made her admire the woman even more for trying to fit in, rather than travelling in the first class section. It reminded her of what Billy had told her about Davy wanting to join up with the local lads, even though it meant missing out on the officer training he'd have had if he went with lads from his school.

The party occupied several compartments.

"Who'd have thought we'd need this much luggage for a week?" Clara had a bag at her feet, as there was no more space on the racks. "I've got more football shirts than I have dresses. Perhaps I should wear those to the evening dos we're attending."

The others laughed.

Vi sat quietly, holding Billy's hand and wondering if he was thinking back to when he first travelled to the coast.

When they boarded the ferry at Dover, Billy said, "It's a bit different from the last time I did this."

Vi could tell that his smile was forced.

"I wanted to take you and Tommy to the seaside as we'd always said we would. We still haven't been. Maybe when we get back." This time Billy's smile seemed more genuine.

The team was staying just outside Paris for the next couple of nights and would be playing their first match the day after arriving. Fortunately, both Terence and Audrey spoke reasonable French and would act as interpreters. Audrey said she was glad there was a way to justify her joining the trip. Otherwise it didn't seem fair to all the other families in Billingbrook who had lost sons or husbands in the war.

When Vi saw the welcoming party waiting to greet them, she gasped. "Oh, Billy, never mind all the people, just look at those hats." She tried to take in every detail so she could sketch them later. How wonderful it would be to bring Paris fashions direct to Billingbrook. They sometimes appeared in the papers and magazines, but they never showed this many styles.

They were greeted in faltering English and Vi wished she'd taken the time for Audrey to teach her a few words in reply. Audrey stepped forward, and looked taller and more elegant as she did so. Vi presumed she was passing on greetings from Billingbrook and from the team, from the odd words she caught, but the waiting crowd seemed delighted to be addressed in their own language.

Over the next few days, the girls barely stopped. Between the matches against the French teams, sightseeing and official receptions, the time passed quickly. They played four matches, and there were good crowds at every one of them. Vi had little chance to think about the shop, but she was missing Tommy and sent him a postcard every day.

The French teams they played against were good, but the Billingbrook girls held their own and won two of the matches. Whilst, of course, Vi loved the football, the highlight of the earlier part of the week was the cabaret they went to in Paris.

"Just wait until I tell Ena. Those dresses and the singing. Oh, Billy, I do hope we can go again one day." Vi felt like dancing along the street when they came out at the end of the performance.

"We've never even thought of going to the theatre in Billingbrook before, never mind Paris." Billy chuckled. "It's a bit different to the local revues we could go to when I was in the army."

Vi felt as though some of the glamour had rubbed off on her as they returned to their hotel. "I have thought about going to the theatre at home, but it's not something we could easily afford to do." Reality would have to wait;

for now she was a real lady, enjoying Paris.

On Friday morning they headed back to Northern France. Whilst the whereabouts of many of the dead was still not known, the team was due to attend a ceremony at a cemetery where a number of the Billingbrook soldiers had been laid to rest, including Private David Moore, Davy.

It was a sombre party who stepped down from the bus when they reached the cemetery near Thiepval. Most of the girls didn't want to walk amongst the neatly kept graves. There were no headstones, but each had some form of marker showing who was laid to rest there. Vi was touched by how well kept the cemetery was, and by the flowers that bloomed all around them.

After a brief ceremony led by a local dignitary, and with prayers said by a local priest, most of the party stayed close to the entrance. Vi went with Billy and Davy's parents across the graveyard, through row after row of graves, until their guide stopped at the one where Private David Moore lay buried.

Audrey's shoulders heaved as she gulped tears of loss. Terence stood by her side with his arm around her, his face ashen.

Vi supported Billy as he stepped forward and laid flowers on the grave.

"Goodnight, brave soldier," he said in a shaky voice. "And to Stan, and every last one of the men who didn't come home." He stepped back, took his stick, and then stood away to one side.

Vi didn't know what to do. Seeing the hundreds of graves had shocked her to the core. Of course she'd known there were thousands dead, but it was one thing knowing it as a fact on paper and quite another seeing it laid out before you so starkly. She waited quietly and thanked God that Billy had been one of the lucky ones.

It was a very quiet party which re-boarded the bus to head for their final night's hotel.

"Audrey and I have decided to make a donation to the Imperial War Graves Commission," Terence said to Billy. "We want to support the work they're doing making sure there are suitable resting places for all our soldiers. We're some of the lucky ones, knowing where our David is. Maybe one day there will be a marked grave for your friend Private Bradley."

Billy wiped his eyes. "That's very kind of you. Thank you."

Vi looked around at the countryside they were travelling through. There was still evidence of the barbed wire and the aftermath of war. They passed buildings which were derelict, damaged beyond repair by the shells. Even though the war had been over for nearly two years, it gave her a glimpse of the life that Billy had endured; the life which had led to years of nightmares, and she shuddered.

CHAPTER 25

Saturday 31ˢᵗ July 1920 - Kidnapped General Rescued: Road Fight - The Daily Mirror

By the time the train pulled back into Billingbrook that Saturday, Vi was more glad to be home than she had been to arrive in Paris. They went back with Alf to Ivy Terrace with their bags, before going to collect Tommy and Nipper from her parents.

Vi wasn't sure which of the two had missed them most, as both boy and dog came barrelling straight into her and Billy when they arrived. She was as ready to cling to Tommy as he seemed to be to them.

Ena was there with the baby when they went in. Vi was pleased to see her. It meant she could find out how the week had gone at Hats and Haberdashery without any delay, and she was almost as ready for news on that as she had been to see her son; but Tommy definitely came first.

Once she and Tommy let go of each other and they'd answered the immediate questions about their journey, Vi turned to speak to Ena. She frowned. Ena had taken baby Queenie and left without so much as saying goodbye.

"Did I say the wrong thing?" Vi asked, turning to Mam.

"I shouldn't take it personally," Mam said. "I expect she needed to get back."

Vi looked at Billy, who had a very worried expression on his face.

"You don't think something's happened, do you?" Vi asked Billy as they were on their way home. "I mean, in the shop."

Billy let out a heavy sigh.

"You don't trust her, do you?" Vi realised her voice sounded angry.

Billy nodded. "I'm sorry, but no, I don't."

"I didn't want to believe you when you said she might be stealing from us. You don't really suppose she is, do you?" Vi bit her lip as she waited for Billy to reply.

"I don't think they were innocent mistakes that needed training," Billy said.

They were quiet as they walked. Vi was trying to come to terms with Billy's thoughts. She hoped he was wrong. "What makes you so sure?"

"The till has never balanced on the days she's covered. It's only ever a few pence here and a shilling there, but there are always differences, and the overall balance in the till is always lower. I'm not really sure all the sales are written in the ledger either. Our sales never seem quite so good when Ena's in the shop. I did try to explain to you."

"They're bound to be lower if I'm not there. People make appointments to see me." Vi couldn't bear it if Billy was right. When he'd talked about it before she'd blocked it out. She knew Ena, and whilst she might not be bright, she'd always been honest. That was why she'd put all that extra time into making sure Ena understood exactly what she was supposed to do. It was just a matter of training. Wasn't it?

"The lower figures would make sense, if it was only the orders for hats which were down; but it's the small items like buttons and thread too."

Vi's heart sank. She wanted to argue with him, but she

knew he was good at what he did. It was why she was so happy for him to look after the business side.

"I didn't have enough proof. If I'd pushed the matter without being able to prove it, then we'd just have argued more, and I didn't want that. I hate seeing you upset."

"I'm upset now," Vi said, pouting. "Do you think we should go to the shop tomorrow, even though it's Sunday? We can at least pick up the books and check through what's there."

"It might be a good idea. Sorry, love."

Vi couldn't stop thinking about what Billy had said. The way she saw it, if Ena had asked her for help with money, she would have tried to do something. Surely her sister must know that? She knew it was hard for her. Percy wasn't exactly the reliable type, in and out of work. Mind you, he was a lot better than that brother of his. They'd often wondered which side of the line he was treading. Given what she knew of the Mayberry family, it wasn't so hard to believe that Ena might have been tempted, but never from family. That wasn't how their parents had brought them up. Didn't that count for anything?

She slept badly that night, wondering what they'd find out the following day. As she lay awake, she said a prayer asking for there to be a much simpler explanation to Ena's odd behaviour, and the discrepancies Billy had noticed. She also hoped Billy knew what they should be looking for in the figures, as she really didn't have a clue where to start.

Vi felt mean going out after breakfast and leaving Tommy behind, so soon after coming back from France. She was tired from their travels and would have preferred a quiet day at home, but she could not wait any longer to find out whether Billy's suspicions were correct.

When she turned the key in the lock of Hats and Haberdashery, her hand was shaking. The window display looked exactly as she'd left it, which she was pleased about.

"We'll start with the ledger and the bank book," Billy said.

As they stepped inside, Vi didn't need to look at the figures. "Billy!" She felt her legs turning to jelly and staggered over to the counter for support. "Where's it all gone?" She looked around the shop, at the gaps on the shelves where there should have been rolls of cloth. Three of her sample hats were missing from their stands, and the till wasn't just empty; it was completely missing. She sat down heavily on a stool. Even her nightmares hadn't prepared her for this.

"What are we going to do?" Vi could hear the wail in her own voice. How could she open the shop the following day without any stock?

Billy ran his hand through his hair and looked around. Letting out a low whistle, he went over to Vi and took her hand. "I'm sorry, love. I should have insisted we found someone else. I didn't want…" But his voice trailed off.

Vi nodded and felt shame wash over her. "What do we do now?"

"Well, we need to make a list of what's missing." Billy walked around the shop as he spoke. "And then we ought to go to the police."

"No, please don't." Now Vi felt rising panic. It was one thing realising her own sister had stolen from her, but she couldn't go to the police. "We should go round to talk to Ena."

"Would you mind if I talk to Terence?" Billy asked, turning another full circle and shaking his head. "We could really do with someone with more experience on this."

"But she's my sister. How can I tell other people what she's done?"

"Vi, love, she's depending on you not telling anyone. That's how she thinks she'll get away with it. As it is, we're going to have to use all the money from our savings to cover the loss, if we aren't going to report the theft. Even then there might not be enough."

Vi felt the tears falling. Just as she thought they were ready to move to a bigger house. She didn't know how much was missing, but she guessed paying it back wasn't going to leave them a lot to spare. She could see the sense in asking Terence Moore for some advice, but she really didn't want anyone else to know. Until this, she thought she and Ena were close. How could she ever trust her sister again?

Over the rest of the morning, she and Billy took an inventory of what was in the shop and what seemed to be missing.

"I noted everything we bought. If we use that and the records of what's been sold, we should be able to work out what's gone, but that relies on the sales records being correct. At least this way we have something to check it against," Billy said as they reached the last drawer of haberdashery.

"Do you think Terence and Audrey will mind us just turning up on a Sunday lunchtime? Perhaps we should go home first." Vi would have done almost anything to delay having to explain what had happened to anyone, even if she could see the sense in it.

"If I go home now, I won't want to come out again." Billy looked at her. "Sorry, love. I know this is hard."

Vi sighed heavily and turned in the direction of the Moores' house.

Once they'd finished explaining, Terence nodded. "I can see why you don't want to go to the police, but that's the only way you can recover anything. An insurer won't pay out without that."

"I know." Vi couldn't look at either Terence or Audrey. She couldn't help feeling that Ena's behaviour reflected on her, and the rest of the family too, and that was unbearable. Her parents were good people. They might be poor, but they'd never do something like this.

"I did wonder…" Audrey said, "Oh, I should have said something, but it wasn't anything I could put my finger on. Just little things. I presumed she had some arrangement with you. I should have checked. I'm sorry."

"You're sorry?" Vi said, shaking her head. "Why should you need to be sorry? This is my sister. It's my fault."

"This is not your fault." Terence spoke firmly. "You weren't to know. It's just a pity it's gone this far. I can understand why you don't want to go to the police, but I do think you need to talk to Ena. In my experience, and I've had problems in the factory to know, I doubt you'll get anything back. From what you've said about what's been taken, I suspect this was planned and it will all have been sold on by now. It may even have been stolen to order. Billy, tomorrow, rather than coming to the factory, spend the day helping Vi sorting out what reordering is needed and getting the shop straight. You'll need to change the locks too. We can talk when you know the final numbers, but if you need a hand, we'd be happy to lend you the money." He looked to Audrey for her agreement, and she gave a swift nod.

"Thank you," Vi said quietly, trying desperately not to cry. She felt as though she'd let Billy down by not listening to the concerns he'd raised, but she really had thought she could trust her sister. It was going to be hard, but she'd give up the football so she could cover the shop. Audrey couldn't do all of it on her own. All Vi's other friends were teammates, so she couldn't offer the job to them, and if she couldn't trust family, she didn't think she'd be happy to employ a complete stranger to work there.

Neither she nor Billy felt much like eating until they'd sorted things one way or another. When they left Terence and Audrey they headed straight to the Mayberry family house, which wasn't far from where Vi's parents lived. Vi wondered if Ena would open the door to them. She and Billy didn't speak as they walked. They both seemed to be lost in their thoughts.

When they arrived outside the small terrace, Billy knocked on the front door while Vi stood to his side.

Percy opened the door. Leaning against the door frame blocking the entrance, he said, "What do you want?"

"We'd like to speak with Ena," Billy said, and Vi could see he was clenching his fist.

"Would you now? Well, she ain't here, so you can't." Percy's voice was taunting as he spoke.

Vi heard Queenie cry in the room behind Percy, and then distinctly heard Ena's voice hushing her daughter.

"It sounds to me as though she is there," Billy said.

"And what are you going to do about it, cripple?" Percy laughed at Billy.

Vi cleared her throat and came forward. "I'd like to see my sister, please."

Percy slowly took his weight off the wall, took a pace back and closed the door, leaving Vi and Billy standing outside.

Vi hammered on the door, but the only effect was that Queenie started wailing more loudly.

"Come away, love. You won't do any good."

The weight of sadness in Billy's voice cut straight through Vi. He'd lost an arm and a leg fighting for his country, and now it had left him unable to stand up for his family. Vi was more angry with Percy for what he'd said to Billy than she was about her sister's theft. How could he be so cruel? A man who did everything to avoid going to fight himself. She stepped down to the pavement and took Billy's hand.

"Now what?" she asked.

Billy shrugged. "We could talk to your mam and dad."

"No," Vi said, rather more firmly than she intended. "I don't want to drag the rest of the family into this. It's between me and Ena."

"Then I guess we go home and count what's in the piggy bank."

Vi was relieved that Billy sounded resigned to what had happened rather than cross. She wouldn't blame him if he were, but he always had been slow to anger, and she was thankful. He was a good man.

It took weeks to get the shop back into shape. They saw nothing of Ena in that time, and Vi missed her, despite everything. She'd tried going to the house again, but no one would even open the door to her now.

Vi worked all hours in an attempt to make up for the money they'd lost, and took no time off for football, except if they practised on a Wednesday evening when the shop was closed.

"You'd better choose a new captain for the team," she said to Alf at the start of September. "There's our first cup match of this year in two weeks, and there's no one to work with Audrey in the shop. She did mention a friend from the WI, but I guess as she's said no more about it, the lady wasn't interested."

"I've been thinking about that," Billy said. "Why don't I do it? I know it means I won't be there to support you in the game, but do you honestly want to give up?"

Vi shook her head sadly. "I still want the chance to lift that cup before I hang up my boots. But you've worked so hard on the coaching; it doesn't seem right for you to miss out when this is my fault."

"No," said Billy firmly. "I want to do it. I'm sure we'll find someone else in time, and I want to see you win just as much as you do. Besides, Tommy would miss being the team mascot."

Vi still felt a little shiver of excitement hearing the team called Billingbrook United Women's Team. Many of them were still the former Caulder and Harrison staff team, but somehow it was different. They weren't treated the same as the men's team, but it was still more official sounding.

This season, for the first round of the cup they had drawn Blackburn at home. Vi smiled, remembering back nearly five years to their very first match at Whittingham Road, when Blackburn had beaten them by three goals to their two. This time, the expectations on the Billingbrook team were much higher after their overseas trip. It might only have been local teams, similar to their own, that they'd played in France, but they were still referred to as international players by the press. At least playing on through the summer had helped to keep them all fit.

As they walked out onto the pitch ahead of the match, Vi could have sworn the cheering from the crowds was even louder than it had been the previous season. She couldn't help but smile. Looking at the faces of the other girls, they clearly felt the same way as she did. From the point the game started, however, she was under no illusions they would need to work hard to beat this Blackburn team. The opposition were playing as though they had nothing to lose, and threw themselves into every opportunity.

By half-time there was no score and, in contrast to the start, Vi walked off the pitch with her head down, feeling sad that Billy wasn't there.

"You can do this, Vi. Do it for me."

"Billy?" she said, looking up in surprise. "What are you doing here?"

"I'll tell you later, but I promise the shop is in safe hands and is open for business. Now put a smile on that beautiful face and give them hell."

Vi laughed and nodded. She turned to the others. "You heard that, girls, we're going to give them hell."

It was an altogether different Billingbrook team which took to the pitch for the second half. Vi came alive knowing Billy was cheering her on. She called instructions to the girls and led by example. After ten minutes of the second half they had scored two goals, and had no intention of letting up. By the full time whistle, the scoreboard showed four goals to Billingbrook and none for Blackburn. They were back, and Vi was determined to make the most of it.

"So what did you do to the shop?" she asked Billy as they left the ground.

"You've got Audrey to thank rather than me. She had

it all planned. When I arrived, she introduced me to a dear friend of hers from the Women's Institute. Quite honestly, I don't think I'd have argued with Mrs Ringwood for anything. She seemed very efficient and scared me as much as Matron at Billingbrook Hospital." Billy pulled a face of mock horror.

Vi laughed.

"Audrey said she was sorry you hadn't met Mrs Ringwood ahead of today, but she only received her reply last night and there wasn't time to let you know. Mrs Ringwood is going to call in on Monday to meet you properly. I would trust that woman with my life, and I've only just met her," Billy said.

"I used to think I could say that about Ena," Vi replied.

By their away match against Calderley in October, Mrs Ringwood had become a regular part of the shop team and seemed very happy. If Vi was honest, she was slightly scared of the woman, or at the very least in total awe of her. Her brisk efficiency kept them all on their toes, and things were starting to go well.

Vi had grown to hate playing Calderley. She'd never forgotten some of their tactics in earlier games, and went into the matches expecting the worst; that made her nervous, and less likely to play at her best. Despite that, the team put in a solid performance, and when the whistle blew, Vi felt an enormous sense of relief. They had scored three goals to Calderley's two. It wasn't a wide winning margin, but that didn't matter at all; it was a win. Calderley were out of the cup, and Billingbrook were through to the quarter-finals.

CHAPTER 26

Monday 15th November 1920 - Seven Mile Queue Of Pilgrims At The Cenotaph - The Daily Mirror

To Vi's surprise, Billy was whistling when he came into the house one Monday evening in November.

"Whatever's put you in such a good mood?" she asked as she folded the last of the clothes from the rack in front of the fire.

"Close your eyes and put your hands out."

Billy was grinning broadly, and Vi really wondered what he'd been up to. She obliged and put out her hands. She felt something two or three inches long, but slim and quite heavy for its size.

"Keep your eyes closed and tell me what it is," Billy said.

Vi ran her fingers along the item, from the curved top with some sort of string threaded through, along the shaft to the irregular edge, which stuck out at the end. "It's a key."

"Got it in one. Now guess where the lock is that it fits." Billy was laughing now. "Oh, and you can open your eyes."

Vi looked down at the key, it was similar to the one for the back door of Ivy Terrace. "Billy, is this what I think it is?"

Billy nodded, his grin broad. "It's just for you to look

at. We don't have to have this house if you don't like it, but it's empty now and we can see it as soon as we like. If we want it, it's ours. If we don't, then we'll start looking for somewhere else."

Vi flung her arms around him. She had so many questions she didn't know where to start. "Where is it? Does Dad know? How big is it? Can we afford it? How did you find out about it? When do we move?"

"Stop, stop." As Billy tried to calm Vi, Nipper had picked up on her excitement and was barking madly, which brought both Alf and Tommy to the kitchen.

"I thought we were being burgled with all that noise," Alf said.

"Come and sit down." Billy took Vi's hand. "Let me tell all of you at the same time."

"Hang on." Vi extricated herself so she could fold the clothes horse out of the way and then followed.

"Dad already knows most of this, but I didn't want to raise your hopes again if we couldn't afford to do it," Billy said, looking first at Vi and then at Tommy. "It's a three-bedroom house. It's much bigger than the one we were looking at before, and even has a small garden. Dad would come with us, if that's all right? That's how we can afford to do it. He'd give up this place and help with the costs of the new one. If you decide you like it, then it would be possible to move in before Christmas."

"Will I have my own room?" Tommy asked.

"Yes, you would," Billy said.

"Can Nipper sleep in with me? In case I'm scared."

Vi looked from her son to the dog and nodded. Tommy began jumping up and down with excitement.

"When can we see it?" Vi said, turning to Billy.

"It would be best to see it in the light. Terence says I can have Wednesday afternoon off to take you over there."

Vi felt her face would ache from how much she was smiling, but she just couldn't stop. Of course she was happy for Alf to be part of it. She'd been worried about leaving him on his own, and he was an important part of their family.

She began thinking of all the things she'd need to do in preparation. When they lost all the money in the summer, she put any hope of moving out of her head. She didn't think it was going to be possible for a long time. Maybe this wasn't the right house, but she was hoping they might all like it and that they really could be in by Christmas.

Wednesday afternoon couldn't come soon enough for Vi. Because she was scared of being disappointed, she spent the time telling herself all the things which might be wrong with the house and which might mean they couldn't take it. Tommy was at school, so she, Billy and Alf went immediately after they'd finished lunch. She couldn't have waited a moment longer. They even left the washing up until later, which felt very decadent. Whatever would Elsie have said? Vi smiled at the thought.

There was a low wooden gate leading from the pavement into the small front garden. The gate could do with a coat of paint, but that was easy to sort out.

"I could build an archway across here and grow roses around it," Alf said with a wistful look in his eye.

"And I could cut some of the flowers and have them on the windowsill." Vi was picturing yellow roses in a small vase.

Billy handed the key to her. "You go first, love."

Vi's hands were clammy as she took the key. She was glad it turned easily in the lock as she was shaking. She opened the door wide and took in the dark hall which lay ahead. The light from the front door showed it to be tidy but a little tired. Wondering where to start, Vi realised that the kitchen was probably the most important for her to decide if she could make the house work for them. She guessed it was a similar layout to many, and that the kitchen would be at the back of the house, through the door at the end of the hallway. Alf and Billy turned right into the front parlour, as she walked down the hall to find the kitchen.

"There's a pantry," she shouted with delight on finding the door from the kitchen to a narrow room with shelves along the walls, and a stone slab at the end to keep things cool.

The more she looked around, the wider she felt her smile become. Her face was aching from smiling so much. Then she went out of the back door into the yard and garden. "Oh, Billy, Alf, come and look at this."

It didn't take Vi long to feel sure they could be very happy living in the house. She'd taken her tape measure with her, just in case, and began measuring the windows for new curtains.

"Can we really afford this?" she asked, turning from Billy to Alf and back.

"It won't be easy. We won't have much money to spare for a while, but I think we can do it," Billy said.

"Then let's take it and move before Christmas." A surge of excitement ran through Vi as she said it.

"Don't you want to look at anywhere else?" Billy asked, resting against the wall in the back room.

Vi looked to Alf, who was smiling as broadly as she was. "No. I think this house is just perfect."

Billy came over and hugged her. "We'd best finish the measuring then, so you can make those curtains." He took the end of the tape measure that Vi was holding and went toward the window.

Back at Ivy Terrace, Billy sat down to write to their existing landlord to give notice, while Vi went next door to tell Tessie and Mrs Brown. She'd miss them being neighbours, but with Tessie working in the shop and still walking out with John, she'd see them almost as much as before.

In amongst all the excitement, there was barely time to think about the football. In the circumstances, Vi was glad the team had been drawn at home for their quarter-final match. Between packing boxes, making curtains for the new house and working, there simply weren't enough hours in the day. Their opponents for this round of the cup were from Manchester and, judging by the newspaper reports, they were a strong side.

On the day of the match, Billy and Alf went to the ground earlier and took Tommy with them, leaving Vi to walk on her own. She was grateful for half an hour to clear her head of shop business and think about the game ahead.

She still had the same bolt of excitement stepping through the gates at Whittingham Road. Even though the men's team were playing regularly again, the women drew large crowds and the matches were popular. They'd raised hundreds of pounds for the hospital over the years, and she was proud of that too.

The girls were playing well. The trip in the summer brought them together, and as they left the field after another win, Vi started to believe this might be their year to win the cup.

The semi-final would be on Boxing Day, but there was too much to do before that for Vi to spend long speculating. Moving into their new home two weeks before Christmas, whilst being a lovely idea, wasn't without complications. For one thing, the shop was busy, and everyone wanted hats made in time for the festive season, many as presents and others to wear to church. Vi did wonder at how appropriate it was for some women to want to outdo their friends in looking fashionable for church, but she was happy to have the sales, whatever their reasons.

"I've labelled the boxes which need to be kept handy. Don't leave anything behind, and don't forget..."

"Vi, I have it all under control." Billy kissed his wife. "Just make sure you remember where to come home to when you close the shop. Otherwise you'll have a long walk."

Vi picked up her coat and bag. "You will be all right, won't you?"

"Stop worrying. The men with the van will be doing all the lifting and carrying, and Alf is here to help too. I'll be fine. See you later." Billy ushered her out of the house.

Leaving Ivy Terrace for the last time felt very odd. She wondered how it would feel to Alf. Then, as she waited for Tessie on the pavement, she thought how strange it would be not to walk to work with her friend. Tessie was now nineteen, and over the five years they'd been friends she'd grown into a beautiful young woman. Vi wished John would hurry up and propose to her so she'd be family; as long as that didn't get in the way of either the football or the shop, of course.

Hats and Haberdashery was so busy with Christmas traffic that Vi put the house out of her mind as she worked; but as she locked up that evening her stomach was churning, and her hands were clammy. She almost ran in her haste to reach the semi-detached house in Bowland

Street. Number sixteen was on the right-hand side. She opened the gate and tried to imagine what it would look like when she and Alf had planted the front garden as they'd like it.

When she went inside, Vi was amazed to see how hard the boys had worked. Even Tommy was busy helping to unpack and put things away, although it might have been better if he'd been tasked with keeping Nipper out of the way.

Vi felt anxious as she put Tommy to bed that night in the small room at the front of the house. "We're only next door if you need us, and Nipper is here to look after you."

Tommy looked at his mother and frowned. "No, Mam, I'm looking after Nipper. We'll be fine. We have our own room when we stay with Aunty Audrey and Uncle Terence, don't we, Nipper?" Nipper jumped onto the mattress with Tommy.

Vi smiled. He seemed so grown up for nine years. "Grandpa will sort a bed out for you in the next week or two, so there's something to put this mattress on."

"It's better here," Tommy said, yawning. "It's easier for Nipper."

She laughed. How silly of her. Why hadn't she realised that was what he'd think?

Vi was glad they hadn't invited her family over to their house until New Year; by then she hoped it would be straight. She hadn't seen anything of Ena and Percy to ask if they would come. She wasn't really sure she wanted them in the house, and she was sure Billy didn't. Not including them didn't sit comfortably with Vi, even after all that had happened. She didn't even see them on Christmas Day, as they'd left her parents' house before she arrived.

"I don't know why they had to hurry off," her mam said, but then she didn't know what had happened. Vi wasn't going to spoil the day by telling her.

The Billingbrook girls had been drawn to play at home for the semi-final match on Boxing Day. Billy and Vi went to the Moores' for a Christmas drink before the match, although Vi settled for a cup of tea, as a sherry before her big football game seemed like a bad idea. Tommy was going to the ground with Alf, and then after the game, the whole team had been invited back to the Moores' house for what everyone hoped would be a Christmas celebration of the team going through to the final.

Except for the match itself, Tessie had talked about nothing else than their little party all week; even John had been invited to go with them.

It wasn't far from where Terence and Audrey lived to the football ground, but Terence suggested the four of them go in his car. He and Billy sat in the front, while Audrey and Vi went in the back. Vi had been in the car a few times now, but she still felt a thrill of excitement whenever she did.

Even Billingbrook looked beautiful when the sun peeped out from between the showers, as it did when they turned a corner driving out of the town centre.

"Steady on," Terence shouted, and Vi turned her head in time to see an automobile veering toward them from the other side of the road. It wasn't stopping. She gripped the door handle to brace herself as the vehicle hit the front of Terence's car and skewed them around into a tree on Billy's side. Vi's heart was thundering in her ears, and she realised Audrey was screaming. It was as though everything was happening in slow motion, and Vi's first thought was how out of character it was for Audrey to scream; then she turned her head to see Terence slumped over the steering wheel of the car. Vi was sitting behind Billy. Not only was the car caved in next to Terence, but it was Billy's side of the front which had hit the tree.

"Billy?" she said quietly.

There was a dazed grunt in reply.

The world seemed to return to normal speed, and Vi realised she couldn't just sit there. She had to get help. She turned her door handle. The door opened a fraction, but she would need to use force to open it wide enough to get out. She took her football boots out of the bag and put them on. Then she turned her feet to the door and kicked with all her might. The door made a grinding sound, but moved far enough on its hinges to create a gap.

"Audrey, come this way." But Audrey seemed stuck to the spot. Vi looked around frantically for help. Being Boxing Day, there were very few people on the street, and this wasn't a residential area. The other car was still blocking the road, and there was no sign of the driver of that car getting out either. Vi was relieved when a cyclist stopped to offer help, and then peddled away as fast as he could to fetch the police and medical support.

Vi wondered what she could do. She didn't think Audrey was hurt, just hysterical. She went back to the car and gently guided her out.

All Audrey kept wailing was, "Terence, Terence."

"I'm sure he's going to be fine," Vi said, though she was just as worried about Billy. Then she heard him.

"Vi, can you help me get this damn door open."

"Oh, Billy, my darling Billy." She tried pulling at the door, but it was wedged against the tree.

"Are you injured? Are you all right?" Vi tugged again

at the door, but fruitlessly.

"My leg's trapped. I think it's broken," Billy said.

Vi began to panic. With only one leg it would be impossible if anything happened to the other. "Oh, God, Billy, no."

He turned his head and looked at her. "Not my good one. It's my wooden leg that's broken. It doesn't hurt at all."

As relief washed over Vi, she found herself laughing uncontrollably. Or was she laughing? Her body was shaking violently and she was gulping down air, but she didn't feel humour in the situation. Her teeth began chattering. She hadn't realised that other people had stopped, but someone wrapped a blanket around her, and she became aware that there was a policeman taking over the situation. Meekly she allowed herself to be guided away from the car and onto a seat.

She had only a vague sense of what was happening as men pulled Billy and Terence out of the car and into an ambulance. They must have taken the other driver as well, and eventually another vehicle took her and Audrey to Billingbrook Infirmary.

"I need to send a message to Billy's Dad," Vi said to the nurse. "I need to tell them where we are and what's happened. He'll be worried."

"All in good time, Mrs Dobson," was all the nurse said, continuing her work with no-nonsense efficiency.

Vi and Audrey were given tea and checked for any injuries. Apart from shock, they had both suffered only minor grazes and bruises. Then they sat together, waiting for news of Billy and Terence and the driver of the other vehicle.

Billy was brought out to them, being wheeled in a chair.

"No news of Terence?" he asked.

Vi rushed over to him. She shook her head.

"Bad business. From what the policeman said, they think the other driver was blinded by the sun as he came around the corner and didn't see us or where the road went. He's alive, but I don't know any more than that."

Eventually a doctor came out to them. "Mrs Moore?"

Audrey got up.

"Your husband is asking for you."

Audrey burst into tears, and Vi put an arm around her.

"You mean he's alive?" Audrey asked.

The doctor smiled. "He'd have some difficulty asking for you if he weren't. Yes, madam, he's alive, but…"

Vi's heart sank. She hated buts.

"… he is badly injured, and it will take a long time for him to recover."

Now that Vi knew everyone was alive, her mind turned to Alf and Tommy. She hadn't even been able to get word to them as to what had happened. Then she thought about the football match. Was there any possibility the team could have won?

CHAPTER 27

When Vi and Billy went home from the hospital, Tommy came running to greet them. "Granddad said you'd be here soon. You missed the match."

Tommy showed no reaction to his Dad being in a wheelchair, and both his parents looking somewhat dishevelled.

"You missed the match," Tommy repeated without missing a beat. "We're out of the cup."

Vi felt the tiredness of the day's events and the disappointment of the news come crashing down on her. She saw the look on Alf's face as he stood behind Tommy.

"Are you all right?" he asked quietly. "I was worried."

Vi gave a half smile. Alf had always been one for understatement. She could see by his face that he'd been beside himself, but he'd still managed to keep Tommy calm, and she was grateful for that.

"I'll put Tommy to bed while Billy tells you what happened." Vi took Tommy's hand and led him along the hall.

"Can you bring my spare leg down?" Billy called after her.

Whilst Tommy got undressed, she took the old wooden leg down to Billy. It would do until the hospital could provide him with a new one that would be a better fit. Before Vi went back to tuck Tommy in, she heard a tapping at the back door.

She opened it to find Tessie and John standing there. Tessie wrapped Vi in a big hug. "Thank God, you're all right. What happened? We were worried sick when you didn't turn up, and then we went to Mr and Mrs Moore's house and there was no one there. The others left, but John and me waited, thinking you'd come back eventually. It was Mrs Moore who found us and said there'd been an accident. She was in a right state."

"Go into the back room, I'll be back down in five minutes. Let me sort Tommy out and I'll tell you the whole story — if Billy doesn't tell you first."

John gave Vi an awkward hug as he went past, which made her smile.

When she came back down after saying goodnight to Tommy, Tessie was in full flow.

"We just didn't know where you were. I wanted to come and look for you, but the referee said if we didn't start the match, then the Bolton girls would be given a bye. Mr Dobson," Tessie nodded to Alf, "said that whatever had happened, you wouldn't want that. Anyway, John said he'd go to look for you and we should play. We were awful, Vi. It was as though God had given us all two left feet for the afternoon. Nellie came on in your place. We were all so worried about you. I kept looking to see if John was coming back, and... well... the Bolton girls made the most of it. Sorry."

"How many did you lose by?" Vi felt a lump in her throat as she asked.

"We did score one, goodness knows how, but they got three past Edith." Tessie shrugged and looked very remorseful.

"It just wasn't to be," Alf added. "The good thing is that you'll be all right. I don't mind saying now that Tommy's in bed, I was worried daft. I just kept telling him everything would be fine, and you'd be home soon. I didn't know what else to say. I just hope Mr Moore will come through all right."

Vi kissed Alf's cheek. "You did a great job. He doesn't seem to have been worried at all, and we're fine." She looked across to where Billy was trying to fit his old leg comfortably. "Well, almost."

"I'm going to the hospital," Billy said the following day. "I need to see how Terence is."

"Perhaps I could come with you. I'd like to check on Audrey," Vi said. "Just give me five minutes."

Alf came out of the back room. "Tell me what needs to be done here. Tommy and Nipper can give me a hand."

"Thanks, Dad," Vi said. "If you can keep an eye on Tommy it'll help."

Alf turned to Tommy. "In which case, young man, you can help me digging our new vegetable plot at the end of the garden."

"Nipper will be good at that," Tommy answered, grinning.

Alf groaned. "I fear he might."

Audrey was sitting by Terence's bedside when they arrived at the hospital. She looked as though she'd been there all night. She must have returned after Tessie had seen her. Vi was surprised that Sister had allowed her back in.

"I'll take you home for a while," Vi said, taking

Audrey's arm. "Terence is asleep, and Billy can sit with him."

"He's lost a leg." Audrey spoke in a matter-of-fact tone, but Vi could see her lips quivering.

"A man can take wanting to be like me too far, you know," Billy said.

Terence opened his eyes and grunted, not as asleep as they'd thought. "You're going to have to stand-in for me."

Billy sat down heavily in the chair which Audrey had vacated. "You mean..."

"I mean you're going to have to run the company until I'm back."

Billy let out a low whistle. "You will tell me what to do, won't you?"

Terence nodded.

"I'm probably more use helping you with the leg, to be honest." Billy ran his hand through his hair.

"You can do that as well. I'm going to need it. One other thing..."

It was clear to Vi that Terence must have spent his waking moments working out how to move forward. It was no wonder he'd done so well when that was his attitude.

"We're going to need a driver and a new car. I asked Audrey, didn't I, darling?"

Audrey nodded. "I don't much feel like driving after what happened yesterday. I'm sure I'll get over it, but I'm not ready just now."

"I wonder if maybe Dad would take it on," Billy said. "He's already done some driving in Maud's dad's Morris Oxford. What do you think, Vi?"

Vi grinned. "I think he might insist on a peaked cap, but I suspect he'd love to do it."

Whilst Terence continued to talk through with Billy what needed to be done, Vi walked Audrey home and left her to get some rest.

Now that Vi knew Terence should be all right, she was struck by the disappointment of the team being out of the cup. She felt herself welling up, and looked around to make sure there was no one who might see her. She wasn't ready to give up. She'd give it one more season. She was so deep in thought that she was outside Ivy Terrace before she realised she'd walked back to the wrong house. She broke into laughter and decided she might as well have a cuppa with Mrs Brown and Tessie while she was there.

Over the next few months, Billy worked long hours. He was either at the factory keeping the business running, or he was with Terence helping with his rehabilitation and getting him walking again. Vi hardly saw him, but when she did he was happy, and that meant a lot to her. One of the benefits of Alf taking over the driving was that the automobile, when not in use on company business, or for the Moores' social engagements, was parked at the Dobsons' house, and Terence had kindly said they could use it. It certainly made visits to her own family easier to fit in.

By April, Terence was back in action and life was beginning to return to normal. Terence made sure that Alf still had time to coach the football, and they had matches at intervals against neighbouring teams. The one thing which continued to disappoint Vi was that she'd still seen nothing of Ena. It wasn't just that she missed her sister; she still wanted to understand why Ena had stolen from them. Queenie would be sixteen months old now, and Vi was sad to have missed so much of her growing up. Her own mam had been asking to know what had gone on between the girls, but Vi still didn't have the heart to tell her the whole story.

It was a Wednesday afternoon toward the end of the month, and Vi was making the most of the time away from the shop to weed a patch in the front garden where Alf planned to plant some flowers. He'd been growing quite a few plants from seed, ready to make a border by the path, but until the risk of frost had passed, they would stay safely under the glass cold frames at the back of the house. Nipper started barking, and Vi looked up to see what it was about. She wiped her hands on her apron and moved a stray strand of hair out of her eyes. Then she looked over the gate.

"Ena!" Vi scrambled to her feet.

Her sister was pushing a child's wheeled chair and carried a number of bags over the handles and others on her shoulder. She put them all down in a heap on the pavement, looking utterly dejected. "Please, I didn't know where else to go. Can we come in?"

Vi's heart was beating hard. She didn't say anything, but went to help Ena and led her into the kitchen.

Ena sat in the chair, shaking, while Vi put the kettle on. She wanted Ena to drink some hot sweet tea before she started asking her any questions. Whilst the tea brewed, Vi went to find a blanket and wrapped it around Ena's shoulders. Queenie was, thankfully, asleep in her chair, so Vi left her safely there.

Ena looked up at Vi with big soulful eyes. "He made me do it. I'm sorry. Really, I am."

Large tears were rolling down Ena's cheeks, and Vi didn't think her sister was enough of an actress for them not to be genuine. "Made you?" she said gently.

Ena nodded. "He said he wouldn't love me anymore if

I didn't do things for him. Said he'd throw me out, leave me in a gutter."

Vi frowned. "Why didn't you come to me for help then?"

"I couldn't live on what I earned on a Saturday in the shop. I had Queenie to think of and nowhere to go. You know there's no room at Mam and Dad's, and back then you had no spare space. Where else could I go?" Ena was gripping tightly to her now empty cup. Vi took it from her and poured a refill.

"And what's changed now?" Vi asked.

Ena frowned at her and looked around, as though it should be obvious. "You have all this now. There's room for us. It won't matter if I'm not earning anything when you're doing so well."

Vi took a sharp intake of breath. "Just tell me again what you're thinking."

"Well," Ena said, looking to be choosing her words carefully. "I could do a bit of housework for you, and maybe look after Tommy, but you wouldn't need me working as well, would you? I could stay at home and bring up Queenie. I could even do an hour or two at the shop if you needed me to."

"Oh, no." Vi stood up and started pacing the kitchen. "You've worked all this out, haven't you?" She loved her sister, but after what had happened, she certainly didn't want to take her in. What would she say to Billy; and Alf, come to that? She looked carefully at Ena; the tears had stopped, and she looked in complete control. Maybe she was a good actress. "How long have you been planning this little stunt? No, you can't stay here. We don't have room either."

"Come on, Vi. This house is big enough. Besides, I can't

go back now, and there's nowhere else I can go." Ena broke down sobbing.

This time Vi wasn't fooled by her theatrics. "Don't you think you should have talked to me before doing something as rash as this?" What was becoming clear to Vi was that her sister was intent on being manipulative, and that no one else's feelings mattered. Now what was she going to do? Ena would simply have to go back to Percy. If she'd only just come from the house, he probably hadn't even noticed their absence yet.

Billy came in through the back door. "Is everything all right? You've left the gardening things in the middle of the..." He stopped and looked at Ena. "What is she doing here?"

"I need to talk to you, in private, but..." Vi hesitated; the housekeeping tin was on the shelf. She didn't want to leave Ena in the kitchen with money around, but what else could she do? She was hit by the fact that if Ena stayed, it would always feel like that. She would always wonder what was going to disappear. Even if she rebuilt her trust in Ena, she'd never trust Percy, and how did she know his hold over Ena was broken? "Let's just go into the garden." At least she could keep an eye on Ena through the kitchen window.

"She is not staying under our roof," Billy said after Vi had explained.

"No, I've said that, but what are we going to do with her?" Vi was racking her brains, but could think of no solution.

"She's brought this on herself. As you've said, she seems to know exactly what she's doing. She isn't our problem, Vi. Not after what happened. She might be your sister, but that does not make us responsible for her."

Vi began to feel divided loyalties. She knew Billy was right, but under it all she had never completely stopped loving her sister. They'd been close once. "And what about Queenie? None of this is her fault. Poor lamb doesn't even know what's happening."

Billy shrugged. "Ena should have thought about that. This is Percy's responsibility. He should be paying for his wife and daughter. Either that or she'll have to get herself on her feet. I only came home to pick up some papers I'd left here. I'm going, and I really don't want to see her still here when I come back." Billy went through to the hall and picked up an envelope, then walked off down the path without saying goodbye.

Vi's shoulders slumped. Her insides felt as though they were unravelling in different directions, with Billy and Ena holding one end each. After how Percy had treated Billy, and then the theft on top of that, how could Vi blame Billy for reacting badly; but she wasn't used to him laying down the law. They were a partnership, and his reaction stung.

Alf came in shortly afterwards. "I've seen Billy, I know what's happened. I don't want to see any trouble between the two of you. You've been kind to me, Vi, I'm not going to stand by while this comes between you. I have an idea, and if you'll permit me, I'd like to see what happens when I suggest it."

Vi was speechless. She had no idea what Alf was thinking, but nodded meekly. He couldn't make the situation much worse.

"There is one thing I need to ask first. Are you prepared to look after Queenie for a few days?"

"Pardon?" Vi wondered if she'd heard right. "Look after Queenie? Well, yes, but..."

Alf didn't wait for anything more. "That's settled

then." He marched into the kitchen. "Ena," he addressed her in an authoritative tone. "Dry your eyes and let's stop the acting."

It reminded her of an occasion when Alf had needed to stop Billy's mam from wallowing years before. She wondered how Ena would react to it. It had certainly worked on her mother-in-law.

"Now, leave Queenie and her things here with Vi. She'll be well looked after for a day or two. Then bring your necessaries and come with me. We'll find you somewhere to stay for a few nights, whilst you find yourself a job and sort yourself out. You aren't going to be able to do that with Queenie in tow, and you aren't staying under this roof."

Vi was ready for Ena to protest. Even she could see that it would be possible for her to keep Queenie with her and simply bring her to their house during the days, still allowing her sister to look for work. She was about to intervene and say something to mollify her sister, but to her horror Ena divided the bags into two piles and without argument, or so much as a backward glance to Queenie, Ena picked up her own bags and followed Alf out of the kitchen.

As Ena walked away down the path, any sympathy Vi had for her sister evaporated, and she looked at her niece who now seemed to be in her care. She had no idea how that was going to work. How would Queenie react when she woke up to find her mam gone and in her place an aunt she'd hardly met? Vi shook her head and sighed. She'd always been told she was good with children; she just hoped her niece agreed. At least Ena was, for the time being, out of the way; but for how long?

CHAPTER 28

Wednesday 27th April 1921 - German War Crimes Inquiry at Bow Street - The Daily Mirror

When Billy came home the kitchen was empty, and he breathed a sigh of relief. He stiffened as he heard a child giggling, and went along the hall in search of the sound. Through the open doorway he saw Tommy sitting on the floor, playing with his young cousin, and both of them were laughing. Nipper's tail was wagging madly, and Vi was sitting on a chair looking pensive. There was no sign of Ena.

He coughed and they all turned and looked at him. Vi stood up and came to the doorway to talk to him.

"Ena?"

Vi shrugged. "Your Dad's taken her somewhere. I don't know where. We're going to look after Queenie for a couple of days while she sorts herself out."

Billy nodded. It wasn't ideal, but he was glad the child would be well cared for. None of this was her fault, poor mite. It was certainly easier than finding Ena there.

"She looks happy enough."

Vi groaned. "She wasn't when she woke up and found her mam gone. It took a while to convince her that Aunty Vi would have to do."

"What will you do with her while you're at work?" he asked.

"I have absolutely no idea. I'm waiting for your dad to come back. I was going to ask him to take me to see Mam or Mrs Brown to find out if either of them could help. I suppose to ask Mam I'm going to have to tell her the whole story. Perhaps it's time I did that anyway. I could go now you're back, but it would be quicker in the car."

Billy nodded. "Let's hope one of them can help. We can't afford her getting in your way." He went into the room and looked more closely at his niece. She was a pretty little thing. He knew Vi would enjoy having her around, although it might make it feel harder that they hadn't been able to have more children of their own, especially when Queenie left again. He found himself smiling as he watched Tommy with her. If he was being honest, he liked having young children around too.

It was another hour before Alf returned. "We found your Ena a nice little bed and breakfast for a week. It's near the town centre, so she can easily cover most places looking for work from there. How's the little one doing?"

"See for yourself," Billy said, leading his dad to where Queenie was now curled up asleep, with her head on Nipper and Tommy sitting nearby.

Alf raised his eyebrows. "Well, that didn't take long."

Vi joined them. "I need to go over to Mam and Dad's to see if they can help. I think I should take Queenie with me. It's better she sees familiar faces than wakes up again with another new face."

Billy was relieved; he didn't feel quite ready to take on looking after Queenie on his own. It wouldn't be so bad with two hands, but as it was he could be very clumsy.

"I was wondering…" Vi got no further in the sentence.

"Righto," Alf said; understanding the question. "Just give me five minutes and I'll be ready."

Billy thought it might be best for him to stay out of things, but Vi said, "You will come, won't you? I think you might help when it comes to telling them what's gone on - at least our part of it."

There would be no easy way for them to tell Mr and Mrs Tunnicliffe about Ena's behaviour.

"I'll wait in the car," Alf said when he parked outside their house. "It'll help to stop there being too many fingers on the paintwork."

Billy realised his dad wasn't joking. He guessed there weren't many cars parking up around here. He opened the car door for Vi, making it easier for her to carry Queenie.

Vi's mam stood up from the chair as they went in. "Hello, love." A look of total confusion washed over her face. "Whatever are you doing with...?"

Vi passed Queenie to her grandmother and the little girl held out her arms enthusiastically. "It's a long story. I think I'd best make some tea and we can sit down. You can take one out to your dad too, Billy."

"Oh, Billy lad, tell him to come in. No, I'll go." Vi's dad was on his feet.

"I think you should be here for what I need to say, Dad, but you can go to see the car while the tea brews."

Frank Tunicliffe's beaming grin made him look many years younger as he almost skipped out of the room to see the car.

None of the children seemed to be around, except for Queenie, which was a blessing, but Billy was still concerned to be talking about Ena in front of her, even though she was only sixteen months old. Vi appeared to have had the same idea; and after the tea, she changed Queenie and put her down for a nap. Billy just hoped she'd drop off.

Frank came back in when Billy took tea to his dad. Billy was grateful when he took charge of the situation.

"Now; begin at the beginning, love. What's been going on with our Ena?"

Billy noticed that Vi's dad started from the assumption this would all be down to Ena, which might mean he was more prepared for what was to follow than Billy had feared.

As Vi laid out events, Frank Tunnicliffe simply nodded and grunted in appropriate places, while Vi's mam interjected with exclamations of, "Well I never," "Oh you poor dears," "Lord have mercy," "I feel so ashamed," and "That girl's never been right since she took up with that Mayberry boy."

Once Vi's parents had been brought fully up to date, they all fell silent. Billy simply waited. They needed time to digest everything before they started asking questions.

"Why didn't she come here?" Mam asked, focussing on the immediate problem and saying nothing about the theft.

"Queenie, love, she knew we couldn't fit them in easily. It's hard enough feeding the mouths in the house at the moment." Dad was gentle as he spoke to Vi's mam.

"We could have made things stretch."

"I dare say if it weren't for feeling we need his wage, our John would have asked Tessie to marry him by now." Dad sighed.

"You don't think that, do you? Oh Lor', of course he must wed if that's what he wants. We'd manage."

Vi's mam seemed happy to follow the change of topic, and Billy wondered if she was trying to block out the subject of Ena.

"There's more to this than just where our Ena stays,"

Dad said, coming back to the main subject. He turned to Vi and Billy. "We should help cover the cost of what she stole." He went across to a jar on the mantelpiece.

"Dad, no. This isn't your fault." Vi went over to her dad. "We've not come to talk about the money. We only needed to tell you, so you knew what had gone on, but we don't want anything. All I came to ask is if Mam can look after little Queenie while I'm at work."

Dad turned to Mam, who was looking dazed. "Queenie, love, what do you say?"

"Of course she can come here." Vi's mam went over to the sleeping child. "She could just stay here."

"No, Ena brought her to me, and I think it's only fair that's where she finds her. I'll bring her over first thing and pick her up on my way home." Vi looked very determined.

Billy was surprised by how quickly Vi reacted to the suggestion.

"We are her grandparents," Dad said, as if to reassure Vi.

Billy saw the look of disappointment on Vi's face and smiled. She was enjoying having little Queenie to look after. "She's nice company for our Tommy. He quite likes having a little playmate."

"Righto," Dad said, as though that was a perfectly reasonable explanation.

It would at least mean mother and daughter didn't start a tug of war over the child.

"And where's Percy in all this?" Mam asked.

"That's a very good question. We've not seen hide nor hair of him." Billy grimaced. "I could go round there…"

"No," Vi interrupted him. "After the way he spoke to you the last time we tried that, you'll do no such thing. I think we should wait and see if he comes to us."

Billy nodded. He suspected Vi's reaction was as much that she didn't want to give up the child to Percy's care as anything, and she was probably right. The thought of him turning up on their doorstep wasn't a good one either. He didn't trust Percy at all, not even where his own daughter was concerned.

Billy was expecting to find Ena on the doorstep wanting to see her daughter the following day; but two days had passed, it was now Friday, and there was still no sign of her.

"Do you think I should check she's all right?" Alf asked, when Billy came in from work. "I do feel at least partly responsible."

"I think Ena's the one who is responsible for the decisions she's making at the moment. But I suppose a check can't do any harm. I know Vi's worried," Billy said.

"I need to collect Terence from the station, I'll do it on my way." Alf picked up his jacket and hat and went out to the car.

"Just don't go bringing her back here," Billy muttered under his breath once his father had closed the door. Something was niggling away at him. He suspected Ena had been badly treated by Percy, but he just had a feeling that she was more in control of what was happening than anyone around her realised, and that worried him.

It was a couple of hours before his dad returned, and Billy was pleased to see he wasn't accompanied by Ena.

As Alf unbuttoned his jacket, he said, "There was no sign of Ena, but her landlady says she's in good health and looking for work. She's not booked to stay on beyond the week yet, but she talked about staying if she can find work. At least until she can find a more permanent residence."

Billy let out a low whistle. "Maybe I was wrong. That all sounds like she's doing the right things. I'm just surprised she's not tried to see Queenie."

"I did leave a note for her. I said that Queenie is with her grandparents during working time, and if she wanted to see her then it might be easier to go there."

Billy smiled. "Thanks, Dad. That was a good idea."

The rest of the week passed, and there was still no word from Ena.

"I'll drive over and see what's happened, shall I?" Alf said. "She'll either have needed to move on or be paying for herself by now. You'd think she'd be ready to make proper arrangements for little Queenie. I didn't really expect her not to show up for this long."

"Neither did I," Billy said through gritted teeth. "I've no idea what Vi thinks."

"Billy," Alf said when he came back later. He ran his finger around his collar as he spoke. "Can I talk to you?"

Billy went to join his father, who was indicating they should go outside. He took his hat off the peg and followed.

Alf didn't start talking until they were along the path and out onto the pavement away from the house. "Let's go for a drink. I think we need some thinking time."

Billy's heart sank. "Break it to me."

Alf gave him a sidelong look. "She's gone."

Billy stopped where he was. "What do you mean 'gone'?"

"I mean she's taken all her things, left the lodgings and given no forwarding address." Alf shook his head as he spoke.

"Without Queenie?" It was a stupid thing to say. Billy

knew full well that it was without his niece. She was still safely at their house. "Did she leave any idea of what she was doing?"

"Well," Alf said, "there was a suggestion she might have joined a travelling theatre group."

Billy spluttered. "What? Now what are we supposed to do?"

"And what do we tell Vi? Sorry, lad," Alf said. "The child could always go to her grandparents. But from what I can see, we're all rather enjoying having her around, and she already goes there while Vi's at work."

"Vi's become very close to her. I think I know what she'll say. Tommy has too, although how long he'll appreciate his young cousin sleeping in his bedroom is hard to know." Billy had no idea what to think. "You're right, I think we've all grown fond of the poor little thing. She needs some stability in her life. It's not as though her father has come looking for her." Billy had been trying not to become too attached to Queenie; even he was worried what would happen when Ena took her away. But if Ena had gone... "I'll talk to Vi, see what she wants to do. How can a mother simply leave a child?"

"I don't think Ena knew what she wanted or what she was doing from the little she said. It sounds like she's had a pretty bad time of it. Maybe she'll straighten herself out and come back," Alf said. "In the meantime, I'm sure we'll all do our best to help."

They didn't walk as far as the pub, but simply walked around the block before returning to the house. Tommy had gone out on his bicycle, so Vi was alone with Queenie.

"Vi, love," Billy said, not knowing where to begin. "It's Ena..."

Vi almost snapped as she replied. "What about Ena? Is

304

she here?"

"No, love. She's gone. She's not coming. As far as we know, she's left the area." Billy watched carefully to see how Vi would react.

Vi's eyes closed and she let out a long breath that she seemed to have been holding. Then she took a few deep breaths.

"I thought..." she hesitated. "I thought you were going to say she was here to take her daughter back, and I don't want Queenie to go."

"Do you think you should talk to your mam and dad first, love? Maybe Ena's left word with them." Billy went and sat beside Vi.

She looked up with tears in her eyes. "She can stay here, can't she? With us?"

Billy looked across at Queenie with her beaming smile and sighed. "I don't know, love. Ena might have made other arrangements, or she might come back for her daughter. Maybe Percy will come for her."

A tear dripped down Vi's nose as she nodded. "But otherwise, you will say she can stay, won't you?"

Billy wiped away a tear that was tumbling down Vi's cheek. "Yes, love. If Ena's gone and there's no other arrangement, little Queenie can stay."

No one knew where Ena had gone. The remaining weeks of May and early June passed with no word from her, and no sign of Percy. Queenie simply became Tommy's sister, and Billy and Vi doted on her as they would have done a child of their own.

In late June, a letter finally arrived from Ena.
'Dear Vi,
I'm sorry. I had to get away. One day you'll understand.

Ena'

"And it says no more than that?" Billy asked Vi when she showed it to him. "There was nothing else in the envelope, and nothing written on the back?"

Vi shook her head. "That's it. No address. No mention of Queenie. Nothing."

"This is something I will never understand." Billy read the letter again and examined the envelope. "The envelope's postmarked 'Torquay'. Where's that?"

"I've no idea. I'm just glad Queenie is too young to really know what's going on. I wonder if Ena will ever come back. It won't be good for Queenie if her mam just comes and goes."

Billy had little doubt that Vi was right on that point, but he didn't trust Ena one bit.

CHAPTER 29

Wednesday 22nd June 1921 - The King Opens Ulster Parliament To-Day - The Daily Mirror

Despite her concern for her sister's well-being, and her constant worry that Percy Mayberry would turn up on their doorstep, Vi was happy. Most days Alf took her to leave Queenie with the child's grandparents in the morning and then drove her to Hats and Haberdashery. The days he was busy, Vi didn't mind the walk; extra exercise was always useful. If she thought no one was looking she would trot at a gentle run, made easier by the shorter skirt length she now wore. Gone were the days when she had to hitch her skirts up to do anything more than a sedate walk and, as she wore sensible shoes for standing in the shop, she made the most of it.

Terence was working regular hours again, and it meant that Billy had a little more time. Vi loved the fact that he took Queenie out now and again, and Tommy and Nipper usually went with them. Queenie really did seem to have completed their family, and Audrey was thrilled to stand in as an extra grandparent when the child's own grandmother couldn't take care of her.

This morning, Vi was walking to work. It was such a beautiful sunny summer's day that she hadn't wanted to do anything else. She'd left Queenie with her nanna and was now well on her way to Hats and Haberdashery.

"Vi."

Vi turned to see Tessie running along the road, waving her arms madly. Vi frowned and waited. She couldn't decide if Tessie looked distressed or happy. For the moment, she just looked a little wild.

"Vi," Tessie called again, somewhat needlessly as Vi was now waiting for her. "He asked me."

Vi was about to open her mouth to ask Tessie what on earth she was talking about, when realisation dawned. "When? Mam never said. Oh, Tessie, that's wonderful, congratulations." Vi wrapped her arms around her soon to be sister-in-law and felt Tessie still jumping up and down with the excitement.

She pulled back from her friend and took her hands. "I really am so very happy for both of you. Where will you live? Oh, I have so many questions."

They carried on walking arm in arm toward the shop.

"He was waiting until after you'd dropped off Queenie before he told your mam and dad. He knew I wanted to tell you, and your mam's never so good with secrets."

Vi laughed. "That's an understatement. When did he ask you?"

"He was already at home when I got there last night. Mam greeted me grinning like I don't know what and then just left the room. He'd been over to ask her permission. Isn't that sweet? Anyway, he was ever so nervous and had an awful job getting any words out. He did it proper like, got down on one knee and everything. He hasn't bought a ring yet; he says we can go to a jeweller when he gets paid on Friday."

The two of them were in party mood by the time they arrived at the shop, and Vi decided she could redo the window display as part of their celebration and maybe do a bit of a wedding theme. There must be lots of young couples tying the knot at this time of year. "When are you getting married?"

"We'll have to have the banns read and that takes a few weeks. Then there's my dress; I do want something special if I can."

Vi thought for a moment. "I could make it for you."

Tessie gasped. "Oh, Vi, would you? I could help."

"I'd love to."

"We thought maybe we'd get a date in September; that would give us nearly three months. We need to talk to Reverend Smith." Tessie paused, biting her lip. "Would you be my matron of honour?"

Vi reached out and took Tessie's hands in hers. "Tessie, I'd love to. Thank you."

"John's going to ask your Billy to be his best man, and I thought maybe your sisters Katie and Lizzie would be bridesmaids, and what about little Queenie too? She'd be so sweet."

"It's a good job you're not getting married until September if there are all those dresses to make." Vi was thrilled that Queenie would be included, and started thinking about something that would suit her to wear. It was no good making anything too soon, as she was growing so fast.

Over the next few weeks, the girls spent all the spare moments when the shop wasn't busy working on the dresses. At least being out of the football season there were fewer other distractions taking place.

Vi and Billy accompanied Tessie and John to All Saints church on the Sundays when the banns were read. On the first of those Sundays, Tessie, in her excitement on hearing their names read out, elbowed Vi rather sharply in the ribs.

Vi gave out a little yelp. Several people sitting in the pews in front of them turned and scowled, leading Vi and Tessie to giggle nervously. Reverend Smith, or Florrie's uncle Anthony as they knew him, looked down from the pulpit and raised his eyebrows. Vi tried hard to look suitably chastened in return.

The wedding was fixed for Saturday 17th September, and in the weeks beforehand there were hardly enough hours in the day. The one time they didn't use for sewing was Saturday afternoon football practice.

"I really think we need to win the cup this year, if I'm ever going to," Vi said to Billy as they watched some of the new younger players warming up. "I'll have enough on my hands with bringing up Queenie and running the shop."

"Then you'd best train hard. Tommy and Nipper are looking after Queenie." He nodded in their direction. "So today you can focus on the football."

"Yes, coach," Vi replied, and kissed his cheek before running onto the pitch. She turned around and called to him, "You're a hard task master, Billy Dobson, but if I want to win, you are completely right."

Although they'd had no matches over the summer, Vi still worked hard on her fitness. During some of the long summer evenings she'd even gone up to the recreation ground to do extra running. Alf was happy to look after Queenie, and Billy had been going to encourage her. It wasn't so much the long distances she wanted to work on, but the sprinting. She already had the stamina to keep going for the length of the match, now she hoped that speed might give her the edge.

By the start of the football season, none of the younger girls could beat Vi in either a sprint or over a longer distance. She was as ready as she ever would be.

Some of the teams had changed since the previous season, but there were still twenty-four taking part, with eight having a bye in the first round. They waited eagerly for news of when their first match would be.

Alf went up to the Billingbrook United ground ahead of their practice at the start of September to find out who they'd be playing. The girls all waited at the training ground for news.

"Who do you think it will be?" Tessie asked.

"I don't know if it's better to get some of the hard teams out of the way first or save them for later," Billy said.

"Oh, I hope it's not Blackpool in the first round." Vi couldn't stay still as she waited for news. "I don't want a bye either. I want to win fair and square."

"We don't want that Dick, Kerr team from Preston. They're supposed to be really good," Tessie said.

"He's here," Edith shouted as Alf pulled into the recreation ground car park.

Vi watched him as he went over to talk to Billy. There was a lot of arm waving and she frowned. From what she knew of Alf, something was clearly wrong. She ran over to them.

"Is there a problem?" She could feel her heart pounding, not from running but overwhelming anxiety.

Alf looked pale.

"You could say that, love. I'd probably best come and talk to all of you."

Vi bit her lip as they walked back across the field, saying nothing.

Alf coughed to get the attention of the rest of the team. "Right," he said and sighed. "Now, in the past our first

311

match has been on the last Saturday in September."

There were general murmurings of assent.

"Well…" Alf took a deep breath. "This year it isn't."

"Have we got a bye?" Clara asked.

"No." Alf sighed heavily again. "There's no easy way to say this, but we've been drawn to play Rochdale in the first round…"

Maud punched the air.

"Is that good?" Annie, one of the new girls, asked.

Maud stopped and looked at her. "I don't know, but it's not Blackpool or Preston."

They all laughed.

Alf held up his hand for silence. "That's not all you need to think about. The match is not on the last Saturday of September. It's on the 17th. The same day as Tessie's wedding."

A collective gasp ran around the team, and they all turned to look at Tessie.

There was a slight wobble to Tessie's voice as she said, "Reverend Smith said that's the only date that was free." Tessie stood completely still, and no one spoke. Then she cocked her head to one side and asked, "Are we at home or away?"

Alf frowned for a moment. "We're at home, but…"

"Well, that's fine." Tessie looked defiant. "The wedding's at midday. If we can have kick off no earlier than two o'clock, we should be able to get there in time, shouldn't we, Vi?"

This time the gasp was followed by all the girls talking at once.

"Would you really?"

"On your wedding day?"

"What will John say?"

Tessie was looking a little less certain now. "John knows I play football. That's how he met me. He'll be all right about it, won't he?" She looked to Vi.

"I think maybe you should talk to him first," Alf said gently.

"Well, we can't miss out on the cup, and as most of the team will be at the wedding, we'll just have to manage both on the same day. Who's in?" Tessie shouted.

The whole team cheered, and with a war cry Tessie led them all back onto the pitch to practise.

Alf looked at Vi and shrugged.

Vi smiled. "Tessie will keep our John on his toes, that's for sure, but I think he'll agree with her on this one. I'm not sure Mam will see it quite the same, but maybe the whole wedding party can watch us play. Dad will have to save his accordion playing until afterward. We can have a bit of a knees up when the match is over."

Once they'd all run off some of the nervous energy, Alf called them back together to talk about their approach to the match. "As we don't know how they play, we need to be prepared for anything. We take this one game at a time and start by assuming they could be as good as Preston, or as dirty as Calderley."

For the next couple of weeks before the match, they arranged to practise for an hour on Wednesday evenings as soon as they'd all finished work.

"Just keep your head, Vi. You girls can do it this season," Billy said as they walked home.

"Can Queenie be a mascot too?" Tommy asked.

Vi smiled. "I'm sure I can make her a little football kit to match ours. Although she may well be tired after being one of Tessie's bridesmaids."

Queenie had no idea what they were talking about, but

giggled anyway.

"I just hope having the football and the wedding on the same day doesn't go wrong," Billy said. "Has your John said anything?"

Vi raised her eyebrows. "Honestly? He said watching a game of football was far better than having to make a speech."

Billy laughed. "I suppose there is that. Although I thought we might still be called on to do that later."

Vi had been trying to think of anything that could be a problem, but nothing had come to mind.

There was very little time to think about what could go wrong over the next couple of weeks. Vi and Tessie worked every hour they had, either running the shop or making the dresses for the wedding.

"I'm just glad we started these in plenty of time," Vi said as she held up the finished wedding dress for Tessie to see.

"It's perfect." Tessie clapped her hands together and looked dreamy-eyed.

"Try it on," Vi said. "Then we need to put it away until Saturday."

There were customers in the shop when Tessie came back out in the figure-hugging white dress.

"Well, there's my answer," one of the ladies in the shop said. "I came in to ask if you knew anyone who made wedding dresses, but I see that you do. My daughter will be getting married in December. I wonder if we could make an appointment for you to show her some options."

Vi was astounded. While she was a very competent milliner, she'd never seen herself as a seamstress and dress designer; Tessie's had been a one off. She was about to answer that unfortunately that wouldn't be possible, when

Tessie moved closer to the lady so she could see the dress better and said, "She's ever so good. This is all her own design."

Vi crossed her fingers and went to fetch the diary from the desk.

By Saturday morning, everything was in place. The dresses were finished, and everyone looked a picture.

Alf was acting as chauffeur for the wedding party, and Vi had found white ribbons to tie to the car to make it look perfect. He'd already taken Vi's sisters, Katie and Lizzie, to All Saints Church, and having collected Vi and little Queenie, he drew up in front of their old house on Ivy Terrace to collect Tessie from next door.

"Do I look all right?" Tessie asked as she came out of the front door. "Mam insisted I came this way. It makes me feel important before we've even started."

Alf escorted Tessie to the car and opened the door for her.

"I could get used to this." She looked anxiously at Vi, who was getting back in beside her. "Is John at the church yet?"

"He'll be there, but I've not been to the church yet so I've not seen him." Vi made sure she and Queenie weren't sitting on any of Tessie's dress before the car set off.

"He was already there when I dropped the girls," Alf said. "He's keen, I'll say that for him."

Tessie let out a yelp of excitement.

There were about twenty-five who'd been invited to the wedding, including the bride and groom. Vi noticed a few at the back of the church who she didn't recognise, and guessed they'd come to see the show; and wish the couple luck, of course.

Alf was taking several important roles during the day. Having left his chauffeuring duties for a while, he was ready to walk Tessie down the aisle; Vi didn't think she'd seen him looking quite as happy as he did when Tessie asked him if he would take on the role. Vi followed close behind them as they processed through the church, with Katie, now thirteen years old, taking charge of her younger sister Lizzie and little Queenie.

When Vi reached the front of the church, she caught Billy's eye and her heart missed a beat as she remembered their own wedding day. He patted his pocket which made her laugh. They'd made sure he had the ring hours ago, but still he needed to check. She moved to the side, to the seat beside Mrs Brown. Tessie's mam was already sniffing into a handkerchief and the service hadn't even started.

Tessie and John finally finished saying their vows, and Vi gave the first thought to their need to arrive at the football match on time.

As she watched the happy couple walk back down the aisle, Vi felt a thrill at having played a part in bringing them together. They went out of the church onto the steps of All Saints, and Vi was surprised to find a reporter and photographer from the *Billingbrook Mercury* ready to capture the details of the happy couple and their families. The photographer invited the girls who were part of the team to gather around the couple for the photograph, and Alf and Billy stood to either side. Once that was done, Alf gave a nod to Vi, her signal that it was time for the girls to start heading to the match.

Alf would drive some of the girls to the football ground immediately and then come back for Vi, Tessie, Billy and John. One way or another, they should all be there and ready for the game. Those who were spectating would follow on behind, but even walking they should be there for kick off.

"Hang on," Tessie called. "I need to throw my bouquet first."

All the girls gathered around the steps and Tessie turned away to face the church itself. Vi was looking at Tessie as she tossed the small bunch of flowers, dotted with sprigs of rosemary, over her shoulder to the waiting, giggling group of girls. Tessie threw the flowers quite a long way, and Vi turned to see who had caught them. When she saw the woman at the back of the group holding the bouquet, she gasped.

"Ena. What are you doing here?"

CHAPTER 30

Saturday 17th September 1921 - The Irish Crisis: Dublin's Ray of Hope - The Daily Mirror

Vi looked around to see where little Queenie was before making her way to Ena. She had at most twenty minutes before Alf returned to take her to the football. What if Ena took Queenie away while Vi was at the match? Vi felt bile rising in her throat. It was three months since she'd heard anything from Ena, and five months since Queenie had moved to live with them. Would the little girl even remember her mother after that long? Tommy had been scared he'd forget his dad when his dad went away to fight, and Tommy had been four years old then.

Vi's fists were clenched as she reached Ena. She felt guarded on what to say. "Hello."

Ena leaned across and kissed Vi's right cheek and then her left in a flamboyant manner. "Darling," Ena said.

Vi blinked. She most certainly was not used to Ena calling her darling, or the affected tone that her sister was using.

"Are you back for good?" Vi asked in a faltering voice. All she really wanted to know was what were Ena's intentions for Queenie?

"Ena." Vi's mam came over to greet her daughter. "Well, there's a lovely surprise." Mam lifted little Queenie up to Ena's height and turned to look at her

318

granddaughter. "Look who's here, Queenie. It's your mam."

Ena reached out to take Queenie, who promptly let out a howl.

Vi bit her lip. She was torn between relief at little Queenie's reaction and wanting to reach out and comfort the child.

"Vi. Vi." Tessie was calling her. "We need to leave. Alf's back already."

"What? Now?" She turned to Ena. "We'll talk after the match finishes."

"If I'm still here," Ena replied.

Her sister's words were ringing in her ears as Vi dragged herself away to join Tessie and Billy. What if Ena left, taking Queenie with her, before the match even finished?

Arriving at the football ground still dressed in her matron of honour dress and carrying her football kit bag felt very odd to Vi. The stadium was beginning to fill up before the match, but there was enough time to change and settle down before the game started. It wasn't the wedding that was on Vi's mind though, it was little Queenie. All she wanted to do was run away from Whittingham Road and make sure that Ena couldn't take her daughter away. She tried to remind herself that it wasn't her decision to make. Ena was the child's mother, however she'd behaved.

"Vi," Billy said quietly. "From your face you're worrying about Queenie."

Vi turned to look at her husband.

"You have to think about the football. The team can manage without me, though. I'm going to make sure everything's all right. I'll bring little Queenie back here with me and won't let her out of my sight. You will need to talk to Ena later, but for now, think about the match."

Vi gave a weak smile. She was grateful for Billy's perceptiveness, but even so, concentrating on the game would not be easy.

Rochdale was a smaller club than Billingbrook, but they had strong support and many of their fans had travelled to the game. The Whittingham Road ground was full when the girls came out of the changing room. To the surprise of the whole team, except Alf, it appeared, a brass band began playing *'Here Comes the Bride'* as they stepped out onto the pitch. Vi dropped back and pushed Tessie to the front of the line of girls as they went out. Tessie began waving to the crowd and cheers rang around the stadium.

As the match kicked off, the other girls, except Vi, were in buoyant mood. Vi's mind was definitely not on the football. She could tell her play was ragged, and the game seemed to be going on around her rather than her being part of the action.

"Vi, we need you," Tessie shouted as Rochdale restarted the game after the ball had gone off the pitch.

Vi looked up at Tessie, but her heart just wasn't in it.

Twenty minutes of the game had gone by and neither team had scored.

"We should be three goals up by now," Annie said. "Come on, Vi."

But how could she 'come on' when all she could think about was her perfect little family being broken up?

"Vi! Vi!"

This time Tessie was pointing as she shouted. Vi followed her gaze. Billy was approaching the side of the pitch and with him were Vi's mam and little Queenie. Vi ignored the game restarting and ran over to them.

"Mammy," little Queenie shouted, and held her arms

outstretched to Vi.

Vi blinked. Queenie had never called her Mammy before. She wanted her to say it again and again. She scooped Queenie up and held her. She looked to the others. "Ena?" she said.

Billy shrugged. "Gone again, we think. There's certainly no sign of her."

"She said something about wanting to see Queenie before going to Paris," Mam said. "Though how the likes of our Ena would be going to Paris I've no idea."

"Paris?" Vi shook her head. She held little Queenie away from her and gave her a beaming grin. "I love you." She pulled her niece back to her and kissed her. "But now, Mammy has a football game to win." She handed Queenie back to the girl's grandmother, gave a little wave, and ran backward from them toward the game. After a little distance she turned around and let out of whoop of joy. "We've got a game to win, girls. I'm back."

From then on Vi ran the length and breadth of the pitch, chasing the ball, tackling and providing excellent passes to her teammates; Rochdale didn't stand a chance. By the time the girls left the pitch, the Billingbrook team had secured their place in the next round by winning by four goals to one. The Rochdale team were a young team, not just in age but in the length of time they'd played together, and Vi couldn't help but think they would be a team to watch in the future.

"Well done, Vi," Billy said as she came off with a broad grin on her face. "One game down, four to go."

"It'll be me out there one day," Tommy said. "In the Billingbrook United team."

"I hope so," Vi said. "I should be very happy when I hang up my boots to be able to watch my son play, or my daughter come to that." She looked at Queenie. If Ena wasn't taking the child away, then Vi would very much like her to be a permanent part of their family.

As the nights became dark earlier, evening training had to stop, but Vi still exercised at home in addition to their practice sessions. Walking Nipper helped too; he had longer walks than most dogs in the neighbourhood.

Their second round draw was away to Manchester. It would be a big fixture for them, without the advantage of being on their home turf.

"I'm really sorry," Edith said the Saturday before the match. "I won't be able to come. I can't leave my granddad for that long, and there's no one else to look after him on Saturday."

"Surely there's someone? Can't you ask a neighbour to help?" Vi started thinking about who else they could ask.

Edith shook her head. "His mind's not what it was. He gets really funny with anyone other than the family. Sorry."

Vi closed her eyes, coming to terms with the fact she would have to play in goal. She hated being in goal. Edith was so much better at it than any of them, but Vi had more experience than the others and generally did quite well. "Right," she said, turning to the rest of the team. "We'd best spend today with you all kicking as many balls at me in goal as you can."

Billy gave her a reassuring smile. Nothing about winning this cup was proving easy. Vi really didn't want to be knocked out of the cup because she failed in her goalkeeping skills.

After the practice was over, Vi asked Alf and Tommy, every spare waking moment when it was light, to try kicking balls past her in their small garden. She wasn't doing badly, but a well-placed ball would easily find its target.

When match day arrived, Billingbrook had laid on a special supporters' train and the team was taking as many of its fans to watch the match as possible. Audrey and Terence were going by car and taking Vi's dad and John. Queenie was with her grandmother, to avoid her tendency to run out onto the pitch to find Vi when she was playing.

Despite being ten years old, Tommy still enjoyed being the team's mascot and held his head high as he led the girls out onto the pitch. Vi wondered how much longer he'd be happy to do that before he started to feel self-conscious. She wondered if he was dreaming of a day when he would lead a team he was part of, and thought how proud that would make her.

Manchester were tough opposition, but the Billingbrook girls were up to the task, and Vi was glad to see the team matching the Manchester girls stride for stride as the game moved up and down the pitch. The fewer shots on goal she had to face, the happier she would be. When the girls went off at half-time there was still no score, and Vi's skills had not been greatly tested.

"It's a good job we have a strong defence," she said to Tessie. "Ethel was a real find. She's come on so much in the few weeks since she joined the team. Let's hope she stays."

"If she keeps playing like that, one of the other teams will be enticing her away. There's girls being offered all sorts to move to other teams," Clara said.

"How times have changed since we all worked together. We'd best get back out there and see what we can do." Vi left the changing room, ready to restart.

Alf was waiting for them outside. "I want to make some changes. We need you back up front, Vi, if we're going to win this. I've spoken to Ethel and she's happy to go in goal."

Vi breathed a sigh of relief and limbered up, ready for some serious running. She just hoped that Ethel would be all right.

Despite covering the entire pitch, it wasn't Vi who scored the first goal of the match; it was one of the Manchester team. Ethel was better in defence than in goal, and Vi was beginning to wonder if Alf had made the wrong decision. She looked across to him, expecting him to signal for her to go back in goal, but he indicated very clearly that she should stay up front; instead, he dropped Tessie back to give Ethel more cover.

As the game progressed, the Manchester girls slowed down. Vi couldn't decide if they were tired or trying to protect their lead. There was only one way to find out; Billingbrook needed to step up the pace. She indicated her intentions to Clara and Eva, and they started passing the ball in diamond patterns, stretching the Manchester defence and pulling them out of position.

The girls worked their way up the field and Clara, in a neat and fast manoeuvre that they'd practiced many times, passed the ball to Vi, then received it back again in a position where she could immediately shoot for goal. When the ball found the back of the net, Billingbrook were back in the game.

Ten minutes later they repeated the exercise, and this time it was Vi who scored the goal. When the final whistle blew, with Billingbrook winning by two goals to one, Vi felt an enormous sense of relief. There were eight teams left in the cup, and she was starting to believe that this might just be their year to win.

"Don't let Vi see that," Billy said, handing the newspaper to Alf.

"Don't let me see what?" Vi had just come in from work and was walking through the hall.

Alf took his pipe from his mouth. "There's a report here saying that sport is not only 'unseemly' for women to play, but..." he turned back to find his place in the column, "...'detrimental' to women's health."

Vi snorted with laughter. "I presume the report was written by a man."

"Some doctor," Alf said. "You'd think he'd have more sense. Maybe he should come to watch you play."

Vi shook her head. "You'd think after all we did during the war, men would have more sense than to suggest we aren't capable."

"Oh, he isn't saying you're not capable. He's saying it's bad for you." Alf shook his head.

Vi sighed. She'd probably prefer it to say women weren't good enough to play. That was easy to prove wrong, but some silly notion about it doing them harm was much harder to dispel. She'd been playing for six years and was as fit as she'd ever been. She went to take her things upstairs and thought no more about it.

Hats and Haberdashery was already busy even before the Christmas build up. Vi and Tessie had quietly gained a strong reputation as the place to go in Billingbrook for any millinery requirements. They hadn't progressed the wedding dress idea; the lady who saw Tessie's dress came in to say her daughter's wedding had been called off and that was the end of the matter. Thankfully, Audrey still enjoyed helping out, but she and Tessie also persuaded Vi to take on additional part time staff; these ones came with good references and enabled Audrey to attend the matches, as well as covering busy times.

Vi felt the most settled she'd been for as long as she could remember. She'd even stopped expecting to find Percy on the doorstep looking for either Ena or Queenie. But, despite how happy she felt generally, the one thing she still wanted to do was lift the cup.

In the quarter-final in November, the girls were drawn against Bury. Thankfully, Edith was back in goal and, whilst anxious, Vi was more positive than the previous month. For one thing they would be playing at home. On Saturday 5th November the Billingbrook team were ready to take on their opposition. If they won this, only two matches would stand between them and the cup. The women's competition was running up until Christmas, with the final over the festive period so that it didn't clash with the men's major matches.

"Where's my kit?" Vi was running through the hall on the Saturday morning.

"It's here, I've got it. Now will you just stop worrying? You know you can beat Bury. You can do this. Take a few deep breaths and then we're ready to go," Billy said.

Vi grinned. He was used to her routine by now; she was always nervous on match day. She stopped where she was in the hall and breathed deeply. "Right, I'm ready."

From the minute she ran out onto the pitch that day, Vi didn't stop. She'd show whichever silly men thought sport was bad for women just how wrong they were. She could even hear Billy cheering her on when she was close to his side of the pitch. He'd be lucky to have a voice after that much shouting. Perhaps watching was more damaging to health than playing. But then, she was giving him plenty to cheer about. She scored two goals in the first half.

In the end, her team came away with a victory of three goals to one.

"Did you see her run?" Tessie said, slightly out of breath with excitement. "She's a bloody demon when she gets going."

Billy laughed. "I really can't think of my wife as a demon, but she was bloody brilliant."

The week following the match was busy. It wasn't helped when on Wednesday morning Vi had to send Tessie home due to sickness. "You get yourself to bed, and don't come back in until you feel well enough."

Vi couldn't help thinking Tessie had been looking a little peaky for a few days and hoped she wasn't going down with anything serious. Unless Tessie was expecting, but Vi put the thought out of her mind; Tessie would have said something if it was that.

Alf went to the Whittingham Road ground ahead of their practice on Saturday to find out who they'd drawn in the semi-finals. Vi was waiting anxiously with the rest of the team, but there was still no sign of Tessie. She decided to go over to Ivy Terrace after training to find out if all was well.

Alf finally pulled up in the car and came over clutching a piece of paper. Tessie and John were walking across onto the field at the same time. Alf called everyone to order.

"I've got some news you will all probably be happy about," Alf shouted, drawing out the tension. "We've drawn the new Stockport team, away."

The girls started cheering. It was the best news the team could have had. "Then let's hope Calderley knock out that Preston team," Billy said. "They've gained quite a reputation."

"I don't think we'd much fancy playing Calderley in the final if they do, but it might be our best hope," Vi said, turning to find Tessie.

It was John who responded rather than Tessie, which was most unusual. He clapped his hands together to get everyone's attention. "Tessie's got some news for you all as well."

"Not just me, silly," Tessie pushed him shyly. "What John's trying to say is that I won't be able to play in the semi-final. I'm really sorry, Vi, but we're expecting. You're going to be an aunty again."

CHAPTER 31

Saturday 12th November 1921 - Enlarged Armistice Day Number - The Daily Mirror

As the rest of the girls started cheering, Vi simply stood there, dumbstruck. Tessie wasn't ill; she was expecting a baby. She wouldn't be on the team anymore, at least not that season, and there'd come a point when she'd have to stop working in the shop for a while too.

Vi hugged Tessie. "I'm so happy for you both. You'll be a wonderful mother." She turned to John and with a broad grin added, "You could have waited until after the cup final though."

John's face reddened, making all of them laugh.

As the others came over and congratulated Tessie, Vi began to work out what to do. For now, the shop could wait. Tessie had been part of the football team from the start, they knew each other's moves almost before they realised themselves. Not having Tessie there meant she had to put her trust and faith in the new girls in the team like never before. Ethel! Ethel was the most versatile player Vi had seen in a long time, not just in Billingbrook, but any team. She was young though, would she cope?

Vi went over to talk to Alf. "I don't know what you're thinking, Dad, but I'd like to try Ethel up front with me."

Alf was quiet for a moment, but from his nodding Vi knew he was mulling it over. "And move Clara back into defence?"

Vi nodded. "We know Clara's a good defender, she's done it often enough, but we can bring her forward when we want three up front."

"And we can bring Annie forward when we want all guns blazing." Alf gave a stronger nod. "Let's try it today and see how it looks."

As the practice session progressed, Vi and Ethel gradually grew used to communicating with each other. Vi couldn't help thinking that Ethel was a star in the making.

"You have one more practice before the semi-final," Alf said as they came off the pitch.

"Unless Ethel could make Wednesday afternoon?" Vi turned to the girl for an answer.

"I'll tell them I'm sick if I have to. What time?"

They set up to meet on Wednesday, together with whichever of the other girls were free. Vi was sure this would work. Then she went over to Tessie and linked arms as they started to walk toward their homes. "Now I can ask you all the other things, like when's it due?"

Tessie grinned. "April or early May."

"But you only got married in September." Vi grasped why her friend was grinning. "Tessie Tunnicliffe, and you never told me."

"I'll still work in the shop, and Mam says she'll look after it so I can come back to work after. It'll be a while though. I can make hats at home while I can't come in."

Vi was glad that Tessie wanted to carry on. It wouldn't be easy with the baby, but her friend was reliable, and Vi knew they'd need the money.

By the time of the semi-final, Ethel and Vi had spent a

number of hours training together. Ethel had even gone to Vi's home on the Sundays to discuss how they worked on the pitch. They were as ready as they could be in the time they'd had.

It wasn't an exciting game. The Billingbrook team played with more caution and less flare. They were all adjusting to their new structure, and no one wanted an upset at this stage of the cup. Vi was grateful that so many of their own supporters had travelled to the match, and she could hear them in the stands, even though Stockport had a good following.

By half-time, neither side had scored. "If you carry on like this," Alf said in an uncharacteristically sharp tone, "you won't deserve to win. This isn't the best you can do." He didn't say anything further.

Vi looked around her at the other girls. They all looked stunned. "It's down to all of us," Vi said. "We've been playing it safe, but that's not what we do best. I'd rather lose having played well, and given the crowd something to enjoy, than win having played badly. Who's in?"

There was a moment's hesitation, in which Vi desperately missed Tessie, before Ethel led a rally call and the girls' mood shifted.

"All for one and one for all," Edith shouted.

"Where d'you get that from?" Clara asked.

"I dunno, but it sounds good," Edith said.

They all laughed, and as they walked out onto the pitch their whole team attitude had changed.

Whilst they may not have played quite as well as if Tessie had been on the pitch, Vi was happy with how the second half went. The crowd responded to their change of pace, and it wasn't long before Vi scored the team's first goal. Not everything went their way, and although Ethel scored her first goal for Billingbrook, Stockport scored as well, leaving the final score at two goals to one in Billingbrook's favour. They were through to the final of the Cup, and had four weeks to return to top form.

Vi couldn't wait for the news of how the other semi-final had gone. She was desperate to know whether they would be facing Preston or Calderley.

The late newspaper carried the results, and as soon as it came out she went to the newsagent for a copy. "They did it," she shouted to Billy, who was waiting outside with little Queenie. "Calderley won." They might be Billingbrook's arch enemy, but nothing would make her happier than beating them to lift the trophy.

"Let's just hope the referee can keep them in line," Billy said. "You wouldn't be happy if they won by foul means."

Vi hadn't thought of that. Surely it couldn't be allowed to happen again.

As November rolled into December the shop became very busy and, except for Saturday's practice, Vi had no time to think about the football. It wasn't just the shop; this would be Queenie's first Christmas with them, and she wanted to make it a very special family time. It would also be the little girl's second birthday, and Vi couldn't believe how quickly she was growing up. She was wondering whether Ena was really in Paris, as they'd heard nothing from her since her brief visit in September. The bell rang and Alf came in.

"Dad, what is it?" Vi put down the hat she was working on and hurried to the front of the shop. It wasn't like Alf to come in when they were open. His face was pale. "What on earth has happened? Is Tommy all right? Queenie?"

"I'm sorry." With a shaking hand, Alf passed her a

letter on Billingbrook United headed paper.

Vi frowned. She could tell by his face that she didn't want to read it, but took it anyway.

"I'm sorry, Vi, love," Alf said.

Still not wanting to look at the sheet, she asked, "Whatever it is, does Billy know?"

Alf shook his head. "It seemed right to come to you first."

Vi began to read. "But they can't... what... I don't understand. What does it mean?" She read again the resolution from the Football Association which was included in the letter.

'Complaints have been made as to football being played by women. The Council feel impelled to express their strong opinion that the game of football is quite unsuitable for females and ought not to be encouraged. Complaints have also been made as to the conditions under which some of these matches have been arranged and played, and the appropriation of the receipts to other than Charitable objects. The Council are further of the opinion that an excessive proportion of the receipts are absorbed in expenses and an inadequate percentage devoted to Charitable objects. For these reasons the Council request the clubs belonging to the Association to refuse the use of their grounds for such matches.'

"It's over, Vi." Alf took the letter back from her. "I went up to the ground as soon as I'd read it. The Football Association has banned women's football from all their members' grounds. The Club has no choice. They can't have a women's team anymore."

"But we aren't paid to play. I know Caulder and Harrison covered what we lost by not working our shifts, but we weren't paid any extra. We didn't get paid anything when we went to France. I know our travel was covered, but we couldn't have afforded to go otherwise, and the matches raised money for charity. We represented our town, our country, when we went to the war graves. They aren't being fair." Vi just couldn't understand what they were objecting to. "How is it men can be paid to play, but we can't have our expenses covered?" She thought times had changed, and that women could be treated with some respect for what they could do. "I suppose that makes my decision for me. I'll just have to retire after the cup final. I feel sorry for the others though." Vi sighed heavily.

"Vi, love…" Alf's voice was shaky, and he sounded as though he was struggling to get his words out. "There isn't going to be a cup final."

"Don't be silly, of course there is. It's already arranged." Vi frowned. Alf wasn't making sense.

He shook his head. "You don't have the support of the football club anymore, and you don't have a ground to play at. What's more, you don't have a referee or linesmen either."

"But…" Vi paused as Alf's words began to sink in. "But we have to play. We damn well have to play, and we're bloody well going to win."

CHAPTER 32

Tuesday 6th December 1921 - Ladies' Football - Banned By The Football Association - The Lancashire Daily Post

Tessie came forward, clearly having overheard the conversation. "Why have they done it? Why are they being so cruel?"

"I don't know, love. I heard someone at the Club saying they think it's too popular and they're worried about losing so much money from the men's game, but that was a few weeks ago and I don't know if he had anything to base it on. I suspect the reasons they're giving are just an excuse."

Vi's temper flared. "How dare they? How bloody dare they? We were fit to work in a dangerous munitions factory all hours God sent when it suited men's needs. Now we want to do something for ourselves and it's not convenient to them. How bloody dare they? Tessie, I want you to take the rest of the day to round up the girls and get them to a meeting at our house tonight. We've not come through four years of war to be told we can go back to sitting pretty at home. It's been bad enough that so many women can't find work and nobody really seems to care, but this is too much."

"I'll drive you, love. Terence doesn't need me for a few hours." Alf folded the letter and put it in his pocket.

Vi turned to him. "Dad, can you make a list of all the

things you think we're going to need in order to go ahead? Oh, and can you write to Calderley to say we will still be expecting them to play, and we'll let them know the arrangements soon. The match was drawn to be played in Billingbrook, and played here is what it will be. No men sitting in offices in London are going to tell me that I can't play football. If I can stand up to the Calderley football team, I can stand up to the bloody Football Association."

It was difficult squeezing everyone into the front room that evening as all except Eva managed to attend. Tessie was still as much part of everything, even though she wouldn't be playing, and had already explained to them briefly what had happened, so there was no need to go over the basics.

"I think we should go to London and march outside their offices," Edith said.

"That's easier said than done if no one is paying the costs anymore," Annie said.

"There must be money from all your games. I know that you were doing it for charity, but your costs were supposed to come out first. Did the Club say anything about the money they were holding?" Billy asked his dad.

"No, lad," Alf said, looking as dejected as Vi was feeling.

"I'll go up and ask tomorrow," Billy said. "I'm sure if I explain to Terence he'll let me have some time."

"Can we still wear our Billingbrook United kit?" Clara asked. "I can't afford to buy a new one."

"I'll ask about that too," Billy said, starting to make a list.

"I don't think the kit is your biggest problem." Alf coughed to clear his throat. "Where are you going to play the match?"

"We could use the Caulder and Harrison ground," Vi said.

Alf shook his head. "At a push, but it's not really suitable for the cup final. There are no stands and not many people would be able to see. We need to find somewhere bigger. We also need a referee that both teams will accept, but who isn't working under the football association. And given that it's Calderley you're playing, they'll need to be good. I'm sure each team could supply a linesman."

"Calderley don't play fair at the best of times." Vi sighed. "I'm sure my dad would be our linesman if we asked him."

By the end of the discussion, it was clear that finding a ground and a referee were the biggest problems. They had nineteen days left to find solutions.

"Tessie," Vi said, "can you cover the shop first thing? I'll see if Audrey could come in to help, but then I want to go to the newspaper office. Maybe they could run a story." Vi just couldn't believe that despite everything they'd done, the chance of the cup was going to be snatched away from them now.

"I'll go up to Billingbrook Hall hospital to see if Major Tomlinson can apply any pressure," Billy said. "After all we've raised to support them, I'm sure he'll want to help if he can."

"I have never been so insulted in all my life," Vi was shaking the water off her umbrella and standing in the doorway to the shop. "What are you doing here?" She turned and saw Billy waiting for her.

"I'm on my way to see the football club, but had

something to tell you. You go first."

"I went to the *Mercury*'s offices. I asked to see the editor and was told without an appointment that would not be possible. So I asked to make an appointment. I had to explain what it was about, and the next thing I knew one of his... his..." She paused, trying to find a word, "lackeys came out and said they had already spoken to the football club and would not be able to help us. Even though we raise large sums for charity, they won't even consider our story. Apparently the editor agrees that it is not 'seemly' for women to play football. They've been happy enough to carry the reports of our games, but oh no, now we want their help..." Vi was so cross that she was having difficulty unbuttoning her coat.

Tessie came over and began to help her, as though she were a dresser in the finest of dress shops.

"Well, I may have some good news," Billy said.

"I hope so, I really do." Vi slipped her arms out of the sleeves and allowed Tessie to take her coat.

"Do you remember a long time ago Terence asked if I liked rugby league, and said he'd take me to a match sometime? With the football we've never got around to it. I'd completely forgotten until he said something this morning. He doesn't really talk about it, but I think that's because he used to take Davy. Anyway, he suggested that as half the proceeds were due to be going to the hospital, we could approach Major Tomlinson for him to ask the rugby league club if we can use their ground. They aren't affected by the Football Association ruling, so it shouldn't cause them a problem. I'm going to see Major Tomlinson as soon as I've finished at Billingbrook United."

"Oh, Billy." Vi clapped her hands together.

"It's not certain, so don't bank on it, but there's a

chance. I'm on my way to the Club first to talk about money, and see if they can suggest how we can find a referee." Billy planted a big kiss on Vi's cheek and left the shop.

Vi sank down onto a chair. Tessie, bless her, had made a cup of tea and it was already waiting on the table.

"It's not over yet, Vi. You can still do this."

"I hope you're right, Tessie. I hope you're right." Vi blew on the tea to cool it and wondered whether they were going to be thwarted in their cup bid yet again.

"I have good news and bad news," Billy said when he came in that evening.

"We've found a ground?" Vi turned to him in anticipation.

"Sorry, love, I shouldn't have raised your hopes quite that much. It's too soon to have heard back about that. It's unlikely we'll have an answer before the weekend. I have been to the football club though." Billy reached down to fuss Nipper, who was welcoming him home as he did every night. "The Club says it can't discuss the money from previous matches with us. That's the bad news. I've no idea if it was all paid to charity or went into their books, and there's nothing I can do to find out. Some must have gone to charity, or I'm sure the hospital would have said something. Anyway, that's the bad news. The good news is that they've said you can play in your existing kit for the cup match if it goes ahead. You'd need new kit if you keep playing beyond that."

Vi felt relieved. With the best will in the world, she'd have found it hard to find time to make new kit in the run up to Christmas. She already had more orders through the shop than she really had time for. "That's one we can discuss later then. This is probably my last year, but I want to go out on a high and not fizzle out. I don't know what the others will do, but I think that will be for them to decide."

Billy nodded. "Is Dad around? I could do with him taking me somewhere in the car."

"What, at this time of night?" Vi was horrified. She'd already prepared their meal and felt worn out from the day.

Billy laughed. "No, not today. There's an errand I need to run tomorrow."

Vi didn't ask him anything further, as she assumed it was to do with the factory.

She found it hard to concentrate at work, wondering if they could solve all the problems in time. It was one thing finding a ground, but they'd still need to let people know of the change of venue and sell tickets. She was glad Billy understood bookkeeping, as there seemed to be all sorts of things to take into account, including fees on the tickets that needed paying to the Government. He was going to have to learn fast.

"Calderley are on standby to play and are happy for us to make the arrangements," Alf said, almost before he was through the door of Hats and Haberdashery on Thursday morning.

"Oh, thank goodness." Vi came out from behind the counter. "Did they say anything else?"

Alf shrugged. "Only that if they come up with any suggestions, they'll let us know. I can't stop, Billy's waiting for me in the car. Calderley haven't said if they've found a linesman. I'll ask them again when I write with details."

"Well, at least they won't argue with anything we come

up with." Vi went over to the window and watched her father-in-law go.

"Vi!" Tessie said, taking Vi's hands away from the mannequin. "If you smooth that material down anymore, you'll wear it out."

Vi looked at Tessie, then realised what she was doing. She didn't feel much like working, however many orders they needed to complete.

The day dragged even though they were busy, and Vi was glad when it was time to close up.

"What are you looking so happy about?" she asked Billy when she found him walking Nipper to meet her that evening. "Do we have somewhere to play?"

"Better than that."

"How can anything be better than having somewhere to play the game?" Vi frowned.

"At the end of the day, you could play the game at the Caulder and Harrison recreation ground if there was absolutely nothing else, but what you cannot do is play without a referee, especially against Calderley. And I have found you a referee." Billy grinned.

"One that will be acceptable to both sides?" Vi had no idea where you would even start to find someone.

Billy nodded. "This morning I went to the barracks and spoke to Major Tomlinson. I know I'd seen him yesterday to ask him to write to the rugby club, but when I came away a thought struck me. Major Tomlinson has agreed that Sergeant Cooper, who takes the lads for their physical training, can be our referee. I met him and can assure you there will be no question of either side cheating."

Vi hugged her husband. "What a brilliant idea. All we need now is a venue."

The following Monday, Alf received a letter which

confirmed that Billingbrook Rugby League Club would allow the match to be played at their ground, but only as a one off, as it seemed even they didn't want to fall out with the Football Association. They also agreed to help with the ticket sales to make things easier.

That evening, Alf wrote to the Calderley team with all the information and then drafted an advert to appear in the *Billingbrook Mercury*. The match was on.

The days in the shop were so busy leading up to Christmas, but Vi's mind kept turning to the football. Her initial reaction had been frustration that the game was at risk, but as she'd considered the whole picture, she'd realised there was far more at stake than just the football. Every time she thought about the Football Association's decision, she felt a wave of anger. Hadn't women proved themselves, or did everything they'd done during the war really still count for nothing in a man's world?

That wasn't how she wanted things for little Queenie growing up.

"Vi." Tessie broke into her thoughts. "There's a lady in the shop asking to talk to you."

Vi put down the bow she'd been about to sew into place and straightened her dress. "Did she say what it's about?"

Tessie shook her head. "I said there are no appointments for hats until January, but she said it wasn't about that."

Vi raised her eyebrows and went to where the lady was waiting. The woman cut an imposing figure, standing as though she were commanding operations, while waiting for Vi.

"Ah, Mrs Dobson," she said, holding out her hand. "I'm Mrs Lofthouse, Mrs Peggy Lofthouse."

"How do you do?" Vi shook her hand and waited for further explanation.

"Mrs Dobson, you may wonder why I'm here. I'm the local representative of the National Union of Societies for Equal Citizenship..."

Vi listened carefully, but this left her little the wiser.

"Our members are very interested in the work you and the other girls have been doing within women's football, and the recent decision by the Football Association. As a fellow campaigner for women's rights, we wondered if you'd be prepared to come along and talk to one of our meetings about your experiences."

Had she heard right? She didn't see herself as a campaigner of any sort. She simply wanted to be able to play football. Did it really have to involve a struggle for equality to do that? Before this week she'd thought campaigning was just about being able to vote and own property.

Mrs Lofthouse was continuing. "I know many of our ladies have been inspired by the work of you and your team, and we'd like to know more about it."

Eventually, Vi found her voice. "That's very kind of you, Mrs Lofthouse. I'll have to think about it. It's not the sort of thing I'm used to."

Mrs Lofthouse nodded. "Here's my card. I'll call in to see you again when you aren't so busy. Please think about it. Yours is an important story, and one that women need to hear about."

The lady said goodbye and left the shop, but her words continued to ring in Vi's ears long after she'd gone.

On Monday 26th December 1921 the Billingbrook Ladies' Football Team prepared to do battle with their arch-rivals from Calderley.

"It's like playing away," Edith said, "being at a strange ground."

"Most of the grounds are still strange to me," Ethel said.

Vi looked at Ethel. How sad that all the talent the young girl had wouldn't be put to good use after this game. "It's really odd, the ground being smaller than Billingbrook United. Billy says all the tickets have sold." Vi was doing some stretching exercises, trying to prepare herself for what lay ahead. It would be odd having her dad as one of the linesmen, but he'd been thrilled to be asked. The other linesman was the father of one of the Calderley team, so there was no question of any favouritism overall.

By the whole Billingbrook team's agreement, given that all three had been part of so many of their practice sessions, Tommy led them out onto the pitch, with Queenie toddling one side of him and Nipper bounding back and forth on the other. The crowd cheered as the girls followed them out.

Sergeant Cooper stood ramrod straight, ready to blow the whistle for the start of the match, and Vi felt as though she should be standing to attention.

"I want a clean game. Do you all understand?" he barked to the teams, and they readily agreed.

This was it. Only this game stood between Vi and lifting the cup. She took a deep breath.

For the first part of the game, the teams were playing cautiously, sizing each other up. Vi didn't want to spend too much time running further than she needed to, as she hoped that her team might have more stamina overall. The way they were playing probably wasn't making for the most exciting match to watch, but today Vi was too focussed on the end result to worry quite so much about the beautiful game.

They were twenty minutes into play when a slip by Annie let a Calderley player through. Edith came forward as the Calderley girl bore down on the goal. Before the girl had the opportunity to change approach, Edith stuck out her foot and deflected the ball over the goal line for a corner. Vi shook herself. They were never going to win if they only played a defensive game. Hadn't they learned that in the semi-final? A goalless draw wasn't an option today.

Once they'd recovered from the corner, Vi moved the girls into a more attacking formation. "We'll take the game to them and see what happens." Her excitement at the change of tactics seemed to ripple across the field, and the Billingbrook team upped the pace. Vi crossed the ball to Ethel, who found some space and crossed it back. The crowd were cheering as Vi passed the ball to Clara, who deftly kicked the ball past the Calderley goalkeeper, scoring the first goal of the match. They were one goal up as they went in at half-time, but there was a long way to go.

Whatever the team talk had been for Calderley during the break, it had clearly worked. Their team came out onto the pitch as though each of the girls was two inches taller and twice as wide. They were giving it everything they had. Vi couldn't see how they could possibly keep up that pace for the whole of the second half, but perhaps they didn't need to. Ten minutes in and they'd equalised. Now it could be anybody's game.

As the second half progressed, it looked as though no one was going to break the deadlock. There had to be a winner. There were only a few minutes until the whistle for the end of the ninety minutes, and unless the match was going into extra time, someone needed to score.

The girls weren't letting up. The ball was passed to Vi, but there was a Calderley player bearing down on her. She passed the ball as fast as she could. Ethel had space; it was just possible that this could be their opportunity.

Vi watched with horror as a Calderley player made ground on Ethel and looked more intent on playing the player than the ball. Ethel didn't seem to have seen her opponent. The challenge from the Calderley player took Ethel's legs from under her and she landed with a thud on the ground. Another Calderley defender cleared the ball to a midfielder.

Vi's heart was pounding; where was the referee? This couldn't happen to them again. Calderley couldn't get away with it. She squared her shoulders in anticipation of needing to protest. There were medics on the pitch attending to Ethel who was still lying on the ground.

Then he was there. Sergeant Cooper had blown his whistle and was standing in front of the Calderley girl, as solidly as though he were a wall, while she shouted at him. He seemed to be indicating that she should leave the pitch. For once the referee was in control and wouldn't accept unfair play.

"Yes," Vi said quietly, under her breath. Ethel would have a penalty. Then she realised that Ethel was being carried off the pitch. Someone else would need to take the spot kick, and that someone was her. Vi felt her legs starting to tremble. With so little time left, this would almost certainly decide the game if she could kick the ball across that line. Vi nodded to the referee in acknowledgment that she would take the kick and, still trembling placed the ball.

The crowds waited in silence as Vi took a few deep breaths, looked first to the ball, and then at the Calderley goal and goalkeeper. What was it Alf said? 'Aim for where she least expects.' That was easier said than done. Then in her mind she saw the scene playing forward. She remembered that the goalie had previously made a great save diving to her right. Vi gambled that the keeper might be less adept on the left. She would aim just inside the post. Taking a deep breath, Vi sent up a silent prayer, took three paces forward, and kicked the ball. As the ball passed the keeper's outstretched arms, Vi sank to her knees. It was the goal they needed.

"Get up, Vi," Clara shouted. "We haven't finished."

Vi shook herself and scrambled to her feet. Focus. One slip now and they'd lose the advantage. Those last three minutes were the longest Vi had ever known. When Sergeant Cooper blew the final whistle, you could probably have heard the cheering right across Billingbrook.

She felt dazed as the girls hugged each other, and Nipper ran onto the pitch to join in the general melee.

As Vi held the cup aloft, all she could do was grin. Despite their antiquated ideas, the Football Association hadn't stopped them. She just hoped that one day, the men in charge of football would wake up to the error of their ways and celebrate the women's game as the equal of the men's. In the meantime, she would talk to the group Mrs Lofthouse had invited her to, and to any other group which stood up for women's rights. This was about more than a cup, and more than a game of football.

She looked around for Billy and beckoned him to join her at the front. The war hadn't stopped them. Billy's injuries hadn't stopped them. Influenza hadn't stopped them. Ena's theft hadn't stopped them. She and Billy were a team, and they stood shoulder to shoulder in everything they did. This was about equality.

THE END

POSTSCRIPT

The Football Association banned women's football from their members' stadiums on 5th December 1921. The ban lasted for fifty years and was lifted in 1971. It has taken much of the subsequent fifty years for the game to be re-established to a level where it can take its rightful place alongside the men's game.

The reasons stated for the ban were spurious and unjust, claiming it was injurious to women's health and that not all the money raised was going to charitable causes. The first of those does not warrant comment. The latter needs to be considered in the light of the unreasonableness of expecting working class girls to forgo income and cover their own travel costs in order to play for a team. This was especially relevant at a time when the men's game was already, at least in some part, professional.

Although a women's football body was established, the damage had been done.

It is a delight to see the growing strength of women's football today. I hope that future generations of girls will have the choice to play the game that was not afforded to schoolgirls in my era.

Ros Kind
August 2021

PLEASE LEAVE A REVIEW

Reviews are one of the best ways for new readers to find my writing. It's the modern day 'word of mouth' recommendation. If you have enjoyed reading my work and think that others may do too, then please take a moment or two to leave a review. Just a sentence or two of what you think is all it takes.

Thank you.

BOOK GROUPS

Dear book group readers,

Rather than include questions within the book for you to consider, I have included special pages within my website. This has the advantage of being easier to update and for you to suggest additions and thoughts which arise out of your discussions.

I am always delighted to have the opportunity to discuss the book with a group and for those groups which are not local to me this can sometimes be arranged as a Skype call or through another internet service. Contact details can be found on the website.

Please visit http://rjkind.com/

SOURCES OF INFORMATION

This is not a study of history, so I may not have provided every last reference in the manner you would like, however the following have all been interesting and useful sources if you want to do any further research yourself.

BBC History Magazine
Roger Domeneghetti - From The Back Page To The Front Room: Football's Journey Through The English Media - ISBN-13: 978-1910906064
Tim Tate - Secret History Of Womens Football - ISBN-13: 978-1782197720
Gail J Newsham - In A League Of Their Own: The Dick, Kerr Ladies 1917-1965 - ISBN-13: 978-1782225638
Kate Adie - Fighting on the Home Front The Legacy of Women in World War One ISBN-13: 978-14444759709
Patrick Brennan - The Munitionettes ISBN-13: 978-0-9555063-0-7

Dick, Kerr Ladies' Team
https://en.wikipedia.org/wiki/Dick,_Kerr_Ladies_F.C.
www.dickkerrladies.com/

General History sources
www.bbc.co.uk/history/british/timeline/worldwars_timel ine_noflash.shtml
www.paimages.co.uk/collections/1041

British Newspaper Archive
www.britishnewspaperarchive.co.uk

Hat factory conditions

www.worldwar1luton.com/blog-entry/unhealthy-conditions-hat-factories

Munitionettes history
https://en.wikipedia.org/wiki/Munitionette

Working hours
https://www.bbc.com/worklife/article/20190912-what-wartime-munitionettes-can-teach-us-about-burnout

Songs
https://en.wikipedia.org/wiki/Music_hall_songs

ALSO BY ROSEMARY J. KIND

Violet's War
While Billy's fighting for King and Country, Violet's fighting for the right to play football.

The Blight and the Blarney (Prequel to Tales of Flynn and Reilly)
Whatever it takes to stop your family from starving.

New York Orphan (Tales of Flynn and Reilly)
How strong are bonds of loyalty when everything is at stake?

Unequal By Birth (Tales of Flynn and Reilly)
How far will Daniel and Molly go to fight injustice and is it a price worth paying?

Justice Be Damned (Tales of Flynn and Reilly)
How do you fight for justice against those whose interests it does not serve? William Dixon is about to find out.

The Appearance of Truth
Her birth certificate belonged to a baby who died, so who is Lisa Forster?

The Lifetracer
Connor is out of time to stop the murders. Now his young son's life is in danger – Who is The Lifetracer?

Alfie's Woods
The power of friendship and the difference it can make to us all.

ABOUT THE AUTHOR

Rosemary J Kind writes because she has to. You could take almost anything away from her except her pen and paper. Failing to stop after the book that everyone has in them, she has gone on to publish books in both non-fiction and fiction, the latter including novels, humour, short stories and poetry. She also regularly produces magazine articles in a number of areas and writes regularly for the dog press. As a child she was desolate when at the age of ten her then teacher would not believe that her poem based on 'Stig of the Dump' was her own work and she stopped writing poetry for several years as a result. She was persuaded to continue by the invitation to earn a little extra pocket money by 'assisting' others to produce the required poems for English homework!

Always one to spot an opportunity, she started school newspapers and went on to begin providing paid copy to her local newspaper at the age of sixteen.

For twenty years she followed a traditional business career, before seeing the error of her ways and leaving it all behind to pursue her writing full-time.

She spends her life discussing her plots with the characters in her head and her faithful dogs, who always put the opposing arguments when there are choices to be made.

Always willing to take on challenges that sensible people regard as impossible, she set up the short story download site Alfie Dog Fiction which she ran for six years. During that time it grew to become one of the largest short story download sites in the world, representing over 300 authors and carrying over 1600 short stories. Her hobby is developing the Entlebucher Mountain Dog breed in the UK and when she brought her beloved Alfie back from Belgium he was only the tenth in the country.

She started writing *Alfie's Diary* as an internet blog the day Alfie arrived to live with her, intending to continue for a year or two. Fifteen years later it goes from strength to strength and has been repeatedly named as one of the top ten pet blogs in the UK.

For more details about the author please visit her website at www.rjkind.com For more details about her dogs then you're better visiting www.alfiedog.me.uk

ACKNOWLEDGMENTS

As always thanks to my writing buddies - Patsy, Sheila and Lynne - who make an enormous difference to my work. Also, my husband Chris for your support, encouragement and improvements - thank you.

No book would be complete without mention of my wonderful cover designer Katie Stewart. I am so lucky to benefit from her skills.

Alfie Dog Fiction

Taking your imagination for a walk

visit our website at www.alfiedog.com

Lightning Source UK Ltd.
Milton Keynes UK
UKHW021451221121
394397UK00006B/185